THE IRON SNAKES

Jenny Maxwell

WARNER BOOKS

A *Warner* Book

First published in Great Britain in 2000
by Warner Books

A CIP catalogue record for this book
is available from the British Library.

ISBN 0 7515 2905 2

Typeset in Palatino by M Rules
Printed and bound in Great Britain by
Clays Ltd, St Ives plc

Warner Books
A Division of
Little, Brown and Company (UK)
Brettenham House
Lancaster Place
London WC2E 7EN

Jenny Maxwell is a Scot, was born in Egypt, educated in England, and lived in Germany until recently. She now lives in the Black Country. Her first novel, *The Blacksmith* (1996), was chosen for the W H Smith Fresh Talent promotion, and was followed by *The Black Cat* (1997), the second novel in the Blacksmith trilogy.

Also by Jenny Maxwell

THE BLACKSMITH
THE BLACK CAT

To Sally Watson
My good, true friend
who has never abdicated the responsibility for
her own life

ACKNOWLEDGEMENTS

I have, as always, received generous help from many people as I wrote *The Iron Snakes*, but I would in particular like to thank the following.

Dr Barry Hitchcock, of the Highcliffe Veterinary Practice in Hadleigh, who never seemed to be thrown by my questions, no matter how strange. Dr Adrian Kemp, of the Siam Surgery in Sudley, who was generous, not only with time and excellent ideas, but also with the loan of reference books. Mrs Debbie Arbon, who read the manuscript, and had intelligent comments and suggestions to make. Any mistakes still remaining are there despite the assistance I received; I do not always take advice.

Last but not least, my family, who understood.

PREFACE

Lonely was a word I heard people use about my life here, lonely, and unnatural. Women said it most often, particularly married women.

Not that they went so far as to suggest I should find myself a husband. I doubt if they considered it possible. But the hard physical work, and the muscular strength they imagined it entailed, this was something strange. It was this that was unnatural.

I was never lonely, and although I am very strong I don't often need that strength. I don't often use it. A farrier doesn't wrestle with horses. No matter how strong we might be, we wouldn't often win a contest against an equine opponent.

Nor am I the first woman who's shod horses and mended farm implements in the forge at Anford. A historian came here a little while ago, and he told me of another woman, the wife of the blacksmith at Anford. The smith was taken off to one of the wars with France and she ran this place for him until he came home a few years later. The local priest threatened her with a charge of witchcraft.

'Why?' I asked.

'The usual reason. She was a strong woman, and she

1

wasn't subordinate to a man. The taint of the old religion.'

I was shoeing a nervous young horse while we talked, so most of my mind was on my work, but I was trying to picture that other woman, and I wondered whether she and I had faced the same problems, and how she had handled them. People who won't pay their bills. Men who feel they should advise us.

The witchcraft threat had come to nothing, the man said. Without somebody to shoe the horses and make and mend the tools the local economy would have collapsed, and the priest's word was law only when there weren't more important matters to consider.

'When the smith came home he was told his wife was a wicked woman, evil in the sight of God, and he was ordered to beat her.'

'By the priest?'

'I think so. I can't remember if it was the priest or the Lord of the Manor.'

A car drove up the lane, the engine roaring in low gear, and the horse jerked his head and fought for his hoof. I gripped it hard between my knees, and spoke soothingly until he was still again. There was sweat on his neck and his eyes were ringed in white, his ears still flicking.

The young man drew in his breath to speak again, but I raised my head.

'Could we not talk for a moment?'

He looked at the horse, and nodded. I didn't have to explain.

I went on rasping the hoof, keeping my movements as steady and even as I could, and after a little while I felt the horse's head come down, and he lipped at the back of my shoulder, tasting, and smelling. He was quiet again.

'What happened?' I asked.

'When the smith came back? I don't know. I could guess, if you like.'

'Go on, then.'

'This is a grossly unacceptable practice among historians, you understand?'

'Except on every second Tuesday,' I agreed, and he grinned at me.

'You've met us before. Yes, well, I would say the smith's wife stayed out of sight for a few days, and when she reappeared she affected a slight limp. There might even have been a bandage or two.'

Yes, I thought, that was probably quite a good guess. The smith would have had a bellyful of war by then, he would hardly have been anxious to start one with his wife. A fabricated beating, for the benefit of the priesthood and the aristocracy, was a reasonable enough conclusion.

I released the horse's hoof and straightened up, stepping away from him. He threw up his head and jerked at the rope, tugging from side to side, sweat breaking out on his neck and shoulders again.

'Why's he so nervous?'

'He's only a baby,' I said. 'His dam's a bit highly-strung, too.'

'And hers before that?' He was looking at the horse with a half-smile on his face.

'Probably,' I agreed.

I'd wait for a while now before I approached the horse again. I'd let him grow tired of fighting the rope. He was young, not very strong yet. The muscles in his neck would start to ache, and, as long as nothing else happened to frighten him, he'd stop soon, and step towards the ring to which the rope was tied. As soon as that happened the strain on his head and his neck would ease. A connection would be formed in his small brain. Stop fighting, stop pain.

Wind in the chestnut tree, the leaves sighing quietly, the long grass on the banks of the stream stirring, silver on the green, the young horse shivering the skin on his shoulder as a fly settled on it; distracted by the fly, he moved forward, dropping his head. Soon I would pick up another foot, slowly, and gently, but once I had his foot off the ground I would not release it. I would grip it between my knees, and he would be off balance, unable to use his strength against me.

'I'd thought about generations of people at Anford forge. Generations of horses hadn't occurred to me.'

But I've thought about the horses who've been here. This forge is mentioned in the Domesday Book, but nobody knows how old it is. It's sandstone and black oak, and the floor is made of great sandstone slabs, golden flagstones, worn and scarred. Draught horses, pack ponies, warhorses, palfreys. Carriage horses and hunters, showjumpers and steeplechasers, children's pets and millionaires' status symbols, standing on the golden flagstones, briefly moving through the great river of history that has flowed through this place.

Ninth century, maybe? they've suggested, but it's only a guess. Who could know? And suppose they're right; what stood here before the sandstone and the oak? Anford's on a crossroads, all four of the ways lead through valleys, and the stream runs deep and fast. I think there's been something on this piece of land from the time man first worked iron with fire and water.

I was glad that young historian had come. Now, when people remark that mine is an unusual job for a woman, I can reply.

'I'm not the first.'

Horses, and farm machinery, and gates to make, garden tools to mend, special orders for something different, everyday work from people who'd rather pay more now for craftsmanship and save three times the money in the end.

It's the horses I love the most, and the racehorses best of all.

But I don't often travel, so I only have the racehorses when nobody else can be found. The big racing stables have their own farriers, and even the smallest ones insist on the farriers coming to them; taking racehorses to a forge is almost unheard of.

When I was an apprentice, I had no option; where the master goes, the apprentice follows. I hated it. I hated the riding schools most of all, the children whispering behind their hands, their eyes bright with laughter. And the racing stables too, where some of the lads had looked me up and down with open contempt on their faces.

Now, I can stay here, and if people want their horses shod they come to me. Here, I can face them, and they can look at me, they can even murmur to each other, or whisper, and I don't mind. It's not so bad now. I'm known around here, perhaps even respected. I no longer hunch my shoulders and make myself as small as I can when I go into the village shop or when I meet strangers. I can travel if I need to, or in an emergency, but I prefer to stay here. I don't earn as much money as those farriers who go to their customers. I have enough, and it doesn't matter.

Occasionally the racehorses come here. Sometimes a farrier's ill or injured, or booked elsewhere, and then there's a telephone call: three horses on their way to Hereford, or Worcester, will that be all right? At five in the morning?

Half-past four on a summer morning, the flowers smell wonderful, and sometimes there are deer on the grass verges of the lane. When I see them it's as though there's been a blessing on the day. I watch for a little while, and then I have to cross the gravel from the cottage to the forge. At the sound their heads lift, and they're gone, fleeing into the shelter of the dark woods.

I go into the forge and light the fire, set out my tools, and then I stand in the door drinking my coffee and looking around at the place I love. The paddock and the garden, the sandstone forge, and the red-brick cottage. It's not a pretty house, it's square and low under dark Welsh slates, but Uncle Henry left me this place when he died. I wish I could

5

tell him how much I loved him, and what his gift has meant to me.

The two gates at the end of the gravel drive, I made them when I was only fourteen, and I hung them. I suppose I should replace them; they're not much of an advertisement. They're not quite straight.

But I don't have to tell children not to swing on those gates. It would take more than four or five children to make them sag. I made them strong, as Uncle Henry taught me, and I made them to last, as I make everything, as he did before me.

I hear the horsebox as it turns into the lane from the main road, and I check, quickly, that I have everything I need, that the forge looks clean and tidy, that the concrete path and the square have been swept. Racehorse trainers notice.

I'm ready when they arrive, and watching as the beautiful animals are led down the ramp, watching the way they move, looking for that extra measure of caution that means more than care, that means soreness in a leg or a foot. The travelling lad and the trainer are watching too, but this is my field of expertise, and I can see more than they can, I can spot this sort of trouble before they do.

I work quickly with racehorses, I don't like to keep them standing, they can become restless. It's a simple job, changing the heavier steel shoes they wear for training for the light racing plates that may give them those few extra paces of speed when they need it. As I begin I run my fingers down the hard, slim legs, looking for heat, looking for softness, searching for trouble.

Once they're wearing the racing plates I ask their lads to lead them up the flat concrete path, away from me, circle at the end, and then back towards me, and I watch, crouched down, listening to the beat of the hooves, looking at the movement, alert for signals.

Sometimes I can't even say what I've heard or seen, but I know something's wrong; there's a problem here. Stop.

Look, and listen. Lift the feet, feel again, smell the sole of the foot, probe, and look again, and there it is, the little soft spot that should be firm, the warmth where it should be cool, the small and sudden lift of the head to signal pain.

The men mutter and shake their heads. Can he race?

I stand back. This is not my decision, I have played my part now. They will know. They know the horse, they know the owner. A small bruise, he can race, he's tough, but the lads won't be putting their wages on him, not this time. Nothing will be said. The lift of the head never happened; such a little bruise, who could know? Maybe the owner will be told. Maybe.

I check all the horses who come to me, the same routine, a ritual now. Children's ponies, draught horses, hunters and hacks, young foals and old pets, I watch, and I listen, and I look for the signals.

Early summer mornings at the forge, with the dew misting the feathered grass, so lovely, so delicate, the birdsong, the scent of the flowers light and sweet in the still air, the fire roaring softly at my back, and I am so filled with peace and with love for this place I can feel tears in my eyes for the grateful joy of my life here.

1

You'd have to be very dull to live at the forge here without becoming interested in its history. It was once surrounded by the lands of the Gorsedown Estate, which was huge in medieval times, mile after mile of forest and farmland, with three villages in its demesne. The de Meurevilles were a Norman family, and they owned Gorsedown from the twelfth century until the Civil War, when they backed the wrong side and lost their lands. I'm told that a family called Moorfield are their descendants, but they're in Lincolnshire now, with no connection to Gorsedown.

In 1543 Simon de Meureville lost the forge in a game of dice to William Fitzallen. He wasn't a good loser; he refused to allow Fitzallen's men to ride across his land, so Fitzallen couldn't get his horses shod, or his weapons mended, or anything done at his newly acquired forge. He went to the King to complain, and Henry VIII found it amusing, too good a joke to spoil. Fitzallen and his men were still banned from de Meureville's lands, but the smith and his family were granted the right to ride on Gorsedown, so they could meet Fitzallen's men on the boundary and take the horses back to the forge. That right holds to this day.

It was my Uncle John who discovered King Henry's Deed

when his brother Henry wanted to buy the forge. I expect John Mayall put more effort into his searches on that occasion than he would have done for any other client. Henry was only mildly interested; his wife, Ruth, as shrewd a little Welshwoman as ever left the valleys, foresaw a time when riding land would be valuable, and anyway she would never have thrown away an asset. When Henry left coal mining and returned to his original craft he brought a pit pony with him, and Ruth took up her right to ride on Gorsedown lands.

There are no rights of way at all on Gorsedown, and King Henry's Deed isn't shown on maps.

Four square miles are all that's left of the great Gorsedown Estate, with the little bit of land that goes with Anford Forge sticking up into the southern boundary like a thumb. It's changed hands several times this century, and now it's on the market again, with rotting 'For Sale' signs standing at the two great gates alongside the ones stating that Trespassers will be Prosecuted.

The house that's there now is Victorian, and not a very good example of the architecture of its type, so nobody is doing much about trying to save it. The windows have been smashed, some of the tiles are coming off the roof. It will probably be demolished in the end, and I doubt if anybody will mind.

The land is mostly wooded, and now there are brambles and nettles again. Sometimes I take a slasher up there and clear them back from the rides, not because nettles are a problem to horses, but they might hide rabbit holes. I like to know where my horse is putting her feet. She's quite old now, Lyric, but she still gets away from me sometimes, and then all I can do is hang on and wait for her to tire. That takes a while; old she may be, but she's a thoroughbred, and she was bred to stay, even with nearly fifteen stone on her back.

I don't mind when she runs away with me. I may swear

at her, but the lunging heave on the reins and the surge of speed that means she's won again signals my chance to forget my problems. I have little option; I need to concentrate on keeping my balance, on gripping as hard as I can, and on lying low enough to avoid being scraped off by branches.

It's dangerous, it's yet another sign that I'm a rotten rider, and I love it.

There's a hole in the blackthorn hedge up by the west gate, although you have to look very closely to see it. Just there, the bushes are three deep, and the hole is like a tunnel with a zigzag in the middle, quite low. You'd need to be small and agile to get through it, and you'd need to be wearing something thick and tough to protect you from those wicked thorns.

Jansy Neville's small and agile, and she wears leather.

I'd never have known she was on Gorsedown land if she hadn't stopped me one day, tears streaming down her cheeks as she stood in the track in front of Lyric waving her arms at me.

'Missus? Missus? Got a spade, Missus?'

Her dog was down a rabbit hole. It had caved in and she thought he was suffocating. I rode back to the forge, collected a spade, and we dug him out. He was bruised and winded, and he snapped at me.

'What are you doing here?' I asked Jansy.

'Poaching, Missus.'

It had been a fairly stupid question. Jansy had two ferrets in her pockets and there was a net over the warren.

'Don't get caught.'

'Thanks, Missus,' she called after me as I rode away.

Twelve years old, top of her class in maths and biology, and thought of locally as a good little girl, Jansy led a double life. After the incident with the trapped dog she didn't bother to hide from me when she heard Lyric's hoofbeats. She offered me a rabbit once, but Lyric took fright at

10

the smell of blood and refused to let her bring it near. Jansy
hung the rabbit on my gate that night, and a week later
there was a pheasant.

'What do you want to do when you leave school?' I asked
her.

'University. Biology, I love that biology, I do. Then, game
warden, somewhere in Africa, I want to go to Africa, I do.
I'll get those bastards who shoot the elephants.'

She grinned at me.

'I'll know how to find them, won't I?'

Jansy poaches on Gorsedown because she loves it. Her
parents think she's taking her dog for a walk.

'And I am. I don't tell lies, I don't.'

Janice Neville, top of her class in maths and biology, and
a good little girl, never tells lies. Janice will go far.

Jansy will go to Africa, and get those bastards who shoot
the elephants. She'll know how to find them, won't she?

Africa.

Even I, who know nothing about the place and don't
much want to travel, recognise the thrill of the name.

One of my favourite customers has a cousin in Kenya,
and he talks about it sometimes. Lord Robert Halstay has a
chronically lame old steeplechaser I shoe for him, and he
always comes along when his groom brings Black Bear to
the forge, because he enjoys poking around and getting in
the way. Stephens won't let him drive. He's polite and def-
erential to his boss, but it always happens that Stephens is
in the driving seat before Lord Robert reaches the door.

'Hah! You want to drive, do you? All right, Stephens.
Good man. Good man.'

Even Lord Robert has given up pretending that Blackie
will ever be sound again. He hacks him around his estate,
stopping to chat to anybody he meets: checkin' up, he calls it.

'Two old crocks, hobblin' around. Good old lad, Blackie.
Good old lad.'

*

11

Riding stables and a dude ranch, hacks and ponies, and the racing stables, now and then. Wrought-iron gates and window grilles, tools to be mended, major jobs and minor bits and pieces, I'm always busy, and usually happy. I don't mind my own company, and I have Lyric, and a few chickens.

Sometimes I have Arno.

He is the secret I hug gleefully to my chest when he isn't there, when I see the scornful look in a man's eyes, a man who judges me by my appearance, and decides I am a failure. A woman such as I am could never attract a man. And when Arno is with me, even then nobody can believe he is more than a house guest, this Swedish professor who looks like a cartoon artist's idea of a Viking. He must be staying in my spare room, Professor Linssen. Of course, the forge is of interest to him. He is an engineer, working at a very high level on theories of metallurgy; it must be fun for him to go back to the roots of his science, fire, iron, hammer and anvil.

In fact, Arno is a quite hopeless blacksmith.

But he does not sleep in my guest bedroom, he sleeps with me, in my bed, and he is my lover.

He came one evening last summer, as I was closing the forge, the big Riley he drives limping through the gate, swaying, the nearside rear wheel scraping against the mudguard. One of the leaf springs had broken, and Arno was in trouble.

'The garage tells me six weeks,' he said, spreading his hands in despair. 'I must be in Australia in three. They say you might help.'

I was defensive with him. He was so good-looking, I found myself resentful. He must be thinking he could persuade me to work late for him. He would only have to smile, and I would melt. So few men would smile at somebody like me. I would be easy, particularly for him.

'I'm closing,' I said.

'It is late,' he agreed. 'And a beautiful evening. You have

other things to do, of course. May I perhaps work here on my car? I will not disturb, I can be quiet. Tomorrow, you might make me a spring? If you have time?'

His smile seemed friendly, and he had a soft voice. The evening breeze was blowing his hair back from his forehead, dark blond hair, a brown face, blue eyes.

Assuming he had me in the palm of his hand, because I am big and ugly and must therefore be grateful for any crumb of kindness a man might throw me, even a smile.

'Perhaps you'd like to make it yourself?'

He must have recognised the sarcasm, but his smile broadened.

'That is so kind! In your lovely forge? I may truly work in your lovely forge?'

I was trapped. I could not be so rude and aggressive to a stranger as to tell him I had not meant it, but I had never worked with anybody in the forge since Uncle Henry died. I didn't want this.

But I turned the key in the big padlock and threw open the doors, and Arno followed me in, looking around in wonderment.

'How old?'

'Nobody knows.'

'This is almost magical. Truly, you permit that I work?'

He held out his hand.

'Arno. Arno Linssen, on holiday from Sweden.'

'Ann Mayall. How do you do?'

I have made spare parts for cars, vintage and veteran models, nearly always owned by people who do not have enough money to maintain them, but who find the struggle worth while. Usually, one of their first questions is the price, and I will not drop mine simply because they love their hobby; I do not share their enthusiasm for their old cars. I have no great liking for cars of any age.

Arno asked only about the tools and materials, had I some steel of the correct grade? And a welding torch, and

13

cutting gear, and yes, this would do. Not perfect, not exactly right, but it will do, and how lucky for him to find such a kind woman to let him work in her beautiful old forge.

Woman. Not lady, a woman. I found I was smiling, I liked that.

He had overalls. When he's in England he likes to drive the Riley. It's a beautiful car, but he says quite often it stops even when he has not used the brakes, and he has to be prepared.

There was a tool kit, clean steel and wood, all with the faint gleam of oil.

He talked all the time as he stripped off his jacket and put on overalls, dark blue, faded in places, worn, but clean. Everything about Arno seemed clean and cared for, and before he started to work he rubbed some sort of white grease into his hands. Later, he showed me. It stopped the dirt and the black oil from becoming ingrained into the skin and clogging under the fingernails. Arno never minded dirty work, but he wanted to be clean again when it was finished.

Talking, all the time, talking, about his car, about his work, his luck in finding me and my forge, my kindness, the hospitality of the British people, his travels over here. Professor Arno Linssen, from Falun, to the north-west of Uppsala, did I know Sweden at all?

Did I use these big leather bellows for the . . . Ah, the electric fan, clever, to hide it there! Yes, of course, the modern workshop through the door, but please, Ann, may I call you Ann? So long since I used these tools, and I am on holiday. Do you mind?

I helped him to use the forge, although it took three times as long, working with hand tools, as it would have done in the workshop. I turned off the electric fan, and I pumped the bellows for him, and he laughed in delight to find they were in such good condition. Uncle Henry kept them like that, so I oil the wood and the leather when it needs it, and sometimes children like to use them.

He turned off the lights. We worked by firelight, and then I found the oil lamps on the shelf above the door. They were smoky, so Arno trimmed the wicks and wiped the dust from the brass, and we set them on the workbench.

He made me laugh.

He was clumsy with the hammer, rueful about being out of practice, and I smiled. It was more than that: he wasn't good at this work. It was taking far too long, and he wasn't very sure, with these tools. His work was in laboratories and offices; here in my forge he was an amateur.

By the time we finished it was almost dark, too late to start on the car itself. Arno stripped off his overalls and the shirt he'd worn under them, and I turned away, misery taking the place of the enjoyment I'd been feeling, when I'd hardly realised I'd been happy. I'd been working alongside a man, and he'd treated me well, as a colleague, as a friend, as his hostess.

I turned away, because I did try hard not to think of what I could never have, and there'd been the shine of sweat on a well-muscled body, there'd been supple movement of arms and shoulders, lines of shadow and light on a broad ribcage.

We had finished the work, and he would go. He would return the next day and fit the spring we had made, and pay me, and then he would drive away and I would be alone, with the memory of an evening working alongside a stranger who had made me laugh, and who had respected my skills, and had said so. I would never forget it, this time we had had working together, but I knew I would also remember the ache and the misery of knowing there could be nothing more.

Was there a hotel in Anford, or a pub? Somewhere not far?

'You could stay here.'

I had never invited anybody to stay here, only my sister when she'd been ill, and my Uncle John, but I'd never offered hospitality to a stranger.

'Here?'

I wasn't looking at him. I was staring at my feet, and I could feel my shoulders hunching defensively.

What was he thinking? A woman inviting him to stay overnight in her home, what would he think? What did he think I meant?

And what did I think I meant, asking him?

'I've got a spare room,' I said. 'If you'd like, you can stay.'

I glanced across at him, quickly, and lowered my eyes again before he could see.

'In my spare room,' I added confusedly.

'Ann, you are so kind. Thank you. I would like to stay.'

I made us bacon sandwiches, which he had never eaten before. He affected to be suspicious, but pronounced them delicious, yet another British invention of genius, comparable with radar and infinitely superior to television. Why were they not served at Maxim's?

I was beginning to wonder if he would ever stop talking.

I made up the bed in the spare room, feeling flustered as I did so, wondering if the sheets and blankets were aired properly. They might perhaps be damp from lying in the cupboard. It was dusty in there, should I have arranged a bowl of flowers? My mother would never have dreamed of leaving a visitor in a room without flowers.

Was the bathroom clean? What would he think if there was a tide-mark? What would he think of me?

I lay awake all night, trying to think of Lyric, of riding her in the park, of the time she'd won the race at Wolverhampton. I tried to think of my work, I tried to plan my vegetable garden.

I saw, again and again, the firelight in the forge, Arno working at the anvil, smiling at me, talking, laughing. I saw the sheen of sweat on his chest as he stripped off his shirt.

16

He was only yards away from me, sleeping in that room with the dark green curtains.

I lay on my back with my hands behind my head, staring up out of the window at the dark summer sky, trying not to think of him. Trying, and trying, not to think of things I could never have.

When I heard the church clock strike four, I began to cry.

I was up at six, doing my best to move quietly so as not to disturb Arno. I crept down the stairs, pressing myself against the wall so the old wood might not creak under my weight. I didn't make my coffee; running water makes the pipes rattle, they might wake him. I went out to the stable block and filled a hay net for Lyric, and brought her in from the paddock, brushed her mane and tail and picked out her feet. I tried to concentrate on what I was doing.

My eyes felt sore, and I was tired and depressed. I felt foolish, told myself I was too old for schoolgirl crushes, I should pull myself together.

But I laid the brush on Lyric's back, and I bent my head and leaned against her neck, feeling the coarse hairs pressing into my hot face, feeling the tears springing again into my eyes.

'I have made coffee,' he said, and I jumped, knocking the brush off the mare's back so it clattered onto the concrete and she threw up her head and stamped.

'I am sorry. I startled you.'

'It's all right. You're up early, for a holiday-maker.'

I tried to speak lightly, but my voice was artificial. I didn't want to look at him because he would see my eyes were red.

'I like the mornings. I put milk in, is that right?'

'That's fine, yes. Thank you, that's fine.'

'Are you all right?'

'Yes. Yes, fine. I have, sort of, hay fever.'

Such a stupid excuse. A blacksmith with hay fever,

grooming a horse, with hay fever, standing by a hay net, with hay fever.

'More, well, a sort of allergy. Nothing much. It's OK.'

'Oh. You are allergic to what?'

To what could I be allergic, in my job, here?

I turned towards him and smiled, taking the mug from his outstretched hand. I would ignore the question.

'It's a lovely morning,' I said, but he was looking at me with his head on one side, an expression of concern on his face.

'Yes, it is a lovely morning. To what are you allergic, Ann? My wife has an allergy also, it was treated. Now she has no problems.'

His wife. I had lain awake all night, thinking of him, and not once had I thought of a wife. Not once had the idea crossed my mind. His wife.

'She doesn't come on holiday with you?'

I could not keep the brittle artificiality out of my voice. I was making small talk, a practice I despise.

'She takes the children to their grandmother for the summer holiday.'

He sipped his coffee, and turned his eyes towards the paddock.

'I can't stand her bloody mother,' he added unexpectedly, and I laughed, surprised.

He smiled at me.

'I can't stand my bloody mother, either,' I said, and then frowned as I considered my words. I'd spoken almost without thinking, and I'd spoken the truth.

I hate my bloody mother. Lucille, I hate you. I hate you.

'Ann?'

'I hadn't realised,' I said. 'Arno, I hate my mother, and I'd never realised until I said that to you. Isn't that weird?'

'No, not very. Why do you hate her?'

'I suppose because she hated me. I didn't know that until I was quite old. In my teens. Then she told me.'

18

I threw the dregs of my coffee away onto the grass by the paddock fence.

'It wasn't her fault. She's very beautiful. She was then, anyway. I don't know now. She didn't know what to do about me.'

He was looking at me, a very serious expression on his face.

'You are not beautiful like the Miss World women, no. But you are magnificent.'

I looked away from him, feeling my face growing hot and flushed.

'Oh. Yes? Oh.'

'I would be proud to take you to bed.'

My coffee mug shattered on the concrete at my feet, and Lyric shied away, her hooves clattering and her head thrown high in alarm.

I turned towards her, snatching at her head collar, although there was no danger of her breaking free, but in my humiliation and anger I hardly knew what I was doing. I could not look at his face. I could not bear to see his laughter.

Lyric tugged hard against my hands, and then dropped her head, her ears flicking suspiciously, her eyes still rimmed with white.

'I am sorry if I startled you, Ann.'

I clenched my fists in the mare's mane. I still had my back to him, and my cheeks were burning with shame and rage.

'Arno. Just . . . just *please* don't. I don't mind a joke, but please don't laugh at me like that.'

'What?'

'Don't laugh at me. Please.'

He threw his own mug down onto the concrete where mine had shattered, and he was shouting at me.

'Listen. You are angry? OK, you hit me in the face, only not too hard please, because I think you are quite strong. You leave that damned horse alone a minute, she's okay,

19

you just listen to me instead. Maybe you tell me to fuck off out of it, if that is how you say it, and I apologise and I go away feeling very sorry, because I like you. But you, you, Ann, you do *not* tell me I am laughing at you. I am *not* laughing at you. Why can I laugh at you when you have been kind to me? What the *hell* you think I am, Ann?'

I was crying again, and I didn't know what to say to him, or what I should do. No man had ever said I was magnificent, no man had ever shown any sign of wanting to take me to bed, and I could not believe it had happened now.

'I'm sorry,' I stammered. 'I'm sorry.'

He fell silent, and I stood looking down, my head hanging in shame and confusion. I could only look at the coffee and the broken china as I tried to control my tears, tried to breathe properly. My chest felt tight and the tears would not stop welling up out of my eyes and running down my cheeks. I brushed them away.

'Oh, no. No, please, Ann. I am sorry, it is me who is sorry. Don't cry. I should not shout at you, I am very sorry.'

He walked up to me, close to me, but I couldn't look at him. I felt so humiliated, so bewildered, and I didn't even want to think of what he had meant. I did not believe this. No matter what he said now, he could only have been laughing at me.

I kept turning my head away, looking anywhere but at Arno.

'Please, Ann, please look at me. Don't cry.'

'I'm not . . . I'm . . .'

'Oh, yes, I forgot. Your allergy. Ann?'

'Mm. Yes. Yes.'

I glanced at him, and he was smiling at me, so I smiled back. He reached out and touched my cheek. I tried not to, but I flinched.

'Oh, Ann. What has hurt you so much?'

'Nothing. Please, Arno, nothing.'

'OK, Ann. Nothing. I hope the coffee mugs were not valuable?'

I managed a laugh, a slightly choked one.

'Woolies' best,' I said.

'What?'

'Woolworth's. Just cheap mugs, not valuable.'

'So, a professor's salary will be enough for replacements?'

This time it was a little easier to laugh.

He said he was hungry. He asked whether bacon sandwiches were also possible for breakfast, and I said I supposed so, why not? But when we were in the kitchen he said he wasn't hungry at all, he'd wanted us to come back to the cottage, and would I please sit down for a little while, and tell him why I hated my mother? And he would make some more coffee.

So I told him about Lucille, my beautiful mother, for whom the opinions of men were of paramount importance. I told him of the times she had taken me to doctors because I was growing too tall, and I remembered as I spoke of it how I had felt then when I heard her say 'freak', and knew she meant me.

Arno stirred milk into the coffee, and handed me my mug. He said nothing, but he leaned back against the kitchen table, and sometimes he was watching me, and sometimes he was looking down at the floor, and he was listening to me.

'She put me on a diet and I got ill. I wasn't fat, I was just big. The doctors had told her diets wouldn't work. She'd asked them. She gave me gin once, it made me sick. I was about seven, I think.'

I thought about that time, trying to remember what Lucille had said, to me, to my pretty, feminine sister, to the doctors.

'"Women shouldn't be too tall. Men don't like it."'

Arno was looking at me, questioningly.

21

'That was what Lucille said,' I explained, and he smiled. One eyebrow lifted slightly before he looked down again and waited for me to go on.

'When I was a child I used to come here. Uncle Henry and Aunt Ruth, I loved it here, I was happy. When Aunt Ruth died Lucille wouldn't let me come any more. I didn't understand why. Then a lot later, Henry's brother, John, he's a lawyer . . . Well, Henry had died, you see. And he left me the forge, so I decided to be a blacksmith, and Lucille . . .'

Screaming at me. So ugly your own father couldn't stand the sight of you. Took one look at you lying in your cot, and he left. You just got uglier and uglier and uglier.

I wish I could have left you, like he did.

Go, then. And may the devil go with you.

I couldn't tell Arno this. My sister Glory had helped me, she'd heard, and she'd helped me, and she'd telephoned Uncle John, and told him. He'd come to the school.

You weren't ugly, he'd said. You were rather a fine-looking baby. But it was quite obvious then that you weren't Peter's daughter. You were at least partly negro.

So Peter Mayall, the third brother, the youngest, had left his beautiful wife, and his beautiful daughter, and the baby his wife had borne to another man, and gone back to the Navy. I'd never seen him.

'I still don't know who my father is,' I said, and wondered after I'd spoken how much of what had been in my mind I'd said to Arno, and how much remained in pain and silence in my memory.

My coffee was almost cold, but I drank it, and I put the empty mug on the draining board, and wondered what Arno would say now.

I gazed out of the window at the paddock, looking at a clump of thistles I'd intended to dig out, and behind the stable block Lyric moved restlessly at the end of her rope, her hay net almost empty.

Arno was watching me again when I turned back, his expression thoughtful and a little sad.

'So much of your spirit is scar tissue,' he said. 'It is a lot of pain, Ann. But you know it is very strong, scar tissue. I think you have a very strong spirit.'

He reached out his hands towards me, and I looked at them, and gave him mine.

'Now I say it again. I would be proud to take you to bed.'

2

Arno stayed with me for three weeks that time, until he had to leave for the conference in Melbourne. I had counted the days we had left, at first believing they were the days to the end, but then he asked me if he could leave the Riley at the forge, if I could make room for it beside my old van.

It was early on a Sunday morning when he asked me. We were lying in bed together, and I had said I would have to get up to feed Lyric, and Arno had nodded.

'Horses eat even when they are not working, this is not good economics when compared to a car. Oh, I meant to ask you, Ann. May I leave the Riley here? Can we make some room beside the van, if we move some of that rubbish in there?'

'Yes,' I'd said, and I'd turned my face into his shoulder and begun to cry again.

That first day he'd been with me, there'd been so many tears. He'd been very gentle, very understanding, and for Arno very quiet. Every time he'd touched me at first, I flinched. Every time he'd looked at me, I waited for words of scorn: I'd been ready for the pain, and the shame. When he touched me, when he stroked me, I'd hardly been able to breathe. He'd been looking at me, looking at my body, stroking my skin, his hand just brushing, lightly, gently, over my ribs, and then he'd noticed.

'Why aren't you breathing?'

I hadn't known what to say. I'd drawn in my breath, and let it out, and then I'd done it again, and again, and then he was looking down into my face.

'Your skin is as velvet, Ann. I have never touched such beautiful skin.'

So I'd watched his hand on my body, and found I was breathing again. But I'd started to tremble, and then to shake, uncontrollably, and he'd stopped stroking me and put his arms around me and hugged me, tight and hard, until I stopped, but by then I'd been crying again.

'I'm sorry,' I'd whispered. 'I'm sorry.'

He'd kissed me, gently and lightly on my lips, and then he'd looked down at me, into my face, and brushed the tears away from my cheeks with the tips of his fingers, and kissed me again.

'Are you frightened?' he'd asked.

'No. I don't think so. No.'

'Do you know what is going to happen?'

'Yes. Of course, yes.'

Then he'd been smiling. There were deep lines at the corners of his eyes, as though he'd spent a long time in bright sunlight, or perhaps looking into the white heat of a furnace.

'So? *How* do you know?'

I'd felt myself flushing again, but I tried not to look away.

'I was very good at biology at school.'

The smile had turned to a grin, and then a laugh, and I found I was smiling, too, although I could feel my face flaming.

'So? I am very pleased, and very proud, that you were such a good student of biology. At school. What did you learn, in the biology lessons at school?'

'Well. You know?'

25

'Ann, I think I know, yes. I do not want to talk about the reproductive system of the rabbit, I want to talk about love, and friendship, and human sexuality, and so now, will you please give me your hand. Thank you, and now will you please *open* your *eyes*, and forget about your school biology lessons.'

He'd talked, and explained, and I'd had to listen, and to look, and to touch, and he'd ignored my embarrassment, and talked, and talked, and I'd called him Professor Linssen, which had made him smile in amusement, but still he'd talked.

Then at last I'd found I was stroking his shoulder, watching my hand on his skin, I was hardly listening to him, just aware of his voice, but looking at my hand, and feeling the smoothness of his skin under my fingers.

When I'd looked into his face, he was watching my hand, too, and then he'd smiled at me, and he'd only spoken once more.

'Use the palm of your hand, Ann. Not just the fingers.'

When he was lying close against me, I thought of the evening before when I had turned away in misery and longing as he had stripped off his shirt, and I felt a sense of wonder, that the body I had seen and yearned for was here: for this moment at least it was mine. Now my hands were on the skin that had shone in the firelight, now I was touching the smoothness, and the suppleness, there was warm breath against the side of my neck, there was hair falling onto my face, and when there was pain there was also a gentle voice, and comforting hands, and a smile of sympathy. My name was spoken, in affection and in friendship, and perhaps even in love, just for now, for this small instant in my life, my name.

'Arno,' I said. 'Arno.'

'Yes?'

'I just wanted to say your name. Arno.'

'Ann.'

26

There was sunlight on our bodies. It was warm, and there was a scent of leaves from the woods in the park, I lifted my face to it, and then bent my neck and rested my forehead against Arno's shoulder.

'Ann.'

'What's today?' I asked.

'Friday. The thirteenth.'

'Arno. I have customers coming.'

'Mm. Yes, all right. We must get up again, and we must work. I must fit the spring to the Riley. And you?'

'Horses to shoe.'

'May I watch?'

'Yes. From a distance, please, Arno.'

He borrowed my van instead, and drove into Cheltenham. He came back that afternoon with two coffee mugs, Royal Doulton, beautiful.

'They're too good to use,' I said, and he shook his head at me.

'Good things must be used. One day they will break. One day you will die, and so will I. Shall I make some coffee?'

That afternoon we fitted the new spring, and I waited for him to say he would go. Instead he asked if he could work in the forge again that evening. He would like to make something, if I would permit.

'Oil lamps and bellows?' I asked, and he laughed.

I lent him my old leather apron. I told him the legend about the cut, made by the jealous tailor when St Clement had forced King Alfred to change his nomination of the tailor as the paramount craftsman and name the blacksmith in his place.

'Do you wear this?'

'No, not now. I used to wear it. I wear chaps when I'm shoeing horses now. They're more practical.'

We didn't work late that night. He said he wanted to make a basket in which he could put a flower pot, but it was too difficult for him, and he gave up.

27

'I'm tired,' he said. 'I lay awake all last night, thinking about you. Shall we go to bed now?'

'Bacon sandwich first?'

But we weren't hungry. We went upstairs, and we undressed, and got into my bed, and then we fell asleep, almost immediately. When I woke in the morning his arms were around my waist, his head on my breast, and he was still sleeping. There was a dark shadow of stubble on his face, and his hair was tousled.

I lay still, studying his face, trying to memorise every line, every plane, every shadow. This would probably have to suffice for the rest of my life, I wanted to remember everything I could.

Light on the smooth skin over his shoulder blade, and the little hollows down his spine, the curve of his buttocks, and the long lines of the muscles in his thighs and calves. Remember this. Remember the warmth of his breath, and the movement of his ribs. Remember the colours in his hair, dark blond, darker shadows where it falls at the parting, the crisp curls at the back of his neck.

Remember.

His eyes were open, he was looking into my face, a slow smile, and I smiled back at him, looking into the blue of his eyes, thinking, the same colour as Aunt Ruth's kitchen flower vase, remember.

'Ann. What are you thinking?'

'Your eyes are the same colour as Aunt Ruth's kitchen flower vase.'

The lines at the corners of his eyes, as they crinkled in amusement, crow's-feet, they call them. Remember.

And remember the touch of his hands, and his lips, and the way he breathes, and his eyes, looking down into mine with a question that I don't have to answer, except with my own hands, and my own lips, and the way I am breathing now, and the way I look back at him.

Remember.

How will I bear it, when he has gone, and I can only remember?

Everything must pass, perhaps even the pain, when he has gone.

Then he'd asked about the Riley. He hadn't asked why, when I'd cried, because it had always been something that had hurt in the past, or some fear he had soothed. He'd held me close, he'd been warm, and comforting, and friendly, and he hadn't asked.

'You can drive it, if you like. I will pay, of course.'

'You don't have to pay, Arno.'

'But yes. I would rather pay you the two hundred pounds a year than this man in London who puts up the rent for his little garage every time I see him. He thinks I am a rich idiot.'

'If you're paying two hundred a year just for a garage, he's right.'

Arno had grinned, hugged me again, and rumpled my hair. I wasn't crying any more. If his car was here, he meant to come back to me. I didn't have to remember; he would come back.

'Not so stupid as that man thinks. At least if my car is stolen from here, I will know you did not have a share of the price.'

I'd been shocked.

'Arno! Would he? Oh, that's . . . that's dreadful.'

'Oh, yes.' He was laughing at me again. 'It is dreadful, that he could be so dishonest, and cheat this stupid, rich, foreign idiot. It is very dreadful. It is also damned inconvenient that every time I leave the car in that garage I have to take so many bits of it home with me. You see, the cost of having them made is nearly as much as the price of the car.'

While we were clearing the rubbish out of the garage to make room for the Riley I asked him about his wife, and he told me I didn't have to worry about Brita. I thought he was warning me not to ask him about her, to mind my own

29

business, but he'd been dragging a broken garden table through the door at the time, and when he came back he explained, without my having asked anything else.

'I am away for many months every year, and Brita would be alone. She has Krisu. Kristian. He's a nice young man, I like him. He's her lover.'

He knocked something over, there was a crash, a cloud of dust, and he was coughing, and swearing in Swedish.

'Do you want to keep these goddamned deckchairs?'

'Yes, I think so. Or . . .?'

'There are worm holes.'

'Oh. No, throw them away, then.'

'I know about Brita and Krisu, and I try not to mind. It is not my business. I do not own her, and if I am not there, I should not complain if he is.'

The deckchairs were thrown through the back door, and Arno was picking at a splinter in the heel of his hand. Uncle Henry and I had sat on those deckchairs on summer evenings, and I wasn't sure I believed they had woodworm. Arno could suffer his splinters. I didn't like what he was saying.

He'd seemed to guess what I was thinking.

'Don't be stiff,' he'd said. 'Our marriage works very well. I love her. Please understand. If you can't, please accept it.'

A week later, he'd flown from Heathrow for the conference in Melbourne.

'I have a week in October,' he'd said. 'May I come here?'

I'd cried that night, alone in the cottage, but I hadn't tried too hard to remember. The Riley was in the garage, under a big dust sheet, its keys on a hook in the forge, my talisman for Arno, who would come back in October.

He comes whenever he can, sometimes just for a day or two, sometimes for longer, and people say to me, how nice for him, this Swedish professor of metallurgy, that you put him up when he comes over here, and keep his car for him. It must be so interesting for him, because of course the

30

forge is very, very old, such a contrast to his modern laboratories.

The villagers like him. He's always so friendly, you'd never think he was such an important man, would you? Miss Mayall's friend Professor Linssen, who stays in her spare room when he's over here for conferences, or when he comes to meet colleagues at the British universities.

Arno is the secret I hug to myself when he isn't here.

When he leaves, for a few days I am unhappy, missing him, feeling alone, and even lonely, which is something unusual, for me. My customers come, and say that I'm very quiet today, a question in their voices, so I summon a smile, and try to talk.

At those times in particular, I do resent strangers.

Strangers come here to pry into the past, and we in Anford are trying to forget that. We're ashamed of the episode that brings the curious and the morbid to our village, and especially to the forge.

If it hadn't been for the fact that Arno had left only two days before, and if I hadn't become so resentful of strangers, so brusque and short with them, I might have taken more notice of the Müllers when they called. They were speaking German to each other, and breaking off their conversation to look at me as though I were something put on display to entertain and interest tourists.

'Can I help you?'

The tone was as sarcastic as I could make it, but perhaps they didn't notice, or didn't understand. Mrs Müller smiled at me. Bright turquoise eyelids and brass-coloured hair, a slightly surprised look about her face. It speaks; this big thing speaks.

She said something else to her husband, again in German, so I turned my back on them both and went into the forge. Perhaps they'd go away.

'Excuse me, please?'

He had followed me, and she was standing slightly

31

behind him, so that she had to crane her head to one side to see past him. She did this often; she had this trick of standing behind her husband and looking out from behind him, as though sheltering, or trying to hide.

'Yes?'

'You make orders?'

'Do you make special orders?' she asked before I'd had a chance to answer her husband. 'Is this correct? To say it like this?'

'What do you want me to make?'

'A door, as the one you have made.'

'A gate,' she said. 'Not a door, Franz, a gate.'

There are four gates on the forge land, and I made them all, but I knew the one she meant. The gate between the paddock and Gorsedown Park appeared in the national newspapers, although nobody had asked me for permission to photograph it. It's held in place by three springs, and you have to exert a lot of force to move it. When you do, it rings. It's covered in leaves and flowers and curlicues, all made of steel, and when they move they clash together. There isn't a straight line on that gate, and there's only one place where you can get a handhold. Those springs are heavy, and they come into play one after the other. Once the gate has been forced past the third spring, it's held open by a steel catch. There's only room for one person to push against the gate. Very few are strong enough to open it, and nobody can do so silently.

It had taken me three weeks to make it, and I didn't want to make another one.

'A thousand pounds,' I said.

'Ja. Yes. A thousand pounds is OK. When can you make it?'

He hadn't even hesitated. She said something to him in German, and he shook his head. She sniffed and turned away, walking back out into the sunlit yard.

An average man, grey haired.

'Are you strong enough to open the gate?' I asked.

'Please?'

I tried to remember what I had learned of German at school.

'*Sind Sie stark genug um das Tor zu öffnen?*'

He spread his hands in bewilderment, and I put down my hammer.

'Come and try,' I said.

They hadn't known about the springs. They pulled at the gate, they talked to each other, quickly and quietly in German so I could neither hear nor understand, and he shook his head.

'Thank you,' he said, and she smiled at me, brightly.

'We will consider a solution to these problem. This. This problem.'

I didn't think they'd be back. I assumed they were on holiday, that they'd wanted to ship the gate to Germany, and that they'd give up the idea.

Somebody telephoned me the next day, a man with an English voice.

'Frau Müller asked me to discuss the order for the gate. Can't it be made with a conventional latch?'

'Yes, of course it can, but then it could be opened silently.'

'Sorry?'

'If you open it smoothly the steel won't move. I mean, it won't shake, so it won't ring.'

'I don't quite understand.'

I'm not very good at explaining, and I was busy.

'You have to jerk the gate to make it ring. It jerks when you hit the springs. Why do they want this gate? Is it for ornament or security?'

'Just a moment, please.'

There was a muffled discussion in German. The farmer who'd come to discuss hinges for his barn doors looked at his watch, pointedly.

33

'Hello? Hello? I'm sorry, I can't hold on any longer, I have a customer here.'

'I won't keep you long.'

Again, the hand over the mouthpiece, the voices muted. I hung up the telephone and switched on the answering machine. I didn't want to make the gate for the Müllers, and Garth Michaelson was a good client.

'Hinges,' I said. 'Four for each door on those monsters, Garth. Going to cost you.'

'Always does,' he answered. 'But at least it only costs me once.'

We both ignored the telephone when it started to ring.

Two days later the Müllers came back in person, with drawings. One plate spring to make the gate vibrate and ring, a latch with three locks, and a catch with a winch, so that a child could open the gate from the inside, if necessary.

The latch was work for a locksmith, and the winch was dangerous. I said I wouldn't do it. The winch could slip, and somebody could be trapped between the slamming gate and its frame.

'But then your gate is also dangerous!' protested Frau Müller.

'Very,' I agreed. 'Much more dangerous than this. But it's mine, and it's on private property.'

'Our gate will also on private property.' Herr Müller, not sounding very sure.

'Will also *be* on private property, Franz. Be.'

Frau Müller smirked at me, inviting my support. Two women against this man, no? And my English is good, isn't it?

I was frowning at the drawings. I didn't notice. Never turn down a customer, you don't know where it might lead. Uncle Henry had said that to me when I was seven years old.

'On private property,' asserted Herr Müller, avoiding the verbs.

34

I didn't like these tourists, and I didn't want to make the gate. It was genuinely dangerous.

'I'm sorry,' I said, handing him the drawings. 'If somebody were to be hurt I could be held liable, even if it was a burglar.'

'But your gate,' he protested. 'Also, you are liable if it is a burglar.'

'Yes,' I agreed. 'I'll probably take the gate down when the estate's sold.'

Frau Müller was no longer smiling. She snapped at her husband and stalked off, her nose in the air. He glanced after her, his lips tightening, and then he looked down at the drawings. He seemed to be about to speak again, but the telephone in the forge rang, and I turned away.

'I'm sorry,' I called back over my shoulder. 'I'm sorry, I don't think I can help you.'

I heard them arguing, her voice indignant and a little shrill, his exasperated. Then there were footsteps on the gravel, and one last exclamation from her.

'Ah, *Scheisse!*'

It was a wrong number, but I didn't go out again after I hung up. I wanted to start work on Garth's hinges; it was quite urgent. One of the doors was sagging, and he'd said he didn't dare use it until the hinges had been replaced.

'God knows what it weighs. Quick as you can, Ann, I need both those doors, can't get the big trailer in through just one.'

It's a medieval tithe barn, a listed building, and Garth has to be careful with repairs or the Anford History Society threatens him with legal action, not entirely jokingly. Garth lets them use it every June for their annual barn dance, their big fund-raising event, so the relationship is friendlier than that between them and most of the other farmers in Anford, who find them a nuisance.

The hinges I was to make for Garth had been designed by the History Society's membership secretary, who was a draughtsman for a firm of architects. He'd done that job for nothing; he'd charged George Fowler fifty pounds to design the locks for his coach house, because George had installed locks made by a modern security firm, and had then told the History Society to mind its own blasted business.

Its business was preventing that sort of thing, and it had obtained a court order against George, which had brought him to the forge, spitting curses. I'd made the housing for the locks, and some sort of compromise had been reached with the History Society.

It's a pretty village, Anford, it is worth preserving, but that takes money. Old houses cost a lot to maintain, so the young people move away to places they can afford, and the pretty old houses are bought by newcomers, middle-aged or retired.

Jansy Neville told me the Müllers had bought a cottage on the other side of the village, and she was furious, although not about the purchase.

'Damned old bitch. Keeps me waiting nearly ten minutes for the paper money last Saturday, her and her airs and graces. Leaves me standing there on the doorstep like I'm a beggar. Late for all the other customers.'

Jansy had come to ask me a favour. Her mother had finally grown tired of the smell of the ferrets and had told Jansy to get rid of them. The dog was bad enough, snapping at the postman; the ferrets were too much.

A home-made hutch containing two ferrets was now at the back of the hay store.

'Oh, Missus, you *are* nice.'

So, the Müllers wanted the gate for a cottage in Anford. I didn't like them, and I didn't want to make another gate. I always do my best for local people, and now they were local people. I might have to make them their gate.

They sent the next drawings by post, dimensions and an outline, with a covering letter that had certainly been translated by someone else. They would be responsible for the frame and the springs; I was to make the main piece of the gate, so it rang loudly when it came up against any resistance. This letter was their assurance that they understood the verbal warnings I had given them, and accepted all responsibility for the use to which they put the gate.

The gearbox on my van had finally reached the point where even Graham Steel said the thing was only fit for a scrap heap. A thousand pounds would be welcome.

'Oh, bugger.'

I typed a note to the Müllers to tell them that their gate would differ from mine in design and ornament, but would work in the same way, which meant only one handhold, and nowhere else where a good grip could be obtained. Also, I added, my order book was full and I would not be able to start work for over a month. It would be June before their gate was ready.

I wrote that with a clear conscience because it was perfectly true, but that evening I started to draw.

By the time I'd finished it was well past midnight, and the Müllers' gate was clear in my mind, and on paper. I looked at my drawings with my head on one side, and a smile on my lips.

It was a vine of sorts, a type I knew well, and disliked, because it was a fast-growing weed I was constantly pulling out of my hedges. It has little white flowers, and I planned to make the edges of the petals sharp. The tendrils hung in spirals, or twined around the stem of the parent plant. It was a tricky, detailed piece of work, but not in the outrageously baroque style of my own gate. This was more realistic; one could believe such a thing had grown.

Moving through the vine, and curling across it to provide a framework, as well as the single handhold, were three snakes.

I tapped my pencil against my teeth as I looked at those snakes. I had no idea why I had drawn them; they had been some sort of doodle as I considered the composition of my design and looked for a way of bracing the fragile-seeming stems. The snakes had grown, an abstract metamorphosis from plant to animal. What had begun as wood or fibre had ended as muscle and skin, animal, coiled around the plant and at the same time supporting it.

Two of the snakes faced each other, their heads inches apart, passive and incurious. The third turned back from the handhold as if towards an intruder, jaw gaping and the fangs standing sharp and clear.

That night I dreamed of snakes in the hedges around the forge, holding the beech plants together, watching each other, and waiting.

I woke in the morning curiously soothed by the dream, with a memory lingering of the snakes, quiet, and not unfriendly, a part of the land. There are snakes in those hedges sometimes, I've seen them in summer, sunning themselves on the banks. When I see them I move away, I give them room. That morning I searched for them, walking along beside the hedges, and I was looking into the beeches, although I've never seen them climb.

I asked Garth Michaelson about them later that day while we were re-hanging his barn doors. He was perched dangerously on the fork lift of his big tractor while his cowman took the weight of the massive oak on the smaller tractor and I called out directions and tried to guide the doors into place with a crowbar. The job needed two more people at least, but that farm's always short-handed.

'Jackson, for God's sake get the damned thing closer to the frame,' ordered Garth, and the cowman dabbed at a lever. The door shuddered and swung, and Garth cursed. I began to wonder whether the hinge would stand the leverage that was being demanded of it.

Jackson muttered something apologetic, and revved the tractor engine for no reason at all.

'Again!' yelled Garth, and once more the rear lift on the little tractor rose slowly, the nose rising as the huge weight settled.

'Stop!' I shouted.

The engine revved again. I braced myself against the long crowbar and glanced up at Garth. He nodded, and I leaned forward and heaved.

The second bolt slammed home, and we grinned at each other.

'Do snakes climb trees?'

'What?'

'Do *snakes* climb trees?'

He shook his head. He couldn't hear over the noise of the engine. Jackson was looking back over his shoulder, waiting for a signal. We'd have to swing the door hard up against the frame to bolt the second hinge into place, and Garth needed to lower the fork lift to be at the right height.

'Ann, lower the lift for me, would you?'

'Not with you on it, no.'

'Oh, get on with it.'

But I wouldn't, and he knew it. He grumbled at me, but he climbed down and did it himself.

'Do snakes climb trees?' I asked again.

'No,' he said. 'Well. What snakes? I mean, what are you talking about?'

'I wish you'd get some sheerlegs.'

'I've got some, they're broken. What do you mean, do snakes climb trees? Some do, some don't. What sort of snakes?'

'Pythons climb trees,' said Jackson. 'So do boa constrictors and anacondas and moccasins.'

'A moccasin's a water snake,' objected Garth.

'Maybe I'm thinking of copperheads.'

'Pythons can swim,' I said. 'I think.'

'That's different from being a water snake. I can swim, but I'm not a fish. I can climb trees, too, and I'm not a squirrel.'

'If you could handle a tractor, you'd be a help.'

Jackson considered taking offence, and decided not to.

39

'I'm a cowman, not a tractor driver. I'm a specialist. I can tell the difference between a redpoll and a shorthorn, which some I could mention can't.'

Garth climbed back onto the fork lift without answering, and Jackson winked at me. I moved the bricks and timbers that braced the door, and stood back.

The engine roared again. Another uncertain dab at the lever, and the huge door dropped judderingly onto the timbers. One of them splintered, and buckled. I looked up anxiously at the single hinge now supporting the entire weight. It was pulled rigidly away from the frame, but it was still level.

The tractor lurched forward, stopped, the small front wheels turned, the familiar roar from the overworked engine, and it backed, the tail lift scraping onto concrete.

Garth screamed at me over the noise.

'Will two hold it?'

'For ten minutes,' I yelled back, and he raised his eyes, parodying a prayer, and then nodded to me.

'Lift,' I called to Jackson, and he looked at me, cupping his hand behind his ear. I gestured, raising one hand palm upwards.

Again he raised the tail lift too quickly, and this time the door swung against the hinge, dangerously close to Garth, who instinctively put out his hands and nearly lost his balance. If he fell he could be caught between the spikes and that massive door. If that hinge gave way the door would fall on him. I'd calculated it needed four hinges, and now it was only supported by one.

Horrified, I watched as the huge structure tilted, as it rocked against the prongs of the fork lift, which dipped helplessly under the weight. Garth was trapped now. He had no way of getting out, and the hinge couldn't hold.

'*Down!*' I shrieked at the cowman. 'Down *very slowly*.'

This time he got it right. The oak was creaking as it rubbed against the frame, and as it lowered I jammed the crowbar into the space under the door, dropped it across the bar of the tail lift and threw my weight onto it. Agonisingly slowly, the door slid backwards, straightening as it moved, and Garth hammered the bolt through the iron and the oak.

He was rather pale, and there was sweat on his forehead that hadn't been caused by physical effort alone.

He looked down at me as the tractor engine died.

'What bloody snakes, then?' he asked.

'Adders, I think,' I answered, and then, 'There should be seven bolts for each hinge. Have you got them up there?'

'Yes. I don't think adders can climb trees. I've never seen an adder in a tree. Can you reach that third hinge?'

I was already tightening the first bolt, so I didn't bother to answer.

'What about grass snakes, then?'

Jackson was watching us, very subdued. He looked a little frightened. That had been an extremely dangerous moment, and it was his fault.

Garth wouldn't blame his cowman. Garth Michaelson's a fair man.

'What do you think, Jeff?' he asked. 'Do grass snakes climb trees?'

'Nope.' Jackson was still uneasy, despite the use of his first name. 'You finished with me now? Can I get back to my cows?'

Garth ignored the request.

'Any snakes in this country climb trees?'

'Not unless they got out of a zoo. We got three snakes in this country – we got adders, we got grass snakes and we got slow-worms. Far as I know, not one of them climbs trees. Course, I could be wrong, I'm only a cowman.'

I glanced at him. His face was red and he was looking across the yard, avoiding our eyes.

'If we want those two heifers ready for the show you'd better go and manicure them again,' said Garth, and as

Jackson hunched his shoulders and walked off he called after him.

'Thanks for your help, Jeff.'

Garth and I fixed the rest of the bolts in silence. Garth seemed to be embarrassed.

It wasn't until we'd finished, and tested the doors, that he spoke to me again. He wiped his hand across his face and gave me a shamefaced smile.

'I have to admit there was a moment then when I was downright glad I didn't buy those hinges they had on special offer at Blake's.'

I'm not good at accepting compliments, even oblique ones like that, so I just looked up at the barn doors.

'I wonder what they do weigh,' I said. 'You'd think they'd get lighter with age, but oak seems to get heavier and heavier.'

The doors of the forge are oak, the same shape as Garth's tithe barn doors, smaller, but even thicker. They're hung on a massive iron frame which Uncle Henry made when he first came to Anford from Wales. The original oak frame is still there, and it's probably strong enough to carry the doors. I suspect Uncle Henry didn't have much to do when he first came. He made a lovely wrought-iron bench which stands under the tree, and it's really comfortable to sit on. It curves against your back, it invites you to relax. Uncle Henry was a great craftsman.

I wondered what he'd think of the gate I'd drawn for the Müllers.

The dream came back that night, the snakes in the hedges watching and waiting, twined around the beech bushes, quiet and friendly in the darkness.

3

Frau Müller didn't like the gate, and she was angry about it. I should not have put snakes in her gate. She had not ordered snakes. I was to make another gate. She would not accept this one.

Accept it or not, she would pay for it, was the gist of the letter I sent in response. I had warned them that the design would differ from mine, and they hadn't asked to see the drawings.

The big agricultural show was only a week away, and I was very busy. Not only were there horses to shoe, there was other livestock; cattle with feet to trim and polish, and a billy goat, an old and respected adversary, who never failed to inflict bruises during the annual contest between us.

Then there was an emergency call from an RSPCA inspector, David Lord. There's a disaster at a donkey sanctuary, please come at once.

'You know I don't travel,' I'd replied. 'Can you bring the donkeys here?'

'It'd be kinder to shoot them. Some of them can't walk at all.'

There was nobody else, David insisted. Yes, he knew I didn't travel, but in this case, please, Ann. For pity's sake, literally, for *pity's* sake. Please.

The place was being run by an old married couple who had meant well, but who had had no idea of what their charitable venture would cost. The animals were in a wretched state. It took a full day I could ill afford, working with the RSPCA and two veterinary surgeons, talking to a policeman, cutting back grotesquely overgrown hooves, treating corns and rotting feet, and in several cases advising immediate slaughter. It was a miserable incident.

The old woman was crying. They had never meant this to happen, but people had brought them donkeys and promised to pay for their keep, and more often than not the promises had been broken. After a month or two the money would stop coming. Letters wouldn't be answered, telephone calls would be met with evasion and lies.

'Will you prosecute?' I asked the policeman as I packed my tools into the van, and he shook his head.

'What would be the point? They didn't mean any harm. We have the nerve to call animals dumb, with morons like that stumbling around on their hind legs.'

The RSPCA had arranged for food to be delivered, but there were eighteen animals to be re-homed, and funds were limited. It wouldn't be long before they'd have to call in the knackers.

'Would you like a couple of donkeys?' David asked me.

'I would not.'

But some of my customers might like a donkey to graze in an orchard or to be company for a retired hunter. I'd ask around, I said. I'd do my best, and he thanked me.

One of the vets was hovering by his car. That old jenny with the cracked hooves, he'd been rather taken with her. She could share the paddock with his goats. If Ann would help him with those hooves?

'Yes,' I said. 'Gladly. I'd be happy to help.'

Nevertheless, I was thoroughly depressed by the time I got home that night to find a letter from a solicitor who represented the Müllers. He claimed it was unreasonable of

44

me to incorporate snakes into a design for a gate, and not to tell my clients I had done so. Their only experience of my work had shown them nothing but flowers and classical designs. They had had faith in me, and I had let them down. Birds or butterflies might have been acceptable; few people, he was sure I would concur, found snakes agreeable.

It was time to hand this over to Uncle John. I needed the money. I'd bought a new van, and my bank balance was too low for comfort. I wrote to him that night, enclosing the solicitor's letter and telling him, as I usually did when I wrote, all my news, especially about the donkey sanctuary.

Everything has to die in the end, but I had a memory I feared might not fade, of a lorry bumping away down the track, tarpaulins over humped shapes, and one pathetic little hoof protruding from under the green canvas.

Sentimentality does so much more harm than outright cruelty.

I was up at five the next morning, trying to get through the repair work before the first of the show horses arrived, and I was beginning to feel panic-stricken by the backlog of jobs that was accumulating. It seemed nothing I had to do was anything less than urgent, most of it critically so.

The grass in front of the forge was growing long and unkempt; I'd had no time to mow it. There were weeds between the flagstones and in the flowerbeds. Uncle Henry's bench needed a coat of paint, and so did the front door of the cottage. It had been days since I'd been out for a ride; I was feeling tired and stuffy from lack of exercise.

I'd welded two farm gates and straightened a garden fork by the time the first pony trailer turned into the drive.

'Would you like a donkey or two?' I asked Jane Laverton as she led her little pinto mare down the ramp.

She was sympathetic, but no. No place for donkeys on a dude ranch. Would I like an old Appaloosa, since we were talking about pensioners? Company for Lyric? Yes?

Jane's a good friend, one of my first customers, and her Bar-J Dude Ranch is a successful venture, and a popular holiday resort. I shoe all their horses, and make any iron-work they need.

'Have you heard about the hippies?' Jane asked as I nailed the first of the new shoes onto the mare's neat little feet. She went on before I could answer.

'I bet they're squatters. They've moved into the old rail-way station. Yes. Well, it's been asking for it, hasn't it? Standing empty since Beeching. I wonder.'

'What do you wonder?'

'If they're lesbians. Well. Rumour has it, you know?'

She laughed.

'I made a New Year resolution, Ann, that I would get you to have a gossip with me this year. I don't break my resolutions, so I'm warning you. Here goes. Do you think they're lesbians?'

'No.'

She waited, watching as I released the forefoot and ducked under the mare's neck.

'Well, go on! *Why* don't you think they're lesbians?'

'I don't think about them at all. I didn't even know they were there until you told me.'

'Three days ago, about a dozen of them and not a man in sight. Of *course* they're lesbians. They must be. And they've got herds of unwashed brats.'

There was quite a long silence by Jane's standards, and I grinned to myself. At last she laughed.

'So there's been the occasional aberration. No doubt by way of unsuccessful experiments. But why do you think there aren't any men about the place? Aren't you in the *least* intrigued? How are her feet?'

'Fine.'

'She's going to win again, my little Minnie. Oh, yes, no bother. Nothing to touch her south of Lancashire.'

I asked again as we were loading the mare into the trailer.

46

'Donkeys, Jane. Ask around, will you?'

She sighed.

'Oh, hell. Why are people so bloody silly? Yes, all right, I'll ask. Yes. Don't hold your breath, most people come to us because they can't afford a horse of their own. Yes, well. A donkey isn't much cheaper to keep, you still need land. Yes.'

The next customer was an hour late, claiming there'd been a crash on the bypass, he'd been stuck in traffic. By then I was already working on another horse, with a second tied up under the tree and a third, which hadn't been booked, still in the trailer.

'You'll have to wait, Mr Taylor. I'll fit you in as soon as I can.'

'I have to be home by ten, I'm expecting a client.'

There were messages on my answering machine. Could I fit in a show pony, their farrier had let them down, two hackney horses, he'd be so grateful, my Arab mare, she's quiet as a lamb I promise, a cob with a bad grass crack, it really can't wait. My gate's broken and the bloody trippers keep getting in, please Ann. Little Peter's darling Welsh mountain pony, he wants to go in for the bending race, you can fit us in, can't you? We can't disappoint little Peter. Any chance of those window grilles a week early? I've got men standing idle.

'I'm expecting a *client*, Miss Mayall. I can't wait any longer.'

'I'm sorry, Mr Taylor. I wasn't responsible for the crash on the bypass.'

'Can I leave him here, then, and pick him up this evening?'

Then the hippies arrived. There were four smiling young women with a group of small children and a baby, and they were leading two donkeys I thought I recognised.

They stopped at the gate, looking in at the men and the horses, at the horsebox and the trailer, and listening to the hectoring tones of the angry Leonard Taylor.

47

'Miss Mayall, *may I leave him here?*'

'Yes, very well. But please take the trailer. You can put the horse in the loose box on the corner.'

'Why can't I leave it here? I'm already late.'

And the apologetic Basil Sumner: they hadn't thought they'd got the entry form for the two-year-old in early enough, they'd been surprised when they'd accepted it, he really would be so grateful.

'Why can't I leave the bloody trailer here?'

'It takes up too much room. I'm expecting three horse-boxes later.'

The young women at the gate were talking to each other, quiet, but smiling and laughing.

'Well, suppose I back it up onto the path, then?'

'*Can* you do the two-year-old? He's quite quiet, really. Well, for a thoroughbred colt, he's quiet. You know.'

Jake Brewer's big horsebox was coming down the lane with four hunters and two showjumpers in it.

'Mr Taylor, will you please get the trailer out of here now? There isn't room for the horsebox to turn.'

The driver jumped down out of the cab and strode towards us.

'Am I supposed to come in here or just block the lane?' he demanded.

'Oh, shut up, Morry. Help Mr Taylor put his horse in the spare loose box and then he can take the trailer home.'

'Why can't I leave the damned trailer on the path?'

'Because Miss Mayall trots the horses up that path to see they're moving right, that's why, as you ought to know.'

'Don't you take that tone with me, my man!'

'I'm not your man, I'm Jake Brewer's man. He'd be glad to get a letter of complaint from the likes of you, can always do with a good firelighter. Maurice Old's the name. Now, do I move your horse, or do you take it with you?'

'*Can* you do the two-year-old, Miss Mayall? Please?'

'Mr Sumner, there are six horses in that box, and they've been booked in for the last three weeks.'

'Seven,' called Morry as he led Taylor's gelding along the path to the loose box. 'He's put that eventer in, too. Said you wouldn't mind.'

'Oh, *Jesus*.'

'Who are those blasted women with the donkeys?' demanded Taylor, as though they were in his front garden. 'What are they doing here?'

'Walk him up the path, please, Mr Sumner.'

'Listen, Lord Muck, you don't get that frigging trailer off the drive I'm bringing the box in anyway. You won't get the flash car past that even without the trailer, I'm telling you.'

'He might,' I said as apologetically as I could to Taylor. 'And there's nothing I can do about it, he's a law unto himself.'

'Yes, well, we'll see what Brewer's got to say about you, Old. I'll be back at five for the horse, Miss Mayall. Good morning to you.'

It seemed the only moments of peace I had were when I was watching horses on the concrete path and listening to the rhythm of their hoofbeats. Sometimes those sounds seemed more comprehensible than human speech.

Basil had to lead the horse up the path three times, because I hadn't been able to hear properly. Leonard Taylor's Jaguar roared away across the gravel spraying stones onto the grass as it went, the empty trailer rocking dangerously as he turned into the lane. Then Morry started unloading Jake's horses, his way of letting me know I'd said nine o'clock and it was now ten past.

'Pack it in, Morry, I'm being as quick as I can.'

'What about the two-year-old, Miss Mayall? My mother's hoping to sell him at the show.'

One of the young women walked across the grass towards us. She was a tall girl, dark, in a long green dress, and she was smiling.

'David Lord told me you'd help us,' she said. 'I think we've come at a bad time.'

'Couldn't be worse,' I agreed. I'd intended to ask them to leave, but her obvious anticipation of my request was disarming.

'The crack in the white donkey's hoof's spread,' she explained. 'It's halfway down the wall now. I've put Stockholm Tar on it, but it needs a sandcrack clip. Unless there's something better?'

'Give me five minutes, and then I'll try and talk to you.'

'I'll talk to you, darling,' offered Morry. 'And you won't have to wait five minutes.'

'Too kind,' murmured the girl, but she was amused rather than annoyed, and the look she turned on Morry was almost maternal.

'Oh, well.' Morry shrugged and walked back to the horsebox. 'Don't know what you're missing.'

'Is he a jockey?'

'How did you know?'

Morry was a steeplechase jockey, nearly six foot tall. Not many people would have guessed.

'Most of them are raving sex maniacs.'

She didn't bother to lower her voice. Morry would take it as a compliment anyway.

'What about my mother's two-year-old, Miss Mayall?' Basil was growing impatient.

I looked at my watch, and then shook my head.

'I can't. I'm booked solid until nine o'clock tonight, and I'll be lucky if I finish then. I haven't got one spare minute.'

'You're shoeing Brewer's eventer, and he wasn't booked in, either.' Basil was petulant. His mother's word was law, and she'd blame him if he didn't bring the colt back shod.

'I'm not at all sure I am, as it happens. But anyway, that's a straightforward job. He's a nine-year-old gelding. You're asking me to shoe a two-year-old colt, and he's never been shod before, has he? No, I thought not. It's not a job I'm prepared to rush.'

That was particularly true of any horses bred on the Sumners' stud. Lady Caroline didn't look for docility in her horses, and her grooms didn't handle the young stock unless they couldn't avoid it. There was a reign of terror on that farm.

'Could I leave him here? In case you get a cancellation?'

'Basil, I've got Leonard Taylor's gelding in my one spare loose box, my mare's in the paddock and she's coming into season. Where do you think you could leave a colt? In the tool shed?'

'Come on, squire,' yelled Morry from the horsebox. 'Your time's up. Come in, number ninety-six, sixty-nine, are you in trouble?'

Basil glared at him.

'*God*, he is irritating. Does he pick his jokes out of the *Beano*? Or one of his ghastly porno magazines.'

'I'm sorry,' I said. 'I'm running late. Good luck at the show.'

'If you get a cancellation, can we have it? Please?'

'Yes, all right. If I can fit you in, I will.'

He sighed, and turned away, reluctantly.

'Mother'll bust a corset. Well, *I'm* not rasping the foul thing's feet, it bites like a crocodile.'

I felt sorry for Basil. Lady Caroline treated him worse than the most junior member of her staff, and had a habit of reminding him that one day all this would be his, in tones that suggested the day would coincide with the end of civilisation as we know it.

The woman in the green dress was standing under the tree, watching and waiting. I looked across the yard at the donkeys, who were cropping at the grass. The white one kept lifting a hind foot and dabbing it at the ground. I'd thought the split in the wall of his hoof might spread, but

51

there'd been no time to do more than pare it down. The hoof was soft and crumbling, it couldn't take a shoe.

'David Lord did warn you about his feet, did he?' I called, and the woman nodded and walked towards me.

'If we can patch him up, he's young enough to work,' she said, and held out her hand. 'I'm Gwen Turner. I'm sorry we've turned up in the middle of the rush hour.'

'It'll be the rush hour for the next week.'

'Oh.' She chewed at her lip. 'That hoof can't wait a week.'

Morry Old pushed between us, leading Jake's favourite hunter.

'Sorry, ladies, but time and horses wait for no man, or woman either come to that, and we've got seven to do.'

I'd already resigned myself to spending my midday break shoeing Taylor's horse. A sandcrack clip isn't usually a long job, but it does have to be done carefully.

'You could be waiting here all day,' I said to Gwen. 'And even then I can't promise.'

She seemed content with that. She went back to the other women and spoke to them, and they led the two donkeys into the shade of the chestnut tree and sat on the grass. The children argued over who should hold the halter ropes, and the women made no attempt to interfere; after a while the raised voices died down.

I don't like having children at the forge. They grow bored, and then they become a nuisance. I try to discourage my customers from bringing children. When I'd told Gwen Turner about the long wait I'd assumed the other women, and the children, would leave.

Jake Brewer telephoned about the eventer. Jake's always been a good friend to me, and it was he who sold me Lyric, warning me about a problem with her knees, honesty I hadn't expected.

'I've got a buyer for him at the show,' he said. 'He'll take him if he does well. Tell you the truth, Ann, I could do with the money. How about it? Can you fit him in?'

'Can I leave one of the others, then?'

'Oh, shit. Well. The bay filly if you have to. Mind, she's in the show, too. Oh, and I wanted to talk to you about gates.'

'Talk to me next week, then.'

It was the middle of the afternoon before I had a chance to look at the donkey, and that was because another customer was late. The children had been very quiet; the women had brought books and paper, and two of them seemed to be teaching the three older ones to read. A little girl was asleep on the bench, her thumb in her mouth, and the baby was suckling at its mother's breast.

Gwen stood up as I approached, and the other women looked up and smiled at me. I went straight to the donkey and lifted his hind foot. His feet were unusually soft for a donkey's, and the crack, as Gwen had said, was spreading.

This couldn't wait.

'He'll have to be shod before he can work,' I said. 'David Lord did tell you, did he? I've never seen a donkey with feet this soft.'

One of the women nodded.

'And he said it would take time for the hooves to grow, and that he couldn't be shod before they had.'

Another woman laughed.

'And that we were mad, and he needed his head examining for letting us have them.'

I smiled at her. At least they seemed to have realism on their side as well as optimism; they knew they were taking a chance.

'Right,' I said. 'Let's stop this crack, and then we can only hope for luck.'

They stood and watched as I worked, the children close and interested, but backing away as soon as I warned them. The white donkey seemed quiet, but I didn't know him well enough to trust him too near to those vulnerable boys and girls; a kick from a donkey can break a man's leg.

I hadn't finished working with the donkey before a Land

Rover and trailer pulled in and drew up in front of the forge, and there was another car immediately behind it.

The Müllers. They were angry, and they had brought the gate.

'We do *not* accept,' said Frau Müller as soon as she was out of the car. 'Our lawyer says we are right. We do *not* accept, we bring it back. We do *not* pay for this.'

Herr Müller was struggling to lift the gate out of the back of the estate car. I didn't go to help him.

'Have you heard what I said?' She was advancing, shaking her finger at me.

'Don't come near this donkey. He may kick.'

She stopped, looking at the donkey doubtfully, and then staring around at the women, who were watching her with interest.

Herr Müller called, and she turned and walked back to the car.

Mrs Shanklin, round-faced and smiling, climbed out of the Land Rover, walked to the back of the trailer, and let down the ramp. She asked Herr Müller to back his car away so she could unload her horse.

'*Moment mal, bitte*,' he snapped, and she looked at him in astonishment.

'Miss Mayall, you must help my husband,' said Frau Müller.

'Not me,' I replied. 'It's your gate. You do what you like, I'm busy.'

Mrs Shanklin came over to me.

'I can't unload Ginger with that car in the way,' she said. 'Why's that man so rude? It was a perfectly civil request.'

She rubbed the white donkey's nose, almost a reflex action, and he pushed his head against her hand.

'He's Snowflake,' one of the children informed her. 'And the other one's George. Was that man rude?'

'Yes, darling, he *was* rude,' said Mrs Shanklin. 'Let's just ignore him. What's the matter with Snowflake's feet?'

'They're soft.'

'Do you mind waiting for another ten minutes?' I asked. 'It's a bad crack, I can't leave it.'

The Müllers had managed to drag the gate out of the back of the car. She was talking angrily in English, not lowering her voice, intending everybody to hear what she said.

'She is mad, that great woman. Snakes, she thinks we want snakes on a gate, she is mad. We *do not pay*!' she shouted at me.

Herr Müller dragged the gate across the drive and dropped it onto the grass. He rubbed his hands and glared at me. He was breathing hard, and he looked rumpled and hot.

'My wife says the truth. You are mad.'

Mrs Shanklin strode across the gravel towards him.

'Now, you listen to me. You can't say that sort of thing. It's libellous, illegal. You can get into a lot of trouble. Miss Mayall's a highly respected woman in this village. Any of that sort of nonsense and you'll find yourself in court.'

'This is nothing for you to do,' snapped Frau Müller. *'Das hat mit dir nichts zu tun.'*

I put down the donkey's foot, and stood up. There was nothing more I could do. The clip would hold the crack and stop it spreading.

'Finished?' asked one of the women.

'For now, yes.'

'Thank you,' she said, and the children echoed her in a soft chorus. Thank you. Thank you. Thank you.

Herr Müller slammed the door of his car and reversed it down the drive and out into the lane. He was still mouthing angrily as he drove away, leaving Mrs Shanklin standing with her hands on her hips, her jaw jutting.

'What a thoroughly revolting person!'

'Try to keep him in a dry paddock, and off the roads,' I said to Gwen, and she nodded.

'He's a nice donkey,' she said. 'Pity about his feet.'

Mrs Shanklin led her cob across the drive. She was brisk and businesslike, and there was nothing she enjoyed more than interfering in other people's affairs.

'I'll be a witness for you,' she announced. 'You're going to have to do something about those people, they're malicious. And what about you lot? You all heard them, didn't you? Are you prepared to stand up and be counted?'

'I hope it won't be necessary,' I murmured. 'I doubt if anybody would take much notice.'

Mrs Shanklin ignored me. She tied Ginger's halter rope to the big iron ring, and went on as though I hadn't spoken.

'Miss Mayall's helped you with the donkey, what about you helping her with her problem? People libelling her like that, it's disgraceful, got to be stopped.'

Gwen looked at me, her head tilted slightly to one side.

'Do you want us to be witnesses?'

'Oh. No, I shouldn't think so.' I made a helpless gesture, and Mrs Shanklin glared at me in exasperation.

'I've got no time for people who won't stand up for themselves.'

Two of the women were crouched over the gate in the grass, running their hands over the iron and talking together.

'Gwen, come and see!' one of them called, and Gwen held out her hand.

'Thank you for helping us,' she said. 'Do I pay now, or what?'

'End of the month will do.' I patted the donkey, and handed her his halter rope. 'Don't let anybody fall in love with Snowflake, will you? Those hooves may never be right.'

'Gwen, come and see the snakes,' one of the children shouted, and Gwen looked across in surprise, then led the donkey away as I turned to Ginger and listened resignedly to Mrs Shanklin telling me I should sue that appalling man and his perfectly dreadful wife.

I began to work with the cob, levering the clenches up away from the hoof and clipping them off, so I wasn't taking much notice of the women and the children. Ginger's a restless horse, and he isn't helped by Mrs Shanklin constantly barking at him to stand still and stop being such a silly old bugger.

His feet are a problem. They don't grow evenly, and I have to level them up every time he comes to the forge. Mrs Shanklin doesn't bring him often enough, and this means he's inclined to stumble for a few days after I've trimmed his hooves. If I could do it once a month the correction wouldn't be so severe, and he wouldn't have so much difficulty in adapting to it. Mrs Shanklin complains about it, but she's sacked every other farrier in the area for the same thing, and she did once admit to me she knew it was her own fault.

'Can't spare the time,' she said crossly. 'Next time I buy a horse I'll get a farrier to check him and the blasted vet can stay at home. He said Ginger was sound as a bell.'

'Well, he is,' I objected. 'When his feet are level he moves beautifully. He got a third last year, didn't he?'

'Highly Commended.' She made it sound like an insult. 'HC stands for Horrible Cob. I daren't jump him, Ann. Are those the hippies the village is having hysterics about, by the way?'

'I don't know. Perhaps.'

'You should have got their address. They might not pay their bill, you never know, do you? But that woman seems intelligent. How strange.'

They were still by the gate. Two of them had stood it upright and they were all looking at it, running their hands over it and talking to each other, and to the children.

I glanced across at them.

'I wonder where they're keeping those donkeys, then,' I mused.

Gwen was writing something on a sheet of paper, which

57

she tore out of a book and impaled on the gate. She looked back towards us, and raised a hand in a friendly gesture before pointing at the paper.

I nodded to her.

'I wonder what *that* says.'

Mrs Shanklin would certainly find some way of reading it before she left, so I didn't reply.

It was quite late that night before I had a moment to read Gwen's note myself. I ripped it off the gate and took it into the kitchen.

Her handwriting was bold and square, and she'd used a thick, black pencil.

'I forgot to tell you, we're at the old railway station, so please send your bill there. If those people really don't want this gate, don't let anybody else have it without offering it to us first, we love it. The snakes are so beautiful. Best wishes, Gwen.'

4

It was late summer and the harvest was a good one that year. I'd been busy, but since the show the pressure of work hadn't been more than normal; gates broken where the heavy combine harvesters hadn't negotiated them successfully, either to be repaired or, more often, replaced. I was proud of the fact that the three biggest farmers in Anford ordered gates from me when they needed them rather than buying the mass-produced ones from the builders' merchants, and some of the smaller farmers were following their example.

It was Jake Brewer who gave me the first order for something out of the ordinary, and he did it because he liked the snake gate. He came over after the show with a bottle of wine for me, because he'd sold the eventer, and because I'd managed to shoe the bay filly as well. Jake appreciates extra effort, and goes out of his way to thank people who make it for him.

'That's a fantastic piece of work,' he exclaimed.

'If you like snakes.'

'Even if you don't. I'll say this for you, Ann, you are damned good at what you do.'

As he'd said when he telephoned, he wanted to talk about gates. Big, double gates for the main entrance to his stable yard, and he wanted the outlines of jumping horses in wrought iron, and he wanted his name, and what did I think? And what would it cost?

Too much. He said he'd settle for his original idea, the one he'd had before he'd seen the snake gate. Barred gates to fit into the arch, and his name.

But he telephoned again later in the day. He'd set his heart on the wrought-iron horses. Could I bring down my price? His gates would be an advertisement for me, wouldn't they? Come on, Ann, what about it?

So I drew the gates for him, and he said, oh, yes. Yes, please. Now, what about the price, you mean bitch? Ah, come on, Ann.

I wouldn't, and in the end he said he'd have the gates anyway and tell all his customers they'd been made in Sweden, so sod you.

Arno telephoned that night as I was remembering Jake's threat, and said he'd been thinking of me. He was in his laboratory waiting for something to cool so he could measure it; what was I doing?

Eating bacon sandwiches, I said, and remembering him.

'You make me hungry. May I come at the end of the month, just for a weekend?'

'Arno, you may come whenever you like.'

Jake's gates took me two weeks. He was delighted with them, and he told all his customers I'd made them, a special commission, just a one-off piece of work, because I didn't usually do this sort of thing.

But I'd enjoyed making Jake's gates, and so I began to experiment with new designs, trying to make them decorative and attractive. I made hinges in the shapes of sprays of leaves, catches in the form of bullrushes, gateposts with patterns hammered into the iron.

Most of the farmers smiled at my gates; they were far too fanciful for the mundane purpose of keeping stock in the fields, or trippers out of them. But when Ken Robertson had his drive relaid he bought a double gate with decorative hinges and a bullrush catch, and he asked me to make the posts a bit different, something specially for his farm. He said his wife had a notion for it. Her name's Rose, so the posts had climbing roses twined around them, and Ken painted them.

'What about decorative horseshoes, then?' Morry Old demanded when he saw one of my gates. 'I'd fancy that on old Barbarian, toe clips in the shape of butterflies.'

And Jake again: the small gate that led from the stable yard to the back of the block, could I make one? And this time, since he'd brought me so much business, what about dropping my price?

The snake gate stood propped against the wall at the back of the forge, and my customers would stare at it, puzzled and undecided. Most of them found it vaguely disturbing, but some liked it. One or two offered to buy it, but I said it wasn't for sale, it was a special order.

'Why's it still here, then?'

Uncle John had written a letter, and was now threatening to take the Müllers to court. They'd ordered a gate, a gate had been made, and the agreed price must now be paid.

'How much would a gate like that cost?' asked one of the women from the railway station. She'd brought Snowflake to have his hooves levelled and yet another crack treated. It was time to suggest they give up. This was costing more than the donkey was worth.

'It was a special order,' I said. 'There's quite a lot of work in a gate like that.'

'Do you think they'd sell it to us?'

'You could ask.'

I was reluctant to condemn Snowflake. Gwen knew she would have to make a decision about him soon, and I suspected she was waiting for me to say I could do no more. The donkey Nigel Armstrong had taken to run with his goats in the orchard was completely sound, but her hooves had cracked as a result of damp bedding and neglect. The dry grass in Nigel's orchard, together with proper care, had cured them. He's a good vet, and he'd known Sally's hooves could be treated.

She was a delightful animal. Nigel had trained her to come when he whistled, something I refused to believe until he demonstrated it in my paddock.

I told him about Snowflake, and he shook his head.

'I remember him,' he said. 'The big white donkey? I think he was born with seedy toe. Have you ever seen a donkey with feet that soft? I don't think I have. Most of them have hooves like iron.'

I scribbled a note at the bottom of the bill I sent to Gwen.

'I'm afraid you're wasting your money. There hasn't been enough of an improvement to justify optimism. I'm sorry.'

She put an answer in the envelope that contained her cheque: 'Thank you for the note. Right, if vets and farriers can't cure him, we'll try witchcraft.'

I smiled, crumpled the note and threw it into the bin.

The children would probably be upset, but really David Lord shouldn't have let them take the donkey. He'd almost certainly only been in the sanctuary in the first place because of his soft hooves.

My sister came to see me that afternoon, with work for me. Glory's a theatre designer, one of the best in the country, and she's won international awards. If there's one person in the world I can say I've always loved, it's Glory.

She wanted big candlesticks for scenery, Jewish style, to set the background tone for a new play about the Holocaust.

'Yes,' she said in tones of mild disgust, 'Another one.'

We spent the rest of the day together, mostly discussing her design and how she wanted the candlesticks to look, but we could have covered that in less than an hour. She was unhappy and tense, and it took some time before she could say what was worrying her.

Glory can't have children, and the man she loves wanted to adopt a child.

'I knew this would happen one day,' she said. 'I don't want children. It's time to split.'

'Oh, Glory, no!'

'Why shouldn't Peter have children if he wants them? He'd be a wonderful father. He's marvellous with Danny. He plays football with him. Cricket. He's teaching him to ride now.'

Peter's an actor, mostly Shakespearian, and he and Glory got to know each other when he was playing Oberon in a production of *A Midsummer Night's Dream* at Stratford. She did the design.

Glory lived here at the forge for a year when she was ill, and I still keep her bedroom ready in case she needs it. There's a drawing table and an easel, some pencils and sketch pads, although she took all her paints with her when she went back to Birmingham.

She lived with Peter for a year or so when she was better, and she still lives with him in Stratford when he's there, but he's very successful now and he travels a lot. Glory doesn't like living alone, so when Peter's away, making a film or appearing in a theatre too far from Stratford to allow him to commute, Glory stays with a friend who has a son. Su-Su and Danny come with Glory sometimes, because there's a bank of clay at the bottom of my paddock. Su-Su's a potter. She digs the clay out of the bank and takes it back to Birmingham in a big plastic sack.

'I thought about buying Danny a pony,' said Glory. 'I'll wait and see if he's really interested first. It might just be a craze.'

'Does Peter know you feel like this? About children, I mean?'

'No. I'm not going to tell him, either. It wouldn't be fair.'

We were sitting at the table in my living room, and Glory was doodling on the telephone pad, shapes and patterns; they were very dense, the blue ink on the white paper, a

63

sign that she's troubled. When Glory's happy, her drawings are light and airy.

'If I told Peter he'd say we should forget the idea.'

'Because he loves you more than he wants children,' I suggested, and she shrugged.

'At the moment, maybe. But he'd always regret it in the end. If we split he'll find somebody else. He'll be sad for a little while, but he'll find someone else, and then he can have children.'

He'd never find anybody as beautiful as Glory. She has thick, curly blonde hair, and it was tied back that day with a dark blue scarf, almost the colour of her eyes. There are a few lines in her face now, but she's still lovely, although pain and stress have made her appear older than her years.

She was smiling across the table at me now, the rather curved, tight smile that means she's fighting tears.

'I won't deprive Peter of children,' she said lightly, 'but in my opinion all brats should be drowned at birth.'

'No chance of a compromise?'

'How?' she demanded. 'How do you compromise on children? Children are all or nothing, aren't they? Commitment and birthday parties and having to be a bloody parent.'

'Nannies and housekeepers?'

She didn't bother to answer. She was very close to tears now, and I didn't know what to say to her.

I thought about the time before I'd left our home for ever, gone back to school after that terrible quarrel with Lucille, when she'd said the things I could not forget. Then, Glory had hardly ever spent an evening at home. There'd always been men for Glory, taking her out to parties, to the theatre, wherever she wanted. She'd been so beautiful then. It had always been she who'd chosen: this man, yes; that one, perhaps. She's very like our mother, although Lucille depends on men, and Glory's never done that.

I haven't seen Lucille for years now.

'There are still times when I wish I'd died,' said Glory, and I flinched.

She reached out a hand, and touched mine. 'Could I come back here?' she asked.

'Always. Whenever you like.'

'Yes. I think I may need a little time here. For a while.'

I made us a salad for an evening meal, and we sat on the lawn and ate it, as we'd often done when she'd lived with me before, when she was ill. Apart from Arno, there's nobody with whom I feel so happy as I do when I'm with Glory, because I know she loves me. She's never lied to me, and sometimes I feel she needs me.

We're so different. She's beautiful, and I'm ugly. She's rich and famous and successful, and I'm hidden here in my forge at Anford, just glad I can make ends meet. She's small and slim, and I'm six foot five, heavy and thickset.

Glory loves me, and I love her. Even though I grieved for her, that she would lose the man she loved, the thought of her living at the forge again made me happy. I found I was looking forward to it.

When I've finished work in the evenings I close the double gates across the drive and put a chain through the bars. I lock the forge doors, the final task at the end of my working day. That afternoon I'd been talking to Glory, and working with her, so the day hadn't ended as it usually did, with my last customer driving or riding away, and I'd forgotten the gate.

'Somebody's here,' said Glory.

It was Gwen Turner, and she was leading Snowflake.

'Oh, damn,' I muttered, but I wasn't really annoyed. I'd grown to like Gwen. I found her air of lazy amusement soothing, and I was flattered by her admiration of the snake gate. I like it when people admire my work.

I didn't stand up as she approached. I was lying on my back on the grass, and I raised a hand to shield my eyes from the evening sun.

65

'Hello, Gwen.'

She smiled down at me. Snowflake bent his head and snuffled hopefully at an empty plate, knocking the fork onto the grass.

'I'm intruding,' she said, and threw a quick, apologetic glance at Glory. 'I wanted to talk to you without any other customers around. I need your help to break the law.'

I sat up, slightly startled. I'd once been asked to make some very strange tools for a man who said he was rebuilding a piece of Victorian machinery, and the police had confirmed my suspicions about their more probable purpose, but I'd certainly not expected Gwen to ask for my help in an illegal venture.

She laughed.

'I don't want to steal anything. I want to turn Snowflake loose in Gorsedown Park.'

'Abandon him?'

This was worse than theft; it was cruelty. Snowflake couldn't fend for himself, not through a winter. He was a domesticated animal, he depended on people.

'No, no! I wouldn't want to lose Snowflake. I'll have to go in myself every couple of weeks or so and find him, and when I do I'll ask you to fix his feet again. I want him to forage for himself for a little while. I think it might help.'

It seemed a strange idea to me. There was nothing wrong with the donkey's diet, so far as I could see. He'd been thin and scruffy when they'd first taken him, but now his coat was shining and he looked big and well. The only problem he had was his crumbling hooves.

I must have looked doubtful. Gwen watched me, her head on one side, and I waited for her to explain, but it was Glory who spoke.

'Su-Su did that with Naomi,' she said, and then she turned to Gwen. 'Naomi's my friend's cow. The farmer said she was barren. Su-Su let her forage for herself in the

66

woods, and they got her into calf the next time they tried. She's had a calf every year since.'

Gwen was looking at Glory, still smiling, but with a questioning expression on her face. She crouched in front of her, on one knee, then reached out her hand with three fingers extended and laid them against the side of Glory's head, on the temple, just above her ear.

Glory was startled, but she didn't move her head away. She just looked into Gwen's face. Gwen was smiling back at her, a very kind smile, and she said something quietly that I didn't hear, then took her hand away.

It had been a very quick incident, a strange one, and I was puzzled by it.

Glory was still sitting on the grass, looking at Gwen, and Gwen stood up and faced me.

'Will you let us in?' she asked. 'I can't do much more for Snowflake myself, and you've already told me I'm wasting my money bringing him to you.'

I should have refused. Gorsedown was private property. It was illegal to turn livestock loose on the land. But I had no reason to love the people who'd owned it, and I couldn't see that Snowflake would do any harm, one donkey on four square miles of woodland and grass that was in any case running to wilderness.

There's only one way in now, and that's through my gate. Neither Gwen nor Glory could open that, so it would have to be me. If Snowflake was to run loose on Gorsedown, I was to be an accessory.

I'd first seen Snowflake immediately after I'd sent three old donkeys one after the other into the shed where a man in green overalls waited with a humane killer, and something in me had rebelled at sending a fourth, this one a young animal with at least some sort of chance of life. The decision, right or wrong, seemed to leave me with a share of the responsibility for him.

Glory looked up and smiled at me, and I laughed.

'All right,' I said, 'but if anybody asks me, I've no idea how a donkey got in there. There must be a hole in the hedge.'

I rasped Snowflake's hooves again, quickly and lightly, leaving as much of the horn as I could. It might have been nothing more than my imagination, but they did seem slightly harder, and there were no new cracks, just the two old ones, gradually growing out.

It was beginning to grow dark as we led Snowflake through the paddock towards the gate, and I went on ahead to open it, leaving Gwen and Glory walking side by side, with Snowflake following closely behind them. That, too, was a little strange; Glory's nervous of animals, she doesn't like to be too close to them, yet she hardly turned to glance at the donkey as they moved across the grass.

The gate chimed as I hauled it back against the springs and the ratchet caught and held it open. The noise could be heard a long way away, but people were used to it; it meant only that I was going for a ride in the park, or coming back from one. Nobody would investigate.

Somewhere away behind the woods a fox yelled, and Snowflake lifted his head, his long ears forward, interested and alert.

Gwen patted him, and slipped the halter off his head.

'I do hope this works. He's such a nice donkey.'

'I'll look out for him when I'm riding in the park,' I said, and then, because I was happy that Glory might be coming back to live with me again, I added, 'I'll carry a rasp. You might not need to go in and look for him every two weeks. That's a lot of land to search, on foot.'

'Ann, you are kind. Thank you.'

I asked Jansy to keep an eye out for Snowflake. She was enthusiastic.

'I'll track him. I ought to learn how to do that, I will too. I'll track him, and I'll teach Cracker. Think I could ride him?'

'No,' I said. 'Not until I've shod him, and that won't be until his feet are better. Please don't, Jansy.'

Jansy was having to be co-operative and obedient, which was not easy for her. One of the ferrets was pregnant, despite her assurance when she'd brought them that they were hobs. I should have checked.

'I'll find homes for them, Missus. I will, honest.'

'Don't let your foul dog pee on my anvil, Jansy!'

'*Cracker!*'

He'd chased the dustman down the path a few days earlier, and Mrs Neville was furious. She'd been told she'd have to put the dustbin out by the gate in future.

'I'll wash it down, Missus.'

'Too right, you will. The disinfectant's on the shelf in the workshop.'

It was Jansy who saw Snowflake next, but there wasn't much she could tell me, because Cracker had chased him. All she could say was he didn't seem to be lame, he couldn't half move when he wanted to.

Cracker wore the subdued and depressed air of a dog in disgrace.

I rode out myself the next day. Jansy had been apologetic about Cracker and Snowflake, but, as always, she'd told me the truth: her dog had chased the donkey. I was concerned. If Snowflake had run far, particularly onto the drive, he could have damaged his feet.

Also, I wanted to check the hedges.

The last people to live at Gorsedown Manor had claimed to be a religious sect. They'd called themselves the Children of God. They'd been criminals, pornographers, and the religion had been a cover, a plausible reason for their demand for privacy. The Children of God had planted blackthorn hedges around their land. The bushes are three deep; it's a wicked barrier, and dangerous. Some of the thorns are as much as an inch long, and if they break off under the skin they can cause blood poisoning.

It's lovely in spring, that hedge, covered with the little white flowers that hide the thorns. Now, in late summer, the flowers had gone. There were only the dark leaves, and it should be easy to see if anybody had tried to break through. Gorsedown's been empty for four years. There's nothing worth stealing, so far as I know, but that wouldn't deter vandals, or poachers, and either of them might be a threat to the donkey.

I rather enjoyed having a purpose other than exercise to my ride.

There are tracks through the woods, and along the inside of the hedges there's a strip of grass, although now it's matted and full of nettles and other weeds. That much land needs a lot of work to keep it from going wild. Even the blackthorn ought to be layered. A hedge is more than bushes planted close together; the branches have to be trained to grow between and around each other, to make a plaited barrier of living wood. It's a skilled job, layering hedges.

As I rode I watched out for Snowflake, and I kept myself aware of Lyric as well; she'd know of the presence of the donkey long before I saw him.

It was a Sunday afternoon, moving towards evening, the shadows of the trees lengthening. Lyric was dancing a little, mouthing at her bit, but not yet trying to run away with me. That could come later, if she became too impatient with our slow pace.

I found Snowflake near the north gate where a stream runs through a corner of the park. I'd hoped he might be there, near water and a wide swathe of grass. Lyric laid her ears back and refused to approach him; she doesn't like donkeys. I dismounted, tied her to a tree, and walked over to Snowflake.

He was muddy, and there were twigs and burrs in the tuft on the end of his tail. He seemed pleased to see me, turning towards me and walking a few paces to meet me. I

70

had some pony nuts in my pocket, so I fed them to him before stooping to pick up his feet.

I was relieved to see there were no new sand cracks, but the toes were still crumbly behind the wall of the hoof, although the soft patches seemed a little smaller. I might be able to shoe him soon. Three nails could hold a shoe, unless the weather broke, when mud would suck it free, and the nails dragging through the horn would do yet more damage.

I released his foot and stood back, looking at him, and wondering. Was there really an improvement, or was it simply that I was in a good mood, and therefore optimistic?

Lyric was becoming restless, tied to her tree, so I pulled a few twigs out of Snowflake's tail, rubbed his forehead where he liked it to be rubbed, and went back to her. At least I'd be able to tell Gwen that he looked all right, and his feet were no worse.

Lyric ran away with me almost as soon as I was in the saddle, and it was two miles before I managed to pull her out of a thrashing gallop. I never cease to marvel at her lovely speed, the beautiful action of a racehorse, her long legs slashing at the ground, the muscles in her shoulders and haunches moving so smoothly under her silky skin, her dark mane flying back into my face.

When I tried to pull her up she still fought me, shaking her head at the pressure of the bit. I turned her up the hill, and she began to tire, the even stride breaking and faltering. Her ribs were heaving and the sweat was running down her dark coat, but when I dropped my hands she raised her head again, and her ears were still pricked.

I swung down out of the saddle and loosened her girths. It was less than a mile back to the forge. She'd cool down on the way if I led her, and then I'd only have to wash her before turning her out into the paddock for the night.

If I hadn't been on foot I wouldn't have noticed the print in the muddy patch under the beech trees.

I crouched down and stared at it. There was half the front part of the sole, with a tread, like a running shoe. Just this one mark in the damp, bare earth on the rise above the path to the forge.

I looked around carefully, searching for more, but there was only the one print, and that was indistinct.

I stood up, looking at it thoughtfully.

Blackthorn is an effective barrier, but somebody determined to get into the park could certainly do so. Even though the hedge is over six feet high, there are places where trees grow close against it. Anybody who could climb a tree, and who wasn't daunted by the drop from the branches, could manage easily. Or a rope, left hanging so the trespasser could escape later, that was even more likely.

A poacher, then. Jansy had competition.

I wasn't particularly worried. This was no organised crime; the real poachers today, the serious ones, are clever and systematic, using four-wheel drive vehicles, and they usually hit the big shooting estates. They take deer and game birds in a fast sweep, and by the time the gamekeepers or the police arrive they're on the motorway, back to the big cities. Hotels and restaurants are a ready market, and may have already placed an order with a supplier who they believe is a trader running a legal wholesale meat and game business.

This, if it was a poacher, was a traditional one, a man with ferrets and a net, possibly a dog, although that would pose a problem if he had got in by climbing a tree.

Probably, a gun.

As soon as I could, I told myself, I would check the rest of the boundary, just to make sure there was no way cars could be brought into Gorsedown. And I'd try to find out who this intruder was, and what he was after. If it was rabbits and pheasants I would turn a blind eye, but if it was some teenager with a twelve-bore shotgun looking for deer, I wanted to make sure he could tell the difference between the sound a running stag might make, and the hoofbeats of my galloping horse.

I wasn't alarmed by the discovery of the footprint, but I was irritated. It was likely to be a nuisance.

I got back to the forge as dusk was falling, and I was thinking of little more than a hot bath and a cold drink after I'd seen to Lyric. I led her through the gate, and turned her to face it before I released the catch and it slammed back against the frame, the steel flowers and leaves clashing and jangling their familiar deafening carillon.

Jansy was waiting in the hay store, sitting on a bale of straw beside the ferret hutch with her head in her hands. She looked up as I turned on the light, and her face was white, her eyes huge and dark with shock.

'Jansy, what's the matter?'

She couldn't speak at first. She was breathing shallowly, and her lips were moving as if they were stiff, as if what she was trying to say was strange to her.

I walked across the room and dropped onto one knee in front of her, looking into her face.

'Jansy? Come on, tell me. What's the matter?'

There were tears welling up in her eyes, and she drew in a deep breath, and managed to say the words.

'Oh, Missus,' she whispered. 'Missus. Somebody shot at me.'

5

I telephoned the police immediately, ignoring Jansy's frightened protests, and telling the policeman who took my call she was too shocked to be brought to the police station. Somebody would have to come to the forge to interview her.

He wanted to know about her mother. I asked Jansy, who shook her head.

'Gone out. Gone to see Gran. Back late, she said.'

'I don't know,' I said into the telephone. 'She's here at the moment, and I'm going to give her a hot drink. Will somebody come?'

Yes, he said, as soon as possible. In the meantime, he'd like a few details.

'They'll know I've been poaching,' she whispered when I put down the telephone, and I smiled at her.

'Not unless you tell them, they won't. You found a hole in the hedge and you went in for a look around. Jansy, listen, nobody's going to give a *damn*. Understand? So there are notices saying trespassers will be prosecuted, so what? Who's going to bother? But somebody shooting at you, that's a whole different thing. We can't just pretend that didn't happen. All right, it's only a stupid poacher who forgot his specs, but I'm not ignoring that.

Somebody has to make a fuss when people get careless with guns.'

It was a long speech for me. She listened in silence, her arms wrapped around her knees. Now and then she shivered, a small movement, quickly controlled.

I made her a mug of cocoa, thick with sweetened condensed milk, and she smiled when I handed it to her. There was a little colour in her cheeks now, and the dark and haunted look had gone from her eyes. Soon, perhaps, this would be an adventure, like the ones she saw on television, where the heroes and heroines ducked flying bullets every two minutes and never thought twice about it.

'Did you hear the shot?' I asked, and she frowned.

'Sounded like a whip, right by my ear,' she said. 'You know, sort of like a crack. Then I looked up, and there was this hole in the tree, all splintered. There was a bit of sap, just starting to run down. I could smell it. So I ran away. Didn't stop to think about it, I just ran. It was a shot, Missus. I know it was.'

'Yes,' I said slowly. 'Yes, I think it was.'

It must have happened while Lyric was galloping through the woods, running away with me. Her hoofbeats would have drowned the noise, or I'd have heard it. We hadn't been very far away. Jansy hadn't got back to the forge much before me. She'd put the ferrets into their hutch, and then realisation had dawned, and with it, shock and fright.

I could only be thankful she hadn't been too scared to run when it had happened. Whatever careless cretin it had been out there with a gun might have tried a second shot at what he'd probably thought was some sort of animal, and that second shot might not have missed.

Jansy sniffed, and sipped at her cocoa.

'All good practice, isn't it?' she said. 'I expect elephant poachers shoot at game wardens, too.'

'Oh, God, Jansy,' I said, and I began to laugh. 'Yes, I

believe they do. Let's hope they're no better shots than pheasant poachers.'

Jansy sniffed again, and a slow grin began to cross her face. Later, there'd be hysterical giggles and laughter, and the fright would run its normal course.

The police, when they came, seemed to share my view that the shot had been fired by a poacher, who'd probably been even more frightened than Jansy when he'd realised his mistake. They'd ask around, they said as I walked back to their car with them, and I nodded politely.

The older of the two men smiled at me.

'Perhaps it's time for a check-up on shotgun licences in Anford,' he said. 'We could ask a few questions. Panic him, whoever it is.'

'That would be something,' I agreed. 'She was very frightened.'

'Hmm.' He scratched his chin. 'Mind you, she shouldn't have been in there. But still.'

'But still, neither should he,' I commented, and he smiled again.

Jansy had finished her cocoa by the time I went back into the cottage, and she was looking happier. Almost pleased with herself.

'Reckon they'll catch him?' she demanded.

'No.'

I drove her home a few minutes later, dropping her and Cracker at her gate and leaving it to her to explain where she'd been to her parents. I'd told her I'd feed the ferrets that evening, since she'd been too busy dodging bullets, and that was when the giggles had started, followed by a brief burst of tears, and then she'd admitted to feeling dead tired, Missus.

She'd be all right now.

I was more disturbed by the incident than Jansy was, and I wondered briefly whether I should discourage her from going into Gorsedown. It was an idea I dismissed immediately; I couldn't stop her, and if I tried I would simply lose her friendship. At least this way she would come to me if she was in trouble, or if anything else happened in the park.

It was a week before I had time to ride out on Gorsedown again, and on that Sunday I went straight to the southern boundary, where Jansy usually tried her luck with the rabbits. I'd hardly seen her during the week, and when she'd come to feed and clean the ferrets I'd always had customers, so we'd had no chance to talk.

I rode slowly along the inside of the blackthorn, and when we reached overhanging trees I stopped and looked for signs. I'm not an expert tracker, but there'd surely be something, broken twigs, a rope, marks on the ground under the branches.

It was a rope ladder I found. It was looped over the branch of an oak, with string attached to it, running through the leaves and into the hedge. I wouldn't have noticed it had I not been looking. The string had to mean he was in the park again. If he'd left, he'd have pulled the ladder back into the tree, the string with it.

I took hold of the trailing end of the string, and backed Lyric away from the tree so she wouldn't be startled. The ladder fell from the branch and hung, bouncing and swaying. It was about fifteen feet long, a home-made affair of uneven rungs made from metal bars and odd pieces of wood, knotted onto nylon rope; adequate but amateurish.

I used the rasp I carried to saw through the rope. Standing up in the stirrups and reaching over my head as I dragged the rasp backwards and forwards across the hard fibres, I calculated the cut end of the ladder would be about twelve feet from the ground, and I doubted if anybody stupid enough to shoot at a child would have the ingenuity to find a way of reaching it. When the last strand parted I dropped the ruined ladder onto the grass and scribbled a note on the back of an envelope. I laid it under one of the metal rungs so the wind couldn't carry it away.

Come to the forge gate.

It was dark before I heard the gate ring, the sound of somebody unsuccessfully trying to force his way through. I took a torch and walked down the paddock path. I was feeling thoroughly miserable. I hate confrontations of any sort, and this was likely to be a bad one.

It was Morry Old at the gate, and he was truculent and defiant.

'What the hell you think you're doing, cutting my ladder?'

'Good evening, Morry.'

'Oh, yeah? Is it, then? You having a good evening, cutting my ladder? What bloody business is it of yours? I'm not doing you any harm. It's not your bloody land.'

'You nearly shot a child last week.'

'Don't know what you're talking about.'

I turned and began to walk back along the path. 'Stay there and think about it,' I called over my shoulder.

'Hey! You can't leave me here.'

I stood on the far side of the paddock, listening to him swearing and trying to force the gate open. There are men who are strong enough to do that, but I only know two: the driver who delivers my steel supplies and Glory's lover, Peter Clements. Morry's tall, and quite powerful, but he's light, and you need weight to brace yourself against that gate. There's not much else for leverage.

He'd have to give up soon. Work in Jake Brewer's stables starts at five, and Jake doesn't like his horses to be kept waiting for their morning feed.

He went on trying to force his way through for longer than I'd anticipated. He was a determined man, Morry Old.

'Miss Mayall! Please!'

As I went back to the gate, the dew on the grass sparkled

in the torchlight. There was dew in Morry's hair, too, and he was looking damp and depressed.

'The child you shot at,' I said before he could speak.

'Look, I've got to get out of here. You want a confession? Right, I shot the Queen Mother, that do you?'

I didn't answer, I just stood by the gate, looking at him, and he threw up his arms and turned his back on me, striding a few paces back towards the woods.

'*Oh, fucking hell!*'

'Where's your gun?'

'Somewhere where you won't find it.'

'Jansy Neville might. She knows this land better than she knows her own garden. Do you like that idea, Morry? A twelve-year-old with your gun?'

He was back at the gate again, staring at me, his eyes narrowed against the darkness. Then he sighed.

'Yeah, she was scared, ran like a rabbit. Well, I tell you, she doesn't know what scared is. I fucking near wet myself.'

That would have to do. I took hold of the gate handle, braced myself against the frame, and heaved, digging my heels into the ground as Morry slipped through into the paddock. Then I released it, and it crashed back against the steel plate.

'Don't know how you can stand the noise,' he muttered.

'Get the gun out of Gorsedown tomorrow,' I said. 'I'll let you through.'

'And then what?'

'Then nothing.'

He didn't believe me. He stood on the path, his head lowered, like a bull thinking of charging.

'If I'm a good little boy and never do it again.'

I shrugged, and pushed past him. I was tired, and I'd had enough of Morry Old.

'You do what you like. One more near miss and I'll go straight to the police. And don't bring your friends along when you go poaching on Gorsedown. You on your own I can just about stomach, half a dozen clones, I can't.'

'*Hey!*'

It was an angry shout, and it stopped me. I stood on the path, my back still towards him, and I listened as he walked up behind me.

'What "one more near miss"? You think it was *me* who shot at the kid? You crazy or something? Why would I want to shoot at Jansy?'

'Who else? You said . . .' But he'd said nothing. I turned and stared at him.

'I told you I fucking near wet myself.'

He drew in a deep breath, hissing between his teeth.

'It's a shotgun I've got. A Webley, a .410 if you want the details, it's enough for me. It was no bloody shotgun that was aimed at Jansy Neville, it was a rifle. And it was silenced.'

Deer, then? Poachers after deer?

'I heard that bullet hit the tree. I'd been watching Jansy, see? She's good, that kid. She was busy, so I kept my distance, just watching. Then there's the bullet in the tree, and she ran. Me, I nearly jumped out of my skin, but I stayed and I watched.'

'Who was it, then?'

'Don't know. Never seen him before. Moved like a shadow, he was in camouflage, he came out just a minute after Jansy legged it. He went over to that tree. Maybe looking for the bullet? I don't know. Then he went. I don't know where. Like I said, moved like a shadow. One moment not there, then I could see him, then he was by the tree, then he was gone. Scared me spitless.'

A silenced rifle. I hadn't even known you could fit a silencer to a rifle.

'He meant to shoot at her.'

Morry's eyes were white in the deepening gloom, wide and shiny.

I looked at him, and I waited.

He drew in another deep breath, and again it hissed out through clenched teeth.

'He did, Miss Mayall. Shoot *at* her. I know it. Not hit her, he could have drilled her right through the temples if he'd wanted to hit her. I know it. He just shot *at* her. Yeah. Maybe he was checking if he'd hit what he aimed at? Hadn't thought of that. Yeah, maybe that.'

I believed him. It hadn't been the shot that had frightened Morry, it had been the man, moving quietly, checking his work, and vanishing.

'Morry, I'll have to tell the police this. They're just checking shotgun licences.'

'Oh, thank you so much. Thank you *very* much, Miss Mayall.'

I didn't know what to say. Surely he could understand how serious this was? They wouldn't bother about Morry Old poaching, I wouldn't even have to mention the shotgun.

'I've got a record,' he said at last. 'I'm on a suspended sentence now. Two years. The filth just loved that, they thought I was going down. You hand them this, I will. Thank you.'

Good grooms are hard to find, and Jake Brewer had to take whoever could do the job. Morry handled horses as though he could read their minds. He rode like an angel, and he made the customers laugh. Gold dust, Jake had called him.

Jake had been a good friend to me. A good friend, and a very good customer.

'Oh, God. What am I going to do?'

Morry sighed, a deep sigh of relief, and touched my arm. 'Thanks.'

He walked away from me towards the forge, quiet and almost invisible in the darkness. Then I remembered, and I called after him.

'Morry, what shoes do you wear when you're on Gorsedown?'

'Welly boots,' he called back. 'Why?'

I stood in the paddock after he had gone, thinking of Jake, and Jansy, and Morry, wondering what to do. Morry Old, Jake's gold dust. A liar, a womaniser, a poacher, a criminal, on a suspended sentence.

I wished I could ride as well as Morry. I'm a good farrier, and I'm glad of it, but there is that one talent I yearn for, whatever indefinable something it is that makes people like Morry riders, while the rest of us are passengers on a horse's back.

Perhaps I could tell the police that somebody had shot at me, that I'd seen somebody running away, carrying a rifle. But I doubted if I could convince them. Now I'd given Morry some sort of promise. What could I do?

I asked Jansy when she came to clean and feed the ferrets, could it have been a rifle? She had no idea. Might have been. She didn't seem to realise it made a difference.

And yes, Jansy knew Morry Old poached on Gorsedown.

'Wasn't him, Missus. He'd have come over and said sorry. Anyway, he's careful. I'm giving him a couple of the ferrets.'

She'd seen Snowflake a few days before, and she'd tied Cracker to a bush and gone over to the donkey, who'd been easy to catch, and who, she said, seemed to be in the pink.

I telephoned Gwen with that news, and she asked if I'd let her into the park so she could look for him herself. Also, was I busy? She wanted a word with me. Could they come?

'I'm closing now,' I said.

'We'll bring a bottle. We're not asking you to work. May we?'

They arrived half an hour later, seven women and rather more children. Gwen was leading the other donkey, who bore a pack saddle, with two of the smallest children perched on top of it. I heard them coming when they were still about a hundred yards down the lane. They were singing, and they seemed to be making up the words as they went along, taking it in turns and greeting each effort with laughter and applause.

As they came through the gate one of the women delved into the bag suspended from the pack saddle, and triumphantly produced a huge flagon, which she waved in my direction.

'Debauch juice,' she called. 'Strictly for the broad-minded.'

It was home-made rhubarb wine, surprisingly good. We sat under the chestnut tree, drinking it from the mugs and glasses I brought from the kitchen while the children paddled in the broad shallows of the stream just below the deep and dangerous patch. I'd been a bit worried about them playing there, but one of the mothers took them over to the stream and showed them where it was flowing fast, explaining about the current under the surface as well as the one they could see, and they listened solemnly, nodding, quiet as she spoke.

'They'll be all right,' said Tessa, the woman who'd brandished the flagon at me. 'These children get enough fun out of their lives. They don't have to go drowning themselves.'

Nevertheless, I noticed there was always at least one pair of eyes looking in the direction of the stream, and every time a child shouted or screamed, even though it was only in excitement, heads turned quickly.

They'd brought bread and fruit as well as the wine, and it was something of a feast we had, sitting on the grass, with the old grey donkey nudging at our shoulders and begging for titbits.

'George?' I asked Tessa. 'Isn't that what he's called?'

'He's nearly thirty,' she said. 'He's our shopping trolley.'

Gwen and another woman I hadn't seen before were looking at the snake gate, Gwen tracing the head of the striking snake with the tips of her fingers and talking quietly. She sensed me watching her, and she smiled.

'Do you like snakes?' she called, and I shrugged, and then nodded. Yes, I do like snakes.

'Symbol of wisdom,' said Tessa. 'We love them. Well, in theory we love them. They give Sal the cold shivers.'

An older woman who was leaning back against the tree with her eyes closed laughed, and moved her head, a small nod of agreement.

'The wisdom of a serpent,' I murmured, wondering where I'd heard the phrase.

'That's why we're here,' said Gwen. I hadn't heard her approaching. 'We do want to buy that gate, Ann, but we can only afford five hundred. We haven't got any more. The Müllers turned it down. They said we'd have to pay a thousand.'

I thought about it. Uncle John had said he was fairly sure we could win a case against the Müllers, which meant they'd have to pay the full thousand pounds, as well as the costs. Five hundred would cover the outlay and my time, but there'd be little or no profit.

'Look,' said Tessa, 'how about this, then? We give you the five hundred, get the Müllers to give you two-fifty, and you drop the rest. How's that grab you?'

'That sounds fine.' I spoke without hesitation. It would be worth it, just to be finished with the matter, and with the Müllers. Also, I wanted my new friends to have the gate; they liked it, and the Müllers didn't. It would do me no good in the long run to insist on customers taking work they disliked.

In fact, I'd almost decided to let the women have the gate for five hundred pounds. The prospect of a court case, which would mean a long delay before I could expect any money at all, as well as bad feeling and wasted time, was not one that appealed to me. I'd try to get the extra two hundred and fifty, but I wouldn't take it to court.

I dropped a note through the Müllers' letterbox that afternoon on my way to see Garth Michaelson. Frau Müller shouted something at me from an upstairs window, telling me I was on private land, I must leave. "You great woman", she called me.

I tried not to let the remark upset me, but I was tense and uneasy when I arrived at the farm.

Garth's was my only appointment that afternoon, paring and rasping the feet of his Jersey bull. I don't expect my customers to bring bulls to the forge, although Bill Friar has brought his Hereford once or twice. I know Garth well enough not to mind working in his bull pen.

Jeff Jackson had hurt his back, so there was only Garth with me. There should be two people to help a farrier with cattle. Short-handed as ever. I was never sure whether Garth was genuinely hard up, or simply mean.

I told him about the snake gate, and the Müllers, more because I hoped talking about it would relieve some of the tension than for want of advice, and Garth listened, frowning and nodding.

'They are making themselves unpopular,' he said. 'They seem to have a lot of money. Maybe they think it makes them special. Was it them ordered your snake gate?'

I finished paring down the sole of the bull's hoof and stood up, holding my hands to the small of my back. He's a heavy bull, and he likes to lean. Garth relaxed the rope that had held the leg off the ground, and the big animal shifted his weight, sighing.

'Yes,' I said, as Garth was still looking at me enquiringly.

'Going to be like the one in your paddock, was it? For God's sake. What are they keeping in that cottage, the crown jewels?'

'Oh, Garth.' I leaned on the bull's back, and looked down at him. 'Sod the Müllers. Somebody's prowling around Gorsedown with a silenced rifle.'

'Deer poachers,' he said promptly. 'So long as they stick to Gorsedown.'

Was there anybody with whom I could discuss all this? A man in camouflage with a silenced rifle, Morry Old convinced it had been deliberate, that he'd aimed at the tree just over Jansy's head? The more I thought about it, the more I believed Morry; he'd been shaken and alarmed by the incident, and Morry's not easily worried.

Sighing, I bent to lift the bull's foot again, and Garth wound in the rope.

6

The Müllers accepted my offer, and sent me a cheque for two hundred and fifty pounds, just the cheque in the envelope, with no covering letter. There was a terse communication from their lawyer in the same post, saying that they were paying under protest, and were bitterly disappointed by the quality of my work.

I telephoned Gwen with the news, and she said she was delighted. She certainly sounded pleased, which helped to lift the low spirits the letter from the lawyer had caused. She told the other women who were in the room with her, and I heard faint sounds of cheering in the background, and children's voices, questioning.

'Ann, could you deliver it? I don't think George could manage that on the pack saddle. Anyway, we want to break a bottle over our snakes' heads, so please come.'

Jake Brewer turned up as I was trying to manoeuvre the gate into my new van. He was riding one of his hunters, hoping I might shoe her on the spot even though he hadn't made an appointment.

'Why the hell should I?'

I'd scratched the paint, trying to push the gate past the wheel arch, and I was in no mood for Jake's scrounging.

He looked hurt.

'Because I'm an old friend. I'd thought.'

He was. He'd been a very good friend to me. He had some right to expect I'd make an extra effort for him.

'Oh. Well, I . . .'

I gestured at him helplessly, trying to think of something to say, as well as a good reason for not doing him a favour.

'All right, Jake. Help me with this thing, would you?'

'So you've finally sold it.'

'It's been sold for weeks. I'm finally delivering it.'

When I'd shod the mare before, she'd been quiet. I was in a hurry, so I suppose I was careless. She bit me, savagely, high up on the back of the arm. Blood soaked through my shirt and the bite hurt.

Jake was shocked, and very apologetic.

'Bloody hell, Ann, I'm sorry. She's never done that before.'

'She'll never do it again, either. Not to me, anyway.'

'Look, you'd better put something on that, it's a nasty one. I'll drive you to the doctor, if you like. Or casualty?'

'It's not that bad.'

But he was worried. He insisted it needed attention, so I let him get my first aid kit out of the workshop, and I tried to roll my sleeve up past the bite.

It was too high, and the sleeve too tight. Jake ripped it open from the cuff to the shoulder. The shirt was ruined anyway.

Dark blood was welling from the broken skin, and it was beginning to swell. Jake dabbed at it anxiously with disinfectant on a pad of cotton wool. I watched him for a while, and then grew impatient. He was doing no good, and he was hurting me.

'Just press it against the cut,' I said. 'Press hard. You won't stop it bleeding by patting at it like that.'

'I hate the sight of blood,' he muttered.

I stared at him in astonishment. He was quite pale.

'I wish she hadn't done that,' he said. 'I'm really sorry.

She must be coming into season. Look, let me drive you to the doctor.'

I held a wad of lint against the wound, and after a minute or so it stopped bleeding. Jake bandaged it for me, still talking about the doctor, or the casualty ward at Cheltenham, which he said was used to dealing with horse bites. He was probably right, but I wanted to finish my work and take the gate to Gwen.

'Well, at least let me take you out for a drink,' he said when I refused his offer again. 'I owe you that.'

'You owe me for shoeing the mare,' I answered. 'If I get bitten it's my own fault. But thanks for the offer.'

He muttered something I didn't hear. He held the mare's head as I finished off her feet, tight up against the bit, so she couldn't reach me again, and when he'd mounted he leaned down out of the saddle and patted me on the shoulder.

'Watch out for that bite, won't you, Ann? I mean, go to the doctor if it's not healing right?'

I was surprised at his concern, and rather touched.

'All right. I'll watch out.'

It took me longer than usual to clean up the forge, because my arm was growing stiff. It was throbbing quite painfully by the time I set off for the village and the promised celebration of the snake gate with my new friends.

Anford station is a small building, with just a few rooms set in a line along the eastern platform. The entrance hall has a little ornamental clock tower over it in the centre. It was the usual layout for a station in a country town, but I'd never heard of anybody using one as a home. I was interested to see what had been made of it. Also, I'd been wondering where they were keeping George. There wasn't any land, apart from a tiny car park paved with concrete, and they couldn't be stabling a donkey in the station-master's office.

The rails had been taken up, sold for scrap, Tessa told me.

On most of the disused country tracks the lines had been left to rust, but in this case it had been easy to load them onto lorries from the road where the level crossing had been. The women had put makeshift fences across the track between the platforms, five of them, and in the first enclosure they'd removed the stones that had supported the sleepers, and heaped them up against the platform in the next pen.

'We'll build walls with all that,' Tessa told me as I stood looking down at the familiar pieces of flint. 'With gates.'

Sal looked at me rather seriously. 'We'd like to talk to you about those gates,' she said.

Two children ran past, swinging between the old iron posts that supported the canopy. The girl stopped in front of me, and stood looking up at me.

'Aren't you *big*!' she said.

'Yes.'

'Why?'

'I just grew that way.'

She considered it, then nodded and ran off after her friend. I watched them, remembering how Lucille had taught Glory and me that it was rude to make personal remarks. I thought about it, and decided I preferred the girl's direct question to the disguised stares and whispered comments I encountered from conventional children.

George stood in the first enclosure in the shade of a tarpaulin, his ears flopping low, eyes half closed in sleep, oblivious to the two small boys who sat on his back and the group of toddlers who played in the last of the evening sunshine only a few feet away. There was a pile of hay in one corner, and water buckets tied to the fence. As yet, no grass had grown on the scraped earth, but they planned to try, Tessa said. They would sow seed later in the year, and turn a couple of the enclosures into vegetable gardens. In the meantime, there were barrels and buckets and an old bath on the western platform under the open-sided shelters, with cabbages and cauliflowers growing in them.

Sal and Tessa showed me around. They'd turned the rooms into dormitories and nurseries, and there were pillows and rolled-up sleeping bags lying on the floors, mattresses with blankets, odd pieces of furniture. Orange crates and tea chests did service as cupboards and bookshelves. There were threadbare carpets over the worn linoleum, curtains thumb-tacked to wooden window frames and looped back with cord or string, posters and children's drawings pasted to the flaking walls.

Children of all ages played in the rooms, running in and out, or sat and read books.

There were hundreds of books. Every surface seemed to be covered with them: windowsills, tables, mantelpieces, there were books everywhere.

'It isn't exactly *Ideal Home*,' commented Sal, 'but we like it.'

I liked it, too.

'By the way, there are only sixteen children,' she said. 'It seems like hundreds until you get used to it. You find you've counted the same one seven or eight times.'

They were renting the place through an agent. They'd have preferred to buy it, but they hadn't had enough money. The rent was low, and they didn't need the sort of house most people wanted. But they did, in the normal manner, want to stop strangers walking into the entrance hall, and it was there that my gate was to stand. They'd already set up two wooden gateposts, an oak sleeper lying across the concrete as a threshold, the two pine posts set into it and reaching to the curve of the wrought-iron arch.

It was a beautiful job. The sleeper had been sunk into the walls on either side and planed and polished, and the posts fitted tightly, the joints solid and immovable.

As we went back into the entrance hall, Gwen came out

of the big room that had been the ticket office, and Sal and Tessa excused themselves. I stood beside the gateposts, admiring the craftsmanship.

'Is this where the gate's to hang?'

'Yes. We're giving it pride of place. What do you think?'

'Fine.'

'One resistance plate?' suggested Gwen. 'Enough to make a noise and stop the children?' And then, catching my expression, she added, 'We do expect to pay for your work! I know this will be extra.'

I was tired. I'd been looking forward to spending a little time with my new friends, and then going home for an early night. Besides, my arm hurt.

'Do you want to hang it this evening?' I asked, and she shook her head.

'We want a celebration for the gate. It was going to be a party, but we've had a bad day. Chrissie's husband's turned up. We're a bit depressed.' She shook her head again, briskly this time, trying to drive away the black thoughts.

'We'll be taking it in turns to look after the children this evening,' she said. 'Keep them away from the worry. Well, that's the idea, but it doesn't work. They always know when something's wrong.'

I didn't know what to say in answer to that, so I went back to the gateposts and looked at them, running my hands down the smoothed wood. If they wanted the springs I'd have to mount a steel frame onto those posts; pine would crack away under the strain.

'You want the gate for security, then?' I asked, and Gwen sighed.

'Yes, I think we do, now. We'd certainly want to know if Zack Paulson came in. Frankly, we'd rather he couldn't. Can you help?'

I couldn't see the point. What was to stop the man walking fifty yards down the road and coming in along the platform? I was about to voice my objections, but Gwen smiled at me and turned and walked away, so I followed her through the hall into the old ticket office.

It was immediately obvious which of the women was Chrissie, because she was crying. She was sitting on a sofa in the corner with another woman beside her, hugging her. The others were standing around in small groups, talking quietly. There was a subdued and depressed atmosphere.

There were more of them than I'd expected, several I'd never seen before, and there were three men as well, talking to some of the women. They turned and looked as I ducked under the doorway, and I felt shy and awkward. I wished I'd made an excuse to Gwen, unloaded the gate and gone home. The bandage felt as if it was beginning to cut into the flesh, too tight; my bitten arm must be swelling again.

'She's brought the snake gate,' somebody said, and then they were smiling at me, welcoming despite their anxiety.

'Can we electrify it?' asked Chrissie, looking up at me with reddened eyes. 'Make it lethal for one nasty bastard with big fists?'

I hesitated, trying to think of an answer to a remark that clearly hadn't been a joke, but one of the men said yes, if she liked, they could.

'Rhetorical question, unfortunately,' said Chrissie.

Gwen was pouring drinks at the ticket counter from a huge flagon like the one they'd brought to the forge. She handled it with expertise, her middle finger slipped through the ring at the neck, the weight supported on the back of her forearm, tilting her elbow to pour the wine into the glasses.

'Of all the damned husbands, it had to be that one,' she said quietly as she handed me my glass. 'He's dangerous. Most of them are just threats, but this one's a mental case. So it seems, anyway.'

No men, Jane Laverton had said. Herds of unwashed brats, and not a man in sight.

Well, there were men in sight now, but perhaps I'd learned the answer to Jane's questions.

I looked down into my glass, watching the bubbles rise in the clear, pink wine.

'Are you all . . .?' I didn't know how to finish the question.

'On the run from violent husbands? Some are worse than others. No, we're not all victims of violence. We're not even all married. Sal never married, she was too busy looking after her father. But violence? Well, it's not that easy, is it? Not all violence is physical, either.'

She looked around, her eyes travelling from one face to another, as though she was counting or checking, and then she grimaced.

'I don't think there's one woman here who hasn't had her life bitched up by some man in one way or another. Zack Paulson's the worst, and now he's found us. Hence, the gloom. And Chrissie's scared to death, as you can see.'

One of the men had his arm around a plump woman's waist, and she was smiling at him. I hadn't seen either of them before. And a tall, thin man with grey hair seemed to be explaining something to Sal. She was listening, looking interested.

I wished Arno was with me. I would have liked to visit friends for an evening, with a man; to be the one listening as a man talked to me, part of a group like this, just normal, a guest in the home of friends.

Somebody had made a cake and iced it, a representation of the gate on the top and snakes curling around the sides. It didn't go very well with the rhubarb wine, but the women were trying to make the event into something like a party. Most of them came over to me and said they loved the gate. They thanked me for letting them have it cheaply. More than one spoke of gates between the pens. They wanted to keep goats. Could I help them? Would it be very expensive?

'Do you know anything about goats?' asked a tall girl with an anxious expression and a breathy voice. 'Are they difficult to keep?'

The thin man introduced himself. Perry Graves: he was a cabinet-maker, and it was he who had fitted the gateposts.

'Oh,' I said. 'I thought they'd done it themselves. It's a good piece of work.'

'Didn't know about the springs,' he said. 'Should have told me. Posts won't take that. Still, can fix. Can't we? What do you think? Iron frame?'

Somebody turned on a tape recorder, and there was music in the room, Janis Joplin's wonderful, ruined voice against saxophone and drums.

Perry muttered something about talking another time, and walked back to the group by the door. There seemed to be something wrong with his leg; his knee twisted as he walked. I found myself wondering what it could be, as though he was a horse I'd been asked to shoe.

Gwen wandered around the room with the wine, filling glasses, and gradually everyone began to smile more easily. Now and then there was an outburst of laughter.

I found myself sitting on a cushion under the window, listening to the music, and Sal came and sat beside me, smiling, but saying nothing. It was a companionable silence. From the other side of the room Gwen raised the flagon, looking at me enquiringly, and I shook my head. The rhubarb wine was strong, and I had to drive home. I wondered if I could ask for aspirin, something for the pain of my arm.

On the sofa Chrissie had stopped crying, and was sitting upright, her hands on her knees, her head tilted back, trying to control her breathing. The girl beside her was talking to her encouragingly, half turned towards her, her face earnest.

The Janis Joplin recording came to an end, the tape flicked out of the spool, and somebody pressed a switch to turn the recorder off.

A few more women and the youngest of the three men came over to join Sal and me, bringing cushions with them and sitting in front of us in a rough circle. One of them was watching Chrissie.

'Maybe we should all learn karate,' she commented, and the young man spoke to her, quickly.

'Teach you, if you like.'

'My husband's a deserter from the Foreign Legion, that's as close to martial arts as I ever want to get,' said a blonde girl, and we all looked at her. Her voice was very clear, perfect diction, and it carried easily over the sounds of talk and laughter.

'Go on, then,' said Gwen warily. 'Not that we'll believe a word of it.'

'Gospel true, because he told me so, and as we all know he never lied to me. "Bess," he said, "if they catch me, I'm a dead man."'

'Shop him, then,' suggested somebody from the back of the room.

'Right,' agreed Bess. 'But Directory Enquiries hasn't got their number. Shall I tell you? Very well, children, Auntie Bess will tell you a story. Are you sitting comfortably?'

'Get on with it, you mendacious bitch!'

'I'm being as quick as I can after three glasses of whatever this is. Bear with the mendacious bitch, she's drunk. I said it was a mistake to put diesel in this. Right then, here goes. Richard wanted to kill somebody.'

'Who?' The same voice from the back of the room. Bess waved a hand impatiently, then swore as wine slopped onto her wrist.

'It didn't matter who, he just wanted to kill somebody and not go to jail for it. Just for the hell of it.'

'Wow. Yuck.' A thin girl in spectacles who was sitting on the floor eating cake. She had an American accent.

'Love your command of the English language, Tam. "Wow, yuck" is just perfect. "Wow" was what I said when I first saw him. "Yuck" came during the wedding night.'

There was laughter, and jeering.

'Bess, if you think we'd believe . . .' 'Pull the other one!' 'You told me you'd been married in scarlet.'

'Darlings, previous experience had nothing to do with it. His particular tastes were a well-kept secret until he'd got my autograph on that bit of paper, then he revealed all, and it wasn't a pretty sight. A few days later he told me about his charming fantasy of looking into the face of a man as he twisted the bayonet in his guts, and what he had done to try to bring that to reality. It involved joining the Foreign Legion.'

'Is that true?' asked Gwen, looking slightly startled, and Bess nodded at her.

'As far as I know. Well, I believed it.'

'You knew the man,' Gwen agreed. 'Go on.'

'He went to Paris and enlisted.'

'Paris?'

'Paris, France,' said Bess in a parody of an American accent, and Tam grinned at her.

'Him and two others, they joined up. They signed a lot of papers, and they were shouted at in the time-honoured manner and marched around a parade ground, and then they were sent down to Marseilles. They thought they'd go on to Algeria from there.

'It was the middle of summer, there was a heatwave, and a very slow train, so it took them three days to get to Marseilles, and they were glad to arrive. But they were told their papers weren't in order, they'd have to go back to Paris to get them sorted out. So they went back to Paris on the same train, and got shouted at again, and marched around the same parade ground for another couple of hours, and then they were put back on the train to Marseilles. The heatwave still hadn't broken. They'd been told it was their fault the papers weren't in order so they weren't entitled to subsistence money, and they hadn't got any of their own. They became very hungry, and very, very thirsty, and when they got to Marseilles they were shouted at some more, and marched around another parade ground, and then they were sent back to Paris again. The papers, you understand.'

Everybody was smiling, and Tam laughed.

'I know those slow French trains,' she said. 'They're shit.'

'On their third trip to Marseilles,' Bess continued, ignoring the interruption, 'they decided they'd had enough of the Foreign Legion, so they deserted.'

There was a ripple of laughter around the room. Even Chrissie was smiling.

'What's the penalty for deserting from the Foreign Legion?'

'Death,' said Tam with relish. 'They stake them out on the sand and disembowel them and fill the space where their guts used to be with sand and leave them in the sun to get on with it as fast as they can. It can take as long as three days to die.'

There were groans and exclamations of disgust, overlaid by laughter.

'Oh, Tam, shut up! That's revolting.'

'"Wow, yuck",' said Bess sarcastically. 'Tam, if I thought for one moment you knew what you were talking about I'd go to Paris personally and tell them where to find Richard.'

'I wish Zack had deserted from the Foreign Legion,' said Chrissie savagely. 'Instead of just getting thrown out of the Military Police for beating up prisoners.'

'Chrissie, have another drink.'

'I'd gouge his eyes out and fill them with sand,' she choked, and I felt my nose wrinkling in distaste.

'He killed their little boy,' whispered Gwen, who'd sat down beside me while Bess was telling her story. 'Told the hospital the child had fallen down the cellar stairs, and that Chrissie was only accusing him of murder because he had another woman.'

'Oh.'

'Then he asked the doctors if he could talk to her in private. He described in detail what he'd do to her if she told anybody what had happened. Believe me, Ann, eye-gouging is relatively mild.'

This was turning into a singularly unpleasant party, I thought, and it seemed I wasn't the only one with that opinion. Bess was looking pensive, and a little rueful; her amusing story had backfired. The other women were talking quietly between themselves, the laughter and smiles gone, and two of the men were standing together, silent, staring down at the floor or into their glasses. Chrissie was crying again, and the young man who'd offered to teach karate was whispering into the ear of the girl beside him. She was shaking her head, looking tired and depressed.

My arm was throbbing, and it felt damp. I tried to look at it over my shoulder, to see whether it was bleeding again. I was wearing one of my few good shirts. I didn't want bloodstains on it.

'Chrissie really is terrified,' said Gwen. 'They were walking home this afternoon. She hadn't even seen him, and then he spoke behind them. "Hello, sweetheart, I knew I'd find you in the end." She nearly collapsed. He just smiled, and walked away. Kate and Ruth almost had to carry her home.'

'How did he find her?' I asked, but Gwen didn't know.

Two more women were squashed into the sofa beside Chrissie and the other girl, one of them stroking her hair. As I watched, Chrissie raised her head. She was staring from one face to the other, as though she could find an answer to her terror there. Then she closed her eyes and leaned forward, raising her hands to her face.

Somebody lit candles in the dark corner where the

flagons of wine stood on the counter, and then there was music again, quiet this time, woodwind and strings. A short woman with square-cut hair came over to ask if I'd seen Snowflake, and Gwen went to the sofa and crouched beside the group.

The music grew louder, and more candles were lit. Darkness was falling; the windows were black behind the light. The frightened woman turned her head and tried to smile, and Gwen laid a hand on the tear-stained cheek and leaned forward to whisper into her ear.

Bess said it was her turn to sit with the children, so I stood up and followed her to the door. It was not the sort of party at which I could thank anybody, and Gwen was occupied with Chrissie.

I unlocked the van and dragged the gate out onto the asphalt, then stood for a moment, gritting my teeth at the pain in my arm and cursing Jake's unpredictable mare. After a few minutes the pain subsided, so I carried the gate into the entrance hall where I propped it against the wall beside a holiday poster of a sheep jumping a hurdle. Come to Sunny Ramsgate.

The music grew loud again as a woman came out into the hall. She glanced across and wished me goodnight before going through the other door onto the platform. From further down I heard children's voices and the sound of running water. Homely sounds, an evening routine, and it should have been comforting and happy.

There was a man standing by the van, a stranger. I'd never seen him before.

'What do they want that thing for, then? That gate thing?'

Was this Zack Paulson? The man who'd murdered his own child, and then threatened his wife with horrible violence if she told anybody?

He stood with his shoulders hunched, close against the driver's door of the van, his arms hanging loosely by his sides, held out a little, the fingers curled. It was a posture of practised aggression. He wasn't very tall, but he was powerful, the muscles in his shoulders and neck heavily developed. He was standing half in the shadow. I couldn't see his face, until he smiled.

'You the *bouncer*, then? You their security guard?'

He wasn't speaking loudly, but he was taunting me, laughing at me. A woman my size was an easy target for his jeers.

I stood halfway between the van and the station entrance, looking at him, wondering if I should go back and warn Gwen.

'Zack Paulson?'

The smile broadened and he stepped forward into the light, rolling his shoulders and flexing his fingers. Look at me, woman. Look at me. See how strong I am. Look at me. Be careful.

Be afraid.

'Been talking about me, has she? Always had a mouth on her. I warned her about that. Don't like mouthy women, I don't.'

I wanted to be sure I'd know him again. Chrissie had been terrified of this man. Gwen had said he'd killed his own child, that he was a mental case.

He began to walk towards me, but he stopped under the lamp, looking at me and grinning. Looking me up and down.

'Want to take me on, do you? Do you, then, bouncer woman? Do you want to take me on?'

I heard something behind me, and I turned my head. Gwen was standing between the two pine gateposts, watching us, and there were more women behind her.

Zack laughed.

'You'd have to be mob handed, bouncer woman. You and the bull dykes. Want to try, do you? Do you, then? Want to give it a go?'

I walked past him to the back of the van. The doors were

still standing open from when I'd unloaded the gate. I climbed in, pulling them shut behind me, and scrambled forward into the driver's seat.

I could hear him laughing as I drove away.

I thought I knew now who it was who had shot at Jansy, and I didn't find that suspicion at all comforting.

7

Chrissie brought George to the forge to have his shoes changed the next day, and asked if she could work in my garden while she waited. Gardening had been her job before she'd married Zack. She said it helped her if she could get her paws into the mud.

Her eyes were swollen and sore, but she was trying hard to smile at me, and she'd come on her own. I found myself thinking she was quite a brave woman.

'Please,' I said. 'Please, do. My garden can always do with some attention.'

George was quiet and sleepy, which was just as well, because my arm was badly swollen. I'd bathed it in disinfectant when I'd got home the night before, and tried to bandage it again, but the dressing had slipped during the night.

It took me far longer than usual to change George's shoes, and by the time I'd finished Chrissie had forked over the entire vegetable patch. There was some colour in her cheeks and her eyes were brighter. She looked almost happy.

'Coffee?' I asked, and she nodded.

She talked as we drank. She seemed to feel she owed me some sort of explanation, or perhaps apology, for her distress during the party.

She knew she'd always been a fool about Zack. Sixteen when she met him, in a coffee bar in Eastbourne. She was a student at the technical college, quite pretty she supposed. Two boys had been pestering her, and one of them was trying to paw at her. Suddenly Zack was there, and there was a fight, very brief. He'd hit them both hard enough to hurt them quite badly, and one had managed to land a single punch that had cut Zack's eyebrow.

'So stupid,' said Chrissie. 'Starry-eyed, that could have been invented for me. My knight in shining armour, that was how I saw him. He came to my rescue and got hurt for me. Hurt! That's a laugh. One small cut. I was mopping up the blood with my hankie. I thought Zack was absolutely wonderful. So strong, so brave, so chivalrous. He was a sadistic thug. He loved fighting. He liked to hurt people.'

I picked up the coffee pot, tilted my head questioningly, and Chrissie held out her mug.

'I got pregnant,' she said. 'I was so ignorant. My mother used to say my husband would teach me "all that", if he was "the right sort". What I knew about sex I learned in the school biology lab. Or behind the bicycle shed. Well, metaphorically speaking. I don't think we had a bicycle shed at my school. Did you?'

I nodded. 'I didn't learn anything behind it, though.'

'Zack married me,' said Chrissie. 'And that's the way it was. He married me. I didn't feel I had any option. He was still my knight in shining armour. He was the one who told my parents I was pregnant. I stayed outside in the car. I was too frightened to come in.

'I just did as I was told. It was a register office wedding, in London. My mother said I couldn't have a white wedding, so I'd better not be married in church. I went along with that. Do you know, Ann, I thought it was against the law to be married in white if you weren't a virgin? I really thought it was illegal.

'We had a week in Blackpool. Zack got into two fights

during that week. That was about normal for him. That was when I began to realise. Then, Catterick Camp. Yorkshire? He was a military policeman. Well, for another four months he was. Then there was a court martial. He hadn't told me that was coming up. They threw him out.

'I knew nothing about the court martial until it was all over. My neighbour, she mentioned "Zack's little bit of trouble". When I asked her what she meant she said, "Oh, you know." She wouldn't say any more. It was his sergeant who told me. Zack had beaten up a prisoner. *Another* prisoner. I think he said that was the fourth. Third or fourth. It wasn't just a quick punch or two either. There's a lot of that. They turn a blind eye. This one, he had a ruptured kidney after Zack finished with him.'

There was a long silence. George shifted his weight in the shadows, shuffling on his new shoes, and then tilted his hip, his head dropping again as he dozed.

'Did you really have no idea?' I asked.

'Zack said his wife was to stay in the house. She was there to look after his home, not to spend her time gossiping with all the other idle tarts. No idea? Well, when John Bright came over and told me about the court martial, what the verdict had been, I wasn't as surprised as I should have been. Of course, he thought I knew all about it. I pretended I did. I was so ashamed that Zack hadn't told me. What sort of a wife could I be? My husband hadn't told me.

'So I asked Zack about it that night. That was the first time he hit me. I didn't see his fist coming at me. I don't even remember feeling it. Just my head cracking back against the wall. It nearly knocked me out. I was confused. There was a lump on the back of my head. There was this huge bruise on my forehead. I couldn't think how I'd got it. I sat on the floor. I leaned back against the wall. I wondered what had happened. It wasn't until the next day I realised he'd hit me. I was feeling so sick. Concussion. I didn't know it then. I'd never had concussion before.'

'Did you go to a doctor?' I asked, and Chrissie shook her head.

'I was too ashamed. I felt so guilty. So inadequate, so useless. I should have known about the court martial. I should have been helping my husband. I should have been supporting him when he was in trouble. I hadn't known anything. I hadn't done anything. I was so useless he'd hit me. I was a complete failure. I couldn't tell anybody. I stayed in the house until the bruise faded. Then I put my hair in rollers. I put a headscarf on, low over my forehead. It hid the bruise. It was summer. I could wear dark glasses for the black eyes, but I had to have a reason for a headscarf.

'Didn't anybody help you?'

'There was a welfare officer, because I was pregnant. Zack was always there when she came. Yes, they did help. They found him a job with a security firm. And a flat, sort of. One room, shared bathroom, in Fulham. It was all we could afford on what he earned.

'Luke was born in Fulham.'

Chrissie's voice became light, a little breathless, and her eyes were no longer focused. She was reciting, quickly, words she'd used before and was still trying to drain of meaning. If you are wounded, think of something else, do not look directly at the damage, at the blood or the torn flesh, turn away and think of something else, it will be easier like that.

'When Luke was two years old he had toothache and he was crying a lot, and Zack was tired and angry, and Luke wouldn't stop crying, and Zack picked him up by the bib of his dungarees, and he hit him twice, and Luke just hung there like a doll and Zack said "Oh, shit", and telephoned an ambulance and said Luke had fallen down the cellar steps and hurt his head.'

Turn away and think of something else, Chrissie. It was my eyes that were filling with tears; hers were dry and hard.

106

'I wish Zack was dead,' she said at last, in her normal voice. 'I wish I was strong enough and brave enough to kill him. I wouldn't mind going to prison for that. I don't think I'd even mind being hanged for it, if Zack was dead.'

Arno arrived a few days later to find me staggering around the forge, complaining of a headache, and with a high temperature. My bitten arm had become infected.

He drove me to the doctor, shouting at me.

'You are intelligent, so why do you behave like a fool, Ann?'

I felt too ill to argue. I leaned back into the Riley's comfortable leather seat, trying to think of something other than pain and my pounding head.

Dr Vincent was out on his rounds, his receptionist informed us, glaring at us over her spectacles. Surgery was between nine and eleven, as it stated quite clearly on the notice by the door. It had been over for nearly an hour. If we'd care to wait, she'd tell *Doctor*, if he telephoned. What name should she give?

'Ann Mayall,' I said, and Arno snapped at the woman.

'And *Professor* Linssen.'

We sat on one of the hard benches in the waiting room, and Arno hissed accusations and questions at me, in between unfavourable comments on the National Health Service. The receptionist kept coming in, apparently to see if we were still there, and when she did Arno would fall silent, and stare at her until she went out.

'*Why*, Ann? What do you think he is here for, this precious *doctor*? And that woman with the spectacles, it is her work, too. Her job. Maybe she forgot.'

He shifted on the bench and crossed his legs.

'My God, the English. If they put these seats in a prison, there'd be trouble, so they punish sick people with them instead.'

'They're not so bad.'

'No? You have to be tough, I think, to use your health service here. How many days ago, you got this bite? How long before you come here if I didn't come?'

The receptionist came in again, straightened the magazines on the table, sniffed at us, and walked to the door. Before she reached it Arno was at the table, rummaging through the neatened stack and complaining there was nothing worth reading.

'So, now you listen to me, please,' he went on once the door had banged behind the affronted woman. 'Are you listening?'

'Yes.'

'You think you are nothing, because your mother thought you were nothing. But your mother is a fool, Ann. So why do you believe a fool? Huh? You think about this, please. But for now, if there's something wrong with my car, you take it to the garage for me, yes?'

'Yes. Arno, please don't shout at me. It hurts my head.'

He kissed me, and brushed the hair off my forehead. It was damp, clinging to the sweat on my skin.

'So, please, Ann, if there is something wrong with my Ann, you please take her to the doctor. For me. Yes?'

'All right.'

When Dr Vincent finally arrived he gave me antibiotics and said I should take a week off work until my arm healed.

Arno became a tyrant, and telephoned all the customers whose names were in my diary to tell them I was ill. The antibiotics made me sleepy, so I went to bed. I woke late in the night to find Arno sitting on the chair beside me.

'Hello, Blue-Eyes,' I said, and then frowned in puzzlement. Why had I called him that?

'Huh. Delirium. You take this medicine the dear *doctor* gave you. Now, Ann. Come on.'

When I had swallowed it, he stroked my cheek, smiling at me.

'"Blue-Eyes",' he muttered. 'You know, your eyes are so dark I can hardly tell where the pupil ends and the iris starts.'

'Lucille has blue eyes,' I said, closing mine. 'All the Mayalls have blue eyes, I think.'

'Ah. So this excellent student of biology might have found a clue here?'

'I'm stupid,' I agreed, and Arno stroked my hair again.

Jake arrived that evening in the Land Rover with a bunch of flowers for me, and an anxious expression on his face. Arno showed him up to my room, which was not something I'd expected, or wanted. Jake stood in the doorway looking uncomfortable.

'I sent that mare to the auction,' he said. 'I *told* you to go to the doctor, didn't I? Didn't I?'

He turned to Arno, appealing for support.

'I did tell her. Offered to take her to casualty, but she wouldn't. She won't be told. It really was a bad bite, but she won't be told.'

'I know.'

'You shouldn't have sent that mare to auction,' I objected. 'You could have got a good price for her. She'll have gone for next to nothing in the ring.'

'She tried to take a chunk out of Toby. Bitch.'

'Mr Brewer, please, have a seat. There is a chair, don't stand.'

'No, I don't want to be a nuisance, just, I thought . . . Well, it was my horse, so flowers was the least . . .'

'I make coffee,' said Arno decisively. 'Sit down, Mr Brewer, talk horses to Ann. For horses I know nothing.'

But he fed Lyric for me that night, and told me he was now a master of horsemanship because he had been neither kicked nor bitten.

I was restless, sweating with fever and unable to sleep. Arno brought me orange juice and sponged my face. He changed the sheets twice, gave me aspirin for the pain, then lay beside me, holding me carefully so as not to touch my arm.

'I love you,' I said suddenly, without thinking.

'Oh, Ann.'

'I know. Brita. It's all right.'

My eyes were closed, I was trying to lie still, because I knew he must be tired, and probably wanting to sleep.

I felt his lips brushing gently across my eyelids. I love you, I thought, I love you. Brita. But I love you, Arno, and I know I'm going to get hurt.

I watched the sky grow light, and Arno slept beside me, and the shadows darkened in the room as the morning came closer.

Gwen and Tessa were my next visitors, and after that I refused to stay in bed, fever or not. If people were coming to see me I wanted to be in the forge, or if Arno stood in the kitchen door with his arms braced against the frame and refused to allow me through, at least downstairs in my living room.

'I don't like strangers in my bedroom,' I explained.

'Maybe you don't have enough fun in your life.'

He'd gone shopping the next time Jake called, this time with a box of chocolates with a picture of a foal on the lid. I was in the forge, tidying up, wondering whether I could start work again. The fever had nearly gone, but my arm was still stiff and swollen and it hurt every time I moved.

Jake laid the chocolates on the workbench and pushed them towards me, looking embarrassed.

'Don't know if you like them. You better now?'

'Much better. I'll be working again soon. Have a chocolate. Not the orange creams, they're my favourites.'

He laughed and seemed to relax, but then grew serious.

'Got bad news, Ann. Well, not *disaster*, but it's not good.'

'What's happened?'

'That white donkey. Morry found him yesterday. Somebody's shot him.'

110

Zack Paulson, I thought. You bastard. You utter bastard.

'Probably poachers,' Jake was saying. 'Might have thought it was a white deer. They're rare, but they happen. Albinos.'

'Oh, Jake. Poor Snowflake.'

'You put him on Gorsedown, didn't you?'

'Yes. Yes, I did. You know, his feet were getting better. They really were.'

Jake said nothing, and after a moment I began to grow angry.

'There aren't any deer on Gorsedown.'

'Maybe you haven't seen . . .'

'Listen, Jake, I've been riding that land for a long time now, you know that. There are no deer. You can believe I might not have seen them if you like, but do you think I'd never have seen any sign of them? No slots in the mud? No chewed trees? I know what the signs are, I know a bit about deer.'

He shrugged, but he looked thoughtful.

'There's no way to get a car in there, either. Deer poachers, my foot. What does Morry say?'

'Not a lot.'

'I bet. Jake, I don't want Jansy Neville finding Snowflake.'

'Well, I don't . . .'

My anger and sadness were beginning to turn to rage. A harmless, friendly donkey, and that psychopathic cretin had shot him. Because he liked hurting, he liked to frighten, he was a sadistic thug.

'Where was he shot?' I demanded.

'Somewhere near the house, I think Morry . . .'

'I don't mean that. *Where?* Head? Heart? Where was he shot? Or did that bastard get him in the guts or the kidneys or something?'

'Oh, I see. Head. Nothing . . .' Jake was looking at me curiously. 'What bastard? You know who did it?'

I ignored the question.

111

'Morry won't say anything, will he? He'll stay right out of it, damn him. So I suppose I've got to find poor Snowflake, and tell the police. And what will *they* do about it?'

'Ann, I . . .'

I didn't hear what Jake said because my hammer was in my hand and I swung it hard down onto the anvil in my anger and frustration. Violent pain shot up my arm.

'*Aah, bugger! Oh, bugger, bugger, bugger.*'

I dropped the hammer and turned away, clutching at the wound. Tears were suddenly in my eyes and rolling down my cheeks.

Snowflake. Dear, friendly Snowflake, who I wouldn't send into the shed to the man with the humane killer, because he was young and I'd been saturated with death that day. He'd been getting better, his feet were harder, and now he was dead, with a bullet through his head.

'Ann . . .'

'Yes, what? Oh, damn.'

'Look, Ann, don't be . . . Oh, come here.'

Jake was pulling me around to face him, and there was a handkerchief in his hand.

'Here, take this, come on. I'm sorry. Really, I am. I didn't know you'd take it like this. Come on, Ann, animals die, you know that. Ann? Come on.'

'I'm all right. We've got to get Snowflake out of there, and what do you mean, animals die? They don't have to die like that. You wouldn't be so damned calm about it if it was Barbarian, would you? If someone put a bullet through *his* head, what about that?'

'Yes, well Barbarian's a . . .'

'Barbarian's worth a lot of money. Barbarian's valuable. And Snowflake's just a donkey, and a reject at that.'

'I didn't shoot him, Ann.'

I'd been shouting at Jake, and I'd not even realised it.

'Sorry, Jake. I'm sorry. That wasn't fair. You didn't know the donkey. He was nice. I liked him, and he was getting better.'

Jake was still holding the handkerchief out, and he smiled. 'Look, do you want this, or don't you?'

It wasn't very clean. I shook my head. 'No, thanks. I'm all right now.'

But my arm was hurting badly and my head was beginning to throb. I wished Jake would go away, and then I thought of Snowflake, of getting the carcass out of Gorsedown. I'd probably need his help.

'I can't manage the gate,' I said. 'Not with my arm . . .'

'No, right. Well. Oh, you mean . . . The donkey. Ah, yes. Well. I don't know.'

Arno came back, drove the Riley into the garage, and walked into the forge through the workshop. He looked at me, then at Jake, but he said nothing. He watched my face, and waited for me to tell him what had happened.

'Snowflake's dead. Somebody shot him.'

'And so you are sad. Yes, I see.'

I could feel my face hot and dry; the fever was coming back. And when I moved my arm I couldn't help wincing.

'I've got to get him out of Gorsedown and I can't open the gate.'

'He's not your donkey, Ann. This is not your problem.'

Tears of frustration and weakness were stinging my eyes again, and I wanted to go away before I began to cry.

'Maybe not, Arno, but please solve it for me. Please. Use the brilliant mind for this, not just for metal. Please?'

He smiled, and his shoulders lifted slightly in a brief shrug.

'Please,' I said again, and then I couldn't stay in the forge any longer. I held my hand over my eyes as I walked past Jake and out into the sunshine, but I was sobbing with pain and anger and sadness by the time I reached the door of the cottage.

It was half an hour before Arno followed me into the kitchen, and at first he said nothing. He touched my cheeks where the tears had stained them, and then he unbuttoned

113

my shirt and carefully eased it down over my arm. I watched his face as he frowned.

'The *dear doctor* maybe should come here.'

'No.'

'OK. I just rope you and tie you and drag you to hospital. Or we see if my grandmother's remedy still works.'

Strips of towel soaked in boiling water, laid over the infected area and bandaged in place, changed every half hour. It should have scalded, but it was soothing, and Arno made me drink something bitter. Mostly tea, he said, and some herbs. Mint; the others, he did not know the English names. But they were in my garden.

'I have to tell Gwen about Snowflake,' I said.

'I telephoned her. They are all very angry, I think.'

He was wincing as he laid the fresh towel on my arm. The hot water was scalding his fingers.

'Jake believes you know who did this.'

'Yes. I'm not sure, but I think I know.'

I was absolutely sure. I was sure it was Zack Paulson who had shot at Jansy, and I was sure he had killed Snowflake. I hadn't even bothered to wonder whether there could be another explanation.

Arno was watching my face again, but he didn't ask me any questions. He bandaged my arm, and handed me the mug.

'Tomorrow this man Morry Old will go into the park. He will push the gate and I will pull. This will work?'

'Oh, yes. Yes, the two of you . . . I mean, you could probably, on your own . . .'

He smiled, and shook his head.

'I do not think so. But I will survive this shame, not being as strong as you. Anyway, it is not for you to worry about. Jake brings a horse who is very quiet, with something he calls a trace, and we drag the donkey back here. Somebody called Johnson will be here with a lorry.'

So simple. Such an easy answer, but I hadn't thought of it.

'The women who owned Snowflake, they said this is all right. So now, please, Ann, you go to bed. Just sleep a little. Or I have to try to be a caveman and drag you off to hospital, and I do not think I will be very good at that.'

I slept through the afternoon and the night, waking only when Arno put fresh hot towels on my arm and gave me the tea to drink. He was beginning to look haggard from tiredness, but when I asked him he only shook his head. He was fine, he said. Now sleep, Ann. Sleep.

I woke to bright daylight to find him beside me, still dressed, lying on top of the blankets with his head turned away from the window, deeply asleep. I slid out from between the sheets carefully, so as not to disturb him, and he sighed and muttered, but he didn't move.

I stood looking down at him, thinking how much I loved him, how happy I was when he was here with me, and I tried not to think too much about the future.

When I went down to the kitchen there were sprigs of herbs wilting on the table, mint and hyssop, lemon balm. The kettle was standing filled beside an enamel bowl, with a strip of towelling lying ready and a clean bandage rolled tight against it.

My arm was still swollen and painful, and it was difficult to move. There had been no overnight miracle cure, but I had slept, and the headache had diminished to a dull blurring behind my eyes.

When Jake arrived with the Land Rover and trailer I told him Arno was asleep, that he'd been up all night. Jake thought he might just manage the gate himself. Maybe.

'How are you?' he asked.

'Better. Thanks.'

Morry was already at the gate, waiting, and he and Jake opened it without too much trouble and fixed it back against the holding catch ready for their return. Morry complained about the noise, said he couldn't see why I needed a gate like that now.

Partly because of people like you, I thought, but I said nothing. I was wondering if the noise had woken Arno.

I didn't go with them into the park. Jake led the cob, and Morry walked beside him, his hands in his pockets, his shoulders hunched. I watched them walking down the path by the beech trees until they crossed the high bank and dropped down the other side, out of sight, walking towards the track that led to the house.

Arno was lying exactly as I had left him. I listened to him breathing, slowly, deeply. I wanted to brush the hair out of his eyes but I was afraid I'd wake him, so I crept away and went down into the stable yard to wait.

It didn't take them long. They came back the same way, over the bank under the beech trees, Jake leading the cob, Morry beside him, still with his hands in his pockets and his shoulders hunched, and behind them, lurching over the rough ground, the sad, hunched shape that had been Snowflake. Weak tears sprang into my eyes again, and I brushed them away. I am not a sentimental person, and I do not usually cry easily.

I don't think either of them noticed when they reached the paddock gate. They weren't really looking at me. Morry was still staring at the ground, sullen, and Jake was busy with the cob.

'That Johnson, late as usual,' he said. 'Old, you take Smokey back to the yard, I'll wait for the lorry.'

Old, he'd called him. Not Morry. Jake's a first-name man, unless he's angry.

'Coffee?' I asked, and Jake nodded at me, unsmiling. Morry said nothing. A quick glance in my direction, a short shake of his round head, and he was leading the cob towards the trailer, the chains of the traces clinking on the concrete.

Jake followed me into the kitchen and stood in the doorway. Leaning against the frame, he watched me as I lit the gas.

'He knows who did that,' he said. 'He knows. He won't say.'

I had no answer to that, and after a moment Jake went on.

'You're right, it's not poachers, and Old says there are no deer on Gorsedown, so I suppose that's right, too.'

I suppressed my annoyance at the remark, and scooped instant coffee into the mugs. 'Why do you think he'd know more about what's on Gorsedown than I do?' I asked mildly, but he didn't seem to have heard.

'Now he's got a girl in Gloucester pregnant and he's trying to borrow money off me for an abortion. I don't hold with abortion.'

He stamped irritably, kicking the heel of his boot at the threshold and pushing his hands into the pockets of the old flying jacket he wore for everyday work.

'I'm sick of him. Rides like an angel, can't keep his hands off women. Always in money trouble. He borrowed fifty off poor old Toby last month, Toby's seen the last of that, daft mug. And he won't tell me who shot that donkey. Says he doesn't know, lying bugger.'

He looked up at me, and his jaw was thrust out aggressively.

'So, you tell me, please, Ann. Who was it?'

'Zack Paulson,' I said.

'Who's Zack Paulson?'

I paused, considering. How much of this story was mine to tell?

'He's the husband of one of the women at the railway station,' I said at last. 'Ex military policeman and, according to her, a sadistic thug.'

Jake was looking at me, frowning.

'Do you know him?'

'We've exchanged a few words.'

He raised his eyebrows at the tone, and would have spoken again, but instead turned his head, then jerked it at me.

'Fred Johnson, in his own sweet time as usual. Do you want to stay in here, or come out and help?'

I followed him out into the yard, and watched the big fat man climb out of his lorry, puffing, and hitching at his braces. He was late, he said, because the fan belt had gone. He'd had to wait for the engine to cool down. Couldn't expect him to wreck his engine for a donkey, could we?

So now, if I'd be so kind, he'd like to use my telephone, so his missus could get off her fat backside and go down to the garage and get him another fan belt. If I didn't mind.

'You can winch that carcass up into the truck first,' snapped Jake. 'After that, we'll see.'

The knacker was surprised at Jake's tone. He stood up straight, his mouth open, blinking.

'All right, squire. No need for that. No need.'

I watched Snowflake jerking up the ramp of the lorry, and nodded when Johnson asked again about the telephone, this time politely. Then I crouched down beside the carcass and rubbed the leaf mould out of one of the hooves.

'Look, Jake,' I said, sadly. 'It really was almost better. I could have shod him. I could have got four nails in there. It would have been enough, on dry ground.'

Jake stood, his hands once more stuffed into his pockets, looking down, and nodding. He shifted his feet in the straw, scuffing at the wooden slats.

'Ann?'

'Yes?'

He was uneasy, he couldn't keep still. I looked up at him.

'What is it, Jake?'

'Well, I meant to ask you yesterday, but you were upset. I mean, about the donkey. Snowflake. You know, when I brought you the chocolates?'

'Yes?' I was watching him, wondering what was worrying him. 'They're very nice chocolates,' I added, although they were still on the workbench in the forge, almost untouched.

He was looking at the toe of one of his boots, as though something of interest was to be seen there.

'Have you ever thought of marriage?'

It seemed a very strange question.

'Well, I suppose so,' I said. 'What do you mean? Whose marriage?'

'Well, yours. You know.'

Still looking at his boot, he glanced at me, and then looked away. His face was red, and he brushed one hand across his forehead.

'Oh. Oh, no. No, Jake. I've got a mirror, I don't think about my marriage. I don't think anybody would want to marry me.'

I could have shod Snowflake, I thought. I could have brought him out of Gorsedown and shod him, and he'd have been safely back at the railway station, with George.

'I would.'

Jake was looking at me, almost defiantly.

'I would,' he said again. 'I mean . . .'

And then he was talking fast, about how we'd known each other a long time, how he'd always liked me, hoped I liked him. Didn't I?

I was staring at him in amazement.

'Jake? Are you asking me to marry you?'

He nodded. Then he said he hoped I'd think about it. He'd always liked me. Thought we could make a go of it. Not a romantic sort of man, not good at this sort of thing, you know, proposing and all that, but very fond of me. Please think about it?

He was crimson with embarrassment. He still had his hands pushed hard down into the pockets of his jacket, and all I could think was, how amazing, somebody wants to marry me. Jake Brewer, he's asked me to marry him.

'Jake,' I said, when I could think of something to say, 'Jake, thank you. But I don't believe I want to marry. I've

119

never thought about it, you see. I mean, I don't want to marry anybody, it's not that I don't want to marry you.'

Then I looked around, and slowly I climbed to my feet and turned back to him.

'I suppose I've had romantic daydreams. I suppose, anyway, when I was a teenager. But I must say, Jake, it never occurred to me that somebody might propose to me in the back of a knacker's lorry over the body of a dead donkey.'

8

Summer became autumn, and autumn began to carry the threat of winter. The ground was hard underfoot in the early mornings, and the breath of the animals hung in the air in front of their faces. The leaves and berries in the hedge turned yellow, then gold, and then bright, fire red.

Lyric's coat grew long and shaggy, her forelock a heavy clump of hair falling between her eyes. There was grey on her muzzle now, and hollows in the bones of her face. I rubbed her forehead with the heel of my hand and she pressed her head against it, blowing softly, and then turned to lip at my jacket.

I'd have to clip her before I rode her again, a tedious job that neither of us enjoyed. But I was too busy for riding. I was working until after dark every evening, so Lyric grazed in the paddock and her dark coat remained long and shaggy, with only the worst patches of dried mud brushed off it when I had a few minutes to spare for her.

I was turning work away, something I'd never done before. A builder had asked me to make garden gates, fifteen of them for an executive housing estate, each one to be individually designed please, Miss Mayall, they're to be a selling point for the houses, so they're to be just a bit special, know what I mean?

At a special price, which was to remain a closely guarded secret, and there might be something in it for me if I played my cards right, never know where something like this could lead, know what I mean?

That executive housing estate was being built on Ashlands, which had been a nature reserve, a lovely piece of woodland and open heath. Jake Brewer had used it for training his eventers and hunters, and something very underhand had been done about planning permission, according to him.

So I wrote to the builder and told him I couldn't make his gates.

He telephoned me, incredulously indignant. This could be *big* money we might be talking here, this could *lead* to something.

'But I'm already doing as much work as I can handle,' I said. 'Know what I mean?'

I told Jake I'd turned down the job, and he said that was great. Then he shuffled his feet, and asked if I'd thought any more about our conversation.

He'd mentioned it once or twice since that morning, always looking a little shamefaced, and finally it had sunk in: he'd meant it. Jake wanted to marry me.

Had it not been for Arno I'd have assumed it was a taste-less joke. But Arno wanted me, so perhaps Jake did, too.

'It would be easy for me to love you,' Arno had said to me sadly on the night before he left. 'I cannot let it happen. Dear Ann.'

I'd told him I loved him. I'd been feverish, but not quite delirious, not then, and it had been true.

'I love you.'

He would be back some time before Christmas. There was to be a conference in Birmingham and another in London; he could only attend one of them, he was not yet sure which.

'Please take the Riley to the garage and Ann to the *dear doctor*.'

'I'm all right now.'

His arms around my neck, our foreheads pressed together, so close we could not see each other. My skin against his, mine pale, like cream, he'd said, his darker.

'Are you part Negro, too?' I'd asked.

'I don't think so.'

'You're darker than me, except for hair and eyes.'

Burn scars on his hands and wrists, from when he was a student; he'd been careless. Not any more, he said.

'Did you go to the doctor?' I asked, and I felt him smile, felt his lips move against my cheek, the breath quicken in a laugh.

'I went to the hospital in an ambulance, with the blue lights and the bells.'

'Oh, yes?'

'You don't believe me, do you?'

I wound my fingers into his hair and pulled his head back so I could look into his face.

'Not a word.'

He was grinning down at me, the lines at the corners of his eyes etched deep, not from looking into the hot sun or a furnace, but from laughter, and from smiling.

'So I'm a damned liar. Too bad.'

He twisted his head free from my hand and buried his face in the side of my neck. I ran my fingers down the line of his back, feeling the bones under the skin, wondering why wanting him made me drowsy.

'Is this the same for all women?'

'Yes.'

Lips, and hands, and voice, and smiling eyes. Slow, rolling movements, my legs curling around his, my arms around his body, holding him close, a low, moaning sound, is that me? His hands on my shoulders, pushing me away, pushing me down, my eyes opening, he is smiling down at me, and I turn my head, slowly, as I hear his voice.

'Ann?'

'Yes. Oh, yes.'

Now I do not think, I can only feel, but his movements are deliberate, considered, he is careful and attentive, and when I open my eyes he is watching me. I touch his cheek, and he turns his head and kisses the palm of my hand, but his eyes never move from my face.

For what is he waiting?

'I wish I could teach you to fly,' he says, but the words skim past my ears, and I do not heed them.

There is an echo of sadness in his voice that lingers.

He will come back some time before Christmas.

Jake Brewer stands leaning on the door of the Land Rover, and says he hopes I'll consider what he's said. He's always thought very highly of me. Always liked you, Ann. Sorry I'm not very romantic.

I should have repressed the urge to tease, but I didn't.

'A proposal in the back of a knacker's truck over the body of a dead donkey,' I said, and if his responding smile was somewhat wry, at least it was a smile.

'I brought you chocolates the day before.'

'So you did.'

'Unfortunately, your friend Professor Linssen turned up too soon. I didn't have a chance.'

My friend Professor Linssen will be back some time before Christmas, and the thought makes me kind.

'Dear Jake. If I wanted to marry anybody, it would be you.'

He and Clive Ulverton had put Lyric back in training when she was a ten-year-old and I'd been too badly injured to ride her, and too sick with worry to care about anything except her. She'd run three times, and on that third time she'd dug herself out of a too careful jump at the last, and she'd fought every inch of a heartbreaking uphill run to the winning post to beat the favourite by a head.

It had been Jake who'd persuaded me to let Clive train her for those races, when they'd both been concerned about

124

me, and wanted me to have at least some fun during that dreadful time.

'Dear Jake.'

'Give us a kiss, then,' he said, and I leaned over the top of the Land Rover's scarred door and brushed my lips briefly across his cheekbone.

He kicked at the gravel with the heel of his boot. 'I'm going to ask again,' he said, making it sound like a threat. And then, a little anxiously, 'Hope you don't mind?'

I shook my head.

'It won't be in the back of a knacker's truck. Thanks for turning down those gates for Campbell. He's a right slimy bastard.'

Campbell had seen the snake gate, and had asked one of the women where they'd got it. Perry Graves and I had hung it as soon as my arm had healed, because Gwen had been really anxious about Zack Paulson since Snowflake had been shot. She, too, seemed to be in no doubt that it had been he who had killed the donkey.

'What will it be next?' she wondered.

'Where can we get another donkey?' asked Tessa. 'Old George's that lonely!'

I might try to think about that when Zack had gone, and in the meantime we had to keep him out of the old station.

One spring only, and then the catch. Noise was what they wanted, and enough resistance to stop the children running out into the road. As for somebody coming along the tracks, the geese would give ample warning of their approach.

When Gwen had asked me where she could buy geese, I'd laughed, realising at once their main purpose. She'd laughed too, at my quick recognition. Better than watchdogs, and who could possibly object? A lot of people kept geese for the Christmas market.

'What about the children?' I'd asked, and she'd said they had to learn how to avoid danger sooner or later; better to learn by watching out for the geese, who would only inflict a few bruises, than by dodging traffic in the cities from where most of them had come.

Or by dodging fists, which some of them had already learned.

Chrissie seemed to be coping with her fear. She refused to stay out of the village and would even go out on her own; if she seemed nervous, if she jumped at sudden noises, she did at least try to disguise it. Since that night, when she'd been in a state of shock following her first encounter with Zack since she'd left him, I'd seldom seen her with anything other than a smile on her face.

I'd seen no sign of Zack on Gorsedown, although I watched for him. When Morry Old brought Jake's horses to the forge I asked him again to describe the man with the rifle, but he was vague; it had been getting dark, he'd been in the shadows of the trees. What description Morry did give could have fitted Zack; I could think of twenty other men it could have fitted, too.

'You think he shot that donkey?' asked Morry.

'Don't you?'

He shrugged. He was still nervous, and certainly not prepared to risk any sort of admission that might tempt me to tell the police.

But Zack was still in the neighbourhood, although nobody knew where he was living. He made no attempt to approach Chrissie if there was anybody with her, or even nearby. Now and then he'd be there, in the village, standing in the main street, looking around. If he saw any of the women from the railway station, he'd grin; he'd watch them as they passed, looking them up and down, but he rarely spoke.

They did their best to ignore him, and Chrissie said little about him, to them.

'He calls me "unfinished business". He says he'll get around to me soon.'

She was spreading lawn clippings around the stems of the young plants in the vegetable garden, and I was watching her, marvelling that she had managed to make so much more grow in that little patch of ground. There was enough for her to take vegetables back for the children now, and still leave all that I needed.

'What does he mean by that?' I asked, and then I noticed that her voice had taken on the light and brittle quality it had when she was trying not to think too much about meanings.

'He says he'll kill me.'

Don't speak for a moment. Let her keep silent, let the thoughts drift away.

She believes him.

Count to fifty, and then ask.

'Has anybody else heard this?'

A quick shake of the brown curls, but her head was still bowed down, turned away from me so I couldn't see her face.

'Only when I'm alone.'

And then she was talking about the vegetables, shying away from the subject of Zack. She'd told me, because she'd needed to tell somebody, but didn't want a discussion.

This can't be true, can it? I wondered. But he'd killed his child. What was to stop him, if he thought he could get away with it? What would stop a man like Zack Paulson?

I left Chrissie alone in the vegetable garden, and went back to the forge, wondering, and very troubled.

I made the frame for the snake gate, and Perry sunk it into the posts, chiselling out the wood with slow strokes, silent as he worked. Then he laid the steel against the pine, looked it up and down, and pushed it into place. It fitted so closely it hardly seemed to need the bolts.

We worked together to hang the gate, levering the spring out of the way, adjusting the ratchet, testing and checking, and then, when it worked as it should, we stood back and smiled at each other.

'I suppose it'll just have to do,' he said.

I was surprised. I tested the gate again, looking for looseness, for play in the joints, sagging, but I could find nothing. It all worked perfectly. I looked questioningly at Perry, to find him grinning at me.

I've always been slow-witted when people make jokes.

He came to see me a few days later, riding a tricycle that towed a small trailer. I tried not to stare at it, but I'd never seen a man on a tricycle before.

'Haven't got the balance for a two-wheeler any more,' he commented as he pushed it up to the wall of the forge, and I nodded, as though I'd understood.

He'd brought three old wrought-iron brackets, two of them broken, the third almost rusted through. They were from a Spanish table he was restoring. He wanted me to make new ones.

'New in fact, not in appearance,' he said. 'Eight of them. The other five are missing. Look, they're none of them quite the same. See? Maybe whoever made these wasn't as good as you.'

It was the first of several pieces of work I did for Perry. I found I liked him. I liked his dry sense of humour, his quietness. He asked if he could watch me working, and I said I didn't mind. The few questions he asked were intelligent; they sprang from a desire to learn. He wasn't just making conversation. But usually he just watched, and worked out the answers for himself.

Sometimes he'd bring his own work, if it was small enough to fit into the trailer, and he'd sit at my bench by the forge window, carving or sanding, while I made whatever it was he needed.

He came from Sheffield, he said. He'd been in the Merchant Navy, but he'd left that when he married, and set up his own carpentry company. It was doing well. He'd bought a nice little house for his nice little wife from the proceeds of his nice little business.

'Nearly drove me mad.'

I hammered the punch against the hot iron, three sharp blows, and put the metal back into the forge.

'Were you missing the sea?'

No, he wasn't missing the sea. It was solitude in the evenings he'd missed. He liked to be alone at night, and his wife had done everything she could to make a good home for him. To make his home the place where he'd want to be.

To be a good wife to him, in fact.

'I looked into the future and I saw year after year of her pretty little face smiling at me across our living room. Nice hot meals every night, lovely clean home, Susie dressed in a pretty frock with her make-up all just right, and I thought, I'd rather be dead.'

He'd stayed with her for seven years, playing the good husband. He'd paid off the mortgage with the profits, he'd taken her on holiday every year, Greece or Spain, there'd been investments and insurance, and Susie had talked about children.

'Then I got cancer, and Susie turned herself into the perfect nurse. I couldn't take any more.'

I looked at him. The late afternoon sun was shining through the window onto his face, and his eyes were sunken into deep hollows. His hair was thinning, and there was a grey shade to his skin.

He turned his head and caught me watching him. He grinned.

'You can't see the skull yet. You're slacking off. I need that T-brace tonight, not next Monday week.'

No sympathetic platitudes for Perry, then. It was information I'd been given, not an appeal for compassion.

Snowflake had been shot, Perry was dying, little Luke Paulson was dead, and his murderous father was in Anford, probably with a rifle.

129

I broke the T-brace, and had to start again.

That night I threw the windows of my bedroom wide open, and wedged them with wooden blocks. I lay under them staring up at the windy sky, shivering with the cold even under my thick blankets, but I felt crowded, claustrophobic from other people's fear and anger. I listened to the wind and I watched the clouds, and when they broke it seemed as though it was they that were still and the stars were hurtling past, wheeling and plunging through the black sky.

Later it rained, and still I lay under the open windows, feeling my face cool and wet and my hair clinging to my forehead, grateful for the clean coldness of the night.

Peter Clements came to see me the next day, back from playing a demon in a film in Italy. I was glad he had come. I like Peter, and he's good for Glory. I was beginning to hope they'd stay together, that he'd realised how she felt about children, and had chosen her instead.

As soon as I saw him pulling into the drive my spirits lifted, but the happy feeling didn't last. He hugged me in greeting, wandered around the forge for a while looking at work I was doing, and then asked me about Glory, and children.

'Did she ever want children? I mean, before those perverts carved her up? Did you ever talk about it together?'

What could I say to him? How could I turn this away? I felt as though the sun had gone behind a cloud.

'I try not to think about things I can't have, Peter. I don't talk about them. Glory knows that.'

I spread out my hands, and stared him in the face. I'd promised Glory I wouldn't tell him what she'd said. I'd try to get out of this, but I wouldn't lie to Peter, either.

'Look at me. I don't think I'm likely to have children, do you? So Glory and I don't talk about it.'

He didn't turn away, he stared straight back at me. Peter is a very determined man.

'You must have talked about her injuries when she came back here. What did she say about children, please, Ann?'

I drew a deep breath, and closed my eyes. I could still picture my sister as she'd been then, her face grey and sweating with pain, her attempts to smile at me, lips drawn back from clenched teeth.

'She said she was barren, so that was that. Finish. Those were her words, Peter. And we didn't talk about children again.'

When I opened my eyes he was still looking at me. His expression hadn't changed, but I knew Peter well enough to feel the depth of his sadness. Had she started to drift away from him? I felt my hope for them growing smaller. Oh, Peter, please. Please make a lucky guess. Change your mind, tell her you can't fit children into your life.

'Dear Ann,' he said. 'I love you, my big sister.'

'Glory used to call me that.'

'I know. Come to Stratford and rewire the flat for me.'

I smiled at him.

'Stay here and rub down Uncle Henry's bench,' I countered.

He grimaced at me, but he'd already said he had the day to himself, so after a few protests he dragged the heavy iron bench into the forge and set to work with sandpaper.

'Will you do the flat?' he asked.

'I'm not an electrician.'

'Glory said you could, if you would. If you had time. Save a poor struggling actor a few hard-earned pennies?'

'Peter, you *are* a liar. How much did that enormous car cost?'

Before he could answer, Chrissie came in. She'd been working in the garden since early that morning, and drinking brandy, to keep out the cold, she claimed. That and the sharp wind had brought colour to her cheeks and made her vivacious, and a little reckless. She looked at Peter, frankly appreciative.

'Hello, handsome.'

'Hi, sexy,' he answered, glancing up from the bench.

'Would you two like a formal introduction?' I asked. 'Or just the key to the hay store?'

'I've seen you somewhere before,' said Chrissie. 'Have we met?'

'In my dreams.'

Chrissie's eyes began to sparkle, and she leaned against the workbench and folded her arms, grinning. I'd never seen her look so bright and happy.

'But all my dreams are about trees, so where have I seen you?'

He turned his head and smiled at her.

'Sitting in a holly bush?'

I went into the workshop and turned on the lathe. A flirtation with Peter would lift Chrissie's spirits, but I hoped they wouldn't fall again too painfully.

Later that afternoon when Peter had gone she told me they'd talked about Zack and Luke.

'Isn't he easy to talk to? You'd never think he was so famous.'

'You recognised him, then.'

'In the end, I did. I felt such a fool. He's really nice, isn't he? And he hasn't made a bad job of rubbing down that bench, either. Why had I always imagined actors could never do anything else? God, Ann, I fancy him *rotten.*'

'Have a black coffee and a cold shower instead.'

'Is there any more of that brandy?'

'You've had enough.'

'Not while I can still stand, I haven't. There's a wind like a knife in your veg garden. I *want* that man, and I want him *now.* Is your sister the jealous type?'

'She's never had to be.'

'Oh. Oh, shit, that sounds ominous.'

Chrissie leaned back against the door frame and

stretched, reaching her arms up high over her head and rolling her shoulders.

'Oh, well, I can always dream. Damn. I thought I was over men for good. But don't you ever wonder what he'd be like?'

'Does brandy always have this effect on you?'

I was laughing at her, but this time I felt happy about her question. I'd have been embarrassed, before Arno. I'd have changed the subject, because I did try, then, not to think of things I thought I could never have.

She sighed, and raised her eyebrows at me.

'Yes, Chrissie, I have wondered,' I said, and it was true. I had wondered what he'd be like, my sister's lover. That afternoon I'd watched him, sweeping the flagstones, rubbing down the paint on the bench, I'd talked to him, and I'd listened to him, and I'd thought of Arno, and I'd wondered about Peter.

Once I'd asked Arno, when you're with me, like this, do you ever imagine you're with another woman?

He'd been falling asleep by then, but he'd opened his eyes, and smiled at me.

'Ann, you have been listening to the wrong sort of dirty jokes.'

'I want some more brandy,' said Chrissie. 'If I can't have that fabulous hunk, I want some more brandy. I wonder if he's as good as he looks.'

Tessa asked me again about another donkey, as a companion for George. She insisted he was lonely, although every time I saw him he seemed to be half asleep. Gwen said Tessa had a bee in her bonnet about George, but they did need another donkey, if I had any ideas.

'Why don't you get goats?' I asked. 'I thought that was a good idea. They'd be company for him, too.'

But they needed something that could pull a cart, and George was too old and too small for anything heavy. Coal had to be brought in for the winter, the delivery charges were outrageous, and firewood.

I telephoned Jane Laverton.

'Have you still got that old Appaloosa?'

'Yes, why? Do you want him? Please?'

'No, but the hippies might. Could he pull a cart?'

'Grief! I've no idea. I don't think he's . . . Oh, just a minute, yes, he was. Yes, when I bought him, the man said he . . . Yes. Well, I mean, he'll be out of practice, I've had him, what is it now? Yes. Fifteen years, yes. Would they look after him?'

'They won't take him unless they're sure of that.'

'Ann, I don't want old Gerry getting shot, either.'

There wasn't much I could say in reply to that. Zack Paulson was still in Anford.

'Gerry won't be out on Gorsedown,' I said, but I wondered if that would be enough to stop Zack. Gwen had already mentioned their worries about George; the pony would be no safer.

But Jane agreed they could have Geronimo if they wanted him, so they all met at the forge, where they could try him with the donkey cart in my paddock. Jake came too, and I was glad of that; we needed an expert.

'Friends of yours,' he said. 'Yes, I'll help, friends of yours.'

I was more touched by that than by anything else he'd said.

The pony was skittish and tricky, curving his back at the touch of the crupper and threatening to kick when he felt the weight of the cart. Jane held his head and talked to him, and after a while Jake slapped his back with the reins and he started, hesitantly at first, trying to back up, but at last he leaned into the collar and pulled.

'Oh, *isn't* he an old darling?' exclaimed Tessa. 'Look at him! What a poppet.'

'He won't kick, will he?' asked Gwen. 'I thought he looked as if he might. We can't have that, with the children.'

'Gerry kick? More likely to take up tennis,' said Jane. 'Yes, well, that seems all right. Yes. Want him? Not for riding, is he? He's too old for that. Yes. But he can manage that little cart.'

They led him back to the village, the cart loaded with nothing heavier than a few bales of hay, and Jake said he knew where he could lay his hands on a nice little palomino gelding, if Jane was interested, half broken and no nasty habits.

'Yes, I might be. Yes, if he's not too big. I'd like to see him. Yes.'

But when Jake had gone, she shook her head.

'He'll have to be good. But maybe, yes. Poor Jake.'

'Why poor Jake?' I asked.

'Things aren't going too well for him. Yes, since he lost Ashlands, you know? Used to train his hunters and eventers? Yes, well. Paddock jumps aren't the same, are they? Jake had a name for hunters with some jumping sense. Any coffee in that pot?'

I poured her a mug, and listened.

Jake had always had at least two horses in the top ten in the October hunter trials, and it had been his big opportunity to sell good horses at a high price. This year, he'd had nothing. There was nowhere for him to train them. He'd sold one promising five-year-old, for about half what he could have got for him if he'd been decently prepared. And he had a stable full of fit young hunters, waiting for customers who hadn't seen Jake Brewer's name in *Horse and Hound* this year. Those customers would now be going to Jake's rivals, whose horses were fit to jump in tough hunting country and who had learned something of their business.

'Didn't he tell you? He tried to get permission to ride on Gorsedown. Yes. Nothing doing. Some sort of legal hassle about liability in the case of injury. Yes, I think that was it. Only the blacksmith, under the terms of King Henry's Deed.'

135

'The blacksmith and his family,' I said. 'Or hers.'

'Yes, well, your sister doesn't ride, does she? How is she, by the way?'

'She's all right. I'll tell her you asked after her.'

I wanted Jane to go, then. I wanted to think about what she had told me.

Perhaps I needed to face the truth about myself again. Jake didn't want me. No man would, not for a lifetime. Not for marriage. Jake needed Gorsedown, to train his horses, and the only way he could ride on Gorsedown was as a member of the blacksmith's family.

I sat on my anvil looking down at the golden flagstones of the forge floor as I had so often sat when I needed to think, when something was troubling me. At such times I would let my mind drift, musing on the thousands of horses who had stood on those huge blocks of stone, whose hooves had worn them into a landscape of shallow hills and valleys. As my eyes wandered over the familiar shadows I would find the anxiety and the unease lifting, so that I could think clearly and find the answers I was seeking.

Couldn't Jake have told me? I would have helped him, if I could. He didn't have to trick me. We'd always been friends, Jake and I. Or so I'd thought.

I did wish he'd told me the truth.

9

Eight white Shetland ponies were due at the forge in less than an hour, on their way to Birmingham for a rehearsal. Cinderella's white horses in miniature, could something be done to protect the stage floor? Rubber shoes, perhaps? The stage manager understood perfectly that the ponies would be a draw, but what about his new teak planking?

'Why do they need shoes at all?' I'd asked, and he'd fallen silent in surprise.

'*Can* they work barefoot?'

He'd sounded very doubtful, and I'd smiled. I like people who don't pretend to know.

The woman who owned the Shetland ponies had agreed they could work unshod, but she'd been ruthless with the stage manager's ignorance. Their hooves were to be trimmed every two weeks by a professional farrier, at the theatre's expense, and once the run of the show was over, the ponies were to be reshod, ready for their summer work.

I'd been sent a contract, and I'd signed it in some amusement. Now I was involved in show business, too, and Glory had sent me a cardboard black cat that she'd painted, one of the mascots she was known to distribute to casts before press night. I'd stuck it to the wall of the forge with a small piece of putty.

I swept the yard and checked that everything was clean and tidy, with all my tools in the right place, sharp and properly oiled.

The lorry was late. They should have been here ten minutes ago. I intended to keep the ponies' shoes, the ones that weren't too worn. The Riding for the Disabled group could have them for nothing. Every penny counted with that group, and they needed two new saddles.

Where was that *damned* horsebox? It would be dark soon.

It was a cattle truck, driven by a man who later admitted he'd never handled livestock of any sort before.

'Bloody little sods!' he yelled as he jumped down out of the cab. 'Kicking my bloody lorry to matchwood, bloody little sods.'

He strode around to the back of the lorry.

'Are they tied up in there?' I tried to ask, but my voice was drowned in the crash as the ramp hit the gravel. I saw immediately that the ponies were loose, and milling around, squealing and kicking.

'Don't open the gates!' I shouted, but I was too late.

'Bloody little sods!'

He had no chance of avoiding them. As soon as the first gate showed clear daylight the ponies charged it, and the driver was thrown off the ramp, arms and legs flailing, to land on his back on the grass.

It was almost a stampede, straight down the ramp, which was bouncing under the strain, little hooves cracking down onto the wood, and then they were loose, on the gravel, and swinging back past the tree. At the sight of the open space in front of them their heads went down, short and powerful hind legs gathered under compact bodies. Two strides later they were flat out, galloping across the grass towards the cottage.

I sprinted for the front gate. If they got past me they'd be out in the lane, and then anything could happen. It was only three miles to the big ring road round the town.

They're double gates, and I managed the first one. The ponies were galloping across the lawn in front of the forge. They swerved as they approached the hedge, the leading pony skidding on the grass but keeping her legs, and then they headed straight for me. I shouted at the little mare, waving my arms, and she threw up her head, her eyes white-ringed, startled and scared.

But I had no time to close the second gate before they were on me, and although seven of them did shy away from me one of them broke free from the herd and hurled himself at the narrowing gap.

I made a wild grab at his mane, but it was hopeless. He was too excited, and moving too fast. All I gained was a slicing cut on the insides of my fingers from the tough hairs; it stung painfully.

'You insufferable cretin,' I said as I approached the driver, who was still sitting on the grass. 'You unspeakable idiot, what the hell do you think you're playing at?'

'Uh?'

'Why were those ponies loose? Why did you let them out?'

'How was I to know they'd do that? Crazy bloody wild animals, how was I to know? Kicked my lorry to bits, nearly killed me, bloody little sods.'

I stared down at him.

'Have you ever handled ponies before?'

'No.'

He sounded slightly ashamed, but then his spirit returned.

'No, I bloody haven't, and I never bloody will again, nei- ther. I didn't want to do this run, I told them, bloody animals, I *hate* bloody animals.'

'Why a cattle truck?'

'Because the bloody horsebox's in a ditch the other side of Hereford, that's bloody why.'

The ponies had slowed to a canter, but they were still too excited to be caught. I'd have to go and look for the one who'd got away. If I rode Lyric I'd stand a better chance. She'd let me know if he was around, and if I had to chase him at least I'd win the race.

'I've hurt my wrist,' whimpered the driver.

'Oh, get up. OK, it's probably not your fault, but you'll have to telephone the owner and tell her what's happened.'

'The hell I will! Anyway, she's not there, she's in hospital.'

'Telephone your depot, then. Somebody's got to know.'

'Why don't you do it?'

'Because I've got to find the missing pony before it gets dark or he causes a pile-up on the bypass, that's why.'

'I've hurt my wrist,' he whimpered again, but I ignored him, left him sitting on the grass and went to saddle Lyric. She was muddy and shaggy, but I had no time to do anything about that.

'Don't open any gates or try to touch those ponies,' I called to the man as I led her across the drive. I was coiling a halter for the pony and clipping it to her saddle.

He nodded. He was looking worried, and a little shame-faced, so I relented.

'Make yourself a cup of tea if you like.'

'Ta,' he answered, nursing his wrist ostentatiously. 'Bloody animals. I *hate* bloody animals.'

The ponies were trotting up and down the paddock fence looking for a way in as I led Lyric through the gate, closed it behind me, and swung myself up onto her back. It would be at least another hour before I could be sure of catching them. They were too upset and excited to be approachable before then, and if I tried too soon I'd set them off on another wild gallop around the garden.

I trotted Lyric down the lane in the direction in which the pony had bolted, staying close to the verge and looking for hoofprints. There are a lot of horses and ponies around

Anford. It would be difficult to distinguish between the prints, but on a muddy patch a hundred yards further on I did find fresh tracks that I guessed had been made by the little white Shetland. He was still heading for the main road.

I resisted the urge to hurry. Once Lyric warmed up she'd be hard to handle, and I needed her to be quiet if I was to approach the pony.

The road twisted between high hedges, blind corners and sharp bends every few hundred yards, and there was no sign of him. I could hear traffic, the sounds of heavy lorries.

Perhaps I should have been worrying about the people in those vehicles, the ones who might be injured if the pony caused a crash, but I could only think of him. Powerful, stocky little body, but so dreadfully vulnerable, and a loose pony, bewildered by the noise, could bolt into a stream of traffic, and then he'd have no chance. It was nearly rush hour, when the road would be at its busiest.

More hoofprints on the verge by a drainage pipe, still heading for the road. Were they his? I couldn't be sure.

At least he was white. It was getting dark now, but he should be easy to see, even from a speeding car or lorry. Perhaps he'd turn away when he became aware of the noise. Perhaps he'd stray into a field, if there was one with an open gate.

But he'd been bolting. He might not even hear the traffic until it was too late, until he'd charged straight across the road, into the path of whatever steel menace was hurtling towards him.

There were tracks up into the woods. Each time we passed one I pulled Lyric in to the side of the road, and scanned the ground hopefully for fresh hoofprints.

It was unlikely. A bolting pony usually runs in as straight a line as possible.

We were less than two hundred yards from the bypass when I heard the sounds I'd been dreading: car horns, and tyres squealing. I stopped and sat still, listening, waiting for the crash of an impact.

More car horns. Somebody shouting.

And then hoofbeats, fast and growing faster, on the lane coming towards me, a frantic tattoo on the hard road.

I turned Lyric so she was facing back the way we had come, and she started to dance, pulling at the bit, trying to circle, trying to get away from me.

Louder now, and still faster, and I stood up in the stirrups, craning my neck to see over the high hedge.

It was him, and he was panic-stricken, galloping flat out back down the lane, his head stretched out in front of him, his mane and tail streaming, straining every muscle in his efforts to flee the predator his instincts told him had threatened him.

Lyric was fighting at the bit now, hearing the hoofbeats and wanting to run. I let her move forward, dropped my hands, and she broke into a trot, pulling again, and shaking her head.

I was looking over my shoulder.

He came around the bend as Lyric plunged, almost dragging the reins out of my hands, and his feet slid on the tarmac, leaving him scrambling frantically as he tried to keep his balance.

'*Whoa!*' I screamed at him. '*Whoa, there!*'

He couldn't hear me. Panic had blinded and deafened him.

Lyric plunged again, and then half reared, catching the pony's fear as he charged towards us. I tried to hold her, but she heaved forward, throwing her head from side to side, and I couldn't control her any more. They were running together, the tall thoroughbred and the little pony, and Lyric was fighting the bit, trying to get away.

I dragged her head in, speaking to her, using my voice to try to break through her fear, using the soothing words she knew, but her ears were flattened and she wouldn't respond.

Oh, God, don't let a car come now. Please, God, don't let there be a car now.

I had Lyric's chin pulled in hard against her chest and her neck was sharply bowed in front of my face. I nudged her over to the side of the road, closer to the little pony, and I kicked my foot free of the stirrup and swung it at his shoulder.

'Whoa, pony,' I called. 'Whoa, pony. Whoa, baby. Steady, now. Steady, baby.'

He flinched away at the touch of my foot, and I had to ease Lyric back into the centre of the road. There was a deep ditch. If he went into that, he could break his legs.

Please don't let a car come now. Please, don't let there be a car.

Lyric was drawing ahead of the Shetland, and I dragged at her mouth, side to side, trying to unbalance her to slow her down. The pony's nostrils were flaring and reddened, his coat was dark with sweat, and foam was flying back from his mouth, but he stretched out his head again and tried to keep pace with her, his eyes rolling as I pulled her to the side, into his path.

'Whoa, there, pony,' I called back to him. 'Good baby, steady, pony, whoa, now. Whoa, there.'

I could hear his breath. He was gasping. As I glanced over my shoulder again I saw him throw up his head, his mouth gaping as he dragged air into his labouring lungs.

'Whoa, there, pony. Steady, boy. Steady, baby. Whoa, now.'

Was he beginning to hear me?

But Lyric was pulling ahead of him, and I couldn't hold her.

'You *bitch*!' I spat at her. 'You damned, stubborn old *bitch*, will you damned well do as I ask *just for once*? Now *whoa*.'

I let the reins slide through my hands, and then I snatched savagely at her mouth. She snorted in protest, shaking her head.

'Whoa, Lyric. Please, Lyric, whoa.'

The pony was behind us now, and then I heard what I had been dreading. The sound of a car in the lane, heading towards us.

Oh, God, no. Please, let him slow down, please make him stop. He's going to hit us.

The engine note was rising, a gear change, and there were headlights flickering through the trees. The car was coming faster, and I couldn't stop.

I let Lyric swerve across the lane, then I swung her back to the other side, and again, twice more. The pony was drawing closer and trying to follow.

The car headlights, it was getting darker. It was coming faster than ever, straight towards the blind corner. It was going to hit us.

'Oh, *Christ*!' I screamed. 'Lyric, please, *stop*!'

I only saw him for a brief moment as the car came round the corner. He made a crazy silhouette against the lights, almost a parody of a running man, and my impression was of a series of strange movements. One moment he was on the grass verge, arms high, half turned back towards the wood as though watching for a pursuer. A stumble, and he seemed to be crouching, his body and his legs black angles against the white glare.

And then the wild leap, high, and I thought I heard a scream.

I don't believe he ever saw the car.

Tyres were squealing on the road, and I was blinded by the lights and fighting the plunging mare. The car was out of control, broadside on and sliding towards us, and Lyric dragged her head free. Two huge strides and she was in the air, reaching out for the far bank, a crashing landing in the brambles and she stumbled, almost on her nose, throwing me forward onto her shoulder, and then she recovered her balance, and staggered upright.

Behind us I heard the pony sliding down into the ditch,

little hooves scrabbling for a purchase, and then he scrambled up the bank and into the brambles alongside Lyric as the car spun full circle and crunched hard into a tree on the other side of the road.

Lyric seemed to have gone berserk. She spun round, squealing, lashing out at nothing; I saw her eyes, white-ringed and maddened, in the reflected lights of the car. The pony tore past her, his head stretched out, eyes bulging and mouth gaping, a picture of pure terror, and then Lyric dragged her head free and bolted after him.

Behind me I heard a woman scream after us.

'Oh, stop! Please, come back and help me!'

I could do nothing but cling on, keeping my head low over Lyric's neck as she bolted. She overtook the pony within a few strides and was lurching through a patch of brambles which dragged at her legs and whipped painfully at my face. I could feel blood from the scratches running warm down my cheeks, and with it, tears.

Why was I crying? Why were the hairs crawling on the back of my neck? Why did I not want to stop this perilous flight through the darkness? Why did I, with Lyric and the exhausted pony, want only to be as far away as possible from whatever it was back there in the black woods and the night-stricken fields?

I saw the bank in front of us, and I felt Lyric try to gather herself for a jump, but it was too late, she was galloping too fast. Her feet hit the bank halfway up, her head came down, and I rolled over her shoulder, landing on my back on pine needles and soft mud.

Lyric lay on her side, her ribcage heaving, and then slowly she raised her head.

The pony had stopped at the bottom of the bank. I could hear his agonised breathing, and when I turned to look I saw him standing, stiff-legged, rigid, his head stretched out, mouth still gaping.

'All right, pony,' I said. 'All right, baby. All right now.'

145

Lyric pulled herself to her feet, and I used the stirrup leather to help myself up. I stood for a moment, clinging to the saddle, shivering, before I turned and led her down the bank to the pony.

He let me buckle on the head-collar, standing still and quiet as I fumbled with the stiffened leather and the old brass fittings. When I mounted Lyric and turned her back towards the road he was reluctant to move at first, but I spoke to him again, encouragingly, and after a moment he took a pace forward, and another, and then he was alongside us, his head drooping with weariness, but doing his best.

They're brave little ponies, Shetlands.

There was a blue light flashing. A police car had pulled up behind the other car, which was still slewed across the road, its side crumpled from the impact. A woman was leaning back against the police car, her arms wrapped around her chest, her head lowered. She was rocking forwards and backwards, slowly.

At the sounds of the hooves she raised her head and called out: 'Why did you run away? Why? I needed help.'

It was Mrs Wilson, from the boarding kennels in the village.

'My horse bolted,' I said. 'I'm so sorry.'

One of the policemen walked across the road towards us.

'Did you witness the accident?' he asked.

'Yes. Yes, I did. It's a bit confused. There was a man, I think. He ran into the road.'

'You saw him,' cried Mrs Wilson. 'Tell them I couldn't help it.'

He was lying on the verge with a blanket over him. The other policeman was standing by him, drawing something in a notebook.

'You're bleeding,' the first policeman commented, looking up at me. 'Your face. Were you involved in the accident?'

'No. Only brambles.'

'Tell them,' cried Mrs Wilson again. 'Please, Miss Mayall, tell them I couldn't help it.'

'He ran into the road,' I said. 'Mrs Wilson couldn't avoid him.'

'And you were out riding? A bit late for that, wasn't it?'

I was too tired to explain. I was shivering, and Lyric was trembling with weariness under me. I kicked my feet out of the stirrups and slid to the ground, holding her mane to steady myself.

'I've got to take the horses home,' I said. 'I'll make a statement there. It wasn't Mrs Wilson's fault.'

'You're hurt.' He made it sound like an accusation. 'You'd better wait for the ambulance.'

I shook my head. I wanted to get away from there. I wanted to go home.

'The horses,' I said, and I was crying again, a memory of terror creeping into the corner of my mind. 'I want to go home now please.'

'Did you recognise the man?'

'No.'

Now the tears were coursing down my cheeks, and I tried to rub them away. That silhouette, that thing, turning, and crouching, and leaping to its death against the lights.

I don't want this.

'I want to go home.'

The second policeman was beside me, and he reached out a hand to run it down Lyric's sweat-soaked neck.

'All right, love,' he said. 'In a minute. We'll see you home in a minute.'

There were more blue lights as another police car came slowly around the bend in the road and stopped. Doors slammed and there were new voices, one of them a woman's.

'I don't like asking you this,' said the policeman who was stroking Lyric. 'I'm sorry to ask, love. But could you take a look at him? There's nothing horrible to see, I promise. Could you take a look, and see if you know him?'

'Can I go home then?'

'Yes. We'll see you home then. That's a nasty cut on your face, that needs looking at, but we'll see you home.'

Somebody came over to hold Lyric and the pony, and the kind policeman took my arm and led me over to the shape by the side of the road. I saw Mrs Wilson turn away and raise her hands to her face.

He bent down, looked at me questioningly, and when I nodded he turned a corner of the blanket.

'Yes,' I said. 'I know him. His name's Zack Paulson.'

10

There was an inquest a month later. Mrs Wilson saw me in the hall outside the coroner's court and came over to say she was sorry, but how lucky it had been that I'd seen the accident. Lucky for her, she meant. What a tragedy, such a young man. Only thirty, she'd been told. How dreadful.

I would, please, say she couldn't have avoided him, wouldn't I? She'd been told this coroner was very unpleasant about road accidents. So, if I could make it clear she'd had no chance of missing him, she would be so very grateful.

I wasn't sure we should be discussing it. Also, she'd been driving too fast. I remembered my horror as I'd heard the gear change, the rising engine note, and seen those lights racing towards the blind corner.

But when the coroner asked how fast the car had been travelling, I said I didn't know. I really couldn't judge. I'd been trying to control a frightened horse and catch the pony.

'Nevertheless, you saw the man?'

'Yes, I did see him. I saw him on the grass verge, and then he seemed to jump into the road. The car was only a few yards from him.'

'Might he have been frightened by your horses?'

Uncle John had warned me about that question, and I was ready.

'No. We were on the other side of the road. If anything, he was coming towards us.'

Jansy had found his rifle in the park, lying on the track. She'd brought it to me, very excited about it, but not connecting it with the dead man. I telephoned the police, and a sergeant came a little while later to collect it.

The same sergeant gave evidence at the inquest.

Zack Paulson's fingerprints had been found on the stock. The gun was a Lee Enfield .303, and it had been stolen some years previously from the barracks at Catterick in Yorkshire. It seemed that Paulson had run from Gorsedown Park, yes, that was private property. He had been trespassing, yes.

No, there was nothing to indicate why he had dropped the rifle and run.

There were thorns embedded in Paulson's flesh: his face, his arms and chest, the fronts of his thighs. Blackthorn, the pathologist said. He had no opinion to offer as to how the victim had sustained these injuries.

Paulson had died as a result of head and chest injuries. His body had been identified by his estranged wife, Christine.

The coroner said the driver of the car, Mrs Hermione Wilson, was apparently not to blame. He sounded rather disappointed.

The verdict was accidental death.

Chrissie had come to the inquest, and had sat at the back of the room between Bess and Tam. Some of the other women were there, all listening intently to the evidence.

Afterwards, Chrissie asked me if there was anything I hadn't told the coroner. She was looking very white, and tired.

Yes, I thought to myself, there was a great deal I hadn't

told the coroner, and that I never would tell anybody. The impression I'd had of fear in those silhouetted movements. The terror of the horses as they'd fled the scene, and my own feelings. My skin crawling, and the hairs rising on the back of my neck. Lyric's exhaustion after only half a mile of galloping.

I shook my head, but I wouldn't look at Chrissie.

Bess spoke to her.

'He was a threat to us,' she said. 'Come away now. It's over.'

Glory was staying with me. She'd come down a few days before the inquest, because she knew I'd be dreading it. I hate appearing in public, where people can stare at me and I can do nothing to defend myself against their ill-mannered curiosity.

That night we sat in front of the fire in my living room, and we talked.

'What do you suppose Bess meant, when she said he was a threat to them?' I asked her.

By now she knew the women quite well. Since she'd met Gwen at the forge on that summer evening when we'd turned Snowflake loose on Gorsedown she'd visited them several times, although she admitted she found the children tiresome. Once or twice she'd even stayed there.

I'd been glad, even though it had meant she wasn't with me. Glory doesn't make friends easily now. She seems to be suspicious of strangers.

'He was certainly a threat to Chrissie,' she said after quite a long silence, when I looked at her questioningly. 'Didn't you know he'd said he'd kill her?'

'I know that,' I replied. 'But Bess made it sound like an explanation. Almost an excuse.'

Glory shook her head, slowly. She didn't know.

'I've never heard them make excuses. Even when they couldn't help me, there were no excuses.'

'How did they help you?'

151

'They're healers, you know that.'

Did Glory need healing? I wondered. Her injuries were beyond repair. She'd told me, many times, that she was as fit and well as she could ever be, and that she was content. She enjoyed running, she was fast and strong. She could both sprint and keep up an almost tireless lope for mile after mile.

'Do you still run?' I asked, and she nodded.

'Sometimes. When I have the chance.'

What was to be healed? She couldn't have children, but then, she'd never wanted them. It was Peter who wanted children.

I didn't like questioning Glory. I thought, perhaps if I sat quietly she'd tell me what she'd meant, about these women who had been my friends, and who were now hers. She seemed to know far more about them than I did. Healers, she'd said.

Two of them were nurses. One was some sort of doctor. Hilda, was it? Or a therapist, I couldn't remember. Was that what Glory meant by healers? Somehow I didn't think so. Chrissie was a gardener, and Sal a secretary. Or some sort of office work. Tam translated, three languages somebody had said, but there was nothing of healing in that. Most of them went out to work during the day, leaving the children at the station with two women I didn't know very well. Gwen had said they were nannies, real trained nannies, and bloody lucky the group had been to find them. A primary school teacher and a laboratory technician. How is this healing?

'What are you thinking?' asked Glory.

'I'm wondering about you and Peter. You said you might leave him, so he could have children with somebody else.'

We were drinking wine. Neither of us had ever enjoyed spirits. Glory smiled into the firelight. Her eyes seemed to be a darker blue than ever, but perhaps it was because they were sunken.

152

'I don't want to leave Peter, and he wants to stay with me.'

That's good, I thought. Oh, that's good. But what about the child Peter wants? What about the child?

'Did you know they're pagans? Witches, in fact.'

I was shocked. I stared at her, aghast.

'Gwen? And Bess, and Hilda? All the women at the railway station? Witches?'

'Yes. You didn't know?'

'No!'

It was a horrible idea. I couldn't believe what Glory had said. Why was she still friendly with them, if she'd found out something like that?

'What do they do?' I asked, and she looked up at me quickly, hearing the disgust in my voice.

'What do you mean?'

'Black masses? Devil worship, that sort of thing? Desecrating churches and graveyards?'

'Devil worship? No, of course not. Nothing like that. Actually, they don't believe in the devil. They don't really believe in God, or not in the way the Christians do.'

I remembered some of the things I'd read about witches. Could my friends really be like that?

'Ann?'

I looked at her, and she was smiling at me, but she seemed to be very serious. 'Did you hear what I said? No devil worship, no desecrations, none of the Sunday newspaper garbage.'

Had she known I was thinking about the newspapers? Suppose the press had found out about this?

'They're white witches then, are they?' I asked, and Glory became impatient.

'White witches, black witches, please, Ann. Purple, pink, or orange witches. I think they're green witches. They do no harm, they try to do some good. They're cautious about that, too. They're not so arrogant as to be sure what good is, or how to do it.'

153

I tried to understand that, but it seemed wrong. Doing good, not doing harm, why was it so difficult to understand?

'People used to give gypsy children money, so they could claim they'd been begging. The magistrates could order the children to be taken away from their parents and put in the workhouse, where they'd be brought up as Christians. Those people thought they were doing good. The Lord's Work, they called it.'

I sat in silence, wondering. Witchcraft, Satanism, Voodoo, weren't they all bad? The Black Arts, that was a phrase I'd heard: dirty superstitions, a nasty excuse for perverted orgies. Dead babies left in wild places, excrement on church altars.

'They're healers,' said Glory, quietly. 'That's what they try to do. They say they're just at the beginning. They're trying to learn. So much has been lost over the years. Some people are researching it now. Gwen's one of them, and so's Melissa, have you met Melissa? These people are my friends. I'd thought they were yours.'

I'd hurt her feelings. I felt I had to try to make amends.

'If they're helping you, they're certainly my friends,' I said.

'What do you know about witches?' I asked Jansy that evening when she came after school to sweep out the hay store and restack the bales. She was saving to go to university, and came when she could.

'I'll need a bit behind me, I will,' she'd said.

'Fairy story or proper witches?' she asked. 'Can I chuck these two out? Look, they're all black and rotten in the middle.'

'Yes,' I said. 'Put them on the manure heap, they'll make compost. What do you mean, proper witches?'

'Old gods,' she said, lifting one of the bales by the strings and carrying it to the door, bumping it against her knees as she went. 'And goddesses,' she added. 'More goddesses than gods, aren't there? Anyway, that's proper witches, that what you meant? Can I bring Cracker in here? There's mice.'

How had she learned about witches? I wondered. Religious education at my school had been strictly Christian, and anybody who wasn't a Christian was either evil or unfortunate, or both.

That night I showed her Uncle Henry's notebooks, in which he'd drawn the feet of horses he'd shod, showing deformities and abnormalities. There were notes in his neat, square script, describing what he'd done to try to correct them, and the effects of his experiments.

Jansy sat at the workbench, her head propped in her hands, the notebooks open in front of her between her elbows, her lips moving as she read.

'Good, isn't it? He must of known a lot.'

'Must have, not of. Grammar's going to matter at university.'

'Must have, then. What's the difference? I want to do biology, not flaming poetry.'

Jake had been to the forge, sometimes bringing horses, sometimes just to see me.

Occasionally he repeated his proposal. 'I wish you'd marry me,' he'd grumble. 'I don't see why you won't.'

Hilda and Gwen came a few days after the inquest, with sketch plans and measurements for the gates they wanted to hang between the enclosures on the old track. I thought about what Glory had said, and then I asked.

'Glory said you're witches. Is that true?'

'Yes,' said Hilda.

'We're trying to be,' Gwen amended. 'I don't think we merit the term yet.'

No, nothing to do with devils, or dead babies, or the desecration of churches. Some witches, the more militant of them, thought a church was desecration enough without anything they could do to it. They said churches were a desecration of places that had been holy for thousands of years before Christianity came to Britain.

Witch, Wicca, the wise way, learning what they could about the earth, trying to live as the earth meant them to live. Some of them worshipped the earth as the Great Goddess, the mother.

'Is that what a witch is, now?' I asked. 'Somebody who worships the earth?'

Gwen said, not necessarily. Would I like to borrow some books?

I made an evasive answer. I didn't want to read about religion. When I read, it's about my own work, or I lose myself in a novel. I didn't want to start studying anything new, particularly something as heavy as a new religion.

'Snakes come into it sometimes,' said Gwen after a long silence. 'That's why we had to have the gate you made. It sang to us.'

Strange way of putting it, I thought, but her words rang true in my mind, like a bell finding a harmonic, and echoing.

Yes, I thought, these women were my friends.

It took me two weeks to make the gates, because I wanted to do something extra for them, something a little special. They weren't as ornamental as the snake gate. The sides and bases were square and strong, and there were bars to give safe footholds for the children, who wanted to climb on them. I went to the library and asked for a book on paganism, and I looked at the illustrations, and copied them in a form I could work in iron.

Between the bars and the uprights were double spirals, stars, a crescent moon, and a flying crane. The library book said they were pagan symbols. I read a few pages here and there, still uneasy about the idea of witches, but I told myself it was just another religion. I wouldn't have minded if my friends had been Muslims, or Buddhists.

The following Sunday afternoon was spent down at the railway station hanging the gates. Everybody was delighted with the work I'd done. Bess and Tam hugged me and said I was a genius.

Perry was there, and he looked desperately ill. He'd been in hospital, having chemotherapy, but he'd discharged himself.

'Rather be dead,' he said. 'You lot do me more good, you make me laugh.'

'We can't cure you,' Bess replied, but he just shrugged.

After that, we neither talked about his cancer, nor avoided the subject. When he grew too tired to work he handed over to someone else and sat on the edge of the platform until he could continue. His only complaint was that they'd run out of rhubarb wine.

It was a happy afternoon, and noisy, although Gwen had promised it would be quiet; two of the women, Erica and Sue, had taken all the children to the seaside for the day. Nobody worked too hard, and by the time we were tired the job was finished. We sat on the edge of the platform or on upturned buckets in the pens eating *chilli con carne* and drinking red wine or fruit juice, talking about gardening.

Not a steeple hat or a ragged black cloak in sight, I thought, and I smiled to myself.

Glory thought the gates should be painted. She talked about the colours with Sal, who seemed enthusiastic, and Tessa said the children should be allowed to join in. They liked painting, too.

Peter sat on the platform with Chrissie beside him. They were listening to Glory and Tessa, and Chrissie said something to him which made him smile.

Hilda and Gwen massaged Perry's back, not vigorously or hard, more like stroking, and they were talking to him, quietly. Now and then one of them would laugh.

I put my bucket closer to the wall of the platform and leaned back, resting against the painted concrete. I couldn't help but feel at ease with these people. They had accepted me; I would have to accept those things about them that I could not understand.

When the children returned, in two rented minibuses driven by Sue and Erica, I decided to leave. I'd enjoyed myself. I was very happy, and a little relieved that my gates had been an acceptable present, but I was tired, and in no mood for noisy children.

The shadows were quite long on the grass by the time I got back to the forge. I'd walked up the lanes behind the village, and I hadn't hurried; it was a fine evening.

Arno was sitting on the bench in the sun, his chin propped in his hands, his elbows on his knees.

I was so glad to see him that I couldn't speak. I could only smile at him, and wait for the answering smile on his own face and the hand that reached out to touch my cheek.

'Hello, my Ann.'

'Arno.'

We stood and smiled at each other, and I wondered briefly why he hadn't telephoned. I was too glad to see him to ask. Whenever he came, it was something like relief that he was there again, as though everything was all right now.

'I'm hungry,' he said.

'Bacon sandwich? Fresh coffee? And, Arno, I've bought a proper coffee percolater. No more instant coffee.'

'Have you broken the new mugs yet?'

I shook my head. I'd never told him I only used them when he was there.

'Blue Mountain coffee,' I said. I was gabbling, I was so pleased to see him. 'In Royal Doulton mugs, and best Wiltshire bacon, not that rubbish they import from Italy.'

'Mother's Pride bread?'

I was laughing helplessly, but he was still just smiling at me.

'What else? I can't make bread.'

'It sounds wonderful, Ann.'

158

'I've cleaned the Riley. It's running well, too, and I charged the battery.'

We were in the kitchen, and it was filled with the smell of coffee and frying bacon. Arno was leaning back against the table, as he always did when I was cooking and there was nothing for him to do, his arms folded, smiling quietly as he listened to me.

The bread was warmed, as he liked it, and there was mustard, Dijon for him, English for me. Coffee, brown sugar, everything as it should be.

'Breakfast's ready,' I said. 'Not bad for eight o'clock in the evening.'

Again, the smile, slow and affectionate, but he wasn't laughing.

'Is there a conference? Where is it? London?'

'No. This time I came to see you.'

I didn't look at him as I handed him his plate. Knife, fork, yes, everything was as it should be. Coffee poured into his mug; he'd help himself to milk and sugar.

Why did those words sound so ominous? He'd spoken very quietly. This time I came to see you.

No.

The words of a song, I couldn't remember them all, but they made sense, what I could remember. Tell me no secrets, was that it? Tell me some lies. Don't give me . . . I forget. Give me alibis.

I told him about the white Shetland ponies. I tried to make it sound funny, the driver lying winded on the grass as the little herd stampeded around the forge, and me chasing off after the pony on Lyric, a racing thoroughbred in pursuit of a Shetland.

But I didn't know how to end the story, so I just said I'd caught him in the end.

He listened, looking at me, looking away again, eating his sandwich, drinking his coffee, listening to me.

'Ann?'

159

'No. Listen, the women in the village, you know the ones I mean?'

Say anything, but don't say goodbye, that was the final line of the song, wasn't it? The one that gave it all its meaning?

I told him they were pagans or witches, I wasn't quite sure, I didn't actually know much about either, let alone the difference, but I'd made them some gates, and the gates had symbols in them, symbols of paganism, or witchcraft, maybe both, there was a double spiral, I think that's a symbol of the mother goddess, and she's the Earth, or maybe I've got that wrong, and the crescent moon, that's Diana, the virgin huntress, that's another aspect of the Goddess, but there are three aspects, there's Diana, only she has other names as well, and the earth mother, and I think she's usually called Gaia, she's the one with the spirals, and then the old woman, which is death. I don't think . . . I don't know if there's a symbol, I don't . . .'

Say anything, but don't say goodbye. Arno.

'Hecate,' he said. 'In India, Chamunda. Not many witches would name her.'

'Oh. That's why they didn't mention . . . Is there a symbol?'

'Sometimes. Sometimes a skull.'

I managed to laugh, just a small laugh.

'I wouldn't put a skull on the gate.'

'No. Ann?'

No, Arno. No. But I was dumb, I could say nothing, I could only look at him.

'My Brita has Alzheimer's disease.'

160

11

We sat up all night on the sofa, and Arno told me about his wife, his dear Brita, who was losing her mind from premature senile dementia. And he talked about the children, who weren't old enough for a burden this heavy.

He needed to talk, and he needed me to listen, so I leaned against his shoulder and felt his arm warm and heavy around me, and I did listen.

When the fire died down I made it up again, and when I went back to the sofa Arno held out his arms to me, so I lay against him, and for a while we were silent. Then he went on talking, and I listened, and tried to accept.

After he fell silent I thought of the first night we had spent together, when I had woken in the morning thinking that was all there would be, and that I must remember.

My cheek was against his shirt, it was cotton, a little rough, blue, and it was faded on the collar. Remember.

The way he breathes, his sad eyes as he looks at the fire, the way the flames reflect the red tints of his dark blond hair, I must remember. His voice, the accents, the small imperfections in his English, why had I never tried to learn Swedish for him? Remember.

It is the last time, this is all there is. So remember.

When he asked me to sell the Riley for him I did cry, although I had tried very hard not to.

He stroked my hair, and he was silent then. Had he known what that old car had come to mean to me? The promise of his return? Now that promise could no longer be kept, and the talisman must be taken back. Nothing lasts for ever, I told myself as I tried to control myself, nothing lasts for ever.

But the crying went on, and the question I could not keep from my mind. Why? Why?

It had happened quite suddenly, he said at last, when I was quiet again. It was unusual, for it to be so sudden. Now, Brita was finding it difficult to manage. She'd had to stop working. She was anxious about the children. She needed him at home.

'Will you have to stop working, too?' I asked him, and he shook his head.

'Not now. Not for a little while, at least. Just, every day, to see that nothing has been forgotten. To help the children.'

I should be thinking about his children, I should be thinking about Brita, feeling sorry for them. I could feel very sorry, for Arno, and for myself, but for his wife and his children there was nothing. How could I be so cold and unfeeling? I was losing my lover, but she was losing her mind.

'Does she know you're here?'

I felt him shake his head, and then he spoke.

'No.'

Had she ever known about me? Perhaps she'd never asked, never wanted to know. Why the extra days after the conferences in England? Where do you go for those weeks in the summer, when I take the children to my mother?

In her place, would I have asked?

Oh, yes. But in her place, I would have been jealous, and angry, and I would have tried to stop him. He would have had to have kept me a secret, and he wouldn't have been very good at that.

162

Suspicion and bitterness and angry accusations. Fidelity or nothing, and I thought, there would have been nothing.

Brita was wiser than I could have been.

'Do you think I should have told her?'

I had no answer. What could I say?

'I must say goodbye to my magnificent Ann. Also, I must withdraw from the project I had been invited to lead, in which universities in Melbourne and Moscow and London, and perhaps California, are to co-operate. Yes, I must do this. But everything I give up is as nothing against what is being taken from her, from . . .'

His voice broke, and I reached up my hand to touch his face, and found his cheeks wet with tears. All I could think was, he is crying for her. Not for me, he is crying for his wife, for his dear Brita.

'No,' he whispered a few minutes later. 'No, I will not speak of these things, not to her.'

He loves her more than he loves me.

You always knew that, I said to myself. You always knew that. He never loved you, he told you, he couldn't let himself love you. He was always honest about it.

Tell me no secrets, tell me some lies. Don't give me reasons, give me alibis.

But I love Arno. Why did this have to happen?

When he leaves this time, I'll never see him again. He came to say goodbye. How long do we have left? How much longer can he stay?

He hadn't brought a suitcase. Perhaps he hadn't meant to stay. When I'd first seen him, I should have noticed; and why hadn't he telephoned to say he was on his way? He'd always done that.

How long will he stay?

Until daylight. Once or twice I almost fell asleep, but I pulled myself back. This is all we have left, every moment counts. Stay with him, and remember. Everything you can, because this is all you have left.

A taxi to the station, a train to London, and then a flight back to Sweden, and Brita.

It was raining as we stood by the window, watching for the taxi. There was nothing more to say, and I didn't even want to remember this, although of that time it is now those moments that are the most clear in my memory.

The taxi drew up in the lane and Arno turned and kissed me, quite quickly, and then he was walking away, and I stayed by the window and watched him as he crossed the lawn and went down the drive and climbed into the car.

He was gone, and there was nothing.

Two Royal Doulton coffee mugs, a pair of dirty plates. I washed them, I dried them, and I put the mugs back on the high shelf where I kept things I didn't use except on special occasions, alongside Aunt Ruth's kitchen vase that was the same colour as his eyes.

Fresh coffee, and bacon sandwiches because he'd been hungry.

I raked the fire, and took the ashes and embers out to the heap at the back of the garden. Cinders for drainage for a path through the kitchen garden, ashes for the dustbin, but they were still hot. Still hot, from the fire: we'd sat in front of that fire and held each other through the night.

The ashes were still hot.

There was rain on my face, and tears.

He'd be at the station now. He'd be standing on the platform, waiting for the train that would take him to London. He was still less than ten miles away from me. Arno, still quite near.

'Arno.'

I unlocked the forge and threw the big doors wide open, and I made up the fire. I used the wood and leather bellows, because that was how he'd liked the forge to be used, as it had been for hundreds of years. I laid out my tools, everything ready for a working day.

He'd be on the train now. He'd be sitting by the window,

164

and looking at the green fields of England as the train rattled through them, leaving the West Country behind. What would he be thinking?

Further away now. The train to London, quite fast, every second taking him further away.

'Arno. My Arno.'

It had stopped raining. The wet gravel under my feet shone in the morning light, the roof of the cottage gleamed as though the slates were black. The sun was beginning to break through the clouds. It might be a fine day.

This time yesterday I'd been finishing the gates for my friends the witches. I'd been welding the last of the stars into place, and thinking I'd better be quick, there were polo ponies to shoe, and they'd be here soon.

Had I thought of Arno while I'd been welding those stars?

I'd been quite happy.

Arno.

The cloud was almost gone, and the sky was clear.

I collected a hoe from the garden shed, and I worked down between the rows of onions and early potatoes that Chrissie had planted for me. There was no trace of the damage the Shetland ponies had done, and the garden was in beautiful condition; the soil was almost black, and it broke and crumbled easily under the hoe.

This time yesterday I'd still been happy.

Will I ever be happy again?

There were four horses from a new livery stables that had opened up ten miles away. A new customer, and one that promised to be important, so I had to be very polite, very alert, I had to make a good impression. They were fine horses. I remembered Jane Laverton talking of the charges this stable demanded, and she'd been aghast. How could anybody afford that much? she'd wondered. They'd never find anybody to leave horses there at that price. Would they?

The big bay mare had come from Holland, the woman told me. She'd cost a fortune, but she was a jumper, she could clear the Berlin Wall. Going to the top, all they needed was a sponsor, and there was a packaging materials company who'd said they might be interested.

So, very careful with the big mare, with her good, broad hooves and her strong pasterns.

'Have you tried the new jumping studs from America?'

She hadn't, what were these? Never heard of them, had I got any? So, what were the advantages?

I gave her some, and one of the leaflets that had come with them.

A black colt, careful, Miss Mayall, he's a bit funny. A quarter horse, isn't he super? Yes, the owners brought him over from Kentucky, they're setting up a stud near Wolverhampton, he's only with us for a few weeks. Do be careful, he's quite tricky.

So, tie him up close and keep an eye on that handsome head. A bit funny, a euphemism for downright dangerous.

Do you ever travel, Miss Mayall? Would you come to us? It's not very convenient, having to bring the horses to you.

No? Well, that's a shame. We'll have to see.

A heavyweight hunter, past it now, old Flashy, but his rosettes would cover that wall. He can still move, too. Lots of life left in the old boy yet. Show days are over, though, aren't they, old lad?

A friendly, confident horse, who blew gently into my out-stretched hand and stood calmly as I worked on him.

And my favourite of all our customers, little Zinab. Do you like Arabs, Miss Mayall? Isn't she delightful? You could fit those hooves into a teacup, David said I should ask for a discount because you'd save so much steel on her shoes.

I smiled.

'Working in miniature isn't very good for my eyesight,' I replied, and the woman laughed.

'I'll tell him you said that. But isn't she a little doll?'

She made another appointment: she had two carriage horses, one of them had a problem with his hind feet. Did I think I could help?

'I'll do my best.'

She was coming back. Uncle Henry would have been so pleased. A new customer, a big one, expensive livery stables, an international showjumper in the very first lot they brought us, and the owners know a bit about horses. Not born yesterday. Calls for a drink, Annie love, orange juice for you, whisky for me.

Arno would be at the airport by now, waiting for his flight. Going away.

Please, make this not happen. Please, if there's something that can hear, please. Make him come back. Please.

I scrubbed the tears away from my cheeks.

A new customer, Uncle Henry, I thought. Rich people, with horses from all over the world, Kentucky, and Holland.

But I already had enough customers, and I wanted Arno.

I leaned over the workbench, and I cried.

The telephone rang: it was a market gardener from Chepstow. He'd heard I repaired tools. Could he bring in a job lot he'd bought in an auction up in Birmingham? We could go through them, sort out what was worth fixing and what wasn't? I didn't buy up scrap metal on the side, did I? Pity.

We made an appointment, and I looked at the clock.

He'd be in the aeroplane. He'd be looking out of the window, his last sight of England. He'd be waiting to take off. What would he be thinking?

He'd come just to see me this time. No other reason, just to see me, to tell me, to explain, and to say goodbye.

Goodbye, Arno. I do wish you well. And Brita, too. I really do, I mean it. I love you, Arno.

There was a big roll of cleaning paper on the workbench. I grabbed a handful and scrubbed at my eyes.

This happens to everybody, or most people. Love affairs come to an end, and it hurts. This is so banal, an affair with a married man, and it's ended, and now I'm crying.

He'd be in the air by now.

Get on with your work. Stop moping. This is doing no good.

Four wrought-iron window boxes, to hold pinewood cases, and they were due back that week. If I didn't start now, I'd have to work late every evening to have them ready on time.

I drew several deep breaths and splashed cold water onto my face from the cooling trough. I thought it was probably just as well there wasn't a mirror in the forge, and that I could work alone for the rest of the day.

But it wasn't easy. By the time I was too tired to continue I'd only half finished one of the boxes and cut the iron ready for the other three, and it wasn't my best work. I could only hope it was good enough. There'd be no time to start again.

It was a beautiful night. There'd been a brilliant sunset, and it was warm, almost like summer. I closed my eyes, and told myself I could smell winter. The air was so still I could hear the herons in the woods behind the quarry.

It should have been raining. It should have matched my mood, and been raining.

I went into the cottage and threw myself down on the sofa. This time yesterday he was here, I thought. This time yesterday I didn't know it was all over.

Please, I need a miracle.

This time yesterday. This time yesterday.

I fell asleep in the early hours of the morning, and woke to bright daylight.

This time yesterday he'd gone.

I went upstairs, and I had a shower.

Those were the clothes I was wearing when he was here.

So, you've worn them for two days and two nights, they

must be filthy, they probably stink. Put them to be washed. And wash your dirty hair, too. And scrub your nails, they're black. And clean your disgusting, scummy teeth, and get on with your work, you hardly did a decent stroke of an honest job yesterday.

As I came down the stairs the telephone rang, and it was David Lord of the RSPCA with an emergency. There'd been a fire at a riding school on the other side of Cheltenham, and a place had to be found for twenty-five ponies. A kindly farmer had offered two big fields, but the ponies' shoes had to come off first.

'Riding school?' I protested. 'Surely they can . . .'

'They were fighting the fire all night,' David interrupted. 'They're exhausted, and shocked. Please, Ann.'

They came in relays, in the RSPCA's horse ambulance and in trailers lent and driven by concerned neighbours, and I fitted them in around my other customers. One of the men put up a picket line under the chestnut tree, and the waiting ponies were tethered to it; two women watched them. One came over to me and introduced herself. I'm Amy, this is Carol. Thank you for helping us.

There were three hunters due in later. I had no time to waste.

Some of the ponies were difficult to handle. They were still frightened. Sweat had dried in rough patches on their coats, and now and then they shivered. Any sudden movement had them throwing up their heads, their eyes wild.

Amy was kicked as she untied a piebald gelding, and she cried out in pain, startling all the ponies, who began to plunge, and whinny in distress. It took all three of us to hold them until they calmed down again.

'Poor little things,' she said, rubbing at her bruised shin. 'I hate fire. Poor little things.'

They told me they lived just down the road from the stables, and didn't know much about horses, but wanted to help if they could. Nobody seemed to have realised the ponies would be difficult to handle that day. Amy brought them one at a time, tied them to the ring, and left me to lever the clenches away from the hooves, pry the iron shoes loose, trim, and rasp, and clean.

Bruised knees on a mare, had she fallen? They were sore to the touch, and a little swollen. I turned the hose on them, and showed Carol how to wash them, letting the water run over the swollen joints, soothing and cooling them.

It seemed never-ending, this stream of ponies, and I bent my back, and lifted feet, and pressed the buffer against the walls of the small, round hooves, and the hammer rose and fell, and the pincers gripped the iron shoes, and levered them away from the frayed horn of the hoof. Trim, and rasp, and feel, and look, and smell, and the pony trotting at the end of his leading rope, up the path, circle, back as I watched and listened, and nodded, and then the next pony, tied to the ring as I flexed my shoulders and pressed my hands to the small of my back, and then bent over to start again.

A grazed hock, scraped against a wall, perhaps.

'There's a bottle on the shelf by the window,' I said. 'Green Oils, we'll use that.'

Two more trailers arrived, unloaded four ponies, and took another four away. The last pony refused to go up the ramp. He began to jump about and squeal, upsetting the other ponies, so I stopped everybody and took his rope myself. 'Take one of the others,' I said. 'Take the black, he's quiet.'

I needed experts that day, and all I had was kind neighbours.

The grooms who brought the hunters hadn't heard of the disaster. They shook their heads, dismayed and sympathetic, and set to work taking the shoes off their own charges, leaving me a little extra time to deal with the ponies. But the big horses had to be shod, and none of them were quiet or easy to handle. The kicker lashed out twice as he was being led to the forge, and his temper communicated itself to the ponies, who began to stamp around and tug at their ropes. Again, time was lost as we held their heads and tried to calm them.

My hand slipped, and I grazed the inside of my wrist against a nail. I looked at it, at the little pieces of white skin scratched away from the reddened line, the beads of blood beginning to rise, to merge together.

It was nothing. It was nothing at all; worse things happened every day, sometimes every hour. Why was I looking at it? Why couldn't I wipe my wrist on my jeans, and get on? Why were there tears in my eyes? A stupid little graze, because my hand had slipped, and it was stinging. I couldn't ignore it, and there were tears.

I brushed them away, and I finished removing the shoe, and then I walked away from Carol and Amy and went into the cottage.

I leaned over the kitchen sink, and I could feel myself shaking. I ran cold water over the silly little graze, and dabbed at it with a piece of rag.

Hot coffee, have to be instant, no time to put on the percolater. And a bacon sandwich. Immediately I thought of Arno.

'I was beginning to wonder what had happened to you,' said Amy as I reappeared, and resentment boiled up into my mind. Why me? Why today? And if David Lord could find a farrier to do this work, surely to God he could have found just one or two people who knew something about horses to help her, instead of this useless pair?

Half-past three, and I had a Welsh cob and a Connemara pony coming in at four. Would I have the ponies finished by then? Would I find any more cuts and bruises on their legs?

Trim, and rasp, and feel carefully down the legs, around fetlock and coronet and pastern, look, and smell. Watch and listen as they trot along the path. Uneven rhythm, check again, and there's bad bruising down the inside of a cannon bone, it might even be cracked.

'Do you think he'll be all right?'

'It should be seen by a vet.'

I'd had enough of the ponies. I had other work to do. I could hear hoofbeats in the lane. The cob and the Connemara. How many more ponies were there still to be done? I'd lost count.

I shook my head to try to clear it.

I couldn't remember the woman's name, my kind customer with her nice cob and the pretty Connemara, but she'd heard about the fire and she knew ponies. She tied her own animals to the rings at the back of the stable, and said they could wait. She'd help with the ponies if I'd lend her the tools. She knew how to remove shoes, so I could just trim them up and check the damage.

I was working in slow motion by the time I'd finished. I felt as if I was swimming under deep water, with everything blurred and muffled and seeming to come from a distance. What was her name, this kind woman who knew how to handle frightened ponies?

She helped load the last of them into the trailer, and the pony who'd fought and squealed followed her confidently, head low on a long rein. The one with the bruise, or the crack, had a neat bandage on his leg. Had I done that? I couldn't remember.

Just these two, then. The cob and the Connemara, and then I could close the huge doors and walk through the darkening evening, and then the memories would come.

She asked if there was anything she could do. Was I all right? and I said yes, thank you, I'm all right, just tired. Sorry it's taking so long, and then, when she looked worried, I told her the bill would be the same as last time, it wasn't her fault I was working so slowly.

'That's not what's bothering me,' she answered. 'You look like death, my dear.'

Her kind concern brought the easy tears back to my eyes, and I turned away to hide them against the cob's warm, rough flank.

David Lord turned up as I was finishing. He helped me clean and put away my tools, and he drove my good, kind customer home. It was too dark for her to ride on the roads, so the pony and the cob went into the paddock for the night.

I had to be alert the next day. There was a lot to be done, and I needed to see Jansy that afternoon. I had something important to say to her, quite apart from a fairly fierce suggestion about the hole the ferrets were beginning to chew in the back of their hutch.

'Get here early tomorrow,' I said, 'even if it means playing truant.'

'What for, then?'

'Ask me no questions, I'll tell you no lies.'

Don't give me reasons, give me alibis.

No, not again. I will not let that start up again.

'Oh, and Jansy? Bring your last school report. The last two school reports.'

Lord Robert was bringing Blackie, and it was time Jansy's ambitions were given a boost. She was beginning to wonder if she'd ever make it. Her parents didn't discourage her, but they were hardly being supportive about her desire for a university education.

'Who's going to pay for that, then?' was her father's response, and her mother simply said she'd have to wait and see, dear.

'There's grants,' said Jansy despondently, 'but they don't pay for everything.'

'Scholarships?'

'I'm not *that* good.'

The Nevilles raised no objections to her plan to stay on at school rather than getting a job. They didn't begrudge the contribution to the family budget she could have made. But they didn't intend to pay for her to go to university. They couldn't see the point.

Lord Robert Halstay was not only extremely rich, he was also a kind man, and he'd told me about his younger cousin, John, who had farms in the White Highlands in Kenya.

'Lord Robert, may I present Miss Janice Neville? Jansy, this is Lord Robert Halstay.'

She was shy. She'd never met anyone with a title before, and the formality of my introduction confused her. Lord Robert shook her hand and said he was pleased to meet her, very pleased, indeed, yes. Jansy mumbled, and gave me a slightly desperate look.

'Jansy, would you go and get those school reports?'

This time the look was angry, and she was blushing, but she did as I told her. Lord Robert looked at me questioningly.

'She's bright, and she's ambitious, and she needs some help. She wants to be a game warden in Africa, and she wants to go to university first. Her parents can't or won't help.'

'Hah!'

He was interested, and he preferred to know immediately what was required of him. He had no time for what he called 'fluffin' around'.

Stephens wandered away and took an interest in the paintwork of the Range Rover, and I turned my attention to the splendid old steeplechaser and his special shoe.

Black Bear is one of my favourite horses, one of the first I shod when I came to the forge. He was a Cheltenham Gold Cup winner, but a ruptured tendon ended his career. At one time Lord Robert pretended the time and money he expended on Blackie was an investment, to patch him up ready for the sales, but nobody had been deceived.

I trimmed Blackie's hooves, and checked the palmar

surface of the fetlock for soreness and bruising. I took my time that day. I wanted Jansy and Lord Robert to get to know each other. Now and then I caught snatches of their conversation. Jansy had lost her shyness within minutes.

I heard her talking about her biology lessons, I loves that biology, I do, and how she liked looking at Uncle Henry's notebooks when she'd finished her work for me. She said that she was working for me because she needed a bit behind her for university, and I glanced across to see Lord Robert nodding his approval.

Blackie could carry Lord Robert safely around his estate; although the horse was chronically lame he was calm and sensible, and because of the light work he did he rarely wore out his shoes. This time he only needed his feet trimming, and I could have finished the work in about half an hour, even allowing for the tricky fetlock. I fiddled around with hoof oil, and I tapped at the clenches, the turned-over ends of the nails, and I picked up Blackie's feet and hunted for corns that I knew I wouldn't find.

'. . . get those bastards who . . .'

Jansy's hand flew to her mouth, and her face turned crimson.

Lord Robert watched her, enquiringly.

'Those bastards who . . .?' he prompted, gently.

It would take more than Jansy's explicit indignation to shock Lord Robert.

I heard a grunt of laughter from behind me, and looked up into Stephens's wrinkled face.

'Bring Her Ladyship's manicure set next time?'

'Are you in a hurry?' I asked.

'Not so long as I get home in time to see the football.'

I began to massage the plantar ligaments in Blackie's hind legs. Stephens snorted derisively, and went back to the car.

'. . . three A levels, I'll get that biology and that maths, it's that English language I can't . . .' '. . . elephants in Kenya, now, just before the war I remember . . .' '. . . there's courses in Bristol, I wouldn't mind . . .' ' . . . photographs, m'dear, I'd like you to see those, now when you come . . .'

I slipped into the forge and went on with my work on the window boxes.

Lord Robert told me, just before they left, that he'd been glad to meet my young friend, very glad. Yes. Thought there might be something to be done there.

Jansy said little. Yes, she'd liked Lord Robert. He'd said he reckoned she'd get to university, but she shrugged as she said it; a lot of people had said encouraging things to her, and so far as Jansy was concerned, it was easy to talk.

But on the following Saturday morning she was almost incoherent with excitement. The headmaster had called her into his office after school on Friday evening, and he'd talked to her about bursaries. He'd said Lord Robert had telephoned him, and Lord Robert had been finding out about them.

'Old Hatchet's going to find out more, he's writing letters.'

For Jansy, Mr Hatch writing letters on her behalf was the most extraordinary aspect of the whole business. The headmaster, that remote and slightly fearsome personage, writing letters because of Jansy Neville, because Lord Robert Halstay, a real lord, had found out about her going to university.

'I'm going, Missus,' she said. 'I am, I'm going to university, I've just got to get that English language sorted, and I'm going.'

'What do your parents say?'

'All right by them, long as they don't have to pay for it.'

She drew in a deep breath, and let it out in an ecstatic sigh.

'I'm going to university, I am.'

And then, narrowing her eyes at me, 'You all right? You don't half look knackered. You been funny all week, what's up?'

I've been crying myself to sleep every night, that's what's up, I thought. But I sent Jansy off to limewash the loose box and the tack room, and I tried to push the thoughts of Arno aside.

I do wish you well, I thought. I love you. I wish Brita well, too, but I want you back, I want you back, I do so want you back.

I hadn't tried to sell the Riley. I hadn't started the engine that week, I'd have to do that, I'd have to keep it in good order.

And I'd have to sell it. But not yet, not just yet.

Sunday tomorrow, I told myself, and I'd go for a ride. I'd have a really good gallop, right down the east track from the north gate. It was time Lyric stretched her legs. Flat out, down the hill and past the house, up the curve through the beech woods.

Might even break my neck.

But I didn't go riding the next day, because Peter came to see me and told me that Chrissie was pregnant, and he was the father.

I felt the words echoing around my head. Glory had seemed so happy when I'd last seen her. She'd seemed to think she and Peter would stay together.

'You shit,' I said. 'You utter shit. What about Glory?'

'Listen to me. Please, Ann, listen, and try to understand.'

'Understand what? What more is there to understand?'

I'd been pleased to see him. When the car had rolled to a halt on the gravel, I'd been so pleased. And now he sat in my living room and told me he'd got somebody pregnant. My sister's lover, and he asked me to understand.

'Glory knows about Chrissie. She's happy about it. Happy, Ann.'

It made me even angrier. Glory loved Peter. She was so desperate not to lose him she was prepared to let this happen. She'd forgive him if that was what she needed to do in order to keep him.

What would I have done, or forgiven, if it meant I could have kept Arno?

'Happy? Happy, that you've got another woman? Oh, I bet. I bet she's over the moon about it.'

'I want children,' he said. 'So does Chrissie, now Zack's dead. She's trying to get over Luke, and she wants another child.'

'She wanted you,' I retorted. 'The first time she saw you, what was it she said? "Fancied you rotten", that was it.'

'That's just as well under the circumstances, isn't it? At least we didn't have to wear blindfolds.'

It was the first sign of temper he'd shown since he'd arrived.

'It's none of your business anyway, Ann, so don't start sitting in judgement on me. Or on Chrissie, or Glory either, come to that.'

'Glory's my sister, and I love her.'

'She loves you too. That's why I'm here.'

I could think of nothing to say. I was almost incoherent with fury, and one of my thoughts was that Peter had two women, two, and Chrissie was pregnant. Glory loved him and would stay with him, and I couldn't even have Arno for a few days a year. It wasn't fair. It wasn't fair.

'So, Chrissie's pregnant.' There were tears of rage and pain in my eyes, and I wanted to hurt Peter: because I'd been hurt, because I was in pain, and so he should suffer, too.

'How many more of that gang of tarts have you got pregnant? Your ready-made harem, your baby-breeding factory? "Children", you said you wanted, children, that's plural, right?'

'That's unforgivable, and I'm not going to try to forgive it.'

'Get out, Peter. You selfish bastard, get out of my home.'

He was already walking out of the door, and he didn't bother to reply.

I made no effort to stifle my rage. For the rest of the morning I prowled around the cottage and the garden, every thought angry and vengeful, thinking of things I wished I'd said to him. Chrissie pregnant, and I'd introduced them, I'd laughed at the way they'd flirted with each other. Chrissie, my friend, and she'd seduced Peter. It had been easy because Glory couldn't have children. She'd trapped him with a child.

The bitch had seduced my sister's lover.

How could Peter do that to Glory?

If I'd got pregnant, what would Arno have done?

But I hadn't got pregnant, because Arno already had two children, and he didn't want me to have his baby. He'd never even asked me if I wanted a child, he'd just assumed I didn't.

What would he have done?

Would he have stayed with me, if I'd been pregnant? Would he have told Brita, and would she have stayed with him? What would have happened?

How could Peter do this to Glory?

I took a spade into the paddock and went to work on the thistles, slamming the sharpened steel into the soil, dragging the tough weeds out into the air and shaking the earth off the roots.

That bastard, that selfish bastard. How could I ever have liked him? An *actor*, all the time he'd just been *acting*, pretending he liked me, because he knew Glory loved me, and he didn't want to lose Glory.

'But he wouldn't give up his idea of children. He wants children, and Glory can't have them, but that isn't going to stop our Peter, oh no. What Peter wants Peter has to have, and nothing and nobody's going to stop Peter Clements having what he wants, the spoilt, selfish bastard.'

I was so angry I was speaking aloud, and I hadn't even realised it until I heard the voice behind me.

'Who's a spoilt, selfish bastard?'

'Nobody important, Jake, nobody important. What do you want?'

'Just came to see you,' he said. 'Just a friendly visit. Thistles, eh? Could start on mine when you've got yours out. Got plenty to spare.'

I moved on to another clump, slammed the spade into the earth and trod on it. I felt it grate against a stone.

'You all right, Ann?'

'Fine, thank you, Jake.'

The root broke, and I muttered irritably. The thing would grow again now.

'Just wondered. You know, if you'd thought any more. Ann? I mean, I do wish you'd marry me. Will you? Please?'

I dug the spade into the ground again, and looked across at him as I leaned on the handle to lever the thistle free of the earth. He had his hands thrust into the pockets of his sheepskin jacket, and his tweed cap was pushed to the back of his head. There was chaff in his hair, and he hadn't shaved that morning.

Another stone, a heavy one this time, I couldn't lever the spade past it. If I leaned on it any more I'd bend it, or break the handle.

Why, I asked myself, does somebody as unmusical as me keep getting snatches of popular songs running through her head?

A fine romance.

What do you know about me, Jake? I'm seven inches taller than you, or about that. I probably outweigh you by five stone, and I bet I'm stronger. I keep myself cleaner than you do. Your business is in trouble, and mine isn't.

Does any of this really matter?

No.

Arno's gone, and he won't come back. The good friend I thought I had is a treacherous bitch and I hate her for what she's done, I hate her. I'm alone. So what the hell does anything matter?

180

'Ann?'

'Yes?'

'Have you thought?'

I'm thinking now. You've been good to me. You have been a friend, and friendships are something I do value. There isn't much I won't do for a friend.

'Ann?'

Oh, just a minute, please. I'm thinking. Damned thistles in the paddock. No, I will not start on yours after I've done these, you can dig your own thistles.

What sort of a wife would I be?

Does it matter? That isn't what you want anyway.

If you can't train your young horses you're finished, aren't you, Jake? And only the blacksmith and her family can ride on Gorsedown. That's your only hope now.

But I wish you'd told me the truth. I do wish that.

'Why not?' I said. 'Yes, all right, Jake. I'll marry you. Why not?'

12

Jake and I were married in Cheltenham Register Office a month later, on a day that fitted into the racing schedule. We were to have a weekend in Brighton, because there were two horses running in the last meeting of the season that Jake wanted to see.

Uncle John came, and so did Glory and Peter, although I had no real chance to talk to Glory, except for a few hurried words. Peter kissed me, smiling, and said he wished me all the luck in the world. I thanked him.

Actor, I thought. How can you tell, with an actor? He seemed as friendly as ever, but how can you tell?

I told myself I wouldn't take back a single word of what I had said to him, even if I had once liked him more than almost anybody else I knew. He deserved everything I'd said.

Whenever I looked at him I felt forlorn. I wished none of it had happened.

I wished the women from the railway station were here, I wished they were still my friends, smiling at me and calling me dear Ann, instead of returning the cold look I had given them when I had last seen them in the village.

I wished it was Arno I was marrying.

I wished, and wished, and it turned into a kind of liturgy

of everything I wanted and couldn't have, of everything that had gone wrong and couldn't be put right, of every reason there was for me to look into the future, and find it grey and bleak.

'I hope you'll be happy,' said Glory, and I looked into her lovely face, and wondered: can you be happy? Can you still be happy, with Peter?

Morry Old and Toby Joliot came, representing the staff at Jake's stables, and a woman who turned out to be Jake's mother. I'd assumed both his parents were dead. She stared up at me in obvious amazement, and then turned to Jake.

'You're marrying . . .?

And then she caught herself up, and tried to smile at me. 'My dear, I do hope . . .'

There were friends of Jake's from the horse world, a trainer and his wife and two daughters, a Master of Foxhounds who'd brought a thin, blonde woman he introduced as Lolita, saying she was his mistress, apparently in the hope that somebody might be shocked. There were other people who knew each other, who knew me as the local farrier, and who seemed on the whole to be perplexed by the situation.

'I hope this doesn't mean we're losing our blacksmith,' one of them said, and I shook my head. I had no intention of giving up my work.

After the ceremony we all went to a local pub where Jake had reserved what they called a 'functions room', and two very old women dressed as waitresses brought in trays of sandwiches, and glasses of sweet sherry.

Jake complained.

'I ordered champagne.'

One of the women said she wouldn't know about that, she'd ask.

When it arrived the champagne was warm, and it was in any case German Sekt.

There was a cake. The icing tasted like plaster of Paris.

Start as you mean to go on, I thought, and tried to keep the smile in place.

Morry Old as best man made a predictably smutty speech, and I began to realise I disliked him. Anyway, Toby Joliot had been with Jake for nearly fifteen years, why hadn't he been best man?

I wanted to talk to Uncle John, and I hadn't had a chance. He was standing by the window, looking down into a glass of sherry and listening to Glory with a smile on his face.

'Wouldn't you like some . . . champagne?' I asked, and he looked at me out of the corner of his eye, the smile lifting his mouth.

'I've had some, my dear.'

I tipped the rest of mine into a dusty house plant, and left the glass on the windowsill.

'I think it's very gallant of you even to drink that sherry.'

'It's not that bad. The trick is to pretend it isn't sherry, it's something new. Just been invented, you see, Ann. Now, drink it with that attitude, and you can be interested, if not impressed.'

Was he going to ask me why I was marrying Jake? I wondered. And why the hurry?

Well, time would prove to anybody who'd wondered that I wasn't pregnant.

Jake was talking to his mother, shaking his head as she spoke to him, apparently very earnestly. Was she asking him that question?

'Mrs Jacob Brewer,' mused Uncle John.

'Yes. I'm going to find it difficult to get used to that.'

'You're looking very pensive,' he remarked.

'I've had an idiotic grin pasted across my face all day,' I replied. 'It's nice to be able to drop it for a few minutes.'

Morry was becoming raucous, slapping Peter on the back and making suggestive remarks to one of the daughters of the trainer. Peter was talking to the thin blonde woman, was her name really Lolita? Peter was trying to ignore Morry without being too obvious.

Rides like an angel and makes the customers laugh, was Jake's claim for Morry.

Peter wasn't in the market for a horse, but Lolita might be, and she clearly wanted Peter's undivided attention. Morry was being an irritating distraction.

The Master of Foxhounds was also becoming irritated, although less by Morry than by Lolita's interest in Peter. He was talking to the trainer's wife, loudly, saying nobody he knew had time to sit around in front of a television goggling at matinée idols and poodle-fakers and all that rot, let alone spend an evening at some damned theatre. Anybody worth their salt had better things to do, and so far as he was concerned all this show business rot meant was that a lot of useless idle louts got paid fifty times what they were worth.

'This is turning into trouble,' I said to Uncle John, and he looked at his watch.

'Isn't it time you and Jake were going? You'll miss your train.'

A voice even louder than that of the Master of Foxhounds made itself heard across the room.

'Old, I don't think I care for my daughter being the recipient of remarks like that, if you don't mind.'

'Oh, *Daddy*, it's *all right*. Honestly, you do fuss.'

'It is not all right, Jeannine. Come over here. Right now, Jeannine, and don't argue.'

Start as you mean to go on, I thought again. Why the hell can't Jake keep his blasted angel rider under control?

Jake was still talking to his mother, who occasionally threw a distracted smile in my direction. She looked as if she had drunk too much sherry. It seemed to me she had been raising her glass to her lips in order to give herself something to do in a social setting in which she could find nobody with whom she had anything in common.

'I'll just go and have a word with Jake,' I said to Uncle

John. He nodded, and put his glass on the windowsill alongside mine.

'I must go, my dear. I like Jake. I hope this works out well.'

Jake glanced up and smiled as I approached him.

'There are at least two people in this room who are finding Morry annoying,' I said, and he sighed.

'Oh, Morry's all right.'

I didn't reply, but I stood beside him, waiting, and after another deep sigh he muttered something under his breath and went over to the group by the door.

Mrs Brewer was a little round-eyed, and she kept touching her hat, which had slid backwards so the small veil stood out in front of her face like a peak on a cap.

I smiled at her, finding something rather endearing in her air of startled nervousness and the scared glances she gave me.

'What should I call you?' I asked.

'Oh. Oh?'

'Mrs Brewer's rather formal, isn't it? Unless you'd prefer that?'

She didn't seem to know what to say, so I stood quietly beside her, not looking at her, waiting for her to speak.

Glory had joined the Master of Foxhounds and the trainer's wife, and her lovely smile was working its usual magic. He was explaining something to her, and he seemed to have forgotten Peter and Lolita.

'My name's Sybil. That's best, I think. Don't you?'

I looked down at Jake's mother and found she was staring at me, a determined expression on her face. She would be on good terms with her new daughter-in-law, no matter how much of an effort it took.

'You'd like me to call you Sybil?' I asked.

'That's best, I think,' she said again. 'Don't you?'

I nodded. 'I was hoping it would be your Christian name,' I said.

She took another sip of sherry, and touched her hat.

'Jake's very self-willed,' she announced. 'He always has been, right from the time he was a little boy. A very tiny, tiny little boy. Very.'

'Would you like a sandwich?' I asked.

She drew in a deep breath, touched her hat, and looked up at me.

'I rather think I ought to have some black coffee. Don't you?'

I signalled to one of the waitresses, who looked across the room at me with her eyebrows raised.

'Coffee,' I said.

'Sorry, dear?'

'Coffee.'

'Can't hear you, dear.'

'Then *come here*.'

There was a moment's startled silence, and then everybody began talking at once.

'Who's going to be on top *tonight*, then?' bellowed Morry. 'Better pack the hobble, Jake. That's a filly with a temper, that could be a kicker.'

'I don't want to make any trouble,' said Sybil.

'I do,' I answered, and was pleased to hear her giggle.

'Coffee,' I said to the flustered waitress, who turned towards the door as I spoke. 'Just a moment, I haven't finished. We want *fresh* coffee, not instant, fresh, black coffee, with a choice of milk or cream served separately, and brown or white sugar. Now, do you understand?'

The coffee, when it came twenty minutes later, was certainly not fresh, but it was hot, and it was served as I had ordered. Sybil sipped hers cautiously, twinkling at me over the rim of her cup.

'It's Nescafé,' she whispered.

'I know. Shall we refuse to pay the bill?'

She giggled again, and asked for some more. Then she wanted to meet Peter, because all her friends would ask her what he was like.

'Come on, then,' I said, but she hesitated and said she wouldn't bother, she wouldn't know what to say to him. She'd never met anybody famous before.

Jake should have introduced them, I thought irritably. She was obviously longing to meet Peter. He must have realised.

But Jake was talking to the trainer, quite oblivious to everything that was happening, so I went over to Peter and asked him to come and meet Sybil.

Morry grinned at me, and brandished a can of beer in my direction, some sort of salute.

'Told Jake to take the hobbles,' he said, as though I hadn't heard. 'Can't teach a stud groom anything about bondage sex. Can't have the mares kicking the stallions, so I said, better take the . . .'

'You make the most of it this afternoon,' I said as coldly as I could. 'This won't be tolerated when we get back.'

'You've missed your train,' said Peter as I led him across the room to Sybil, who was looking out of the window and trying to pretend she hadn't seen us coming towards her.

'I know. Do you think I should remind Jake? And put up with Morry's remarks about it?'

Peter touched my shoulder, and I turned towards him.

'Ann, why did you do this?'

He looked worried, and concerned. Acting? I wondered.

'Come and meet Sybil,' I said. 'She's sweet, and she wants to boast about you to her friends.'

It was nearly an hour later that Jake and I finally left for what I suppose was our honeymoon. Everybody had been looking at their watches for some time, and the trainer had finally decided he had had more than enough of Morry Old. He had gathered up his family and walked out, hardly even remembering to say goodbye.

Jake was furious. He'd thought he'd been on the point of selling a two-year-old, but the trainer had hardly been listening; he'd been concentrating far harder on Morry's *risqué*

188

jokes, and had taken very strong exception to his daughter hearing one about a homosexual camel.

'Four thousand quid, that cost me,' Jake kept repeating in the taxi on the way to the station. 'Four thousand quid, I'd nearly got him sold, Ann.'

'Keep him another year,' I suggested, trying to put him in a better mood. Jake had always been an advocate of letting a promising young horse develop before selling him.

'I need the money now, not next year.'

Was he about to tell me of his financial problems? I wondered, but Jake said nothing more, and contented himself with staring out of the window.

Half an hour later, when we were on the train, he asked, 'Are you happy?'

'Oh, yes.'

He smiled.

'Good. So am I.'

It wasn't an awkward silence that fell between us, because Jake and I had known each other too long for that, but I was becoming aware of a feeling of boredom. Was there nothing we could say to each other, away from horses?

'I like your mother,' I said.

'Yes? Good. I don't suppose we'll see much of her.'

I waited for him to explain, but he was looking out of the window again.

'Why not?' I asked.

'She lives in Yorkshire. Richmond. Long way.'

He sat up, and recrossed his legs.

'Might see her if we go up to Sedgwick some time.'

'I'd like that. Have you got any more family?'

'Cousins. Sheep farmers in Australia. Oh, and an accountant.'

I laughed, and he looked at me curiously.

'You make it sound as if he's a jailbird,' I explained, and Jake smiled.

'Well. Indoor work. Idle bugger.' He looked out of the window again, and then added the final dismissive remark.

'None of them have anything to do with horses. I think there's a pony on the farm, something for the kids, nothing interesting.'

About ten minutes later he fell into a doze, his head dropping forward onto his chest.

Sleep well, I thought. Oh, Jake, I hope I'm not going to make you too miserable. I hope Gorsedown's worth this.

I wondered if he'd expected more.

Jake had given me a partnership in the stable, ten per cent, and we'd signed the papers a few days before. He'd been anxious about it.

'It's not worth a lot right now,' he'd said. 'But it will be, Ann. With you behind me, I promise, it really will be.'

Had he expected me to give him a partnership in the forge? I'd never do that; I could never give away part of the forge. Gorsedown would have to be enough.

As I looked out of the window, it began to rain.

I watched the drops sliding down the glass, and I tried to set my mind into a more optimistic frame. I found instead a series of clichés, and I could not banish them.

Today is the first day of the rest of your life, and this is a strange sort of life I'm entering, marriage to Jake Brewer, a man I've known for many years, and yet hardly know at all.

Do you want children? I thought, and then, Jake, I do hope not. I really do hope not.

Wedding presents, lovely cut glass from Glory and Peter, Waterford Crystal, because Peter had been appearing in a play in Dublin, just for two weeks to help start up a newly renovated theatre. I'd run my hands across the surface of the decanters, enjoying the slightly rough sharpness of the beautiful work, wondering when Jake and I would ever use such things.

An antique grandfather clock from Uncle John, the brass face intricately chased. The more I looked at that clock the more there seemed to be to look at, and yet there was nothing fussy about the design, nothing that seemed over-elaborate.

When Morry Old had tackled him about it with the question 'How much did *that* set you back, then?', it had been nothing more than an expression of my own curiosity, although I had gritted my teeth on hearing it.

Uncle John had turned the question aside courteously, but I would have to have the clock valued. It would need separate insurance. Many thousands, I thought, and I wondered why. Uncle John has quite a lot of money, but he isn't usually extravagant with presents. Did he think a time might be coming when I would need money? When I might be glad of something really valuable to sell?

On the other side of the compartment Jake stirred, and sighed.

Toasters, bath towels, cutlery and crockery, no fewer than three stainless steel vacuum flasks, a pair of pigskin shooting sticks, four turquoise nylon lace pillowcases in a heart-shaped cellophane box.

A very valuable antique grandfather clock.

I could grow to love that clock. I felt I could look at it for hours, at the beautiful workmanship on the face, at the delicacy of the machinery behind the glowing polished wood door, and yet it did trouble me that Uncle John had given something worth so much money.

I still hadn't sold Arno's Riley.

I must do that, I thought. When we get home after this weekend, I really must do that.

For a few moments I allowed myself to think about Arno, and to wonder about Brita.

Jake muttered in his sleep. His eyes opened briefly, and he turned his head and fell back into a doze.

It had stopped raining by the time we reached Brighton, but there were clouds low in the sky, carrying the threat of more to come. Jake grumbled about the weather as we waited for a taxi, because heavy going on the track wouldn't give the horses he wanted to see a fair run. He wouldn't be able to tell enough about them.

'Are you thinking of buying them?' I asked, and he put his head on one side, screwing up his face.

He didn't know.

Failed flat racers sometimes made hurdlers or steeplechasers, even if they weren't bred for jumping.

'How much do you think that clock's worth?' he asked a few minutes later. When I didn't answer he made to repeat the question, and then looked into my face, and fell silent.

We didn't speak again until we were at the hotel.

'Uncle John gave us a grandfather clock, not a couple of horses,' I said, and Jake looked a little shamefaced.

'We'll have to talk about money some time,' he said, but I was still too angry to answer.

'I'm going for a walk.'

He seemed surprised.

'Don't you want me to come? Ann, this is supposed to be our honeymoon! We ought to be together. Ann? Ann!'

I walked westward along the promenade because I needed rain in my face, and it was coming from the west. I felt hot with rage, as if my face must be scarlet, so I kept my head down and counted my steps, looking at the paving stones under my feet as I paced along them.

Gorsedown was my real present to you, Jake, I thought, even though we'd never mentioned it.

I'd handed him a package a few days earlier, a neat royal blue presentation box, and he'd been pleased with the gold watch.

I'd had it engraved: 'For Jake, with my love, Ann'.

Neutral and noncommittal, like the kiss he'd bestowed on my cheek to thank me.

Beyond Hove the roads by the sea became mean and shabby and looked as if they'd peter out, so I turned inland and walked along a broad street, still hardly noticing. There were shopping arcades of cut-price supermarkets, charity shops and second-hand clothes stores.

The rain grew heavier, beating up from the asphalt road and paving stones, the wind rising and driving the water along the deep gutters to swirl down the drains.

Portslade, and there was no longer any pretence of a holiday town here. I was in a council estate, and there were smoke-blackened factory chimneys behind the tiled roofs.

Shoreham.

I hadn't brought any money, so I couldn't go back by taxi. I couldn't even take a bus, and my shoes were beginning to hurt. The rain was heavy and I was almost soaked to the skin. My feet were squelching with every step. The shoes were new, but I might as well throw them away. If I developed blisters before I got back to the hotel I'd dump them in a litter bin and go on in my stockinged feet.

Yes, we'd have to talk about money, and when we did Jake Brewer could find himself outflanked. That clock was not going to be his to sell, no matter what he tried. A wedding present is a gift to bride and groom, but if property has to be divided, anything valuable goes to whoever's close relative had given it.

You will not have that clock, nor the Waterford Crystal.

I turned, and began to walk back towards Brighton.

You can have the four turquoise pillowcases, I thought, and hoped it was a sign that my temper was improving. And two of the toasters, I added.

For a while in Hove I sat on a bench on the promenade, cupped my chin in my hands, and stared out at the grey sea.

How desperate was Jake for money, that he'd broached the question of selling the clock within four hours of our wedding? Hadn't he realised I'd be angry? Hadn't he cared?

I liked Jake. I wanted to help him. I'd thought Gorsedown

would help, that it would make an enormous difference, that it would solve his problems.

Had I made a disastrous mistake?

'Are you all right?' asked a policeman.

'Yes, thank you.'

'You'll catch your death, sitting there.'

There was a warning note in his voice. Have an explanation for this, or I won't let it go. A woman sitting on a bench in the pouring rain in a thin frock. Might be a nutter.

'It's a bet,' I·said. 'I haven't caught a cold for nearly fifteen years. If I don't catch one after three hours out in this, I win a hundred pounds. If I do, I win an overdraft.'

He smiled, and walked on.

'Good luck, then,' he called back to me.

'Thank you.'

Jake had left a note in our room. He, too, had gone for a walk, and would see me when he got back.

I had a long, hot bath. I washed the stiff lacquer out of my hair, and what was left of the make-up off my face. Afterwards, I dressed in jeans and a polo-necked shirt. If Jake and I were to get over what might still turn into a quarrel, I thought it would be easier if I appeared as he knew me best, his farrier and his friend, rather than that faintly ridiculous feminine creature, his bride.

I was hungry. The silly sandwiches and the rather unpleasant wedding cake were all I had had to eat that day.

I sat in the armchair and turned on the television. I watched the last part of an old film, and the news, and then I heard Jake's key in the lock.

He was looking sullen and angry, and he hardly glanced in my direction. He went into the bathroom without a word, and started to run a bath. Then he came back, peeling off his wet coat.

'I'm hungry,' I said. 'Shall we have dinner up here? Or do you want to go down to the restaurant.'

'Whatever you like.'

194

'Have you looked at the room service menu?'

'No.'

He went back into the bathroom and locked the door.

I ordered chicken salad with baked potatoes for both of us. The waiter brought it up while Jake was still in the bath, so I let him lay the table, and I turned on the television again. There was nothing much to see: a game show, a cricket match, and a documentary about building materials.

I watched the cricket until Jake came out of the bathroom, and I looked at him, waiting until he glanced in my direction. I smiled.

'I hope the meal's all right. Tell me about these horses.'

He shrugged, and sat down at the little table.

'There's not much point in going to see them, is there?'

I joined him at the table, but I seemed to have lost my appetite.

'Had you assumed I'd pay for them?'

He was opening the bottle of wine and didn't answer until he'd worked the cork free. Then he went through an elaborate routine of smelling and tasting the wine, frowning down into the glass and shaking his head doubtfully.

'The horses?' I prompted quietly as he poured.

'I thought we'd help each other. I thought that was what husband and wife meant.'

I picked up my fork and looked down at the salad. I really didn't seem to be very hungry after all.

'The horses,' I said again. 'Tell me about them. Please.'

So he talked about the two colts, three-year-olds who'd been disappointing on the flat and didn't have the breeding to stay. Jake thought they had the conformation of jumpers, or potential jumpers, to be a bit more accurate, are you listening, Ann?

'I'm listening.'

Jake didn't really see how he could lose, barring accidents. Even if they didn't make hurdlers they'd make hunters.

195

'Hunters need to stay.'

He didn't seem to have heard me. These two colts, if they didn't do well here they'd go to a selling plate. They'd already been entered. Maybe the rain wasn't such a bad thing after all.

'Jake, hang on a minute, I don't understand. You said they weren't bred to stay, and then you said if they don't make hurdlers or chasers you could make hunters out of them. Or did I misunderstand?'

He said he knew what he was doing. Friar's Luck was a born hurdler, he'd stake anything on it. He really wanted that colt. And Deckhand, it was a chance, Ann. It was a chance to get his name back in the winning lists, a real chance.

'Don't you want that chicken?' he asked.

'Not really.'

'Mind if I have it?'

I pushed my plate across the table, and he went on eating, quite voraciously, shovelling the food into his mouth as he talked, his enthusiasm growing as he described his plans for the horses.

Pick them up for next to a song. Geld them, and start them on jumps, you just watch Friar's Luck tomorrow, tell me he hasn't got the action. You just watch him. They'd both be ready for the Spring Meeting at Hereford, the Novice Hurdle, two miles to start, or maybe Chepstow, we'd have to see.

I listened, and I tried to catch his optimism, but all I could think was that the horse world is lousy with failed flat racers looking for something else to do, and jumpers need stamina.

Even he didn't seem to believe what he was saying. There was something forced in his enthusiasm. Was he trying to convince himself, as well as me?

Why was Jake clutching at straws? And why these two horses out of the hundreds that would be on offer later in the season? Not worth their training fees, put up for auction, entered for selling plates, sold to people who didn't know enough not to be impressed by the phrase ex-race-horse.

'Why these two?' I asked.

Because he'd seen them, because he'd talked to people who knew. Because no matter what anybody might say about Jake Brewer, nobody could say he didn't know horses. Was I questioning his judgement?

'Yes,' I said, and he stopped with the last forkful of salad halfway to his mouth, and stared at me.

'You bought a flashy lemon chestnut gelding last autumn. He had shell feet and he was just about worth the petrol it cost to fetch him home. There was the grey filly the year before who overreached so badly she was lame for months. There's only so much that corrective shoeing can do, Jake. Miracles are out. She was going to be the hunter of the year, too, remember that?'

He laid down the fork, looked at it, picked it up again and fed the salad into his mouth.

'Look,' he said, and then paused to chew, still pointing the fork at me. 'Look.'

I waited. His eyes moved across to the window, where the rain still rattled against the glass. He was playing for time, trying to think of a convincing argument.

'Before I buy them, you look at their feet. OK?'

'Well, that is part of my job.'

He grinned at me, a huge and triumphant grin, and raised his glass.

'Right, then. That's a deal.'

I raised my glass in return, wondering why he'd assumed I'd agreed. Was I committed to paying for two racehorses? Would Jake always interpret the smallest concession as total victory?

'We should have champagne,' he said. 'There should be candles. It's not very romantic, is it? Oh, Ann, I'm sorry. I'm not the romantic sort. Would you like candles and champagne? I'll order them, shall I? You just say the word, I'll order them.'

'No,' I said. 'I'm not the candles and champagne type, Jake.'

He leaned across the table and took my hand, smiling.

'You have got lovely eyes, though. You really have.'

'Well, that's romantic, Jake. Thank you.'

He lifted my hand to his lips, and kissed it.

'I'm going to try to make you happy,' he said dutifully.

My reward for giving Jake his own way, I thought as I cleaned my teeth in the bathroom, being told I've got lovely eyes. Is marriage a matter of the carrot and the stick?

I looked at myself in the mirror, looked into the eyes he'd said were lovely.

Arno had said that, too.

Just a little lipstick, the dark browny-orange that was the only colour I liked. And scent, dabbed behind my ears.

I was wearing a plain cotton nightshirt. I'd looked at pictures of silk and lace, and I'd tried to imagine myself wearing them. I'd be like one of those pitiable circus elephants, dressed in a travesty of a pink tutu for the amusement of a half-witted audience.

White wrap-around cotton, then, with something like a sash belt, and if it called one of the martial arts to mind, then that was just too bad. At least I didn't look ridiculous.

And it was new, which was not the case with Jake's pyjamas.

Do not compare, I thought, do not compare. A faint smell of beer: had he been in a pub? Yes, there was the scent of cigarette smoke in his hair. Leaning over me, his weight pressing me down, I could hardly move.

Do not compare, it is unjust to compare him with . . .

Heavy breathing, nuzzling at my neck in the total darkness, one hand fumbling at the sash belt, muttering, pushing away, then both hands tugging until I reached down and untied the slip knot myself.

He turned his back to me. He was sitting up, undoing buttons. Why had he put on a jacket? There were shuffling noises, and the bed shook as he lay down again.

The smell of beer, of cigarette smoke in his hair, and I remember my hands on smooth, clean skin. I remember laughter, and a gentle voice.

'Ann, I love you, Ann.'

These words. I'd never heard them before. I'd dreamed of them, but not from him. Not said as though it was a duty: not like that.

Do not compare.

Hands pushing the cotton wrap away from my shoulders, the breathing heavier, so I sat up and let it slip down my arms, and fell back again, and I tried to relax under hands that pressed, and probed, and I tried to respond to a voice that said oh yes, yes, come on, then. Come on.

Come on, what? Come on?

But I remember. I remember . . .

Grunting, and snuffling, come on, then, come on. Hard breathing, and gasping, and Jake, this hurts. Please, don't.

Do not compare. Keep silent and do not compare, but I remember, I do remember, it was not like this.

This mouth on mine, this tongue in my mouth, why so clumsy? Why must you be so rough? What are you trying to do?

So, move, and try to respond, and touch him, try to be what he wants, try to be . . .

Is this *all* there is? Is this *all* you know? Can you say *nothing* except come on, come on? Please, will you stop grunting, and could you not keep *still* for just one moment?

I will try to do what you want, but I cannot move, I am pinned down, how can you be so heavy? I would kiss you, but your mouth is crushing mine, I can hardly breathe.

'Jake?'

199

'Uh? Ann. Oh, darling, come on. Come on.'

All right, so pretend, and after all, it's not so bad. Yes, Jake, oh Jake, yes. Darling Jake, yes. Come on, then, Jake, come on.

Do not remember, do not compare.

Jake, darling Jake, oh yes, come on, Jake. Come on.

Is there nothing more to say, in the total darkness, under this heavy, heaving body? Is there nothing to do but wait, and listen, and say these meaningless words, until the breathing gets faster and faster, and the words are slurred?

Is there nothing? Is there nothing, Jake?

He kissed me, and he said, that was wonderful, darling, and he rolled away from me.

A little while later his breathing became deep, and quiet, and I lay in the darkness listening to him sleep, staring up at the ceiling and not remembering, and not comparing.

I heard a clock strike three, and I closed my eyes.

I cannot remember my dreams.

13

When I woke the following morning Jake was already up, and sitting at the table reading the sports pages. He was making notes on a sheet of paper.

I lay still for a while, watching him, and then he seemed to become aware of me. He glanced across the room and smiled.

'Hello,' I said.

'Do you want breakfast?' he asked.

'Coffee, please.'

I had a shower while we waited for our breakfast to be brought to the room. I wondered when Jake washed, or if he ever did. There was still the lingering smell of beer and tobacco about him, and Jake doesn't smoke. When I came out of the miniature bathroom I told him there was plenty of hot water, but he just shook his head. He was eating a huge plateful of fried food.

'Don't you want yours?' he asked when I'd poured my coffee and taken it over to the window.

'No.'

How did he manage to stay so thin? I wondered as he helped himself to my breakfast.

'I want to ask you something, Ann.'

There was a challenging tone in his voice. He was

nervous about this question, and was trying to disguise it with belligerence.

'What is it?'

'You're not a virgin, are you? I mean, before last night.'

I stood in silence by the window, looking down at the wet street and the people walking along the pavement. Had I not been so big, would he have expected me to be a virgin, at my age? Had he looked for some kind of bonus? A consolation prize, for marrying the sort of woman who would not normally attract a man?

'No,' I answered at last, and then, 'Were you?'

He didn't seem to notice.

'So who was it?'

The same challenging tone, and he'd spoken quite loudly. I am your husband, I have a right to know all about you. Past, present and future. Also, I had a right to expect virginity from a bride such as you. So, explain, and apologise.

No.

No, Jake, I will not tell you. I will not tell you about Arno. You will have to be satisfied with Gorsedown, and the use of this already-used body, and perhaps with whatever money I can raise to pay for those horses if I can't find something convincingly wrong with their feet.

Why those two horses? Why, out of the hundreds that would be coming on the market this summer, why Friar's Luck and Deckhand?

Jake had been quite fair when he'd said that he knew horses. He'd made mistakes, but he'd made fewer than most men in his position. So, what did he know about Friar's Luck and Deckhand?

'Ann, are you going to answer my questions?'

'No, Jake, I'm not. I won't ask you questions, and I won't answer yours.'

I didn't look at him as I walked back to the bathroom, picking up my clothes as I went, but I could almost feel his eyes on my back. What would he do?

He sulked, but only briefly, because we were going to the races, to see two horses he expected to own. So, although he maintained a stiff silence as he finished his breakfast, he was muttering to himself quite happily as he read the racing pages of the newspapers, and he asked me if I had any ideas about the runners that afternoon.

'Not unless I've shod them,' I answered.

Sometimes I was given a tip, and most of them had been good. Once I'd spotted a cracked sole at the end of a hot summer when the ground had been like bricks. It had been a tiny hairline, and I still don't know how I knew it was there, but I'd probed, and wiped at dust with the side of my thumb, and at last I'd seen it, when one edge had caught the light.

'Look. Here, do you see?'

He hadn't. He couldn't. No, I can't see anything, what am I looking for? And I'd tilted the horse's foot, seeking that raised edge under the early sunlight, and suddenly, yes. Christ, yes! I do see it, I see it now. How the hell did you spot that?

Ground like bricks, and a favourite horse.

'Got a few bob to put on a runner today? Ready Maid in the three thirty. Just don't pass it on.'

She'd come in by three-quarters of a length at fifty to one, and I'd had ten pounds on her.

Sometimes they'd do me a favour, and sometimes I could catch the air of satisfaction and excitement over a particular horse when they came to the forge in the early mornings to have their shoes changed. As the horsebox drove off down the lane I'd stand and watch it, and I'd chew at my lip a little thoughtfully, and I'd consider the horse that had been given that extra friendly slap on the rump as he'd gone back up into his stall. Perhaps later that morning, after I'd looked at the racing page in the newspaper, I'd make a telephone call.

I won more than I lost, but I never relied on a horse-race.

By the time I came out of the bathroom Jake had written down a list of horses he intended to back that afternoon. He read them out to me; two of them came from stables we knew, and both stables had used me on more than one occasion.

'What about Hallelujah Pet?' he demanded. 'Do you know her?'

'Not under that name.'

She might have been Dozy Old Bag when she came to the forge, or Sweetheart, if the lad had been in a good mood, but she certainly wouldn't have been Hallelujah Pet, and Jake understood that.

There was a photograph of one of the other horses, did I know him?

'He comes from Newmarket,' I said after I'd studied the picture and then looked at the text. 'How could I know him?'

'Well, look at the picture. What do you think of his feet?'

Jake was recovering his good temper as the time for the race meeting drew closer.

'Do you want a shower?' I asked. 'The water's really hot.'

'No. What's the time?'

He was lost in the newspaper again.

I wandered around the room looking for something to do, even something to read apart from the Gideon Bible.

There was nothing.

'I'm going out,' I said. 'I want to buy a book.'

'Oh, right. Fine.'

Nothing to say to each other, and nothing to do on our honeymoon. Perhaps it would have been better if I had felt something other than a sense of relief.

We did enjoy the race meeting together, and I watched the two horses through binoculars, for as much as I could see of them. I tried to analyse their actions, and I tried very hard to see what it was that made them so special.

Just a pair of mediocre three-year-old colts. One came in seventh, the other ninth.

'Why?' I asked Jake. 'Why?'

'Did you see anything wrong?' he demanded.

But I was becoming irritated.

'What do you expect me to see when they're in the middle of a herd? Neither of them broke a leg. I doubt if I'd have seen anything less.'

He shrugged.

'You didn't spot anything wrong, so . . .'

'Did you back them?'

'No!'

He seemed affronted at the suggestion.

Perhaps I was being too bossy.

I told him I liked the look of a chestnut filly with white socks. He studied his newspaper, and became perplexed.

'Why?'

'She looks sweet.'

He liked that. He became amused, and indulgent, and he gave me five pounds to put on her. She didn't stand a chance against the favourite, who was starting odds on, but you go on, darling, have a little flutter.

She won.

'Fluke,' I said, and I meant it, but I made a note of her name.

On the way back Jake became insistent about the colts.

'You didn't see anything wrong, did you?'

'Jake, what are you asking? I could hardly see them at all.'

'Why won't you take my word for it?'

I stopped, and a fat woman bumped into me and clicked her tongue in irritation. Somebody else barged past me, ostentatiously squeezing between me and a lamp-post. The pavements were packed with the racing public on its way home, so I sighed, and followed Jake down the hill.

We'd be going home tomorrow. I wished it was tonight.

In the darkness he fumbled and heaved his way through the obligatory sexual ritual, and I tried to respond as I guessed he might expect, or want. I closed my eyes. Please,

Jake, stop telling me to come on. Please, could you try something different? I will not come on, and you're hurting me. I'm not a horse, I'm not being trained to be a jumper when I'm not even . . .

My eyes flew open.

Ringers!

It wasn't even a guess, it was an absolute certainty.

'They're *ringers*. They're bloody *ringers*.'

'Huh? What? Ann, what . . .?'

'Oh, *get off* me. And turn on that light.'

'What are you . . .'

'Those two useless horses. Deckhand, and, what was it? Friar's Luck, they're ringers, aren't they? Jake, will you please *get off me*.'

There was no other possible explanation. Why else would Jake be so determined to buy just those two thoroughly commonplace horses?

'Who owns them?' I demanded as he rolled over to his own side of the bed. 'And what's in this for you?'

'How did you know?' he asked sullenly.

'Because they're nothing, that's why. Why else would you want them? Who owns them?'

'What difference does it make?'

I threw the blankets aside, swung my legs over the side of the bed and switched on the light. Jake put up a hand to shield his eyes.

'I would quite like to know what sort of a racing cesspool you've jumped into, that's the difference it makes,' I said.

'I'm not in a cesspool.' He was sulky, and belligerent. 'I don't run ringers.'

'No, but you buy them up when it starts looking a bit hot for the bastards who do. Christ! You must be a half-wit. Who owns them, Jake?'

'You can read the papers, can't you?'

'Don't treat me like a fool,' I blazed, suddenly becoming really angry. Jake looked startled, and a little frightened, as though he thought I might hit him. 'The real owners, not the mugs with their names on the papers.'

Jake didn't answer. He climbed out of bed and went into the bathroom. I heard the door lock behind him, and a moment later the shower began to run.

The best way to get Jake to take a shower was to pick a fight with him, it seemed. The bathroom was a good hiding place.

Ringers: why hadn't I thought of it straight away? Two dark bay colts, no distinguishing marks, looking not dissimilar to about sixty per cent of all racehorses. But not very fast, certainly nothing like as fast as the two far better animals whose places they occasionally took in races where it was hoped nobody would have sharp eyes.

Even the best of horses can have an off day. The jockey would be seen to be working as hard as he could, but the horse wouldn't quicken. Too bad, better luck next time. Next time, when the odds would be rather longer.

The jockey might not even know. It could shake his confidence a bit, riding something that felt like a water buffalo when only three weeks before Joe Bloggs had brought him in first, but maybe the horse simply didn't like him. It did sometimes happen that a horse would run well for most riders but refuse to go a yard for one man in particular. It was unusual, but not unknown. Or, he'd travelled badly. Or he was incubating some infection, or virus. Or he'd had a hard race last time, and he was scared of hitting the front again because he'd taken a thrashing.

There were a hundred explanations.

One of them was that it was a different horse, but it would be a brave jockey who'd suggest it. All he could do in the unsaddling enclosure was say sorry, he just wouldn't go, and perhaps be grateful the owner and the trainer seemed to be taking it so well.

It was a risky business. It was done under the noses and

eyes of people who lived and breathed horses, and it needed luck. Whispers start very quickly in the horse world, and they can build up into a crescendo in a very short space of time. All it needed was one jockey looking across the paddock at a horse he thought he'd ridden only a few months ago, he didn't carry his head like that, did he? I don't remember that. And then later, how did Lightning run today? Did he hang on the curves? I tell you what, Fred, that's bloody funny, then.

In this case the whispers might have started already, and it would be far, far safer if Friar's Luck and Deckhand, who looked so very like two other horses, were no longer to be found in racing stables, so that enquiries into the genuine ownership of various similar-looking animals might never even start, or, if they did, the horses could not be found, and comparisons could not be made.

Jake came out of the shower looking sulky, and threw himself down onto the bed.

'Are you going to turn that light out? I'm tired.'

'If you like. If you'd rather talk about those horses tomorrow.'

He rolled away from me, muttering to himself.

'Who owns them, Jake?'

'Nobody you know.'

'Try me.'

'Dom Mont-Blering. OK? You any the wiser now?'

I wasn't. Dominic, would it be? Dominic Mont-Blering, it wasn't a name I knew. But then, I wasn't really in the horse-racing world. There were people I could ask.

'Jake? Listen, please. I want to help.'

'Oh, yes?'

But he was listening.

I talked for a long time about a friend who'd sold me a horse I loved. Jake Brewer, who'd sold me my super Lyric, and it had been Lord Robert Halstay who'd said I should go to Jake. Stephens, Lord Robert's groom, had said Jake was as honest as most. I asked Jake, how many customers have come to you because Lord Robert sent them?

He didn't answer, but he was still listening.

How many more of his own friends would Lord Robert send to Jake, if Jake's name was linked to the Mont-Blerings of the racing world?

Jake's an honest horseman, I said, and Jake rolled onto his back again, and stared up at the ceiling. That's little short of a miracle in a world where any dirty trick that can be played on a horse dealer is a joke, something to be shared with a bunch of laughing friends in the pub later. In that same world, anything even suggesting a horse was less than one hundred per cent perfect, no matter what he'd cost, would brand a dealer a thief and a rogue, just like all the other horse dealers, thieves and rogues the lot of them.

'Talk to me, Jake,' I said, and Jake sighed.

'I need the money,' he said simply. 'I need the money. I can't borrow any more. Bills keep coming in, I can't pay them. I have to find wages every week, every time I go into the bank my heart's in my mouth. Manager might come out, ask to see me. I'm over my limit.'

He wouldn't look at me. He was still staring up at the ceiling, but there was something close to desperation in his face.

'Hunters, that's what I do best. That's what I'm known for. How can you train hunters if you haven't got cross-country land? Ever since they built over Ashlands. They might as well have put a bullet through my brain.'

'You've got Gorsedown now,' I said, and he shook his head.

'It's too late. If I don't buy those horses, I'll be bankrupt before spring. I've got to. I don't like it, but I've got to.'

'What's the deal?'

'Buy them, geld them, send them to auction without name or description, and do it fast.'

'Lose them,' I said, and he nodded.

'I get the purchase price back, and anything I make at the auction.'

'Dominic whatever-it-was must be desperate,' I remarked, and Jake nodded again.

'He thought the Jockey Club was a gang of . . . what did he call them? Geriatric chinless wonders, all old school tie and no balls.'

I'd often thought that the Jockey Club was something of an anachronism, the hub of a modern industry run on the old boy network, and quite blatant about it. But while the alternatives contain the Mont-Blerings of the racing world, the old boy network is infinitely preferable. At least most of the old boys base their interest in the Jockey Club on a love of the racehorse.

'I don't care about the others, Jake, but I don't think you should fall out with the Jockey Club. I think they'd eat you.'

Old-fashioned gentlemen, the Jockey Club, and there is nobody as ruthless and single-minded as an old-fashioned English gentleman who believes something he holds to be important is under attack.

There was a long silence, and then Jake turned towards me, and there was a smile on his face, something of the rueful grin I'd sometimes seen before, and always liked.

'It was falling apart anyway. You wanted to look at their feet. I had a word with Deckhand's lad. The bloody nag's got wonky pasterns. You'd have spotted that at fifty yards, wouldn't you?'

'Well, yes,' I said. 'Yes, Jake, I think I would probably have spotted wonky pasterns.'

He nodded, and I added, 'Depending, of course, upon what particular form the wonkiness took. It's a bit difficult, with these highly technical terms.'

He smiled, but it was a rather absent smile.

'How did you guess?' he asked a little later.

'I don't know. It just came to me, suddenly. It was the only possible explanation. Why?'

'Oh, Ann. I wish . . .' He was frowning, and looking away into the middle distance.

'I thought, when that filly won, maybe you knew something about her. She comes from the same stable, did you notice?'

I hadn't noticed. I'd genuinely been trying to humour Jake with my silly 'she looks sweet' reason for backing an unknown horse. She had looked sweet, she'd had the short, blunt face of a foal.

'Well,' I commented, 'that sounds like a stable that's due to get snooped at by some of the old boys' emissaries, doesn't it?'

'What am I going to do?'

His voice was very quiet, with something dangerously close to a choke in it.

I didn't know. I'd never had to think about that sort of problem.

'Can't you raise a mortgage on your land? I mean, there's the house, and stables, and the land, there must be . . .'

'Already done. Crichton says it's mortgaged for more than it's worth now.'

'Crichton?'

'Bank manager.'

He was already over the limit on his overdraft, with bills he couldn't pay and the wages to find. Now he'd turned to me, and asked me what he should do. What could I say?

'Jake, please start by telling Dominic Thing to go and shoot himself. Please. Your reputation for honesty is a real asset.'

He nodded.

'OK. All right, Ann. I'll tell him.'

Still the same small voice, but now his eyes were fixed on my face, and there was something like hope. Did he think I could find the answers for him? He was a drowning man clutching at straws.

'What about your brother-in-law?' he asked after a while.

'Peter?'

Jake nodded.

'Isn't he rich? Famous film star, isn't he? Do you think he might help?'

I'd told Peter to get out of my house and never come back.

'I don't know,' I said. 'I don't know if he's rich. Actors have to try and look as if they're rich, don't they? They have to look successful, but I don't know, Jake.'

And then, because I'd demanded honesty of him, I added, 'I've had a big row with Peter. I'm surprised he came to the wedding. If I asked him for money he'd tell me to go to hell.'

Would he? I wondered. Peter had been a good friend for years; would he still think of my words as unforgivable?

I didn't want to ask Peter Clements for money.

'If we go back to the bank,' I said, 'and we explain about Gorsedown, do you think . . .?'

He was shaking his head.

'I told him we were getting married. I said it meant I could use Gorsedown.'

I'd left it too late, then. I should have agreed to marry him when he'd first asked me. He could have had a few hunters ready for the winter.

'Would the money for the ringers have been enough?'

'For a couple of months.'

And then he almost cried out to me.

'Ann, I'm so tired of trying to find money. Every week, every month, trying to find money. Selling good horses for half their value, just relieved when somebody buys something, any price. Just to pay that week's wages. Just something off the corn merchant's bill. Something on account for the vet. I'm so tired of it.'

'Oh, Jake.'

His voice was almost breaking again.

'I was born in that house. My father and my Uncle Ted

built those stables, I mean it, they built them. No builders, they laid those bricks themselves. I was helping break ponies by the time I was seven. I rode in my first point-to-point when I was thirteen. I never wanted to do anything else. Just horses. Just horses, Ann, it's all I know. Now, I want to give up. Let the buggers at the bank have it all. I just want to sleep, and not worry any more.'

I couldn't offer him anything. I had no advice, no ideas, nothing, but a little word of praise.

'I don't think the horse world can afford to lose its Jake Brewers. There aren't enough of them.'

He gave me a brief, distracted smile.

'Hunters were eighty per cent of my business. It went. The jumpers, the ponies, the dressage, just bits and pieces. You know, Ann, I do evening stables, and I look around, I think, what the hell for? What the hell? But I was born there, and I never wanted to do anything else. I don't know what to do.'

'What happened to Uncle Ted?'

'Sailing accident, he drowned, silly old bugger. Should have stuck to horses.'

'And your father?'

'That could have happened to anybody. Horse fell on him.'

'Maybe he should have gone sailing.'

'Yeah, maybe.'

There was open desperation in the smiles he was trying to raise.

'Do any of your family die in their beds?' I asked.

'Hope not. Sounds like a bloody boring sort of death, that. You got to snuff it, may as well make it interesting. Sort of, on your feet, and moving.'

He was trying to force himself to laugh, and he was still looking at me with something close to hope in his eyes. Did he think there was something I could do?

There was nothing. What could I offer? What ideas could

213

I have that he hadn't tried in the two years in which he drew closer and closer to despair?

'Is the forge mortgaged?'

I had guessed he would ask, and I had my answer ready.

'It never has been, and it never will be.'

He tried to argue.

'I only need about six months, now we can use Gorsedown. Ann, listen, I've got good young horses. Once I get back into the hunter trials I'll be all right. I only need a little time.'

'It wouldn't be enough.'

He clutched at my arm.

'How much could you raise on the forge? Just, if you did. I'm not saying, but how much could you? Just for the sake of argument?'

'Jake,' I said, 'we were married yesterday, and today you've told me you're as good as bankrupt.'

He was staring at me, watching my face, looking for some sign of weakness, some hope that I might be persuaded. I could almost feel his thoughts. You're my wife, you ought to help me. Husband and wife, that's what it means, help each other. You're my last hope. Please, help me.

It seemed like a very long time before he took his hand off my arm and lay back on the bed, looking up at the ceiling again.

'You're my wife,' he said. 'You're my partner, too.'

He drew in a deep breath, and then began to speak quickly.

'It's going to be all right, Ann. It really is going to be all right. I only need a bit of time, now I can train the hunters on Gorsedown.'

But he'd just told me it was too late.

'Your ten per cent, it'll be worth a lot in the end, you'll see. It'll be all right. I'll work hard.'

There was no answer I could make. He'd said it was too late.

'We're partners. It's not a limited company, Ann. Don't you understand? I thought you'd help me. I thought you'd understand. It used to be a good business, and it will be again, I promise. I do promise, Ann. Losing Ashlands, that was the trouble. Gorsedown, that's just as good. It's only time. Only a bit of time.'

'You said they won't give you any time.'

'If you raise some money on the forge, that'll do it. Then I can hold them off, until I've sorted it. Listen, the October . . .'

'No, Jake. I will not mortgage the forge. I won't do it.'

'We're partners,' he said, and his voice was very soft, and his eyes were a little frightened. 'I don't think you understand. We're partners. If they make me bankrupt, they make you bankrupt too. Do you understand? They'll take the forge anyway.'

14

I'd once had keys to both the main gates into Gorsedown Park, but I'd lost them. I hadn't needed to use those gates. I'd always ridden Lyric through the paddock and through my own elaborate confection of wrought iron, my bloody death trap, as Jake called it when we first took his horses into the park a few days after we returned from Brighton.

Lyric had grown accustomed to the noise it made, and Jake had forgotten about it.

We rode the horses along the grass verges to the forge, and then through the paddock, and I dismounted and handed the reins of the fat and lazy cob I was riding to Toby. Jake's grey filly danced nervously at the sounds the gate made as I pulled it open and the ratchet snapped onto the catch, but she was no problem to Jake.

It was when they had all reached the park, when Jake thought fifty yards should be far enough and I let the gate swing shut, that the trouble started. The clashing metal panicked the filly, and her fear was picked up by the other horses.

Two of the grooms fell off, and one dropped the reins, leaving his horse free to bolt into the trees.

Once the others had been brought back under control I could hear the loose horse crashing through the woods, and

216

I thought with horror of the fallen spruce trees, with their spearlike branches sticking out of the trunks at all angles.

'I think I know where he'll stop,' I said, and Jake, still swearing furiously, said I should get up on my bloody horse and go and find out if I was right, then, shouldn't I? In the meantime, he and the others would do a bit of work on the banks under the beech trees.

'Rabbit holes at the top of the hill,' I called back, and Jake swore again.

I kicked the cob into a reluctant canter, and made a resolution that I would not ride him again. After every few paces he'd drop back into a trot unless I kept pounding at his flanks. My legs were beginning to ache with the unaccustomed strain.

I wondered what I would find when I caught up with the runaway. He was a green four-year-old, and he'd had no experience at all of woods and tracks; apart from the rabbit holes, there were gaping caves left by the roots of fallen trees, there were brambles with shoots like wire, there were hazards at every stride for a running horse.

It had been over a year since Jake had been able to afford to insure his horses, and this one, if I remembered rightly, had cost him more than fifteen hundred pounds. It had been one of his best hopes.

I kicked the cob again, and swung my stick hard against his side, which made him jerk his head, but had no effect on his speed. I couldn't understand why Jake still had him in the yard. One of his father's favourite maxims had been that bad horses cost as much to keep as good ones.

The young gelding had come to a halt on a track that ran down to the house between two fir plantations, quite near the clearing where I'd thought he'd stop. He'd trodden on his reins and broken one of them close up to the bit, and there were flecks of blood in the foam around his mouth. His ears were flicking nervously, but as I rode closer to him he laid them back, and moved away, tossing his head.

I slid off the cob and looped the reins over my arm.

'Come on, baby,' I said. 'Poor baby. Just stand, come on.'

Come on, come on, what was that . . . Oh, yes. What was this horse's name? What had that skinny boy called him?

'Come on, sweetheart. Just stand still now. Come on, boy.'

I couldn't remember, and the horse swung his head up and down with his ears flattened menacingly. Was he hurt, then? What was his name? Try to remember his name.

I moved a little closer, and he suddenly turned away from me, his haunches bunching. The cob pulled back in alarm, dragging at the reins, and I dodged behind him as the horse lashed out, squealing.

I gritted my teeth. That had been quite close, and it was unusual for a horse to behave like that. I stood at the cob's head and I looked at the youngster, searching for signs of a wound.

His ears were still flat, and he was moving around restlessly, his head low, nose close to the ground. Once or twice he shook his neck, a snakelike motion, and his nostrils were flaring.

I knew he wouldn't let me approach him. It would be dangerous to try. Somehow, I had to get him back to the others, and then we could drive him into the paddock.

I mounted the cob, and began to ride away slowly, down the track, watching to see if the horse would follow. He moved across the grass, still snaking his head, but he turned away from us.

I stopped, considering. I thought about riding back for Jake, but I decided on one more attempt.

I kept as much distance between us as I could when I rode the cob past him, and he threw up his head, baring his teeth, but he didn't come close to us. After about fifty yards I turned the cob, and I kicked him into a canter. He was reluctant, and he balked as we came close to the horse, but I hit him, and shouted at him, so he put his head down and cantered past, a stodgy and stiff-legged gait, but at least it was movement.

'*Come* on,' I called back to the horse. '*Come* on, fella!'

For a moment I thought the trick had failed, but then he did follow us, the herd instinct taking over from whatever had changed him. He didn't try to catch us, he seemed content to follow, so I listened to his hoofbeats to make sure he didn't veer off onto one of the side paths, and I led the way back towards the forge.

When we reached the others I told Jake what had happened, and he sucked in his breath and swore.

'I can't get close enough to see,' I said. 'Be careful, Jake, I think he's dangerous.'

There were more flecks of blood in the foam around his mouth. I'd hoped it was just a cut from when he'd trodden on the reins, but a small wound like that would have stopped bleeding by now. My initial fear, that he had run into a fallen tree and speared himself on one of the branches, was beginning to grow stronger, and I knew Jake was thinking along the same lines.

'Shit,' said Jake. 'It had to be that one, didn't it?'

I rode ahead and opened the gate into the forge paddock. Toby led the cob through, and then Jake took the filly past the loose horse at a canter, so he followed again, and went with her into the paddock. He wasn't running very straight; he was beginning to weave, and he staggered as he came to a stop.

'Poor old bugger,' said Toby sadly.

We telephoned the vet from the forge, and I said I'd wait for him while the others took the horses back to the stables.

'There won't be much he can do,' said Morry.

'For the insurance, then,' Toby explained, and Jake and I didn't look at each other.

The groom who'd fallen off was looking wretched, and I tried to smile at him. It hadn't really been his fault. He wasn't experienced enough to have been riding the young horse.

'Penance,' I said. 'You've got to ride the slug Jake gave me.'

I watched the horse for a little while as I listened to the others riding away down the lane, but then I couldn't bear it. There was nothing I could do, and seeing him staggering and turning in circles was almost heartbreaking. Only two hours earlier he'd been so beautiful, so proud in the hope of his youth and his strength, and now he was a wretched creature, weakening by the moment, and dying.

He was down by the time the vet arrived, and although his ribcage was still heaving his eyes were glazing and his tongue lolled from his open mouth in the blood and the foam.

After he'd shot him with the humane killer the vet crouched by the carcass, and found what we'd been expecting: a broken-off branch from a dead spruce tree, sharp, smooth and hard. It had probably been lying for years, there was no bark left on it. The young horse hadn't seen his danger, and he'd galloped straight into it. The skeleton of the dead tree would have looked flimsy to him, something he could brush through, as he probably had other trees like it. But that deadly branch had been at exactly the wrong angle; unlike the others, it had not bent away, it had not slid off his sweating hide.

'Into the lung,' said the vet. 'What a damnable thing. Nice-looking horse, too. Poor Jake, if it's not one thing it's another.'

As we walked back to the gate he coughed apologetically.

'You wouldn't have a word with him about his bill, would you?'

The first ride on Gorsedown, and one of Jake's best young horses lay dead in the forge paddock.

It was stupid to feel so depressed, and so guilty. An accident of that type could have happened anywhere, but the thoughts would not be suppressed. It had been my gate that had frightened the horses. It had been my efforts to help Jake that had seen us on Gorsedown at all, and neither of us was happy, neither of us really felt the marriage had been a good idea.

But every evening I'd go back to Jake's house, where a stranger on a casual visit would see the untidiness and the mess as the signs of a busy stables, with no time for trivialities such as houses.

Rust marks around the joins in old radiators, warped floorboards and window frames, damp stains on ceilings below crooked tiles: these told a different story to somebody who knew the truth. These spoke, not just of a shortage of money for repairs, but of a decline in the will to hold it all together. These spoke of the onset of despair.

I'd pointed out cracked stable doors to Jake. Horses had pawed at them and worn the planks, and then the wood had splintered under the impact from impatient, iron-shod hooves.

'Right,' he'd said. 'I'll have to get around to that.'

There was wood, there was heaps of it, offcuts and bits of plank left over from other jobs, boards, even oddments of discarded furniture. He could have done that himself, repaired those doors. Jake was a practical man. Only a few years ago there'd been tubs of geraniums in the stable yard, and the gravel had been raked. Now there were weeds, and rust marks against the walls where drainpipes led to clogged grilles.

There were tins of paint in a cupboard in one of the tack rooms, and there must be brushes somewhere, I'd said.

'Oh, what's the point?' he'd replied.

But that had been on an afternoon when he'd spent two hours trying to sell a horse to a man who might have been interested, but who might, I'd judged, have had nothing better to do with his time than waste other people's. However, Jake had wages to find, and the man might have bought the old piebald. Somebody had to, some time.

Didn't they?

Bad horses eat just as much as good ones, Jake had repeated later that night; might as well send the bloody thing to the knackers. Who wants to ride something that looks like that?

'Why did you buy him?'

It had been a part exchange. The piebald, and five hundred pounds. He'd needed five hundred pounds.

'Would you have done that deal if you hadn't been broke?'

'Would I hell.'

I'd been cooking. It seemed to be expected of me, that I'd put together an evening meal, and at least nobody who ate what I cooked was a fussy eater.

How had it come about that I had worked just as hard as everybody else that day, and now they were all watching television?

How had it come about that I was allowing this?

But I was angry, and I slammed the macaroni cheese onto the table and shouted that I was not doing the fucking washing up.

'Tommy and Glen, you're washing up,' ordered Jake.

I looked around the forge, and thought of lighting the fire. I could get a bit done before they all got back. I should telephone the knacker about the dead horse.

I could at least take his tack off, maybe even clean it. That was something I'd meant to point out to Jake, the state of the tack.

Crown Prince, that had been his name. The lads had called him Mickey. There was the girl from the village who came two mornings a week to do the paperwork, she'd liked Mickey. She'd told me he ate tomatoes. She used to bring him a few sometimes. She'd ridden out with them once or twice, Jake had said, when they'd been short-handed. Not on Mickey, on one of the steadier horses, but she wasn't bad.

222

She'd be upset, when she heard what had happened to him.

I telephoned Fred Johnson, and he said he'd be along some time the next day, if that was all right by me, he'd only just got in and he hadn't even had his bite of dinner.

There'd been an electricity bill that morning, three figures, and it was a red reminder. Jake had looked at it, and pushed it to one side with a fleeting expression of something between anger and despair.

He'd tricked me, and it was I who felt guilty. Why did I still like him?

When he'd told me, and looked at me as though waiting for the answers; when he'd listened to me, and agreed not to buy the horses; when he'd seemed to be handing it over to me, please, Ann, just take it. Just take it. I'd seen something new in Jake Brewer, and I'd ached for him.

Why couldn't I be angry? Surely I had a right to be angry? Why couldn't I raise a single spark of rage?

Poor Jake, trying to hold the land and the stables that his father and his uncle had built. It hadn't been his fault; Ashlands had gone, and with it his chance to train his hunters and his eventers. It really hadn't been Jake's fault. It was so unfair.

I could be cleaning this saddle, I thought. It was scratched, and there was sweat and blood and hair. I could be cleaning it, and the bridle. I could be mending that broken rein. I could be doing that, not just sitting here, feeling sorry for myself. Feeling tired.

It was all such an effort, but I did push myself off the workbench, and I took the saddle and bridle into my little tack room, and washed them. When there's blood I wash tack carefully, because the smell can linger, and it can upset horses.

Where do we find the wages this week? And we're running low on molasses and bran and horse nuts, haven't paid the last feed bill either. And the electricity, that red reminder, where can we find it? What can we sell, and who's buying?

Has it reached the point where we sell Uncle John's clock?

I telephoned Jane Laverton and asked her if she'd like to buy a piebald.

'You could paint him up like a Red Indian war pony,' I suggested. 'He's solid. Long distances wouldn't bother him.'

'Well, yes,' she said, 'but they bother me nowadays. Yes. Well, I don't know. How much is he?'

'To you, three hundred, but if you're asking anybody else, four. He's sound, Jane, but he's not a looker.'

'You're not talking about that ugly fat thing with the wobbly belly and the pink nose?'

'Oh, you've met the new vicar, then?'

She shrieked with laughter, a huge over-reaction to a mild joke, but she offered two hundred for the piebald.

'Two hundred and fifty,' I answered, 'and I'll throw away the bill for shoeing Minnie and Pedro.'

I could hear the horses in the lane, and I went out to wait for them. I was feeling a little happier, having sold the piebald to Jane for a fair price. I hoped Jake would be pleased.

Toby was leading the cob, and my lighter mood vanished.

'I'm not riding that thing again.'

Jake tried to ignore my protest.

'What did the vet say?'

'We found a stake, a spruce branch, in his lung. Jake, I'm not riding that cob, did you hear me?'

He sat on his horse looking down at me, chewing at his lip.

Perhaps I was being unfair to him. He'd just lost a good young horse, and I was adding to his troubles by refusing to ride the cob.

After a few moments he sighed, and looked at the horses. 'None of the others are up to your weight,' he said.

He wasn't being rude. It was a horseman's honest assessment. But I knew that if I mounted that cob he would be my ride from then on until he was sold, and after that it would always be the slow and heavy animals I'd be given to exercise.

I looked across at Morry, who was riding the best horse Jake had ever owned.

'Then I'll ride Barbarian.'

I regretted it almost as soon as I spoke. Barbarian was a hunter chaser, and the pride of his stable. Jake and Morry rode Barbarian. I'd never seen anybody else on him.

Toby's jaw dropped, and I heard one of the others swear softly in astonishment. Morry was grinning, anticipating a quarrel.

Jake's eyes had narrowed, and he was looking at me, not angrily, but as if he was trying to understand what it was that lay behind my outrageous demand to ride his beloved Barbarian.

I looked back at him calmly, wondering how we could break out of this impasse. He or I would have to back down, to give in to the other, and now it was just a case of saving face.

'A fiver says *you* can't get a gallop out of that cob,' I said at last, and saw the beginnings of a reluctant smile at the corners of Jake's mouth. 'And another fiver says Barbarian doesn't get away from me.'

There was still silence, but it was a little less tense.

It was Toby who broke it.

'Baba's an easier ride than Lyric, isn't he?' he asked, almost pleadingly. 'I mean . . . isn't he?'

'Just as well,' commented Jake. 'Lyric carts her halfway round the county.'

But then he seemed to make up his mind.

'Right, I'll take the cob, and I want that fiver in cash, I

don't take cheques from the missus. Morry, you take Jingo, and if any harm comes to Barbarian, Ann, I'll spank you.'

'If any harm comes to Barbarian, I'll let you.'

I could hardly believe he'd let it go, that he'd accepted my challenge with such a good grace and that I was to ride the horse he treasured above all others, the one horse who still kept the name of Jake Brewer alive in his world.

Morry let the stirrups down for me, and held Barbarian's head as I swung into the saddle and gathered up the reins. Jake was already on the cob, who had lifted his head into the correct position, and whose legs were now gathered neatly under him instead of being slack and sprawling as they had been when I'd ridden him.

I was about to lose that fiver. I hoped I'd keep the other one.

But Barbarian was a beautiful ride, calm and sensible, and responsive to every touch of heel or rein. I followed the other horses through the paddock. Jake did turn and watch rather more often than he had done before, but I could hardly blame him for that.

This time, they took the horses over the brow of the hill before I let the gate swing shut, but it was still Barbarian that Toby held when I joined them, and if Jake was feeling nervous about my riding him he hid it quite successfully.

It took him about five strides to get the cob into a reaching gallop, and I could only laugh in admiration. With the other horses held in to a canter I managed to keep Barbarian in the middle of the group, although there was enough weight on the bit to tell me he wanted to be at the front, and would go if I gave him the chance.

I didn't try to jump him. When we reached the end of the track I dismounted, smiling. I thanked Jake for letting me ride him and said I'd take the cob back to the forge and wait for them there.

Jake couldn't quite disguise his relief. As he handed me

the reins I whispered to him, 'I've sold the piebald to Jane Laverton.'

'What? How much?'

'Two fifty, and a few free horseshoes?'

There was nothing that could lift the gloom over the dead horse. The money was a hard enough blow, but we'd seen a beautiful young animal dying, and that was something we all hated.

'It wasn't your fault,' I said to the young groom later. He shook his head.

'Should have been ready,' he said. 'Was my fault, then. It was.'

Later I asked Jake if he was pleased about the piebald, and he said of course he was. But then he turned a tight, hard smile in my direction, and said if I could sell another three like that before the end of this week, we'd be in the clear for about ten days.

'What do you mean?'

It was a letter he hadn't shown me, from the bank. It had arrived two days earlier. No further funds were available, and the manager would be grateful for a meeting with Jake as soon as possible.

I stood in the big, untidy kitchen with the letter in my hand, and I knew I was finally trapped. If Jake's business failed it took me with it, and I would lose the forge.

'It'll be all right,' he said. 'I promise. I only need a little time. Ann?'

Why could I feel no rage? He'd tricked me, and his treachery would take everything I loved from me, and yet I couldn't hate him.

It wasn't only time Jake needed. It wasn't time that had broken the loose-box doors, let the weeds grow in the gravel, the rust stains spread on the flaking whitewashed walls.

'I only need six months,' he said. 'I can do it. You'll see.'

'All right,' I said. 'I'll go to the bank tomorrow. I'll . . .'

227

He came towards me, his arms wide, a smile growing on his face, but I couldn't. I couldn't even look at him. I shook my head, and I backed away from him.

I stood under a hot shower, and I tried to wash away the misery of the dead horse, the worry about the bankrupt stable, and the feeling almost like grief when I thought of the forge. It was the home where I'd always felt safe, where I'd had the pride of belonging to it, and of it belonging to me. I'd inherited it, but I'd earned it too, in the trust Uncle Henry had believed he could place in me.

'I'm sorry,' I said to him. 'I'm sorry.'

Enough for a few more months? Just enough for a few more months, and would a few more months be enough?

I dried myself on a thin and threadbare towel, and I put on a cotton nightshirt, the blue one this time, and then I went into the big, shabby bedroom and lay on the bed and tried to make some sort of sense of what I was thinking, and feeling, and wishing.

Arno, I wish you were here. I do try not to think about you too much, but I wish I could tell you all this, and I wish I could look into your blue eyes and know you were thinking about it. I would know you were using your wonderful brain to look for answers because I had asked for your help.

I never told you how exciting that was for me, Arno. I never told you. I know women find physical strength exciting in a man, and I've felt that, too. But when I could see you thinking, and I know just how fine your brain is, my Arno, and you were thinking for me, I would just melt inside, I felt as if my whole body was warm, liquid fire.

I wish. I wish I could ask you why I feel so guilty. I wish I could ask you if there are any answers.

Why don't I feel angry? He's trapped me in this guilt and this worry but all I see is the grin he gave me when I challenged him to make that lazy cob gallop. And he let me ride Barbarian: why is that so important? Why does the treachery and the trickery seem small compared to the way he nodded and Morry climbed down from that wonderful horse?

Arno, I think I'm praying to you.

I wish I knew what to do.

15

Arranging a mortgage on the forge was not complicated, but it did take time. I listened to the woman at the building society telling me of her difficulties, because it was, technically speaking, a commercial property, and because of its age, and because even the cottage had been built rather earlier than was generally preferred by her organisation, and in the end I interrupted her.

'Should I go somewhere else?'

She was sure some arrangement could be made. She simply wanted to explain, she said, why it might not be possible to borrow on the full value of the property.

I no longer really cared.

I was losing it. My home, the place I loved, I was losing it. Soon it would no longer be mine.

I had tried, once or twice, to picture my life beyond the forge, when strangers had taken it from me, but I couldn't do it. It was as though there was a high, black wall across the road ahead that represented my life.

I would exist beyond that wall, but not in any way that mattered.

Still, I could feel no anger against Jake.

'It'll give me the time I need,' he said. 'Darling, it'll be all right, I promise. You won't lose the forge.'

He'd spoken of his bad luck, and I had tried to sympathise. Yes, there had been bad luck, but there always was; nothing ever ran smoothly all the time, did it?

He'd been impatient with what he'd seen as my lack of understanding. He'd only just stopped short of calling it my stupidity.

'I suppose Mickey wasn't bad luck?' he'd almost shouted.

'How many of your young horses have been killed or injured in accidents over the last ten years?' I'd asked, and he'd looked at me, his expression blank with incomprehension.

He'd never answered the question.

Could he really not see that accidents should play a part in planning? He must have known they did happen, that sometimes horses were lost, or their potential value reduced.

To raise the money, the forge would have to be surveyed, and valued, and then the building society would make me an offer, provided all the other factors were in order.

'We haven't got time,' said Jake angrily. 'What the hell do they mean, it's going to take time? How much bloody time?'

I didn't know.

'Well, why didn't you ask? Ann? Why didn't you ask?'

Because I hadn't greatly cared. It hadn't seemed to matter. I was losing it; the time scale was irrelevant.

I left him stamping around in the yard, and I walked back to my home, unlocked the big doors, and went in.

There was a black iron butterfly stuck to the wall with a piece of dried-out putty. It was the first thing I'd ever made of iron, when I'd been six or seven years old. Uncle Henry had held the piece of molten metal against this anvil with those tongs, and I'd hit at it with a hammer, I couldn't remember which one.

Will they take my tools?

He'd said it could be the forge mascot, and he'd stuck it to the wall. It fell down sometimes, because the putty became brittle in the hot, dry air, but I always put it back again, and remembered, as I did so, the pride I'd felt when he'd named it.

Uncle Henry's forge mascot, and I'd made it.

Well, it could stay. It had no meaning outside these walls. Whoever took the forge could throw it away, put it in the scrap iron bin for Mick Jacobs when he came to collect whatever there was in the way of bits of worthless metal.

The telephone rang, and it was Jake. Would I please go and tell the bank manager I was raising a mortgage? Otherwise we wouldn't be able to pay the wages this week. Get him to extend the loan. The money on the forge can cover it.

'Yes, all right,' I said, but then there was just a small flash of rebellion. 'Jake, if you think I'm simply handing the money over to you to spend as you think fit, you're wrong.'

I put the telephone down, and when it rang again I switched on the answering machine, and listened indifferently to his angry words.

The bank manager also seemed indifferent. The overdraft had been beyond the agreed credit limit for some time. Also, he hadn't, in fact, been given any authority to discuss the stable's business with me, although Mr Brewer had told him I was taking a partnership.

I nodded. I wasn't even looking at him. I didn't much want to discuss the stable's business. I wasn't very interested.

He coughed.

'I think perhaps you were a little ill-advised,' he said gently.

'I wasn't advised at all. The ten per cent was a present.'

There was a long silence, and when I glanced up at his face I thought I saw something of sympathy, and even understanding.

'Difficult for you,' he said at last. 'I do see that.'

As I rose to leave he held out his hand, and he grasped mine for a moment.

'Mrs Brewer, if there is any way in which I can be of assistance, to you personally I mean, I would be pleased to help.'

'I don't want to lose the forge,' I said, and his face went blank.

What could he do? He knew the situation. He was helpless, too.

Mrs Brewer, he'd called me. Mrs Jacob Brewer. I supposed one day I would get used to it, it would cease to raise the mild jolt of surprise. Oh, that's me. Mrs Brewer, my name.

But I didn't like it. I wanted to be Ann Mayall.

And when I got back that evening just as Toby and the driver of a hired horsebox were leading two dark bay colts across the yard, my first thought was that I wanted my old name back. I did not want to be Mrs Jacob Brewer, of the Jacob Brewer who bought ringers from Dominic Mont-Blering, and obligingly lost them as half-trained geldings at a local auction.

'Do you think you can do something about those pasterns?' Jake asked that night, and I told him I'd see him burn in hell before I'd lay a finger on either of his ringers.

'And if anybody asks me I'll tell them, yes, I know where they came from. Dominic Mont-Blering sold them to Jake, and Jake had them gelded and sent to auction without name or description, so have your own story ready, Jake. I've told you mine.'

'I can't afford to pass up the money.'

'Can you afford to pass up your reputation?'

We never did discuss my conversation with his bank manager. We spent the rest of the night exchanging threats and abuse, and I locked myself into one of the many spare bedrooms, telling Jake I was right on the verge of shopping him to the Jockey Club myself.

I'd always liked his honesty, and he'd thrown it away.

233

'I might keep those colts,' he said the next morning when we met in the kitchen. 'They're not bad. Might make hunters out of them.'

'How are you going to pay for them?'

He'd thought I was bluffing when I'd said I wouldn't hand over the money. I looked across at him, and he was staring at me.

'Didn't you get the loan extended?'

'You can pay the wages this week.'

'Pay the . . .?'

And then he began to rage at me.

'How the hell do you expect me to get this business back on its feet? How am I supposed to pay Dom? Out of the fucking petty cash?'

'I don't care how you pay Dom. I'd prefer it if you didn't pay him at all. Send them back again. You're certainly not paying for them with my money. Them or any other horses from him.'

'I've told him I'll take them. I've given my word.'

He was shouting at me.

'I've got to have the money, Ann. Get that through your stupid thick head, I've got to have that money.'

'Then sell some horses. Sell Barbarian, that should raise it.'

'Ann. Listen to me.' His voice was quieter now. 'Come and sit down, and listen to me. Please. Just listen.'

I sat at the table as he'd asked, and I waited, but he had nothing more to say. He could only reiterate that he had to have the money. He'd promised Dom, so he had to have the money.

'You're not having any of mine.'

'I'll sell that bloody old mare of yours, then!' he yelled at me, and I got to my feet.

'Have you ever heard of the Married Women's Property Act?' I asked, recalling a phrase from a long-forgotten school history lesson, and then, aghast, I heard myself add,

234

'If you sell Lyric, so help me, Jake, I'll beat the *shit* out of you.'

I rode Lyric back to the forge that afternoon, feeling sick and ashamed of myself. I'd have to sell Lyric myself before we went bankrupt. I couldn't let her go to an auction. Too old for a serious rider, too difficult for a novice: who would buy my old friend?

Perhaps I could give her away, if that was allowed.

That afternoon I placed a nail wrongly, and lamed a pony.

'I'm so sorry,' I said to the owner. 'Oh, I am so sorry.'

He was more astonished than angry. He wanted to know what had happened, and I tried to explain. There were no excuses.

Such a stupid mistake. How could I have done that? I would, of course, pay the vet's bill. Of course. He should send it straight to me.

Uncle Henry. I'm not only losing the forge, I seem to be losing the craft you passed on to me, the care you instilled into me. I am so sorry, so very sorry.

That evening Jake was wary, speaking softly, almost obsequiously.

'Would you look at Deckhand's pasterns, please, Ann?'

'No.'

'I think they're hurting him.'

He knew I wouldn't leave an animal in pain, but I didn't believe him. The colts had only arrived on the previous evening, and he certainly didn't know Deckhand well enough to judge whether he was in any discomfort from a disability that had, if his stable lad was to be believed, been a problem for most of the season.

'Oh, Ann, please!'

'Unless you're planning to geld them yourself with your penknife, you've got a vet coming out this week. He can look at your damned ringer's pasterns.'

For the rest of the week we hardly spoke to each other,

simply saying what needed to be said, and then falling into a hostile and sullen silence. The vet came out to geld the colts, and Jake tried to tell me what he'd said about Deckhand. We were in the kitchen at the time. I was drying up after breakfast, and when I'd finished I hung up the cloth and walked out. Jake had still been speaking.

He threw something at the door as I closed it behind me.

I opened it again and looked down at the floor, at the saucepan lid lying on the linoleum, then I raised my eyes and gazed at the man I'd married, considering him.

My husband.

A little older than me, dark curly hair beginning to go thin on top, brown eyes deeply set into a prematurely lined face.

He shifted his feet, looking embarrassed.

'I didn't mean it to hit you. I wouldn't do that.'

Was he the sort of man to be violent towards a woman? Had I been smaller than him, would he have thrown something at me before the door had been closing behind me?

'Look, I'm sorry.'

Some people live and work with animals because they need something to dominate, and they can't dominate other people. I hadn't thought of Jake as being one of them. No, I decided, he's not like that. His staff do as he tells them without resentment. They seem to like him.

I'd liked him, too.

'It won't happen again, Ann. I lost my temper, I'm really sorry.'

He'd been a friend, and he'd been honest. I'd thought he was truly an honest man. But it's easy to be honest when there's no pressure. It's easy to be generous, when there's enough money and no need to worry. It's when things go wrong that you learn the truth.

I realised I was still looking at him. His face had turned crimson; he was no longer just embarrassed, he was becoming angry.

I went out of the kitchen and closed the door behind me.

It was my own fault. I shouldn't have married him. I was almost beginning to forget why I had.

I drove to the forge that morning and threw open the gates and the doors, made up the fire and set out my tools.

For the moment at least I could be myself here, and here I would use my own name, not his. I am still Ann Mayall, blacksmith and farrier, and I will not be Ann Brewer, Mrs Jacob Brewer, I will not.

Garth Michaelson was the first to learn of that decision when he came later that day to collect a new coupling for his trailer. I hadn't seen him since Jake and I had come back from Brighton.

'Hello, Mrs Brewer!' he called as he jumped out of his car.

'Mrs Brewer isn't here,' I answered, smiling at him. 'Mrs Brewer can be found in the early mornings and late evenings at the stable yard. Ann Mayall works at the forge, as she always did.'

Garth raised his eyebrows, but he was still smiling.

'Fair enough. Can you come over and do the bull's feet some time this week?'

Garth would not keep that little titbit to himself.

'What's this I hear about you calling yourself Mayall?'

A belligerent demand from Jake two days later.

'It's always been my name. I'm keeping it for work.'

He thought about it, frowning, staring down at his boots as he did whenever he was unsure of something.

'Like using last year's hacking jacket for working days?' he offered a few moments later, trying a smile.

'Like keeping something good for important occasions,' I replied, and the smile vanished.

'Christ,' I heard him mutter. 'Two fucking horses, and we're halfway to the divorce court.'

He sent them to the auction a week later.

It made no difference to the facts, but the atmosphere

between us did lighten a little once they'd gone. I moved back into his big bedroom, into the double bed, and I tried to pretend I liked the way he groped at me, liked the surprisingly heavy weight of his body on mine, liked the routine, the words, the sensations. I tried to feign excitement, I did try. I tried to respond, but I could feel my body turning away from him, a sort of dry withering. Come on, come on.

Soreness: I felt sore, and stiff.

'There's something wrong with you,' said Jake.

'I know.'

Could the friendship survive? Neither of us had ever professed love, but there had been a good friendship, and I'd valued it.

'I think I'll stay at the forge for a few days. The cottage needs airing, it's smelling musty.'

'Oh, Ann. Ann.'

He looked genuinely upset. He was shaking his head, gazing into my face. Then he smiled, something of a plea in the look in his eyes.

'Let's go out for a ride this evening. Lyric and Baba? Would you like that?'

We tried. We were friendly to each other, we rode together when we had time, we talked about the horses and Jake's plans for them, but it was always making the best of a bad job, and we both knew it.

Usually, I slept at the big house, but there were times when the craving for solitude became too much. Then I'd stay at the forge. I'd telephone Jake, say I'd been kept late, I was too tired to drive back. See you tomorrow, or maybe the day after because there's a lot to do tomorrow, I might stay on and try to get it finished.

It was on one of those evenings that Gwen came to the cottage, knocking formally on the front door and saying, when I opened it, that she hoped she wasn't disturbing me.

'Not at all,' I said, and then, because I had liked her so much, 'Won't you come in?'

238

She was very uneasy. She found it difficult to look at me directly, and where once she would have thrown herself onto the sofa and grinned at me, this time she waited until I gestured at it before she sat down.

But she did come to the point immediately.

'It's Chrissie. She's depressed. We've done all we can for her. She's making herself ill, Ann.'

Gwen drew a deep breath before looking me straight in the eye for the first time, and adding, 'And we're afraid for the baby.'

I was sitting back in my armchair, and I stared down the length of my legs at my crossed feet, at the last of the evening light shining on my boots.

What am I expected to do about this? I wondered. Are they asking me to help them save the baby Peter's fathered on Chrissie? I tried to push away the feelings of anger these thoughts always raised when they came into my mind.

Chrissie had been my friend.

Gwen was watching me, waiting for me to speak. I recrossed my legs and cleared my throat.

'What do you want me to do?'

'We want you to talk to her. You two used to be so close. She's feeling very alone, Ann. Peter can't help her with this. You might.'

I remembered Chrissie working in my garden, muttering happily to herself as the dark soil crumbled under her busy hands, sunshine on her brown curly hair, or the rain slicking it against her wet face. I remembered the serious look in her eyes as she studied the young plants, the little nod with which she signified her approval of their progress. There had been joy in her smile as she brought the beautiful vegetables into the kitchen, or as she packed them into her basket to take home for the children.

Until Peter had told me she was pregnant, I'd thought of Chrissie as one of the best friends I'd ever had.

I stood up and reached for my jacket.

'Come on,' I said.

We walked down to the village, Gwen hunched and silent beside me, and I guessed she'd been reluctant to ask for my help in the first place. My rejection of Chrissie had been vehement, and even though Peter would probably not have relayed the more hurtful of my comments, he would certainly have wanted to make sure she stayed away from me, rather than risk a confrontation.

Since then, I'd married Jake. I'd missed my friends, and there'd been times when I would have liked to have had friends.

The snakes had been painted again, green and yellow, the fangs of the one that struck out tipped with black. The leaves were autumn colours now, dark red and copper. I paused, and ran my fingers over my work, wondering who it was who repainted it so often, and what the changes signified, but Gwen had walked on ahead of me, and there was nobody else I could ask.

She was waiting on the platform, watching for me, and as I approached she pointed to one of the doors.

'That's Chrissie's room now. She's in there.'

She was asleep. The room was dirty and untidy, with discarded clothes lying on the floor and on the chairs. Chrissie lay on top of crumpled sheets and blankets, a stained skirt riding up over her thighs, a safety pin holding a gaping side opening together at the waist. She had one arm thrown up over her face, her head turned towards the window, and her hair was tangled and matted.

I moved some books off a chair and sat down. I'd let her sleep. I had nothing to do that really mattered, I could wait for Chrissie.

She seemed to have this room to herself. Most of the women shared rooms, because space was quite limited, but there was only one bed here, and there were no signs of anybody else's possessions.

It was a nice room, I realised, as I let my eyes wander

around it. The dark varnish had been stripped from the old wooden panelling, and the wood had been bleached. There were stencilled patterns on the walls, pale and lively, cream-coloured roses with light green leaves, and the same pattern appeared on a roller blind that was half lowered over the window, the roses in peach this time, the leaves a little darker. The reflected light caught a wide mirror on the side wall, and the colours were warm and peaceful.

It was more than a nice room. It was lovely.

Glory had done this room for Chrissie.

It was only gradually I became aware of it. I looked at the creamy roses, the way the colour blended so perfectly with the faint swirling patterns on the ceiling, and found myself wondering how she'd done that, how she'd achieved the cloudy look using only the different tones of the paint, and why it was so restful and satisfying.

I imagined her sitting sideways on the stepladder, painting the ceiling, comparing tones and colours, working quickly and confidently, knowing exactly what effect she wanted, and how to achieve it.

Then I wondered why she had done it.

Chrissie stirred on the bed, sighed, and was still again, her breathing even and slow.

Glory had done this room because she liked Chrissie, and wanted her to be happy. It was affection and friendship, the desire to please, and Glory had done it for Chrissie.

I couldn't stay any longer. I felt too ashamed.

I'd judged everybody. I'd been self-righteous, and condemnatory, I'd taken some sort of Victorian moral stance and I'd been so utterly blind to the truth I hadn't even understood the love underlying everything I'd learned.

What I'd seen as a cheap and sordid compromise had been quite simply an answer to everybody's needs, and it had harmed nobody. It was I who had done the damage.

Not Peter, not Chrissie, just me. I'd poured my dirty-minded scorn on their happiness, and hurt all the people I'd loved.

I wondered if I had any right even to hope for their forgiveness.

16

She came two days later, very early in the morning. I found her sitting on Uncle Henry's bench when I went out to open the forge and light the fire. She looked ill. Her skin was cold, clammy with sweat, her hair still tangled and unkempt.

'Morning sickness,' she said, trying to smile. 'I threw up on the compost heap.'

'Where better?' I asked, and she started to cry.

I took her into the forge, and I lit the fire as quickly as I could, turning on the fan and sitting her on the anvil, which was as close as I could get her to the warmth. I wrapped my thick jacket around her shoulders.

'Aren't you happy about the baby?' I asked, and she looked up at me, her eyes swimming with tears.

Then she started to talk.

She was incoherent, jumping from one idea to another, trying to explain, sometimes trying to apologise, until I stopped her. She kept breaking off what she was saying, going back to something she'd told me earlier, or thought she'd forgotten to tell me, so it was only gradually I began to understand.

When she'd thought Zack would kill her she'd been frightened, but in the end she'd accepted it. She would die, and that would be the end. And perhaps, if the religions were right, she might see Luke.

She'd started to dream about him. Not about the way he'd died, but everything else, and every morning when she woke up she'd remember the dream, and the idea that she might see him again grew stronger and stronger. At the same time she didn't think she deserved to see him, because she hadn't stopped Zack from killing him.

'How could you have done that?' I asked, and she didn't know, but there must have been something she could have done. There must have been some way she could have saved him.

She would only know when she was dead whether she would be allowed to see Luke again. She'd known it wasn't right to think in that way, and yet she couldn't stop herself. There would be some sort of judgement.

Then all her friends had wanted to help her, because they'd been so worried. She knew her ideas about Luke, and judgement, were wrong somehow, and she was afraid of telling anybody about them, in case they thought she'd gone mad. However, as she saw it, it had been Zack who had killed Luke, and if he sent her to Luke it would be some sort of atonement. It was right that Zack should atone, and it was right that Chrissie should be with her little son. So in the end she'd accepted the idea of Zack killing her.

I listened to her explaining this dreadful logic. I could only think she'd seen it as a way of making her own death bearable, because Chrissie loved life and she had believed Zack meant to kill her.

Then Zack had died.

Chrissie stopped talking, and buried her face in her hands. There was nothing I could think of to say to her, so I waited, and at last she was calm again.

'All I could think was, I'm not going to see Luke.'

There was a very long silence. I thought she was crying again, but she was still and quiet, as though the hurt was

244

too deep for expression. Then she raised her head, and looked me directly in the face.

'I can't talk about Zack's death,' she said.

'All right.'

The day of the inquest had approached, and Glory and Peter had come to see me, and had come down to the railway station, too. Hilda had helped Glory. Not with medicine, nothing like that, but there were ways they were all learning. It was like Chinese medicine; it was a bit like the acupuncture theories, only they didn't use needles.

Glory said it helped her. That, and massage, which they also did, and talking. Maybe it was the talking that helped most.

'Glory talked about you. She loves you.'

Before she'd listened to Glory, Chrissie had always seen me as big and strong, and she'd had some idea it made me invulnerable. She hadn't known I was shy. She hadn't known I hated meeting strangers because the quickly disguised look of amazement still hurt, even after half a lifetime. A woman pays a high price for being big and strong, and Chrissie understood. If she did?

She looked at me questioningly, and I smiled, but when she wouldn't look away from me, I nodded.

One evening Glory had had to go back to the theatre where she was working, and Peter had stayed on. It had been quite late, and they'd made coffee, and when the others had gone to bed they sat at the table, and Chrissie talked. She'd always found it easy to talk to Peter.

When she'd told him about Luke she'd cried. She hadn't cried about Luke for a long time, but the tears had come, perhaps because she still believed she might see him again. Peter had put his arms around her and held her, just to try and comfort her, nothing more.

He'd told her he wanted children, and Glory couldn't have them because she'd been mutilated. Maybe she hadn't ever wanted them. But he did. He wanted children desperately, even though the conventions held that men weren't supposed to feel like that. It was only women, according to the myths, who were desperate for children when they couldn't have them. Peter loved Glory. The idea of not living with her was unthinkable. He'd tried to put the idea of children out of his mind, and not to care, but sometimes he felt as if he was grieving for his unborn children. They'd never existed, never would exist, but that made no difference to his sorrow.

Peter and Chrissie had both been the victims of violence. Her child had been killed by it, and the woman he loved, who might have been the mother of his, had been maimed. It had formed a bond between them. They understood each other in a way other people could not.

'I told him I wanted children, too, and we just stood in the kitchen holding each other. We both knew what would happen. Not then, I don't mean right then. But it was all right. Everything was going to be all right.'

Glory had never said anything to Chrissie about Peter and children. She'd come down to the railway station and she'd sat in Chrissie's room and asked about favourite colours, and what sort of things made her happy. It had never been like a discussion with an interior designer, nothing like that at all. Flowers, and sunshine, she'd said. Summer, when things grew. The colour of an apricot when it's just ripe, and wild honeysuckle in old woods.

'Do you like this room?' Glory had asked, and Chrissie laughed, looking at the hideous brown varnish she'd always meant to paper over.

Peter and Chrissie had gone to Norfolk for a week. They'd stayed in a very old hotel in the country, and for Chrissie it had been as though she was coming back to life.

'He doesn't love me,' she said, 'but he treats me as if he does. Ann, I do love him. I know what Glory means to him. I just want him sometimes, for a little while.'

When they'd come back Chrissie had found her room at

246

the railway station transformed. A company from London had done the preparation and the main part of the work, but Glory had finished it herself, the stencilled roses that were just the colour of wild honeysuckle in old woods, and ripened apricot. The cloudy ceiling, like summer.

'That was how she told me it was all right,' said Chrissie, and I nodded. Yes, that was exactly how Glory would have told her.

'I hoped I wasn't pregnant, because I wanted another week in Norfolk with Peter. But I was. Well, he came down and stayed for a night about a fortnight after I told him. And he took me to France once, when he was filming there. He behaves as if he loves me. Only, he doesn't say so.'

Arno, I thought. You never told me you loved me.

'He won't lie to me. He wants me to be happy, but he won't lie.'

She was looking warmer. There was a little colour in her cheeks, and her face was no longer damp with sweat.

'I'm going to make coffee,' I said. 'Would you like some?'

She didn't say very much while we drank our coffee. She was afraid she'd already said too much. I had to prompt her before she'd continue.

'Peter wants you to be happy,' I said. 'Are you?'

She shook her head, and then made an abrupt gesture.

'It's not him. He's super. He does everything. I mean, all he can, for me. He does it.'

'Gwen said you're depressed,' I suggested after another long silence, and then I looked at her, and saw there were tears on her cheeks again.

'Sometimes I feel lonely,' she whispered. 'Then I think I'm ungrateful. Everything I wanted . . .'

Tears again, but this time she brushed them aside.

'It's just, it's not like a home, and he's not there. All . . . Everything's all together there. I love the way Glory's done my room. But it's just a room. I know it's stupid, but I'm pregnant, I'm allowed to be stupid.'

247

A valiant little laugh, and the tears brushed aside again.

Chrissie could live here, if she wanted.

Everything seemed to go slow, and the thoughts turned in my mind, away from Chrissie and a baby, away from Peter and Glory, and back to the forge. Grey and dismal, and slow, and I checked the words I'd almost offered.

I was losing the forge.

I'd have to live somewhere, and she could live with me.

What could I offer her and a baby? If I couldn't offer a home here, what was there that I could offer?

There was a crack in the corner of one of the sandstone blocks with which the forge was paved. A big shire stallion, Fanfare, had stamped a massive hoof, and I'd heard the stone break. I was looking at the crack, and remembering. The huge black horse, his coat glossy with health and loving care, the caution with which I'd handled him and his brother, not because they were vicious, but because a friendly nudge from one of those magnificent animals could be as punishing as a kick from a hostile one.

Everywhere I looked there were memories.

Scorch marks on the workbench, I knew many of those scars. I'd made some of them myself. The way dust drifted down from the rafters, and the particular swirl when the draught from the door caught the motes, the sunlight through the window, so it was like a pale gold spiral in the air, until the draught died, or the sun went in.

Two old leather and brass head-collars hanging from an iron hook in the corner, mended in big stitches with black linen thread, knotted hard against the scuffed brown leather. Uncle Henry had done that with a brass awl, and Aunt Ruth had twitched an eyebrow at him and said he should stick to iron, leave the embroidery to the experts.

They'd stared at each other across the space of the forge, she with her hands on her hips, he with his arms folded, both of them glowering from under lowered brows, the way they did when a battle of words and wits was about to be joined, and I'd sat gleefully on the anvil waiting to hear who would win this time. Waiting to see who would be chased around the forge and out into the garden.

Where will I live when I lose my home?

'Ann?'

'Yes, Chrissie, sorry.'

'You looked sad.'

'Old memories. What can I do to help?'

There was nothing. She'd like to come back and work in the garden again. Could she cut some flowers to take back with her?

'Take anything you like.'

Jake was supposed to be sending some horses later that morning, and I had some ornamental work to do for a woman in Cheltenham, two plant stands and a trough with her initials worked into them, but I wanted to be with Chrissie for a little longer. I telephoned Jake and told him to bring the horses that afternoon. He tried to argue with me. I told him I was busy, and he said I didn't know what the word meant, I should try doing his job.

'I'll drive you back,' I said to Chrissie when she came to the forge door with a couple of handfuls of flowers, and although she tried to protest she did look relieved. She'd said she had no difficulty in sleeping, but nevertheless she seemed very tired to me.

Bess met us on the steps and smiled at me. She seemed to have forgotten her hostility, and I was glad. I liked Bess.

'We've painted your snakes again,' she said, and I looked at the gate.

They were vipers, with vivid markings down their backs and the suggestion of a glint in their eyes. They were all dangerous now, even the two who faced each other.

Chrissie went in search of something in which she could arrange her flowers, and Bess asked if I'd like something to drink.

249

'Why's everybody so edgy?' I asked, and she looked surprised, and then shrugged.

'You noticed. Well, you would, wouldn't you?'

No, I thought, I wouldn't. Who keeps painting the iron snakes?

But I said nothing, and Bess told me a few things had gone wrong. Sal had gone, poor silly cow. I knew she'd spent the best part of her life looking after her father? Yes, well, they'd all thought it was because her mother had died, but it wasn't. Her mother had left when Sal and her brothers were in their teens. Anyway, her mother was ill, and it was Sal who had to look after her. The two brothers were much too busy, queuing up for the dole and going to football matches.

'Oh, come on,' I expostulated. 'That can't be right.'

But it was. Sal had gone to South Shields to look after her mother, giving up her job and her friends and looking forward to a few more years of being an unpaid drudge. Another girl had been there for a while, I hadn't met her, had I? Rosie? I hadn't missed much. Dozy Rosie. She'd gone back to her boyfriend, because she was afraid if she didn't he'd find somebody else to do his washing and cook his meals. By the time Rosie had left, Chrissie was pregnant.

They'd all tried to stop Sal going, but nobody had said much to Rosie.

'Peter pays a bit extra, so she can have that room to herself.'

'Poor Sal,' I said.

'I suppose so. She's just a born victim. Don't you think so?'

I hadn't considered it in that light. Perhaps she was right. There are people who always seem to be unlucky. It was unfair to blame them, even if they did make their own bad luck.

Jake.

'Sal can come back when her mother dies,' said Bess.

'Is she dying? What's the matter with her?'

'Senile dementia. She's not that old, actually. Sal's only in her thirties, I don't think her mother's much more than fifty. It must be a horrible thing. I hope she doesn't know what it is.'

Bess went on talking about senile dementia.

We were sitting in the old ticket office where they'd had the party. There was sunlight coming through the window. I noticed they'd painted the floor. It was a clever design. The floorboards had been stencilled, or something like that.

When her mother dies. Senile dementia. Not that old.

They were bright colours in that pattern on the floor-boards, quite eye-catching.

'Bess?'

She stopped talking and looked at me. Her bright, blonde head was turned a little, and the expression on her face was disturbed, sort of surprised. Had there been something in my voice?

'What is it?' she asked.

'Bess, do people *die* of senile dementia?'

'Well, yes. Yes, they do. Ann, what's the matter?'

She had an interesting face, Bess. Not beautiful, not really. It was a bit too square for that. Intelligent, though.

'Alzheimer's disease?' I asked. 'Is that what she's got?'

Bess nodded, and the bright sunlight, and her bright, blonde head, and the bright painted patterns on the floor-boards swirled and spun, and I laid my head down on the table and wrapped my arms around it, and tried to stop the swirling, and tried to make myself think.

Oh. Oh, dear God, if you exist, how could I have been so stupid? I didn't know. I didn't even ask.

I didn't know. I didn't know.

'What didn't you know?' demanded Bess, and I realised I'd spoken aloud.

I hadn't even asked.

251

I sat up, pushed the hair away from my forehead, and looked across the table at her.

'I didn't know people died of Alzheimer's,' I said. 'I thought they just . . .'

How do you say that? I haven't got any words now, not for what's happening.

'How long does it take for them to die?'

How long have I got?

She didn't know. It would depend, wouldn't it? It would vary, from patient to patient. Surely?

Another stupid question, with no answer. Stupid, stupid. Maybe I've got the damned thing, too.

'Ann, what the *hell* is the matter?'

'Give me a minute. Just a minute, Bess.'

Where do I start to think again? It's all changed. So stupid. She's dying, he'll come back. He'll come back.

'Ann?'

'No. Let me think. Let me think.'

I can't think. So, just focus. One idea at a time.

He'll come back.

Start there. He'll come back, he'll come back. One day, he'll come back. One day, Arno will come back to me.

I thought I'd lost him for ever. I thought I'd never see him again. But I will, he'll come back to me.

I lifted my head, and I looked across the table at my friend Bess, and I smiled at her, seeing the concern in her face.

'It's all right,' I said. 'I'll explain some time. Not today. "Thank you" will have to do for today.'

'For what?' She was laughing at me.

For lifting the despair. For giving me back my spirit. For making me realise I must not lose the forge, because if I did he wouldn't know where to find me. One day he'd come back to that old place, and it must be me who greets him, not some stranger.

So, Bess, thank you. Everything has changed. The clouds

252

are leaving my mind now. I have to think, and think clearly, and find a way to save my home.

And I will. I will do it. No matter what I have to do, I will save the forge, and I will be there when Arno comes back.

17

Jake brought the horses to the forge himself that afternoon, and said he and I had some things to discuss.

What he meant was that his work was to take priority
over that of my other customers, and I was to set anything
else aside if he needed me to shoe his horses, mend his
gates, or carry out any of the huge range of repairs the
stable might need. He was doing his best to make the business profitable, and he had a right to expect my support,
particularly since he had made me a partner.

'It's about time you understood what's involved here,
Ann.'

I didn't want to quarrel with him. If I was to save the
forge I'd have to work alongside Jake, not against him. I
couldn't let him drag me down, but I couldn't keep all the
anger out of my voice.

'It's about time you started making some economies,
Jake. One of them is finding a cheaper farrier. You can't
afford me. Do you know how your account stands here?'

He knew. He knew he owed me a lot of money now, and
he knew I'd have stopped working for him altogether had
we not been married. I'd probably have been taking legal
action against him.

He sighed.

'Oh, Ann. I can't do this without your support. Seems to me every time I ask you to do something you make excuses.'

I looked at him, standing beside the chestnut mare, so despondent and worried, and my anger died as quickly as it had arisen.

'What's happened this time?' I asked, and he shrugged.

The final demand from the feed merchants had arrived. How much longer was the building society going to take with the forge? Shuffling papers was driving him crazy, and so was making excuses to his creditors.

'I told you,' I said. 'I'm not handing the money over to you.'

He didn't seem to have heard me.

I took the mare's halter rope from him and tied her to the ring. She was a lovely animal. She'd probably be one of the next to go, at about two-thirds of her value, leaving the stables with one less class horse, and a higher proportion of what Jake referred to as no-hopers.

'Send the no-hopers to auction,' I'd urged him on more than one occasion. 'They all eat. Why feed the rubbish?'

Because he'd never recover what he'd paid for them at auction, let alone what they'd cost him since. Most of them had been bought on the same terms as the piebald, a customer saying he'd take a horse if Jake would accept the outgrown pony, the disappointing hunter, the clumsy hack, whatever it was the new purchase was to replace.

A few hundred pounds in the bank, and Jake had had little option other than to accept.

Word had got around. Go to Jake Brewer, he'll take your useless wreck off your hands if you buy something better. You can haggle, too. He'll always drop his price.

I'd be very sorry to see this mare go. I'd watched Morry Old working with her in the jumping paddock, and she'd been good.

'Dom's getting impatient for his money,' said Jake as I finished her and untied the rope.

'What money?' I demanded, but he ignored me and walked up the ramp of the horsebox to fetch the next horse, leaving me wondering how it was that Jake owed Dom money; if Dom was to repay Jake for each horse he bought and lost, why was it Jake who was in debt?

But the following day, when I drove the van into the stable yard as two men were carrying Uncle John's clock out of the front door under the direction of a small man in a camelhair coat, I didn't bother to ask the questions. I drove the van across the front of the big Volvo, blocking it in, and jumped out shouting at them to take my clock straight back into the house before I called the police.

Jake came to the door, saw the van, and vanished back into the house. The man in the camelhair coat turned an expression of mild amazement in my direction, and told me he couldn't be expected to wait for ever for his money. He and Jake had a gentleman's agreement.

'If you're Mont-Blering, what you have is a criminal conspiracy,' I retorted. 'If that clock isn't put back immediately I'll call the police. Then you can try to explain how the debt arose.'

'I doubt if your husband would appreciate that,' said Mont-Blering. 'Or doesn't that matter to a wife these days?'

The men with the clock were still standing on the steps, looking from one to the other of us, waiting to be told what to do.

I walked past Mont-Blering, and pointed at the door.

'Back where you found it, please, and do be careful. It's extremely valuable.'

'Mrs Brewer, please try to be reasonable about this. I have your husband's permission to take the clock in part payment of his debt.'

'Part payment?' I turned towards him, and he took a step backwards. '*Part* payment? You're not by any chance an antique dealer, are you?'

'I'm under no obligation to tell you . . .'

'Put the clock back in the house,' I said to the men. 'I know you're not to blame for this, but if you try to take that clock you'll be committing a crime.'

'Oh, this is ridiculous. I told you, your husband gave me permission.'

'To take my clock?'

'Sorry, sir,' said the older of the two men, 'but if it is the lady's clock I think she's right.'

'You're not paid to think. Put it in the car. If that van isn't moved, Mrs Brewer, it's you who'll be committing the crime.'

The two men lowered the clock to the ground, and the older one folded his arms and glared defiantly at Mont-Blering.

'I'm not a criminal. I'm not stealing the lady's clock.'

'Thank you,' I said. 'Thank you very much.'

I picked up the clock and carried it through the door and down the hall to the place where it had stood. I would have to take it to the forge later; it was obviously not safe here.

There was no sign of Jake. The kitchen door stood open. I locked it before going out into the yard again, ostentatiously closing the front door behind me. The three men were sitting silently in the Volvo, and as I moved the van Mont-Blering started the engine.

I watched them drive away, and then I went back into the house. I was shaking with rage, and with the reaction to the confrontation.

'Where's Jake?' I asked Morry Old when I found him in the tack room. He shrugged, and wouldn't meet my eyes.

It would be bailiffs next, and I wouldn't be able to stop them taking anything they wanted.

I had to co-operate with Jake. Until I managed to raise enough money to buy myself out of the partnership I had to keep his business running, and I couldn't do it if he and I didn't work together.

Glen and Tommy were standing in the stable yard, talking to each other. Glen hid a grin when he saw me, turning away and sliding a hand up over his face.

Idle grooms are just as expensive as idle horses.

'You two, I've got work for you,' I said. 'This yard's a mess. Let's get it cleaned up.'

Paint from the store, rakes and hoes, there were tools all over the place, and none of them had been properly maintained. They were rusty, with splintered handles. There were old paintbrushes as hard as boards, but I found a few that were still usable. There were half-empty drums of bleach under some planks behind the barn, alongside weedkiller and paint and hoof oil, all jumbled together, most of it completely useless. Parts of the place looked like a rubbish tip. It was no wonder people thought they could haggle with Jake.

I set Glen to scrubbing the water stains off the walls of the house and the stables and Tommy to hoeing the gravel and raking up the weeds. Glen was sullen about it, muttering to himself about being a horseman, not a fucking decorator, but Tommy seemed quite happy. He was a nice lad, and even though he didn't ride very well he worked hard, once he'd been told what to do.

There were five men working on the place, including Jake. They were usually busy, but it's mornings and evenings that are the working times in a stable. The afternoons are quiet, with nobody under too much pressure.

I found Toby Joliot dozing in the hay store, and prodded him gently with the toe of my boot until he opened an eye. He sat up hastily when he saw me.

'Are you really tired, Toby?'

He shook his head.

'There are some loose-box doors that need work. They look a mess. Could you sort out some boards and do something about them?'

He wasn't enthusiastic, but he climbed to his feet.

Dear Toby. I could trust him to help, and I might need an ally.

When I went back into the yard Glen had gone. The bucket and brush stood beside a damp wall which still showed mildew stains. Tommy, raking the gravel, didn't look up as I approached.

'Where's Glen?'

'Said he had to mix the feeds, Missus.'

Mixing the feeds was an evening job, not something to be done in the early afternoon.

'Have you seen Jake?' I asked, and he shook his head.

It was time for me to go back to the forge. I had hunters to shoe that afternoon, and I still hadn't finished the plant trough.

'It's looking better already, Tommy,' I said, and he managed a small doubtful smile.

I wrapped the clock in an eiderdown and laid it carefully in the back of the van. I suspected it should only be moved by experts; I might need to call one in to adjust it if I upset the delicate balance of the mechanism.

How much money did Jake owe Mont-Blering? And why, if he was to be paid for buying in the horses and losing them?

Gambling debts.

Just as I had known the horses were ringers, I knew the answer to this second question.

How could he have been so stupid? But at least now I understood how he had been trapped into agreeing to buy the horses.

The girl who brought the hunters that afternoon was known as the Land Rover around Anford, because she was thought to have slept with every farmer in the district. I rather liked her, but I was puzzled by her reputation. She was short, with wide, square shoulders and the powerful arms that come from hours of strapping horses day after day. She had curly ginger hair,

259

which was inclined to turn frizzy in the rain, and small, deep-set eyes.

It wasn't the conventional appearance of a successful seductress.

The first two horses were routine work: removing shoes, cutting back overgrown hooves, replacing shoes. But the third horse had a huge red bow tied to his tail, a ridiculous confection of glittering crimson curls, and the Land Rover was grinning at me as she led him towards me, inviting me to share the joke.

'Kicks,' she shouted in explanation, as though I wouldn't know what a red ribbon denoted. 'Like a fucking pile-driver, actually. Got your bulletproof knickers on, have you?'

'Never go anywhere without them. What about you?'

She shrieked in delight, and the horse threw up his head, his eyes wild.

'Takes too bloody long to get out of them,' she bawled. 'You should be all right with this bastard if you nail his other three feet to the floor.'

Why does everybody send me the kickers? I wondered as I tied the rope up close and bent, a little warily, to lift a hind foot. I hadn't handled this one before, so I didn't know what he was likely to do, or even whether the red bow was the Land Rover's idea of a joke.

It was just as well I'd been ready. As my hand ran down his leg he suddenly pulled it up under his belly, and then it flashed out towards me, a high and scything kick with a great deal of muscle behind it.

'Fucking hell,' squealed the Land Rover as I jumped back out of the way, and the horse flattened his ears and bared his teeth at me. 'Are you all right? Did he get you?'

'No,' I answered. 'Look, let's just keep it silent for a moment, shall we?'

He'd only just missed. I'd felt the wind of the hoof as it had flashed past my thigh, and I found I was breathing a

260

little more quickly than usual. It had been a kick with purpose.

The Land Rover raised her eyebrows, perhaps in resentment at my tone, but she folded her arms, and stood back to watch.

He was a liver chestnut with a smudged white star on his forehead and one white sock. He was quite a small horse, and I hadn't taken any particular notice of him until I'd started to study him, to give myself time to recover, and to think. There was nothing about him to catch the eye. He was just a normal horse.

I drew in my breath, and once again moved towards him, talking to him quietly, hoping he wouldn't catch my unease.

'What's his name?' I asked.

'Polaris. Polly.'

'Polly,' I said quietly. 'Polly. Stand, boy. Good boy, stand, Polly.'

He lifted his head again, rolling a white-ringed eye at me, and a hind foot rose, menacingly.

'Leave it,' said the Land Rover, unfolding her arms and stepping forward. 'Just leave the bastard. Charlie said, give it a try, but don't let anybody get hurt. He's off to the auction next week, and bloody good riddance.'

'Charlie?'

I was looking at the little horse again. Just a normal little horse, and for normal you could almost substitute the word faultless. Not one to catch the eye, Polaris, until he lashed out, or until you took the trouble to look at him. He had a deep, compact body, a short back, and legs that would be straight and strong once the overgrown and wry hooves had been cut back and levelled.

'Charlie Virgo. Look, don't chance it, he's a right bugger.'

Charlie Virgo liked show-jumping. He'd bought a good mare in Ireland three years previously, and with her had been more successful than his own horsemanship had merited.

261

Since then, he'd been trying to find more good horses on which he might add to his victories.

Polaris lowered the menacing hoof and gave a short tug at his rope. I moved closer to him, to his shoulder, where he could neither kick me nor get his teeth at me, and I laid a hand on his withers.

'Polly,' I murmured. 'Polly.'

He knew he couldn't reach me. His ears were flattened against his head and he shifted his weight from foot to foot, but he didn't try to kick.

'Charlie bought him in Holland, stupid prick,' yelled the Land Rover, and Polaris jerked his head at the sound of her voice. 'Thought he looked like a jumper. Bloody thing was doped, I reckon.'

I slid my arm over the little horse's shoulder, leaning against him, leaning over him, and then my other hand was on his neck and I pushed myself off the ground so I was lying across him and he had my full weight on his back. He jerked his head again, but he settled his feet, and although he kept a watchful eye rolled back in my direction and his ears were still flat against his neck, he didn't try to get rid of me.

'Watch it,' warned the Land Rover.

As my feet touched the ground I stooped, continuing the same smooth movement, and before the horse could raise his dangerous hind leg again I had his forefoot off the ground and bent back against my knee. Carefully, gripping it tightly, I turned my back to his head, and then I had his hoof up between my knees, held fast.

'Does he bite?' I asked, and the Land Rover laughed shortly.

'Doesn't bite me, the bugger. Doesn't get near enough.'

The feet were neat, broad and round, but they'd been grossly neglected. The hooves grew over the edges of the shoes, and they were uneven, longer on the medial side, the inside of the feet. He wouldn't be able to move properly like that; his feet would swing outwards.

262

'How long has Charlie had him?'

'About six months. Look, don't bother with him. Last time he was shod they had to tranquillise him. He fell over, nearly squashed the farrier flat. Stupid sod.'

I want this horse, I thought. I want him soon, before anybody else notices.

I let the foot down and stepped aside quickly, before the horse could lash out again.

'I'm not working on his hind feet,' I said. 'If I do the front ones it'll just be a giveaway.'

I knew I was playing a dirty trick on Charlie Virgo, and he'd done me no harm. I could have tied up a foreleg with a stirrup leather. But then, so could the last farrier, and he'd probably tried. We don't usually resort to tranquillisers before we've exhausted all the other methods.

The Land Rover nodded briskly, and together we untied the little horse's rope, and she led him back into the horsebox.

'Tell Charlie I'm sorry,' I called after her.

I am sorry, Charlie, I thought. If I can, I'll make it up to you one day.

That evening I tackled Jake yet again about the part-exchange horses. I wrote down the money he'd allowed for them against the sales, I calculated, as closely as I could, the cost of their keep and multiplied it by the weeks they'd been in the stable, and I asked him just to look at my figures, please, Jake, just look.

Instead, he shouted at me that I knew nothing about buying and selling horses and I should keep my bloody nose out of his business. Also, where was that fucking clock? Dom would have him kneecapped if he didn't pay up, and it was the clock or some money: my choice.

'I'll choose your kneecaps,' I answered, and I walked out of the house and drove back down to the village.

There was a new batch of rhubarb wine at the old railway station, and there was sympathy. My friends listened to me

263

as the darkness fell and the candles were lit and, because it was quite cool, the stove began to glow red in the corner.

Then there was silence, long silence, lowered eyes, and the feeling of thought, working, and merging, and dividing again, and now and then a head would turn, and eyes would meet briefly.

'Could you run Jake's business?' Gwen asked at last.

I'd wondered. He'd spoken the truth when he'd said I knew nothing of buying and selling horses. Jake had inherited a thriving concern, and he'd run it successfully until there'd been a major setback. Then he'd failed to solve the problem, and he hadn't been flexible enough to avoid it.

I didn't know enough about horses to buy and sell them. I'd have to delegate.

Polaris. Polly. Little liver chestnut with the smudged star and the white foot, who didn't catch the eye. Unmanageable and dangerous, needing expert handling if he was to become what I thought I'd seen. Morry Old and Jake Brewer.

'Ann?'

'Yes,' I said. 'Yes, Gwen, I think I could.'

Delegate, but to whom? Who knew enough?

'If Jake were to die, would you inherit?' asked Bess, and they were all watching me; all the eyes were on my face.

Suddenly, I was frightened.

'I'd inherit a packet of trouble,' I answered. 'The bank would foreclose. I'd lose everything. The forge, everything.'

'Isn't there insurance to cover that?'

Who had asked that question? I hadn't seen, somebody sitting in a dark corner.

I was breathing too fast, and I could hear my heart beating. Panic was what I was feeling.

'No!' I said, but I wasn't answering a question. 'No!'

They were all looking at me, their eyes steady on my face.

I'd told them he'd tricked me and trapped me. I'd told them he wouldn't listen, he just wanted my money, that I knew it wouldn't be enough. That I would lose the forge because of Jake Brewer.

'No,' I said again. 'Leave him alone.'

Bess shrugged, and Tam whispered something to her neighbour, who smiled at her, half a laugh stifled behind a lifted hand.

'What would it take?' asked Gwen. 'How would you do it?'

Sell off the useless horses. Sack Glen and Tommy, and run the place with Jake, Morry and Toby, and casual labour when we needed it. Concentrate on good youngsters to get the name of the stable back into the headlines. Make the place look smart.

I threw up my hands, and sighed.

'I don't know,' I said. 'What do you think?'

'Ask Glory,' said Hilda immediately.

'She doesn't know anything about horses,' I protested.

'She knows about money. She's a whiz-kid. Ask her.'

But when I got back to the house that evening, Jake told me, in a tone of casual defiance, that he'd written to Peter to ask him if he'd like to invest in the stable.

'Lend you money to pay your gambling debts to Mont-Blering, you mean?' I responded, trying to suppress my anger. 'Why the hell should Peter help you? And where did you get his address?'

He'd looked it up in my diary. Why shouldn't he look in my diary? What secrets had I got in there that I didn't want him to know about? Come on, answer me that. What was I trying to hide?

Disgusted, I walked away, and that night I slept in the spare room again.

'Why shouldn't I ask my own brother-in-law for help?' Jake demanded over breakfast the next morning. We'd greeted each other, and then, until he voiced the question, everything else had been polite and meaningless conversation.

'How many horses are you sending to the auction next week?' I asked in response, and Jake threw his knife down onto the table in a show of exasperation.

Later, he telephoned me at the forge and apologised.

'I know I shouldn't have looked in your diary. I didn't want a row with you.'

I couldn't think of anything to say. Jake wouldn't believe Peter wasn't rich. Peter was a film star, and all film stars were rich. No matter how often I'd tried to explain to Jake that Peter was an actor, and hardly ever in films, Jake clung stubbornly to his belief. Peter's name had appeared on posters, after the word 'starring', so Peter must be a film star, and therefore almost unimaginably wealthy. Why shouldn't he want to invest in the stables? He might even buy a racehorse. Film stars often owned racehorses, it was good publicity.

I telephoned Peter later in the day and warned him about Jake's letter. He sounded as friendly as ever, as though our bitter quarrel had never taken place.

'I don't think I can help,' he said. 'How much does Jake need?'

'I've no idea. He had some idea you might buy a racehorse.'

Peter laughed.

'Lyric, maybe,' he said. 'If I ever did buy a horse I'd want to ride it myself, not pay somebody else to have all the fun.'

That evening I told Jake that Peter didn't think he'd be able to help, and Jake accused me of trying to sabotage his efforts.

'Why would I do that?' I asked wearily. 'As you keep reminding me, if you go down I lose the forge.'

'I wouldn't go down if you'd stop being so stubborn. Have you got the money from the mortgage yet?'

I had. It was in my bank account, and I would not hand it over to Jake.

'Glory might be able to help,' I said. 'She understands money, Jake. She could advise us.'

Jake didn't need advice, he snapped. He needed time,

and he needed money. What the hell would a backstage worker in a theatre know about horses? And answer his question, please. Had I got that fucking money?

'She knows about *money*,' I repeated. 'She knows how it works. She knows how to make money.'

'So why isn't she rich?'

'She is.'

Jake turned and stared at me.

'She could help us,' I repeated. 'She could tell us what to do.'

'You said she was a theatre designer,' he accused.

Glory, a partner in one of the biggest design companies in the north of England, was indeed a theatre designer. She'd won awards for her designs. Could Jake understand anything about Glory?

'How much has she got?' he demanded.

'I've no idea.'

'Would she lend me money? Enough to pull me through?'

He'd walked back to me, and was leaning across the table, staring into my face.

'Jake, why should Glory lend you money?'

'Not me. Us. Because she's your sister, of course. Ann? *Would* she?

Ask Glory, they'd said. She's a whiz-kid, and I'd wondered, why didn't I think of that?

But I'd always paid my own way, and I'd been proud of it. At the beginning I'd had no money, and a big dog to feed. Uncle John had lent me a shotgun and shown me how to use it. Plod and I had lived on rabbits and winter vegetables from the garden.

'Ann?'

Were I to ask Glory to buy the forge, and rent it to me while I worked my way through the shaming experience of bankruptcy, she'd do it, I thought. Then she'd probably give it to me.

'Ann, will you *answer* my *bloody question? Will she lend me the money?*'

Mortgaged, lost, sold, rented, given back.

A fist slammed down onto the table, and I looked up into Jake's enraged face.

'No,' I replied calmly. 'No, Jake, I doubt if Glory would lend you the money. I told you, she understands money. She'd want to know how you intended to repay it.'

18

Jake telephoned Glory and told her he was in danger of being kneecapped if he didn't pay a gambling debt. He hadn't wanted to worry me, he said, because there was nothing I could do.

Glory doesn't gamble, and she didn't become successful by believing everything she was told. Her questions to Jake were sharp and unkind, and then she telephoned me.

'How much did he ask you for?'

'Fifty thousand. Ann, how true is this?'

I felt sick with rage and shame.

'I've no idea. Glory, listen, I wouldn't give fifty *pence* to save the rat's kneecaps.'

But she'd questioned Jake, and she knew I'd mortgaged the forge.

'I don't want money from you,' I said. 'I dropped myself into this. I was stupid.'

'Do you love him?'

'I've got customers here,' I lied. 'I'll talk to you later, if that's all right.'

I do not love him. I used to like him, and now I'm beginning to despise him.

He was shamefaced and belligerent when I spoke to him that evening. It was my fault. If I'd given him the money from the forge he wouldn't have had to ask Glory. Anyway, I'd said she was rich: what was so wrong with asking a rich relation for help? Why had I mentioned Glory at all, if I hadn't meant him to ask for help?

Hilda had been right about Glory, she is a whiz-kid. If anybody could rescue Jake's business it would be Glory.

'What does she know about horses? How did she get her money, anyway? You said she was a theatre designer.'

Why is the life-jacket this colour?

'She invests,' I said. 'She buys into businesses, and helps run them. She starts things. She knows how to make money.'

'How did she *get* it?' he insisted. 'To start with?'

I didn't know. There'd been a trust fund and she'd taken control of that when she was in her early twenties, but Glory had been well on her way by then. She'd earned a good salary; perhaps she'd saved.

'Will you let her help us?' I asked.

'Oh, don't be stupid. She's already said she won't.'

'Not money. Advice.'

'What bloody advice? I don't need advice, I need money, and I need time.'

I don't want your life-jacket, I'll stick to swimming.

I went back into the kitchen and tried to interest myself in cooking something for an evening meal. Jake followed me.

'Have you got the money for the forge?'

'Yes.'

I wouldn't look at him. I kept my eyes down over the vegetables I was washing, and I listened to him as he shifted from foot to foot by the door.

'There are some horses I ought to buy. In the auction, you know, the one you talked about.'

'I talked about you sending the no-hopers, not buying more.'

An outraged and uncomprehending protest.

'Why did you raise the mortgage if you won't let me use

270

the money? What the *hell's* the *point* of all this? What do I have to *do*?'

I listened to him, listened to the silence that followed his outburst, and then I turned my head and looked at him.

'Is that a serious question?'

He looked tired, scruffy, almost despairing. Why couldn't he at least wash himself? Who could believe in Jake Brewer like this?

He was shaking his head, not a negation of what I had asked, but in genuine incomprehension. Why wouldn't I help him? Why wouldn't I give him the money? Wasn't that why I'd raised the mortgage?

'Let Glory look at the business,' I said. 'Listen to what she has to say.'

'Look at the business?'

His head turned, he was staring through the kitchen window at the big stable yard where Tommy was strapping the chestnut mare, where the wind blew dust and wisps of straw across the cobbles. Where the wood Toby had nailed across the bottoms of the doors was still raw and unpainted, and water stains discoloured the flaking whitewash.

Jake was bewildered.

'Look at the business? What is there to see? She doesn't even *like* horses. She said so.'

'The books,' I explained. 'The accounts, Jake. The money side of it. Let her look at it, and then listen to her.'

'If I do, will you let me have the money?'

All right, I'll grab the life-jacket if you'll do something for me, fair exchange.

'I'll do whatever Glory advises, but Jake, there's a horse in that auction I want you to buy.'

'Huh?'

'The Land Rover brought him over a couple of days ago. He won't cost much, and I want you to buy him.'

He was looking vaguely bewildered.

'You want another horse?'

'No, Jake, not for me. For the stables, to train up and sell. He's hard to . . .'

'*Christ.* Is there anything else you want? Would you like to take over schooling the youngsters? Do you think you can do *that* better than me, too?'

He was genuinely angry. He strode up and down the room, shouting at me, pointing his finger at me, accusing me. Taking everything over. Not supporting him. Antagonising his staff, Glen's a groom, not a cleaner, and Toby's not employed as a carpenter. I wasn't even a good *rider*, let alone talk about training.

'Not me,' I interrupted. 'He'd be far too difficult for me. But you and Morry . . .'

He and Morry had the young hunters to train, not some bloody wild scheme of mine, waste of time and money. And, talking about money, what about those two horses at the auction? The ones *he* knew about, the ones he and Morry could train up, if I would be so *very* obliging as to pull my financial weight in this endeavour, start *helping* him a bit instead of being a fucking millstone.

I could think of nothing to say to him. Even when he stopped shouting at me and stood by the kitchen table, red in the face and still angry, I could only look at him, and wonder.

At the beginning he'd known he'd tricked me. His present to me of a share in the business, a partnership, was a fraud, a way of forcing me to mortgage the forge in order to save him. Had he truly forgotten? Had he now convinced himself he was the injured party? Did he believe the money I was withholding was legitimately his?

'Sell the no-hopers,' I said at last, turning away from him and putting the pot of potatoes on the hotplate. 'Use that money to buy the horses you know about. I'll do whatever Glory advises.'

He walked out of the kitchen, slamming the door behind him, and I looked at it, wondering how I could ever have been foolish enough to marry him. The friendship I'd felt for him was little more than a memory.

'How much do you think these horses will cost?' I asked that evening, and Jake narrowed his eyes as he looked at me.

About three thousand each, he reckoned. If necessary, he should go up to four, but he hoped not more than three. Why?

'If I give you the money for them, will you let Glory look at the books? And will you listen to what she has to say?'

He pulled a face and said he couldn't see what a theatre designer would know about running a stable. But yes, he'd listen. He wouldn't promise to do what she said, mind. However, those horses might turn the trick, get his name back in the winners' lists. Two smashing five-year-old geldings with hunting experience, just a bit of work and they'd be ready for the three-day events. A bit of dressage, he could get treble what he'd paid for them. At least.

Keep your stupid lifebelt, I've found two good straws.

'Glory knows about money,' I repeated, hopelessly. 'Listen to her, Jake. She knows about money, and it's money that's your problem, isn't it?'

It was lack of money that was his problem. All he needed was time, he insisted. Time to get his young horses in shape for competition, then he'd be back on top. But at least I was beginning to see sense, so perhaps there was some hope.

Glory said she could come next week, and of course she'd look, but Jake was right when he said she knew nothing about horses.

'Do you know about all the other businesses you've invested in?' I asked, and I could hear the smile in her voice when she answered.

'I tried to learn about engines once,' she said. 'I learned it's difficult to get dirty oil out from under the fingernails. That's all I can remember of my lessons.'

I laughed.

'If I don't know the business, I make sure I know the people,' she added, and this time there was no smile in her voice.

We both knew Jake, and there was no reason to smile.

All that week I waited for him to say something about sending horses to the auction, some sort of concession in exchange for my promise, but there was nothing. He'd agreed to allow Glory to look at the accounts, and that was it.

Was that enough, for six thousand pounds?

He sold two horses that week, a young cob and a mare he'd bought because she hadn't lived up to her owner's expectations as a jumper. She would go to a stud farm in Yorkshire. Eight hundred pounds for the cob, and three thousand for the mare. At least he hadn't taken any horses in part exchange.

'Can you use some of that money for the two horses in the auction?' I asked, and Jake was horrified.

'You promised!'

'All right. But, Jake, will you look at the horse I want you to buy?'

He shrugged. Yes, he'd look.

He did look at Polaris, one brief glance, and then he moved on.

'Too small.'

'Jake!'

He turned back towards me with an expression of exaggerated patience, and sighed.

'Jake, please take me seriously. Please, look at that horse.'

The little liver chestnut was just as good as I'd remembered. He was compact and powerful, and his bone structure was as near to perfect as anything I'd ever seen.

'Ann, he's too small.'

Jake was right. Successful competition horses are usually quite tall, and Polaris was small, probably not much more than fifteen and a half hands high. A good big horse will beat a good little one. Jake had often said the minimum height for a jumper is sixteen and a half.

But there had been exceptions.

'Some small horses have won,' I said, and he sighed again.

Polaris laid his ears back and swung his head up and down as Jake unbolted the door of his box, and Jake glanced at me, mildly amused.

'I haven't got life insurance.'

'I'll have to do something about that. Be careful, he is nasty.'

Jake's more agile than I am, and quicker to pick up the warning signs, so Polly's hind feet crashed into the wooden barrier rather than into Jake. He caught the horse's head-collar with nothing more than a muttered curse, and jerked his head at me to come and hold it.

'Charlie Virgo bought him in Holland,' I said. 'He's too much for Charlie. Don't worry about the feet, I can deal with that.'

'Why didn't you, then?'

Because I'm dishonest, I thought, but I said nothing, and Jake looked amused.

'Learning the tricks, are you?'

He was running his hands down the horse's legs, and I warned him again, and tried to keep Polly's attention away from him.

'Jake, do be careful.'

The scything kick flashed past Jake's hip as he twisted out of the way, and the horse half reared, his eyes wild and rolling, jerking at my arms, feet stamping and crashing on the wooden boards.

'Come on,' said Jake.

'Well? Is that it?'

'Ann, let's get out of here before he hurts you. He's a rogue.'

He made me leave the box first, standing between me

and the horse as I opened the door and slid through it. Polaris was thoroughly upset, tossing his head and striding around at the far side of his box, still wild eyed, and now sweating profusely. Jake glanced at him, shook his head, and turned towards me.

'Jake . . .' I began, and he put his arm around my waist. I was so surprised I stopped talking, and looked down at him.

He explained things I already knew, but he did try to make it clear, which was more than he had done before. The horse would have to be turned out to grass for at least six weeks, perhaps more, so that he would lose most of his condition, and become slow and sluggish, with a bit of a belly. Then he would have to be ridden, long and low, round and round a schooling ring, until he stopped trying to take hold and run away with his rider, which is what he did, wasn't it? Well, wasn't it? Too hot to hold?

'Yes,' I agreed.

Hour after hour of time-consuming, laborious work for a skilled rider, who could be doing something else. After that, he'd have to be schooled over jumps, which would take weeks. About two hours every day, and it would have to be him or Morry, and they both had other things to do. In the end the result would be a smart little hack, or maybe a hunter, because the horse was just too small to make an eventer or a jumper.

'He can jump,' I said. 'That's why Charlie Virgo bought him, Jake. And small horses have won.'

'He's not worth the risk,' said Jake, beginning to lose patience. 'He's not worth the time we'd have to spend on him.'

Seeing the look on my face, he relented a little.

'But you're right, he is a good horse. On looks, he's as good as anything here. But . . .'

He spread his hands, his head tilting to one side. Had he made it clear to me? Did I now understand why he didn't want the horse?

I had eight thousand pounds in cash belted against my ribs under my sheepskin coat. I'd told Jake that four thousand for each of the beautiful young thoroughbreds was the top limit, and he'd argued, but I'd refused to give way. Any horse is a gamble.

'How much did you get for the bloody forge anyway?' he'd demanded that morning.

'Seventy-five thousand.'

With that much money he could pay off all his debts except the mortgage, some of the interest off that, and still have enough left over to get some good horses. Horses to make people sit up and take notice of Jake Brewer again. What the hell was I playing at? He was working his guts out, day and night, to make the business a success, for both of us, Ann. Not just for me, for both of us. Why are you buggering me about like this? I don't understand. And now you're quibbling about a miserable few hundred for two of the best young thoroughbreds to come on the market for years. God all bloody mighty.

'Once Glory's seen the books . . .' I began stubbornly, and he shouted at me again.

'When the *hell* is she *coming*?'

That Friday, two days after the auction, staying overnight, but she had to be back in Birmingham on Saturday afternoon.

No more time to argue about Polaris, and anyway Jake wouldn't imagine I might have arguments to put forward. Jake had explained, and that was that. The subject was closed. No Polaris.

I followed him back to the auction ring, a dingy building like an outsize bandstand with boarded-up sides. An agent was bidding for the two horses on Jake's behalf; I couldn't see it would make a great deal of difference, but he'd insisted. If somebody saw him bidding for a horse they'd know it was a good one. An agent bought what he was told to buy; nobody could draw any conclusions.

They were splendid horses, tall and strong, with enough bone to suggest they could carry weight, and a look of lively intelligence. I listened to the auctioneer extolling the grey's virtues, his breeding, his potential, and I watched the faces of the crowd, interested and alert. This was not the sort of auction where classic colts changed hands for millions, but everybody wanted to see what the best horses here would fetch.

'Who'll start me at four thousand?' called the man on the podium behind the high barrier. 'Gentlemen? Ladies? Let's not waste time here, he'll fetch a lot more than that.'

'Ann, I've got to have him,' Jake breathed into my ear.

'All you get from me is four thousand for each horse.'

'Three thousand, then? Do I hear three thousand? Thank you, sir, with you. Three thousand I'm bid, three thousand. Do I hear three five? Three five?'

He'd started at more than twice what Jake had guessed, and it was another agent who was bidding.

'*Ann!*'

'Three thousand two hundred, the gentleman at the back. Three thousand two hundred, three thousand two hundred, thank you, madam, three thousand three hundred. Three thousand three hundred, against you, sir, do I hear three thousand five? Three thousand five hundred?'

'Four thousand, Jake.'

'Bitch. You bitch.'

People in the row in front of us turned and stared at us, and I looked back at them, coldly, until they faced the ring again.

'Three thousand five? Three thousand five? Three thousand *four*, yes, sir, new bidder. Three thousand four hundred, three thousand five, against you, madam, three thousand five hundred, do I hear three six? Yes, sir, with you, three thousand six hundred, three thousand six hundred, who'll give me three seven? Three thousand six hundred, do I hear three seven?'

'Just another five hundred, Ann. *Please.*'

Why was I being so stubborn? The horse pacing beside his groom was beautiful.

Every pound I spend will have to be paid back to save the forge. Every pound, and the interest.

'*Ann!*'

I will not. I will argue over every penny, until I know exactly what I'm doing, and that will be when Glory tells me.

'No.'

'Three thousand seven hundred, three thousand seven hundred, all done at three thousand seven hundred?'

The woman in the red coat was talking to somebody beside her, one hand held up, not in a bid, but a demand for time, and the auctioneer was looking at her.

'Against you, madam. Three thousand seven hundred, I'm waiting for eight?'

'Who's got it?' whispered Jake. 'Did you see, who's got the bid?'

'I don't know. I don't even know which one's your agent.'

'Keep your voice down!'

The woman shook her head, a wry expression of regret, and the auctioneer turned back towards the crowd.

'All done at three thousand seven hundred? Going once, going twice, last chance . . .' and the gavel cracked down onto its little stand.

'Sold to Jerome Marshall. Thank you, sir.'

Jake was grinning, savagely triumphant.

'*Got him.*'

The man in the dusty green anorak? Was that the one who'd bid on Jake's behalf? I hadn't noticed.

'Who do I pay?' I asked.

'I'll do it. That leaves four thousand three for the bay, OK?'

'No.'

'*Christ.* Just what are you going to do with that money?'

279

I didn't know. Pay it straight back off the mortgage, if that was what Glory advised. Bring in consultants, start up a rodeo, paint the roofs pink. Whatever she suggested, because she was my only hope, and maybe it wasn't only Jake who was clutching at straws.

I will not lose my home. I will not.

The filly in the ring was dancing, little hooves lifted high, her chin tucked into her chest. The crowd was enjoying her antics, and amused by the difficulties of the man leading her. She had a dished face with a bright blaze, and her pricked ears curled inwards.

The groom pulled her round in a tight circle, and she trotted for him, lifting her knees and curling her hind feet up under her belly.

Jake grinned as he watched her. She was flicking her ears and tossing her head, jerking at the rope, mischievous and flighty, a typical two-year-old Arab.

She was sold for seven thousand pounds, and a whisper ran around the ring. It had been a London agent, bidding by telephone. The little filly was going to Kuwait, to a stud farm.

'Shame,' remarked a woman sitting in front of me. 'Hope they won't be cruel to her. Arabs can be very cruel.'

I remembered the donkeys at the sanctuary, and I wondered what had happened to Polaris, to make him so dangerous and so panicky. I have an Arabian customer, a proud and silent man, who only ever smiles when he's looking into the eyes of his horses. Sometimes I seem to imagine they smile back.

The next group of horses were being sold by the orders of the executors of the estate of somebody. Jake pulled at my arm as the first of them was led into the ring.

'I want to talk to you. Outside.'

I sighed, but I followed him, and we went into the canteen, a dirty shack with a plastic counter, big stained tea urns standing on draining boards behind it, and two tired women washing up thick white cups and saucers.

Jake ordered two cups of tea, and then began to talk to me, but he had nothing new to say. He had to have the second horse, he was doing this for both of us, why couldn't I understand? Why was I being so stubborn and stupid? Was I listening to him?

'No,' I answered, 'but then you never listen to me, either.'

For a moment he looked puzzled, and I thought he would question me, but he simply repeated that this horse was one of the most promising youngsters in the county, maybe even in the country, he'd never have another opportunity like this. How could he get the business back up to scratch if I wouldn't back him? Why was I questioning his judgement?

'Four thousand is my limit for any horse,' I said. 'Unless Glory says . . .'

'Your stupid fucking sister!' he shouted at me. 'Your stupid fucking sister knows *nothing*. She's a stupid theatre designer, the stupid tart's *frightened* of horses.'

I left my tea on the counter and walked out of the canteen.

He caught up with me in one of the alleyways between the boxes, and once again seized my arm. I shook him off. I was very angry. People were looking at us, curious and amused, but Jake seemed to be oblivious of them.

'I'm sorry,' he said. 'Ann, I'm sorry.'

'You're a brat,' I whispered furiously. 'A spoilt brat, Jake, and I'm sick of you. I want, I want, I want, that's your entire thought process. Well, I don't give a damn if you get the horse or not. I don't give a damn. If he goes for less than four thousand, you get him, if he goes for more, you don't.'

I walked away, my feet squelching in the trodden mud, and left him standing, glaring after me.

There was a smell of tar and creosote, and it caught in my throat. It had started to rain, a fine drizzle, but the skies were heavy and grey, and soon it would turn very wet.

Polaris was still in his box, sweating and shivering. He

looked ill. As I leaned over the door he flattened his ears and swished his tail, his head swinging up and down. I guessed somebody had given him a tranquilliser, and I remembered what the Land Rover had said, that he'd fallen on the farrier when they'd last tried to shoe him. This wasn't a horse who could take tranquillisers. Sometimes they have the opposite of the desired effect, and the horse can turn berserk; and sometimes the horse collapses.

Idiots, I thought. Why didn't they check? They only had to ask. They'd never get him out of the box now.

'Polly,' I said softly. 'Polly.'

He was restless and distressed, sweat streaking his dark coat, and his legs were beginning to tremble.

Somebody had come up behind me, and without turning round I asked, 'Do you know where the vet is? I think he ought to come.'

'Oh, *shit*! Poor little bugger.'

Charlie Virgo. He looked genuinely concerned.

'Has somebody tried to tranquillise him?' I asked, and he shook his head, and then shrugged.

'He can't take them. But maybe they didn't know.'

I drew in my breath.

'Charlie, he can't go into the ring like that. I'll give you three hundred for him.'

'Come on, he cost me ten times that.'

'What's he worth now? Oh, go and find the vet.'

Nobody knew what Polaris had been given; nobody would admit to having given him anything. The young groom who'd brought him and the other horses from that stable looked a little too defiantly ignorant, and Charlie stared at him narrowly, but said nothing.

'If I don't know what it is I daren't give him anything,' said the vet. 'We'll just have to wait for it to wear off. I hope.'

'We could put straw bales around the walls in case he

thrashes around when he goes down,' I suggested. Charlie nodded, and told the groom to go and find some.

'Stupid bastard. Just for his shilling in the pound, taking a chance like that.'

Animals used to be sold in guineas, a pound and a shilling, and the shilling was for the groom, or kennel maid, or, for all I know, cattery assistant who'd looked after it. Some people, Charlie Virgo included, hold to the tradition.

Polaris was shivering violently. Every few moments he would stamp a hind leg and swish his tail.

'Three hundred?' I offered again. 'He's cats' meat if he's auctioned.'

The groom was hurrying back along the alley, trundling a wheelbarrow with four bales of straw balanced across it.

'There's more up by the car park,' he said. 'I'll fetch it.'

He looked worriedly into the box, clucked his tongue, and set off at a trot with the wheelbarrow.

'He's not a bad sort,' said Charlie as he opened the door. 'Just thick as a brick.'

Polaris reared as he went in, staggering back and stumbling as he came down. His eyes were wild. I threw the bales of straw into the box, and Charlie piled them against the walls, watching the horse as he did so, and backing away.

'Three hundred,' I said again, and Charlie shook his head.

'Eight.'

'I haven't got eight. I've only got three.'

The groom was back, breathless and red in the face, with more bales of straw. Charlie looked at him, then picked up the water bucket, sniffed at it, and threw the contents over the door, where it splashed heavily onto the soggy ground, drenching the man's boots.

'Fill that,' he ordered. 'And this time just put water in it, nothing else.'

'Sir.'

Polaris lashed out wildly, not aiming at anything, his

hooves clattering into the wooden wall. Sweat was dripping from his shoulders and neck, running down his forelegs. He kicked out again, and then staggered, stumbling down onto one knee. Snorting, he stood up again, but his legs were trembling more violently than ever.

'What would you do with him anyway?' demanded Charlie, piling the straw up into the corners of the box. 'He's not up to your weight, and you couldn't even get his shoes off last week.'

I didn't answer. I broke open another of the bales and shook it out, kicking it against the walls, packing it up as hard as I could to give some protection to the horse's legs. I could hear him breathing heavily, whether from fear or the effects of the drug I didn't know.

'I might have done,' I said at last. 'If I'd really tried. All right, Charlie, eight hundred, but I can only give you three now. I'll give you the other five next week.'

Polaris fell, heavily, onto his flank, and lay with his neck stretched out, shaking, his legs twitching. For a moment I thought he was dying, but then he lifted his head, and struggled to bring his feet under himself. Charlie was beside him before he could rise, leaning on his neck, pushing him down.

'Come and help me.'

The horse was powerless, hardly able to move, his eyes frantic with fear and bewilderment.

'Oh, Polly,' I said. 'Poor little Polly.'

The groom was at the door again, anxious and guilty, watching us as we struggled.

'Go and tell that vet we've found out what the tranquilliser is,' Charlie shouted at him. 'And then, Roberts, you make a lucky guess, do you understand?'

He looked across the horse's body at me, and nodded.

'Right. Eight hundred. And I wish you all the luck you'll need.'

19

Jake said the second horse had cost exactly four thousand, so he hoped I was satisfied. Would I be kind enough to hand over the money, and Jerome's commission.

'You can pay that,' I answered. 'It was your idea to use an agent. You pay him.'

He swore at me, and tried to argue, but I gave him all the money I had left, turned on my heel and walked away.

The vet had given Polaris an injection of something he hoped would act as an antidote to the tranquilliser, but there were no guarantees. The horse was still down, still helpless, hardly able to raise his head.

I sat on one of the bales of straw Charlie and I hadn't broken open, and I looked at my new acquisition, wondering if I'd gone mad. However angry I might be with Jake, however disillusioned and disappointed, I'd never doubted his judgement of horses, and he'd said Polly was a rogue, not worth the trouble. Hour after hour of work for a skilled rider, and even then he probably wouldn't be good enough.

'I only saw him jumping in an indoor school,' Charlie said after the vet had left the box. 'I'll know better next time. Mind you, Ann, he can jump. Five foot six, and there was a lot of daylight under him. God knows what he could clear if he wanted.'

Polaris raised his head again, and scrabbled ineffectually with his feet before falling back onto his side.

'Poor old Polly.'

I'd turn him out in the forge paddock with Lyric. She wouldn't like it, but she'd grow used to him after a while. Somehow, I'd have to make arrangements to have him transported, once he was fit enough to travel. In the meantime, he could stay where he was. Charlie had said he'd fix it with the auctioneers.

'I think your husband's looking for you,' and the catch of the door rattled. It was the vet.

'Thought I'd come back and have a look,' he added. 'Charlie's paid.'

'That was kind of him.'

My voice was tight and dry. Polly looked so helpless. He might die. Eight hundred pounds, and my handsome, dangerous little horse might die. He could be the gamble I'd lost before I'd even started.

Two weeks ago a Canadian had paid seventy-five thousand pounds for a jumper.

My daydreams of Polaris as a winner seemed more than merely far-fetched now; they were ridiculous. Could he recover from something as bad as this?

'If he pulls through,' I asked, 'will there be any lasting effects? Long-term damage?'

'I hope not.'

The vet was frowning as he listened through his stethoscope.

I hope not, too. What sort of an answer is that?

'I think I'd better give him something to help his heart. It's racing a bit. Tricky things, these sedatives, when they go wrong.'

If this were a children's story Polaris would live, and would be so grateful to me for saving his life he would allow me to ride him, and together we would win the coveted Challenge Cup. But I would be small and blonde and

286

pretty, and I certainly wouldn't be a blacksmith. If this were a children's story there would be a happy ending.

'Right, well, I'd better be off. Just keep an eye on him.'

And do what? Keep an eye on him, and do what if something happens? What should I do if his racing heart races faster, until it is hopelessly overstrained?

It was growing dark outside, and a few boxes down somebody turned on a light, a yellow bulb hanging from black rubber flex. Suddenly it seemed as if winter was here.

I cupped my chin in my hands and gazed down across the box at Polly, who shifted his head, stretching his neck. His nostrils distended every time he took in a breath, and his eyes were staring and white-ringed.

Jake was looking for me, the vet had said. What was his name? Sanders? Masters? I knew him by sight, from a practice the other side of Cheltenham. At least he cared about the horse, even if he did express his concern in a series of clichés.

It had been kind of Charlie to pay him. Now the horse was mine, the bills were my responsibility.

Polaris was sweating, and there was a cold draught beating through the wooden slats. I looked around to see if there was something with which I could cover him, and then I peeled off my jacket and laid it across his back and flank. He flattened his ears at my approach, and his head jerked.

'What are you doing here?'

Jake, standing in the door of the box, looking from me to the horse, puzzled.

'What's happened to him?'

'The groom put a sedative in his water. He can't take them.'

Jake clicked his tongue sympathetically.

'Charlie had to take him out of the auction, did he? Shame.'

I looked down at Polaris, wondering if it was wishful thinking that suggested his breathing was easier.

'We've loaded up the horses,' said Jake.

'Yes?'

'Weaver's Dream's a marvel, Ann. Look of eagles. I don't know why they took him out of racing, he didn't do badly. Glad they did, though. Toby's called him Frogface.'

I smiled. Toby always gave his favourite horses insulting nicknames.

'He hasn't decided what to call the grey. "The Greek", that's a damned silly name for a horse, and he's not sixteen three, he's seventeen. I measured him. I thought they'd underestimated, and I was right.'

'I'll build up his shoes,' I offered. 'Make him seventeen one.'

'Teach him to stand on tiptoe?' Jake was grinning.

'Plait his mane down over his withers?' I suggested.

'Ah, that's an old one. They all know that one.' Jake glanced down at Polaris again. 'He doesn't look so good, does he?'

'Better than he was,' I replied, perhaps a little defiantly, and by no means sure it was true.

'Yes? Well, look, we're all loaded up and ready to go, so, if you're coming?'

'I'm staying with Polly.' I drew in a deep breath, and looked across the box at him. 'I've bought him.'

He stared at me in silence for a while, and then frowned, more puzzled than angry.

'But I *told* you.'

How could I come through this encounter without it turning into a confrontation? How could I explain to him why I had done this?

'I didn't want you to tell me,' I said quietly. 'I wanted you to listen to me.'

Yet again, he didn't seem to have heard.

'I've forgotten more than you ever knew about horses.'

It should have been said angrily, but Jake was still euphoric about his two horses, so it was just words, mouthed as something to fill a silence, some sort of answer to assert his superiority.

'I don't think so, Jake,' I said. 'You know more than I do, but there isn't that much difference between us now. I'm a professional, too. My opinions aren't worthless.'

Polaris lifted his head, and this time it didn't fall back onto the straw. This time he managed to pull his forelegs underneath himself, and then he was scrambling to his feet, staggering.

'Look out!' Jake sounded alarmed. 'Ann, get out of there!'

My jacket slipped off the horse's back, and I stooped quickly to snatch it from under him, backing away into the corner as he tried to turn his haunches towards me.

'Oh, *shit*,' said Jake.

'Just shut up,' I snapped. 'God's sake, anybody would think he was a dragon.'

But I did watch the horse quite carefully as I slid round the walls of the box to the door, and Jake opened it for me.

'How much did you pay for him?'

'Less than I paid for The Greek. Or Frogface.'

'I only asked.'

It was true, he had only asked, and not in a challenging tone.

'Eight hundred.'

The grimace was a formality. Jake knew Polaris was worth more than that, even as a smart little hunter.

'He's not fit to travel yet,' I said, 'and he needs a rug.'

'Yes? And are you going to put it on him?'

But he was grinning at me, hardly even thinking about Polaris. Weaver's Dream and The Greek, the horses that would bring Jake's name back into the headlines, these were what was in Jake's mind.

'No. You are, with a little help from me. Or Toby.'

It wasn't difficult, and even Jake admitted he'd handled worse. The horse kicked out a couple of times. Jake caught the anxious expression on my face, and smiled.

'He's upset. I'd kick, too.'

The Greek and Weaver's Dream had been the peace-makers.

We left Polaris in the box at the market, and I padlocked the door. We'd collect him the next day, and take him to the forge.

'Eight weeks minimum,' warned Jake. 'And don't try to feed him sugar lumps.'

'Go teach your grandmother.'

'Go ride your broomstick.'

The euphoria lasted for two days, until Glory came and spent a day looking at the accounts. Jake, tolerant to the point of paternalism, brought ledgers and cash books and piled them onto the dining room table, saying she should ask if there was anything she didn't understand. Then he went out to the stables, and a few minutes later he led the first string out to exercise. He was riding the bay, Weaver's Dream.

Too many horses, said Glory that evening, and the turnover was far too slow. Also, and this in a tone of studied neutrality, she didn't think the Inland Revenue or Customs and Excise would be convinced by the figures.

Jake dismissed that comment as though she hadn't made it, and said horses were his business. They were his stock, if that was how she would like to put it. He had to have them in order to sell them.

'I've done three case studies,' said Glory. 'Horses called Milord, Gravy Train and Tessa. Would you like to see them?'

Jake seemed nonplussed. He knew the horses; what did she mean, case studies?

'You allowed five hundred pounds against a horse you sold to take in Milord. What would you sell him for now?'

'About eight. Give or take fifty or so.'

'He stands you in at four thousand.'

Jake flatly refused to believe her. Glory shrugged, and left the papers on the table, leaning back in her chair.

'He's been turned out most of the time. That costs nothing. Four thousand! Apart from winter feed, he's hardly cost me a penny.'

'Hasn't he been ridden?'

'Well, now and then. Just to keep him up to the mark. Nothing much.'

'Which one's Milord?' I asked.

'Heavyweight hunter, white-legged bay with a blaze. He's half Clydesdale, quite well bred. He's not a bad horse. He had a corn, you put a three-quarter bar shoe on him.'

'I think I've shod him more than once. Haven't I?'

'I'll probably sell him this autumn. He's not that old.'

Jake was becoming defensive. Glory was still sitting back in her chair, rolling her familiar green pencil between her fingers, apparently absorbed in the play of light on the thin bar of painted wood. The damning papers lay on the polished table in front of her.

'He's been out at grass all summer. Now you mention it, he should start working again, it's time to get him fit.'

Glory glanced at him, but then back at the pencil, and she said nothing.

'Four thousand,' muttered Jake. 'That's just daft. Anyway, now I come to think of it, he's a bit better than eight hundred. He's got good breeding.'

'How old is he?' I asked, and Jake pushed his chair away from the table saying we could sit here nattering if we liked, he had evening stables to do.

There were forty-eight horses, Glory explained after he'd gone. Every penny of expenses in this business was related to keeping them, with the possible exception of the competitions. So the arithmetic was simple. One month's expenses divided by forty-eight gave the average cost of keeping one horse. Around that figure you could put the minimum, which was a pony out at grass, and the maximum. Did I know how much Barbarian had cost this business?

'Oh, he's an exception,' I protested. 'He's like advertising.'

'I know,' she said, and she smiled.

When Jake had been successful he had not bought bad horses, or old horses, or anything that couldn't be sold again within a few weeks, or at the most at the beginning of the next season. When his success at the top of the market had failed, he hadn't adapted his methods. If a good young horse had hurt himself in training, the vet had been called, and the expense had been absorbed. He had continued with that policy, but now it wasn't only good young horses in the stable. Seventy pounds here, and a hundred and fifty there, and the horse that had cost a hundred and fifty pounds in vet's bills had only been sold for three hundred.

'He should have gone to the knackers,' said Glory.

'For an infected knee?'

She shrugged.

'Twenty-five pounds from the knackers, or give him to a horse sanctuary and let them worry about him.'

Catching sight of my expression, she added, 'Business, Ann. Making money. Morals or ethics, or sentiment, comes outside that.'

Jake's business methods had worked with first-class horses, but he'd continued to use them when his market had changed. Less than half the horses in the stables were worth the money he was spending on them. Unless he changed those methods, there was no hope.

'Even given time?' I asked. 'Now he's got Gorsedown he can train his young horses again. It's as good as Ashlands. Once his name's back in the winners' lists, he should be all right, shouldn't he?'

She reached for an old account book, turned a few pages.

'Frederick Hoffmann,' she said, 'has bought seven horses in all from Jake, at least one a year. He bought the last one three years ago, and paid nine thousand pounds for it. Since then, nothing.'

'Well, that's typical, I think.'

'Exactly. Has he given up riding? He's found somewhere else to buy horses. He may be perfectly happy with his new dealer. Does Jake imagine he'll be throwing his hat in the air when Jake's back in the headlines? "Oh, great, Jake Brewer's back, now I don't have to deal with John Smith any more"? I doubt if it'll happen. It takes time to build a market, and Jake will have to start again.'

She reached across the table and turned on the lamp. Light flooded down onto the papers, the neatly stacked books, some of them old leather with gold embossing, their corners scuffed. The history of the business, in cold figures. Account books spoke to Glory as clearly as a limping horse spoke to me.

'Two ponies sold to a riding school six weeks ago, one for seventy pounds, the other for a hundred and ten. Three years ago, the cheapest horse from this stable was seven hundred and fifty pounds, apart from an injured one that went to the knackers. There were two ponies, three hundred and five hundred.'

She looked up at me, curious.

'Is there such a big distinction between horses and ponies?'

I nodded, and she returned to the book.

'There's not one record of Jake taking in a horse in exchange, not the way I read it. He's making an actual loss on three out of every ten horses he sells now.'

She looked across at me, frowning.

'Am I telling you anything you don't know?'

'I hadn't realised it was that bad.'

'No. I'm surprised he's kept going this long. It can only be because people like him. Well, he is a likeable person, isn't he? On the whole. What about this gambling debt he talked about?'

'I don't know.'

She was watching me, rather more steadily than I liked.

Her hands were motionless on the green pencil now, holding it poised over a sheet of paper.

'There are some figures I can't understand. There are customers who've sold Jake horses he's sold on almost immediately, at a loss. In auctions. This isn't what he usually does. And the names sound like fiction. Christopher Grey. Martin Jones. About five or six of them. It started just over two years ago. What's this about?'

I told her about Dominic Mont-Blering and the ringers, and she listened, silently, nodding her understanding. She didn't seem in the least surprised, let alone shocked.

'He's the one Jake says will kneecap him.'

'And will he?'

'I've no idea.'

That did startle a brief laugh out of her.

'I'm glad you're not lying awake worrying about it.'

We relapsed into silence again, and I thought about her comment. If it had been Arno who'd been in danger I'd have been frantic. I didn't want any harm to come to Jake. So why was I indifferent? Bad things did happen to people who didn't pay gambling debts; perhaps he'd been telling the truth.

'Uncle John thinks you can get out of this partnership,' said Glory after a while.

'How?'

'He said it was undue influence. You were tricked. A judge would throw it out.'

It took a few moments for the idea to sink in, and then I stood up abruptly, and walked over to the window. There were lights on in the stable yard, and I could hear the squeak from the big wheelbarrow. Somewhere, there must be an oilcan, surely? Hooves clattered on concrete, and somebody laughed. More laughter, three or four people speaking at once.

For better for worse, for richer for poorer, in sickness and in health. I'd married him. I'd made promises.

294

'I don't break my promises,' I said quietly, and Glory asked, 'What was that? What did you say?'

'I don't break my promises.'

What a strange situation this was. I'd married him for reasons that seemed remote now. I'd married a friend I'd wanted to help, who'd been desperate for my help, who'd needed far more than I'd been prepared to give. A trick, a trap, and now there was a way out.

Break your promises, because he tricked you.

For richer for poorer, keeping only unto him.

I'll break that promise. When Arno comes back, I'll be unfaithful to Jake. I don't love him and he doesn't love me, but we understand what this place means, because I too have a place I love.

'You'll lose the forge,' said Glory.

'I will not!'

How can I avoid it? Jake won't change. He'll harass me for the money, and I'll cling to it for as long as I can, letting out little bits here and there on deals that seem possible to me, resisting him on those that don't. In this way, it can only be a matter of time.

'How can we save the stables?' I asked, but Glory just stared at me.

'If you don't break the partnership,' she said, 'you'll lose the forge, as well as the stables. Jake won't change his ways.'

I didn't think Glory would understand. Break the partnership: it is the obvious thing to do. Get out of it. You don't even love the man, and he's hardly earned your loyalty, has he?

She didn't have to say it.

'How do I save the stables?' I asked again, and slowly she shook her head.

'I don't think you can.'

'Please. Please, Glory. Come on, you're the whiz-kid.'

She didn't even smile.

'Please, Glory. Help me. Please help me.'

There were buckets clattering in the yard, water running, and the swish of a broom on concrete. Lights and noise, men working with horses. Evening stables.

Glory spread her hands, a gesture of helplessness, and glanced again at the books which had told her a hopeless story.

'What would you do if this place was yours and you had to save it?' I demanded.

'Get rid of more than half the horses. Sack half the staff. Look for new markets. And even then, Ann, I don't think . . .'

She could not understand.

'Why?' she asked. 'For God's sake, Ann, why? Why don't you just get out of it? You don't even love the man.'

No, I do not love him, nor does he love me, and when Arno comes back I will be unfaithful, and I will not care. Infidelity will mean nothing to Jake. He may mouth objections, conventions will demand it, but it won't hurt him, not as it would if he loved me.

But if I break that other promise, I will destroy him.

20

I moved Lyric back to the forge. Jake had spoken to me again about selling her, because she was getting old. I should sell her now, while I could still raise a fair price for her. I could use the money to buy something younger.

He never mentioned it again, because he saw how upset I was at the idea. Keep her then, love. Keep her, if you're fond of her.

He'd said he wouldn't buy the ringers either.

The Greek and Weaver's Dream were all he had hoped for, and his delight was making him kind. I could see my old friend in this man, with the smile in his eyes and the quick praise for good work.

But she was old now, my lovely racehorse, and there were hollows in her face and grey hairs around her muzzle. Jane Laverton once told me her husband had bought a horse at a horse fair in Yorkshire, quite a good-looking mare, and they'd found the grey hairs had been dyed, and the hollows had had some sort of wax injected in under the skin.

Jake had laughed when I'd told him. Yes, he knew the tricks. Clive Laverton should have looked at her teeth. Clive isn't as intelligent as Jane, and neither of them know as much as Jake does, not about the tricks.

Polaris was out in my paddock, eating the last of the grass. I stayed well away from him, and when I had to go into the paddock he and I kept several yards apart, and ignored each other.

He was showing no sign of losing any condition, and it had been three weeks since he'd arrived. I was torn between pleasure, that he was tough enough to keep fit without too much care and attention, and concern, that it would be several weeks yet before I would dare try to ride him. There'd been the usual squealing and galloping around when I'd turned Lyric out with him, and she'd lashed out at him once or twice. Polly had reared away, fast on his feet and aware of the danger, and Lyric's flying hooves had come nowhere near his shining coat.

Soon I would have to catch him, and do something about his feet. His shoes would start to do serious damage if I didn't remove them.

I gave Jansy the keys to the cottage. She needed somewhere quiet to study, and her father never turned the television off when he was at home. She shared a bedroom with her younger sister.

'Why didn't you go to university?' she demanded.

'Something to do with being too thick.'

That English Language, as she called it in tones of disgust, was still her problem. She'd as good as got That Biology and That Maths.

One of Jake's young hunters developed a curb, a sprained ligament at the back of the hock, and Jake was furious, although mostly with himself. He'd overworked the horse. Now, he'd have to rest him, and the handsome young chestnut probably wouldn't be fit for hard work in time to get him ready for autumn.

I shod him, shoes with raised heels to take the pressure off the damaged ligament, but it was a bad sprain.

'Are you going to take *any* of Glory's advice?' I asked Jake, and he said he didn't think there was much of it he could take. If people weren't buying the horses, he couldn't sell them, could he?

'Send them to auction,' I said. 'Please, just get rid of them. Them and that work-shy bugger Glen.'

He couldn't manage without Glen. Glen wasn't a bad rider.

He bought two more horses. I went with him to the sales, and I looked at their feet and watched the way they moved. There were three he'd wanted, but I shook my head over the bay filly.

He didn't try to argue.

'Thanks for coming,' he said on the way home that night.

'You're welcome.'

I wondered if he would ever pay the bill I sent in every month. He expected to take priority over my other customers, and perhaps that was fair, and natural.

I brought Lyric in from the paddock in the evenings and fed her in the stable yard as I brushed the dried mud out of her thickening coat. Polaris grazed close to the gate, watching her, his ears back every time I came between him and the mare, but not raising his head.

'Please send those horses to auction,' I said to Jake, but I was beginning to lose hope. He wouldn't get enough for them at auction, he replied. He'd already told me that, why couldn't I understand?

Every week they cost you more money.

All the more reason to get a good price for them.

Couldn't Glen paint those loose-box doors? He's not doing anything else, is he?

Oh, all right. I'll tell him.

Glen didn't bother with undercoat, so the gloss straight onto the bare wood where Toby had mended the worn edges stayed sticky, and dust and bits of straw blew onto it. Then it rained, and the paint was dull and streaky.

I'm a horseman, not a bloody decorator. I didn't know, did I?

Polaris followed Lyric into the stable yard and I let him wander around smelling at the doors. He tried to get his nose into Lyric's feed and she bared her teeth and swung her head at him. Disconsolate, he moved away and stood by the gate. When I led her back to it he stepped aside, then shouldered past me as I opened it, hardly seeming to notice me.

'I won't take any more horses in part exchange,' said Jake. 'I promise. Well, Glory said that, didn't she? I shouldn't do that?'

Had she? She'd said he'd never done it while he was successful.

'Ann? There's a final demand for the feed bill. I've got to feed the horses, haven't I? And the wages this week?'

'What about the money from those two mares you sold?'

He became defiant.

'I can't ride with broken kneecaps.'

So, three thousand pounds had gone to Dominic Mont-Blering. And two thousand more would have to be found to save the forge.

'It'll be all right,' he said. 'I promise. Just a bit of time. I'm working as hard as I can.'

It was true. He was working hard, from early morning until late at night, riding out, and schooling, and teaching young horses to jump. He was breaking three-year-olds, trying to get old horses fit, watching the men as they rode and wishing they rode better. Toby could keep a horse going well, but he wasn't good enough to improve a youngster, and Glen was no better. Tommy had become nervous about riding since Crown Prince had died, and was only comfortable in the schooling ring, where he knew the horses wouldn't get away from him.

Morry rode like an angel, and could make any horse look good, if he felt like it. If he was in a good mood. If he was showing off. Anything he could interpret as a reprimand or criticism sent him into a sulky fury, and then he would give an exhibition of an expert horseman barely in control of a bad-tempered useless brute.

'He's costing me more than he's worth in lost sales,' Jake raged after a customer had told him he'd wanted to give his wife a really nice present for her fiftieth birthday, not a broken neck.

'Sack him, then.'

'I can't. He's the only one good enough to break the youngsters. Believe me, I've looked for a replacement. Do you know anybody who rides as well as Morry?'

A few professional jockeys, and they'd hardly accept a job as a groom in Jake's stable.

But they might do some work, now the flat racing season was over.

'Would you pay them?' asked Jake when I made the suggestion.

'Surely there must be some young riders who'd do it for the chance of using your horses in events?' I asked. 'Aren't there? Come on, Jake, there must be.'

Libby Donnington came over a week later, a recommendation from Clive Ulverton, the racehorse trainer. If women were ever going to be jump jockeys, Clive had said without much enthusiasm for the idea, Libby might be one of the first.

Jake gave her three bad horses to ride, and she handled them without apparent difficulty. Good horses can sell themselves, he told her. Bad ones need assistance.

Libby could, and would, ride anything that had hooves, but she knew perfectly well how good she was, and she expected to be paid accordingly. And to ride the best horses in point-to-points and hunter trials.

'You're joking!' said Jake. 'What am I supposed to tell Morry?'

'Tell him to get stuffed,' she said.

'She's a frigging lesbian, and if she comes I go,' said Morry two days later.

'I can't afford her,' said Jake. 'If I put her up on Barbarian instead of Morry, he'll leave.'

Without the point-to-points, Libby wasn't interested. And no, she would not ride the second choices, even though she reckoned she could beat that overrated prat on anything better than a donkey.

'Look for somebody else, then,' I said to Jake, but even I had to admit the hopeful young riders who turned up at the stables having heard he was looking weren't good enough for what he wanted.

'I haven't got time to teach them,' he said, and it was true.

I clipped a leading rope onto Polly's head-collar one evening as he walked past me through the gate when he wasn't taking much notice, and although he jerked his head when he first felt the pressure he fell in beside me and walked quietly down the path and back again. I tied him to the ring and fed him some horse nuts. He was wary, and his ears were flicking, but he didn't try to kick or bite.

I'd had him for five weeks.

He'd cast one of his shoes, and the other was loose. His hooves were frayed and splitting.

Barbarian came fourth in the first point-to-point of the season, a race he should have won, but nobody was to blame. Another horse had swerved into him and nearly brought him down. It had shaken him, and he hadn't recovered in time to make up the ground he'd lost.

Jake was philosophical, if disappointed. These things happen, he said. Fuck it.

Nobody mentioned Barbarian, or Jake Brewer, in the reports.

I took Polly round the stable block to the forge and tied him to the iron ring. His ears were flat against his head as I fastened the rope, but I moved quietly, and he kept his head as far away from my hands as he could. I gave him a few horse nuts, and he took them, although he jerked his head away when I tried to stroke his nose.

I'd tried too soon. I should have left that for a few more days. Now, I'd set him back.

Perry Graves brought an Italian lamp to me and asked me to help him repair it. He looked dreadful, as though he'd come out of a concentration camp. He arrived in a taxi, and he moved very, very slowly up the drive, his feet almost shuffling through the gravel.

I pretended I hadn't seen him. I went on working, swinging my hammer against the iron so I wouldn't hear either. If I saw him I'd have to go to meet him, I'd have to offer to help, and he'd hate it.

I watched from under my eyebrows, just in case he fell. He looked as if he might. How could such a skeleton still be walking? How could it still live?

'Ann?'

'Perry. Good to see you. Sit down, there's a chair . . . Oh, I'll get it, it's in the workshop.'

He was leaning against the door, a plastic carrier bag hanging from his hand.

He was staying at the old railway station, with the women, he said. They helped him. When the pain got bad, they knew ways.

'Witches,' I said, looking at him, and he smiled, and raised his head in agreement.

'But shouldn't you be in hospital?' I asked.

He was dying, anybody could see that. He looked like a corpse already. His skin was a bluish grey in colour, and there were just a few strands of grey hair clinging to his scalp.

'I don't want to die in a hospital.'

'Oh, Perry.'

He held out the carrier bag, his arm shaking, and I took it from him, quickly, before his strength gave out and he dropped it.

'When do you want this?' I asked when I'd looked at the lamp, and his eyes glinted in a shadow of their former amusement.

'I'd like to see it.'

I telephoned two customers who'd been coming that afternoon. Could they put it off until tomorrow morning? I'd be very grateful.

That evening I walked down to the village, carrying the lamp in its carrier bag, and I went to the railway station, walking across the cracked concrete of the old car park and remembering an evening that seemed a very long time ago, when there'd been music and candlelight in the darkening evening, and wine, and a terrified woman crying in the corner.

The iron snakes were smooth under my hands as I stroked the gate, thinking of the work I'd done and the strange story it had started. You've taken me down a few odd paths, you three, I thought.

Somebody was watching me from the shadows outside the old stationmaster's office. Bess.

'Is that Perry's lamp? Come in, Ann.'

'Rhubarb wine?' I asked, and Bess laughed.

'Ah, well! There speaks a connoisseur. Or is it connoisseuse? I suppose it must be. Yes, there's rhubarb wine, but it's still a bit young. I doubt if it'll be given an opportunity to mature. We're taking dipsomania to the level of a fine art.'

There were words of welcome as we went into the office; they were all smiling at me. It was growing dark, and candles on the shelves and the old counter cast warm light and reflections.

'We've missed you, Ann.'

Tam's hand reached up to my shoulder, and I smiled at her.

'Where's Perry?' I asked.

'He's asleep.'

I held up the carrier bag.

'He said he wanted to see this, so I did it this afternoon.'

They all knew what I meant, but there were smiles, and

304

nobody seemed sad. Surely every time Perry fell asleep there must be a question about whether or not he would wake again.

They took it from me, and one of them filled a lamp with oil, and put it inside the wrought-iron frame. It was the wrong age, and I doubt if it was Italian, but once it was lit all that could be seen was the graceful pattern of the lantern. Hilda took it, saying she'd put it in his room so he'd see it when he woke.

'Shall I pay you now?' asked Gwen, but I shook my head. Paying for that work would have seemed like robbing the dead. I didn't want money from Perry.

I wasn't that desperate yet. I had steel and iron in the store, and coal. There was enough feed for Lyric. Were there any bills I hadn't paid? Anything I'd forgotten?

I used to be able to manage this. I used to know, not have to worry, and wonder.

'You're tired, Ann. Come and sit by the window. There's some food in the kitchen. Oh, come and sit down.'

They brought me food, vegetables rolled in a sort of pan-cake with a sharp, rather bitter sauce, and they brought the rhubarb wine. We were all sitting together on the floor, on the thick cushions I remembered from the party, and there was music again, theme music from films, pleasant and rhythmical.

'Why are you so tired?' demanded Tam, and I answered without thinking.

'I'm married.'

Arno had done that once: he'd said something, and I'd answered, and only then realised it was true.

Arno had made me understand I hated my mother.

What had I learned now? What had my own answer told me?

I'd had so much energy before I'd married Jake, and it had all drained away. It had happened insidiously. I'd hardly even noticed it leaving me, and I'd certainly never

305

wondered why. I wanted to cry with weariness now. I laid down my empty plate, and I felt my head falling forward. My shoulders ached, and my eyes were filling with tears.

There were hands on my head, cradling it, pressing gently against the temples, there were hands on my back, stroking and rubbing. Somebody was holding my wrists, and I could hear voices, but the words didn't matter.

I knew they were saying my name, to me and to each other, and there was concern in the voices, and love, and something more, even more than that, something like friendship, which went further and deeper even than friendship, and which demanded nothing, and offered all it had to give.

Lie down: they wanted me to lie down, so I turned on my side and I leaned into the cradling hands.

Somebody was singing, and the music was familiar, although I didn't know where I had heard it before. Surely I knew that song?

I certainly knew these fingers on my head, on my arms, my hands and my feet. This was something I had needed, these sure and delicate pressures, this careful and exact touch, the whispers I could hear but did not have to understand.

I felt as if I was falling, slowly and gently rolling into the welcoming darkness. My heavy eyes closed over the grateful tears, and the singing voices of my friends took me deeper and deeper into the velvet tranquillity of sleep.

21

Perry died a week later in the paddock at the forge, on a lovely frosty night under a bright sky.

He'd asked if he could come, and the women had carried him. They'd borrowed a big car and brought him in that, and then they'd lifted him out of the back seat, four of them carrying him on a blanket along the path beside the stable, through the gate and into the paddock. He couldn't have weighed much by then.

'I've always liked it here,' he said, and just those few words seemed to exhaust him.

Everybody was dressed in thick clothes, heavy jackets and coats, and for Perry there were quilts on a groundsheet, and soft blankets. The women had brought flagons of rhubarb wine, and fruit and bread, the food they usually seemed to eat. It wasn't a party, but there was no sense of sadness, and certainly no tears. Perry had something else to drink, in a mug that had been made for him of a dark yellow clay, and he sipped it through a straw.

Nobody made a fuss of him, but there was always somebody close, to be aware of anything he needed. He watched us, his eyes moving in their deep, dark sockets, and sometimes he smiled. He was obviously in pain, and movement hurt him, but he was content, and quiet.

Part of me felt vehemently he should be in hospital, with strong drugs to ease his pain, but I knew that would have been wrong, and cruel. Perry would rather have the pain, and be here.

'We could be in trouble for this, couldn't we?' I asked Gwen, but she didn't seem to be worried, and by the time the trouble came, if it did, Perry would be away from it.

Lyric and Polaris were grazing in the paddock, the setting sun turning their coats to gold. Now and then they raised their heads, watching us, but they didn't approach. They stayed close to the forge at the other end, near the fence and the gate, moving slowly across the grass, and the sound of their teeth cropping it carried to us on the still evening air.

'It's perfect,' said a red-haired girl who introduced herself as Nell. 'It's just, as if we'd sort of written a list, everything you want for a perfect evening.'

Perry moved, his eyes closing, and Hilda helped him. He winced as she touched him, but he smiled too, and lifted his head to drink from the pottery mug.

'Hasn't he got some painkillers?' I asked Nell, and she nodded.

'In his drink.'

'From the doctor?' I insisted, and she pulled a wry face.

'Well, no. He says they make him stupid. Perry, well, you know Perry. He really wants to live, every minute, right up to the end. He says what we give him is good enough for him.'

Yes, I knew Perry, and I knew what Nell said was true, but I was still worried. Wouldn't it be too cold, later? He was so thin, so weak. Surely he'd feel the cold.

'Could we light a fire?' asked Gwen, and I was relieved. I should have thought of that, a fire.

'Yes, of course. Let's do that.'

Darkness seemed to spring up as the flames rose around the crackling wood, and suddenly it was night. For a few moments there was smoke, and a flurry as the women stood between the fire and Perry, Gwen spreading her long skirt to screen him, but the wood was dry and old and the smoke died almost immediately. But Gwen stayed close to Perry, and whenever anybody threw more wood onto the fire she was on her feet, and ready.

I lay back on the grass, snuggling down into my thick sheepskin jacket, and looked into the night sky.

I was sad for Perry, but there was no sense of the misery a young death usually brings, none of the despair and anger. There was love. He was with people who loved him, and he was where he wanted to be, in the place he'd chosen.

Glory had said these women were healers, and for the first time I began to understand what she meant. There could be no return to health for Glory or for Perry; Glory had been mutilated beyond any hope of repair, and Perry's disease was mortal.

Where would Perry be now, without the witches?

The vision I had was truly dreadful, of Perry lying in a clean, narrow, white bed, drugged almost to the point of unconsciousness, with a pretty woman crying beside him. Tubes and machines, everything clean and sterile, and made as comfortable for him as possible; as comfortable, and as tidy as it could be, with anything unpleasant kept out of sight, to be handled by the professionals, who could remain impersonal about such things.

Perry was not clean, lying on the blanket on the soft grass. Hilda did her best, but nothing could disguise it, and I hoped he was unaware of it. We could not be; the cold wind that kept the drifting smoke away from Perry brought the stench of his disease to us, and we could only ignore it.

We looked elsewhere when Hilda became quietly busy at Perry's side, when we heard the sounds of water and a sponge, and there was a soft moaning, because every touch, no matter how gentle, caused pain.

He'd said the drink in the yellow clay mug was enough. He wanted to live every moment, even with the pain.

They were burning dried rosemary on the fire, and it had a sharp and clear scent. Not quite enough, but it helped.

Tam was asleep, lying on her side on the grass with one arm under her head. Her face seemed to move in the firelight, as though she was talking to herself and frowning over her words.

'I've got some more blankets,' I said to Gwen, but she just smiled and shook her head.

I was feeling sleepy myself.

Sue and Erica were on the other side of the fire. Erica had her arm around Sue's shoulders, and Sue was hunched forward and sideways, leaning against Erica and staring into the flames. Tessa lay beside them, curled up with her knees drawn close to her chest, looking neat, like a cat, and blinking drowsily.

I turned onto my side and looked into the fire, listening to the soft crackling, watching the patterns of the flames. When I closed my eyes I could still see them, a blurring of gold and orange and scarlet. Behind the sounds I heard Sue beginning to sing, the song I'd heard before, and Erica joining in after a few bars.

When I opened my eyes later, the fire had died to crimson embers and there were the sounds of sleep. Bess was standing, and she was naked, the last of the firelight gleaming on her strong, white body. As I watched she stooped over Perry, and lay beside him.

I closed my eyes, but I listened for a little while, and I heard him moan again. There was whispering, and somebody sighed. I heard him laugh, and that was the last sound I heard from Perry, although Nell and Bess went on whispering to him, and there were soft noises, and gentle murmurs. As I drifted off to sleep I heard singing again, but it seemed to come from the trees, and from behind them, from far away, so I knew it was a dream.

310

'Why?' somebody asked. 'Why was that a dream?' and it was daylight.

What had I dreamed?

There'd been the sounds in the night, something like a roaring, far away behind the singing voices, but it had been the wind, hadn't it? Who had spoken?

Nell was standing by the fire, naked, hugging herself and shivering. Her face was very white, and she looked a little sick. Her red hair was clinging damply to her forehead.

'I can't touch him,' she said. 'I'm sorry, I can't.'

Then she started to cry, and Erica climbed slowly and stiffly to her feet, and went across to her.

'He was dead when I woke up. He was lying on top of me and he was dead. I feel sick.'

'It's only Perry.'

'I know.'

Bess was a little further away, wiping herself down with handfuls of grass. Still naked, she was shaking with cold, throwing the grass away from herself as though the touch of it made her shudder.

'I can't help it,' said Nell. 'I can't. I know it's Perry, but I can't touch him, and I feel sick. I think I'm going to *be* sick.'

'Come and sit by the fire,' said Erica, and Sue was with her; Gwen was getting to her feet. 'Wrap a blanket round yourself, you're shivering.'

'There'll be hot water in the cottage,' I said. 'Would you like a shower?' Nell looked across the fire at me, trying to smile, and she nodded.

'And Bess,' she said, and her voice sounded thick and muffled. 'She's got stuff on her.'

She started to cry, her hands up to her face.

'He's dead. He's dead.'

I felt confused, and unhappy. It had been magical, the evening before, the night stars and the firelight, and now in the coldness of the early morning the women were white, and sick, and shocked.

311

What had I expected? The wings of morning? Perry's spirit lifted up to the sky in a flock of flying doves?

Magic in the night-time, and the morning brought reality.

The dead man was lying half off the quilts, one arm stretched out. His mouth was gaping, with something brown and sticky around his lips, and his cheeks were sunken; it was the face of a skull.

Bess had pulled the corner of a blanket across him, and somebody had picked sprays of dried leaves and laid them beside his head.

'Shouldn't I telephone for a doctor?' I asked. 'Isn't that what you have to do?'

'If you would, Ann. Yes, please.'

Gwen, sounding subdued.

I made coffee while Nell and Bess showered upstairs, and I wondered if there'd be trouble when the doctor came, whether he'd refuse to sign a death certificate, or whatever it was that he was supposed to do. He might say the death was suspicious, he might insist on calling the police. Perry should have been in hospital, in the care of the professionals.

Gwen came into the kitchen, looking upset and a little anxious. 'I hate it when people die,' she said. 'I know I shouldn't, but I do. I hate it.'

'Have a coffee.'

'Oh, yes, please. Yes.'

The telephone rang in the living room, and I put my mug on the draining board and left Gwen in the kitchen as I went to answer it.

It was Jake, grumpy because he'd expected me home the night before and I hadn't warned him I'd be staying on at the forge. He said he had work for me to do.

'What work?'

'The jumping paddock gate, Glen backed the horsebox into it. It needs welding. Can you bring the torch up here now?'

Jake's bill was into four figures now. I'd have to buy some more gas bottles soon, I only had two left.

'I'm tired,' I said, and I heard him sigh.

'Aren't we all? Can you do that gate this morning? Ann? I don't like broken gates, they're dangerous. Can you?'

'I can if somebody brings it here.'

He complained and argued. If I'd come back the night before, as I'd said I would, I could have taken it with me this morning. He didn't think he had time. He didn't want to leave the paddock without a gate, suppose a horse got loose?

'Sorry, Jake,' I said. 'No. Only if somebody brings it here.'

I hung up before he could answer.

Gwen had gone back to the other women. I stayed in the kitchen, looking out of the window at them.

The doctor arrived a few minutes later. He was an Indian, quite young, and kind. He followed me out to the paddock, and he smiled at the women before he knelt down beside Perry's body. Gwen answered his questions. She gave him the name of Perry's doctor, and said yes, it was cancer, he'd discharged himself from hospital a few days earlier. He'd signed the papers. They'd advised him against leaving, but he'd wanted to die here. They'd brought him here last night, because he'd said he was dying, and they'd stayed with him. Gwen thought he'd died at about four that morning, but she wasn't sure.

'You are good women,' said the doctor. 'He was lucky that you helped him. I wish some of my patients had nurses like you.'

Gwen looked relieved, and he laughed at her.

'Oh, maybe not all doctors would think so. But I think so. He was lucky, isn't it?'

He told me I could telephone for an undertaker to collect the body, and he came with me to the cottage, where he filled in some forms. He drank a cup of coffee, but then said he had to leave, he had a busy day ahead of him.

313

Nell was still crying when the ambulance came. She kept hugging herself and shivering, and repeating that he'd been lying on top of her until Hilda snapped at her and told her to pull herself together.

'It was Perry,' said Hilda. 'Your friend, remember? I don't think it was much to ask of you, and he won't ask it again.'

When the ambulance had taken Perry away the women began to leave too, Gwen in the borrowed car with Bess and Nell, and the others on foot. After they'd gone I took the hose, and I washed down the place where Perry had died.

I'm sorry, I thought. Sorry, Perry. But the stench was truly horrible, and it still lingered. It would need rain before it became clean again.

The fire had left a big scorched patch on the grass, and I washed that, too, then picked up the wet and blackened wood that was left. When it was dry I'd burn it on the forge. It wouldn't take long for the grass to grow back. Just a little time, and there'd be no sign of the magical night, and the bleak and dreadful morning.

The telephone was ringing again, although it was still early, but I answered it because it might have been about Perry.

It was Jake again, argumentative about his broken gate. It was urgent, couldn't I see that? I could have done it by now if I'd left when he'd called. When was I coming? He needed to know, he had to plan his day, so could I give him a time.

I was upset about the death, and I cut Jake short. I'd only mend his gate if somebody brought it here, and had he looked at his bill?

'Ann!'

He was hurt and incredulous, and I regretted my words.

'Sorry,' I said. 'I'm sorry, Jake. Why can't Glen bring the gate up here?'

'He hasn't got time.'

'Well, *neither have I.*'

It was because I was angry with Jake, and upset about Perry, that I went too close to Polaris, and I wasn't quick enough to get out of the way. I did jump to the side as he kicked, so the hoof that would have caught me squarely on my thigh grazed it instead, but even though I avoided a broken leg the bruise was painful enough.

Polaris was tied to the ring by the forge when it happened, and as soon as he heard my startled and pained yell he jumped forward, throwing up his head and jerking at the rope. I looked up from rubbing the bruise to see him rolling frightened eyes, his head as high as the rope would allow, nostrils flaring.

The pain and anger subsided.

'Poor little bugger,' I said, and then went on, thinking aloud, silly and sentimental ideas. 'Hate everybody, and everybody frightened of you? No friends, Polly? Only Lyric? Somebody's belted you around the head, haven't they? Poor old Polly. Poor lad. Never mind. Let's get those shoes off, and let's not kick again, OK?'

By the time I'd finished this drivel his panic had abated, although he had started to sweat. I fetched a bucket and a sponge and began to wash him, slowly and gently, talking to him as I did so. He shivered as the water ran over his skin, and one ear was turned back towards me. As I reached his back he hunched again, and I stepped away before he could begin the kick.

'Little bastard.'

But the tone was mild, and he wasn't alarmed.

He was tied on a short rope, so he couldn't get his teeth to me as I lifted one of his forefeet, and I used the side of my thumb to rub the compacted dirt away from the sole. I went on talking to him as I worked, and listening, too. He was breathing quickly, his ribcage brushing against the side of my face. His head would be up high again, ears flicking, wary.

I lowered his foot and stepped back, and he was watching

me again, the water still dripping from his neck and shoulders.

Jake had told me a trick with water, for racehorses, to keep the odds a bit longer. Brush them with water the night before, he'd said, brush back against the lie of the hairs. Maybe rug them up like that. Next day, the coat won't lie flat. The horse won't look so good. Poor condition, longer odds.

Or wet them down before you bring them into the paddock, so it looks as if they're sweating. That's another bad sign: overexcited or upset, they won't run so well.

I'd said, surely everybody would be wise to that one? and he'd replied, you wouldn't fool a professional or an expert. But most punters are mugs. Throw around a few buzz-words, a bit of jargon, you'd think they'd taught Lester Piggott everything he knows.

And we'd laughed.

'That didn't hurt, did it?' I said to Polly.

He was too still, too tense, ready to jump or kick. I really needed somebody to help me with him, but I was worried about making him more nervous than ever.

I'd try again.

He let me pick up his forefoot with only a slight, warning jerk of his head and a shifting of one hind leg that might have signified a kick, but then he stood still, only the faster breathing telling me of his fear. The shoe was so loose I didn't need to hammer a buffer against the clenches. I clipped them off with the pincers, and pulled the shoe free, holding it firmly in the pincers so it wouldn't fall and frighten him.

'Good lad. Good lad, Polly. Good boy.'

Lean against his shoulder, pressing, feel the movement as his head rises again, but nothing has frightened him, nothing has hurt him, there is nothing to alarm him.

Until Glen roared in driving Jake's tractor, with the broken gate rattling loose on the flatbed trailer.

'Jake wants it back by teatime,' he yelled as he jumped down. 'Can't get on without it, he says, so get your skates on.'

And he heaved the gate off the trailer, clattering it down onto the concrete path, and scrambled back onto the seat.

'And I should watch out for that horse,' he yelled back over his shoulder as he revved the engine and clouds of smoke blew out of the exhaust. 'Looks a bit spooky to me.'

I swear, I thought, as I leaned against the wall and watched my little horse shuddering with fright, I swear it, Glen, you will see the inside of the unemployment office before the month is out.

'And you,' I said to Jake over the telephone ten minutes later when I'd recovered my temper enough to speak to him at all, 'can wait until I'm good and ready to do your gate.'

'You said Glen should bring it over.' He was resentful.

'I'd just got his shoe off,' I said. 'I didn't have to use a twitch, I didn't have to tie up his foreleg, I got him quiet enough to get that shoe off, and what happens?'

'Ah, I am sorry. I really am.'

He meant it. He'd told me I'd have to handle Polly myself, but he'd wished me luck. He wouldn't have wanted to set back my work on the horse.

'I don't want Glen down here again. You or Toby, maybe Tommy, but not Glen. And not Morry, either.'

'Tommy can't drive.'

Jake wouldn't ignore Glen's behaviour. What would be said I would never know; but there would be an atmosphere of sullen defiance in the house that evening.

I would have to go back. I'd been away for two nights now, and I would have to go back to the house that evening, perhaps cook some sort of meal for everybody.

I went out into the yard and leaned against the wall again, looking at the little liver chestnut horse with the smudged star who'd seemed like a good gamble at the time.

I should talk to him, get him used to the sound of my voice. What do I say to a horse?

So I recited poems I'd learned at school and bits of Shakespeare. Hotspur's death speech, Oh, Harry, thou hast robbed me of my youth. Oh, Jake, you make a damned strange Prince Hal, how is it the very thought of going back to that house makes me feel so weary? Is this how I will be when I am old? I used to be so vigorous, I used to have energy, I could work all day, and still enjoy my evenings.

Why, when I even think of talking to you, do I feel this leaden unwillingness? And yet, still feel no anger?

You don't even love him, Glory had said, and there had been overtones of accusation in her voice.

Dim drums throbbing in the hills half heard, I said to Polly, and remembered hoofbeats on the track as Lyric put her head down and galloped up a finishing straight after a bad jump to get home half a length ahead of the favourite, with Jake Brewer and Clive Ulverton shouting themselves hoarse on either side of me, while I could only laugh with sheer relief that she was over the jumps, and safe home.

It had been fun, and Jake and Clive had put Lyric back into training out of friendship for me when I'd been ill with worry over Glory, as well as quite badly injured myself.

This is a strange thing, this friendship. Had I ever been in love with Jake I would probably be hating him by now. Instead, I remembered he'd sold me Lyric, and told me she had knee trouble. She might break down. She was beautiful, she was a thoroughbred, which meant she could carry my weight, but there was a risk with her knees.

Honest Jake Brewer: you could have painted it on a sign outside the stables, and people would have smiled, but not in derision.

She'd run away with me, had Lyric, taken hold of the bit and set off, she'd given me a quite serious fright. I'd never ridden anything like Lyric before. I'd ridden Uncle Henry's old pit pony, Fag End, who needed a drum roll on his flanks to get him moving, and later a pensioned-off hunter, who dreamed his way around the paddock, and preceded every change of pace or direction with a world-weary sigh.

I'd climbed onto Lyric's back, marvelling at the luxury of a good saddle, and she'd stood quietly enough as I'd slipped my feet into the stirrups, only moving when I collected up the reins, her mouth more sensitive than those of Fag End or the old hunter.

Then I'd clapped my heels into her flanks.

She'd been flat out by the time we reached the hedge at the end of the paddock, and nothing I could do, no signal I gave her, seemed to have any effect other than to make her gallop faster. At the last moment, in desperation, I'd hauled her head to the side, unbalancing her, so she'd refused the jump, and instead skidded round in a tight circle and headed back towards the stable.

At last, just by dragging at her poor mouth to pull her away from the hedges and fences, I'd tired her sufficiently to get her to stop. I'd been quite miserably frightened by the whole experience.

Jake had been sympathetic. Well, she'd been a racehorse, had Lyric, and brakes were not the most important component. Look, tell you what, Ann, I'll come over tomorrow, maybe give you a few pointers. Yes, a riding lesson, all right.

He'd given me three, waving aside my offers of payment. In the end he'd given up, a rueful smile.

'It's not that Lyric's particularly difficult. It's just that you're such a bloody awful rider.'

I'm still a bloody awful rider. Would I ever manage Polly?

I wandered lonely as a cloud, that floats on high . . .

Oh, for God's sake.

'Polly, Polly, Polly,' I said. 'Polly-Wolly-Doodle all the day. Or way. Or whatever, I forget.'

I untied the rope, and he pulled his head away, as far as

he could get it from my hands, but then he followed me quietly when I led him back down the concrete path towards the gate. At least I'd got the other shoe off. Perhaps tomorrow I could get at his hind feet, if I was lucky. Or if, just maybe, Jake would help me.

Morry Old could ride like an angel, but Jake knew horses, from the soles of their feet to the tips of their ears, from the whiskers on their noses to the last hairs in their tails. He'd respected my skills, and he'd been horseman enough to listen to me. He could ride, not with the almost magical touch of Morry, but with the sureness that came from a lifetime with horses. The boxes of rosettes in the tack-room cupboards hadn't been won by Morry; that had been Jake, when competition had been important to him, and it had been so natural to win he hadn't even mentioned it until I questioned him. Then, he'd been a little embarrassed. Yes, well, jumping, you know. A bit of dressage. Um. That flashy gold one? A shamefaced grin. Well, that was a rodeo. In Texas. They reckoned because I was English . . . And he'd shrugged.

'A bronco?' I'd asked, intrigued, and he'd nodded.

'Go on,' I'd insisted.

Ah, well. He hadn't wanted to ride in the rodeo. But there'd been side bets. Well, he'd only been visiting the ranch, just sort of working his way around. And he'd said he could ride.

Jake had started to laugh.

'They'd rounded up strays. Wild horses, about a week before. Most of them were dog meat by then. They'd kept the best of them. A few wild ones were giving them trouble.'

He was scratching the toe of his boot with the heel of the other one, not looking at me, just laughing, and red in the face.

'Nice quiet horses in the English countryside, they thought, so let's play a joke on the limey. Put him up on the sorrel stallion and see how high he flies.'

'But you rode him?'

'I rode three of them, one after the other, to a standstill. So then, there's this rodeo, just a little local thing, but there was some betting. So, well . . .'

He shrugged, and looked at me out of the corner of his eye.

'I wouldn't do it now.'

Now, he watched Morry Old come fourth on Barbarian, and knew it couldn't be helped. He watched me on Lyric, and said nothing while he rode beside me, sitting as though he'd grown in that saddle. He tried to say nothing to Toby, who was doing his best and couldn't do better; he tried to be patient with poor, slow Tommy, who didn't want to ride the good horses any more, and thought he wouldn't be allowed on them. He coached Glen, a little, small faults to be corrected, suggestions, and sometimes loud and angry rebukes.

'Can you help me with Polly?' I asked Jake that night. 'I must get the shoes off his hind feet. I don't want to do it alone.'

He nodded, spooning macaroni cheese into his mouth. How could he eat so much and stay so wiry? Morry counted calories and tolerated hunger, while Toby complained his jeans shrunk in the wash.

'Afternoon?' asked Jake as he laid down his spoon and looked at the empty casserole dish as though willing there to be another plateful in it. 'When the hay's been delivered, I'll come down. Do I smell baked apples?'

He'd given up demanding the money. He knew I'd pay the bills, when I had to, and I'd buy in good horses if he persuaded me they were worth the outlay. I was down to sixty thousand pounds now, and somehow I would have to repay it, if I wasn't to lose the forge.

Nothing had changed. Jake was schooling his horses on Gorsedown, and they were doing well, but the horse world was not flocking back to him, not for the good horses. A hack here, a cob there, a not very good hunter, an old mare for just one more season and then to the stud; but the big money, and the people who had it to spend on horses, they were not coming back.

'It's bound to take a bit of time,' he said, and I agreed.

He'd been worried. He'd telephoned all his old customers and told them he'd got some good horses, and they'd said nice to hear from you, Jake. Yes, great, I'll come over some time, I'll take a look. See you soon.

Jake had promised to help me with Polly, so I brought the horse in from the paddock and tied him to the ring, and then I leaned against Arno's Riley, looking through the window at the deep leather seats, and thinking I really must sell this. He asked me to sell it, and I must do that for him. Perhaps he needs the money, now. Perhaps he's had to stop working, to look after Brita.

Deep maroon paintwork, gleaming under the polish I still, sometimes, rubbed onto it, remembering the times I'd done it because he'd telephoned to say he was coming.

I shouldn't think of Arno. I should sell this car, and send him a cheque, and not think of him again, because I was married now, to Jake Brewer, and I should try to be a good wife.

There'd been a three-day event on the other side of the county. Flycatcher, Honey Girl and The Greek, would I please make sure their feet were all right? He'd heard there were a couple of Australians on the lookout for good eventers.

But the Australians hadn't bought his horses. They'd come with another dealer who'd brought them in a new Range Rover, and there'd been champagne and a lavish picnic, to celebrate the purchase of a lovely grey gelding who'd outshone everything on the cross-country work, and would have won had he been better schooled for dressage.

Perhaps, if he could afford a decent car and could treat his customers properly, instead of turning up in a five-year-old Volvo with a crate of supermarket wine in the back, he'd stand a better chance, said Jake on the way home.

'Why doesn't your Dutch friend ever come any more?' he asked, and I looked at him blankly.

'That professor.'

'Swedish,' I said. 'His wife's ill.'

Jake looked thoughtful.

'Nice car, that Riley. He wouldn't mind if we borrowed it, would he?'

I must sell your car, Arno.

'Yes, he would mind very much. Nobody ever drives that car except him.'

'Well, he needn't know, then.'

Distributor cap in the vegetable rack under the potatoes in the cottage kitchen, and the keys in the bookshelf behind my old school Latin dictionary. You will not drive Arno's car, Jake.

He arrived in the old Volvo, looking a little worried, but when I asked him he said there was nothing wrong. Just thinking, let's get on with this.

Polly flattened his ears as we approached and swished his tail, but Jake spoke to him quietly, and we got a side rope onto him without too much trouble.

'He's calmed down a lot,' said Jake. 'You're doing well.'

There was something wrong. Polly was a little quieter with me, but he'd threatened to kick Jake, and there was no noticeable improvement. Why had Jake said there was?

I cut back the overgrown and cracked hooves and rasped them, and Jake led Polaris up and down the path, walking and trotting. I felt a smile growing on my face, and saw it mirrored on his. The horse's action was straight and even; like his looks, nothing to catch the eye until you studied it, and then it was perfect.

'He's better than I thought,' Jake admitted. 'He's very good.'

'What's wrong, Jake?'

'Nothing.'

The answer had come too quickly, and he knew it. He looked away.

'I've sold Flycatcher.'

'That's good. What did you get for him?'

'Two thousand eight. Well, it's not spectacular, but it's fair.'

He coughed, and wouldn't look at me.

'I bought a mare. She's not bad.'

The smiles had gone, and now I felt desperately tired, more tired than I would have believed possible.

'A part exchange,' I said.

'Not really, no. No, not a part exchange. I might well have bought her anyway. Just because it's the man who bought Flycatcher. I can't promise I never will, I mean, I can't. Not buy a horse because somebody's bought one from me. That's not reasonable. Well, is it?'

Don't question him. Don't ask him how old she is, what he paid, or allowed, for her, who will buy her, don't ask. He's done it. He promised he never would again, but he has.

There really is no hope. Glory said he wouldn't change his ways, and she was right. There is no hope.

'I'll be late tonight,' I said at last. 'I want to go and see some friends.'

22

It wasn't Dominic Mont-Blering who broke Jake's knee, it was The Greek, and it happened on Gorsedown.

I was with them, riding a mare Jake hoped to sell later in the week, Morry was on Weaver's Dream, Toby and Glen on hunters, and none of us knew what made the big grey horse panic, and rear, and then fall back down the bank, with Jake trying to throw himself clear. There was an impression of thrashing legs, a horse squealing, breaking branches, and then a scream, and another, this one broken off short, and the horse rolling over at the bottom of the bank, scrambling to his feet, and turning confusedly in circles until Toby caught him.

Jake was lying halfway down the bank, and his right leg was twisted at an impossible angle. He pushed himself up on one elbow and stared at it, then he fell back. I think he passed out.

All the men were swearing, and the horses were frightened and trying to bolt. Toby held The Greek at the bottom of the bank, talking to him, but something had terrified the gelding and he was jumping around, pulling hard at his bridle, so Toby could only hang on and wait for him to become calm again. Morry had dismounted, and he had Toby's horse and Weaver's Dream, and they were both trying to back off, stiff-legged, with their heads high and their eyes rolling.

Glen's horse was spinning round in circles, and Glen was cursing and dragging at the reins. Twice the horse lashed out, luckily not hitting any of the others, before Glen slid out of the saddle and went to his head, leading him back down the track out of harm's way.

My mare was standing, rigid with fright, tremors running down the muscles of her shoulders. At any moment she might recover, and then she would bolt. I was staring down the bank at Jake, at that dreadful angle of his leg, thinking it was like something drawn on a blackboard in a geometry lesson, thinking that can't happen to a leg, thinking, this is my fault.

Get off the horse. She'll go, and you won't be able to hold her.

Jake opened his eyes and groaned. His teeth were clenched, and he started to hiss through them.

Get off the horse.

I kicked my feet clear of the stirrup irons, and jumped down.

I suddenly realised I was shaking, my skin was crawling with fear. There was a feeling of horror, of dread, and the question over it all, what happened? What happened?

I looked back, almost frantic, and I saw Glen was crying. There were tears on his face, and he was staring around, his head jerking from side to side. He must be asking the same question, what happened?

Morry, white and sweating, was staring through the trees.

'There,' he said.

What? What had he seen? There was nothing, just the trees moving in the wind; there was nothing.

As suddenly as it had begun, it was over. The mare shuddered, and sweat broke out on her body, but slowly that high, terrified head dropped, and she began to breathe.

'Is everybody else all right?' I asked. They were all looking at me.

'Fucking hell,' said Morry. 'Oh, fucking hell.'

'Glen? Are you OK?'

He nodded, and brushed at the tears on his face.

What do we do?

'Glen, ride back to the forge as fast as you can, and telephone for an ambulance. Stay there until it comes, then bring the men here. Cool your horse down while you're waiting, then rug him up and put him in the second loose box.'

What do we do about Jake's leg? Dear God, what can we do about that? A leg can't be like that, it can't.

Glen had gone, his horse galloping fast back down the track. Jake was groaning again, only half conscious. If he moved, he could slide down that bank and do dreadful damage to the broken knee.

But those two good horses, I can't let those horses . . .

'Morry, ride Weaver's Dream and lead The Greek, and get them back to the stables. Watch The Greek, let me know later if he's hurt himself.'

Morry nodded, looking down the bank at Toby, who was still standing at the tall grey's head, listening to me, the colour slowly returning to his cheeks.

'What was it?' he demanded, and his voice was choked.

I didn't know. But it was my fault.

'Toby!'

'Yes, miss.'

Now it was up to me. I would have to manage.

Jake, groaning on the bank, trying to move, trying to look at his leg, not believing what he saw.

'Lie still, Jake. Don't move.'

Toby, searching the bank for an easier way to bring the horse back to us. Morry, with the reins looped over his arms, running the irons up the stirrup leathers on Toby's hunter, and looking at me.

'Jake, don't move.'

Oh, Toby, please hurry. I can't let the mare loose, and I want to get down there to Jake. Come on, please, Toby.

'Jake, *please* don't move.'

Can he hear me?

Then Toby was holding the mare for me, and Morry was riding back down the track. I called after him: 'Pick up a rug at the forge. You can leave The Greek's tack there, use a head-collar.'

Morry turned his head, jerking it in acknowledgement. His face was still white, and sick.

What had he seen?

All I could do was hold Jake where he was, braced below him on the bank, my left foot wedged against a tree root, his arm around my shoulder, and hope that every time he came round it would only be for a moment or two.

I didn't dare touch the leg.

There was blood seeping through the thick cloth of his breeches, a slowly spreading stain.

A compound fracture, then. Of the knee.

Oh, dear God. What have I done?

Nothing. I hadn't done anything. I need help, I'd said. That didn't mean this was my fault.

Toby was walking the two horses up and down the track. Every time he came back he'd peer over the top of the bank at us, his face anxious and concerned.

'All right? You all right, miss?'

Tam had asked, could you run that place on your own, and I'd said, yes. Yes, I could.

Can I? I'll have to.

I hadn't said, do this.

I like him, I'd said. I don't love him, but he's my old friend.

This is an accident, it's a coincidence, pull yourself together.

'You all right, miss?'

328

'Yes, Toby, I'm all right, thank you.'

Can you help me? I'd asked, and eyes had met across the candlelit room, questions I hadn't understood had been in those eyes, and the faces were very grave, and very quiet, and it had been a long time before there had been an answer.

Yes.

What have I done? Oh, dear God, what have I done?

I could hear hoofbeats coming down the track, two horses, a fast canter, and I frowned. What is this? Who's riding on Gorsedown?

It was Glen and a man I didn't know, white trousers rammed into a pair of riding boots, sliding down the bank, mud smearing the cotton.

'Crutchley, I'm a doctor. Oh, dear.'

'Is he going to lose his leg?'

'Let's not be pessimistic. Can you hold him like that?'

'Yes.'

He had something in his hand, shears of some sort, and he was cutting Jake's breeches. He was talking as he did so, trying to distract me. Lovely horse, my old mare, he hoped I didn't mind him borrowing her, seemed the best way to get here quickly. No way to get the ambulance here. Can you manage? Can you hold him? The men are on their way with the stretcher.

More hoofbeats. That would be Glen going to meet them, to show them the way. What about the horses? Left Toby with three of them.

Jake was groaning again, and Dr Crutchley was saying something about an injection in a moment, old chap, just hold on a moment, not long now.

Then Jake screamed, and I was crying.

I didn't mean this to happen. I didn't mean this.

Then what did you think they would do? What did you think? A nice tidy solution to the problem, nobody gets hurt, and happy ever after?

'Sorry, love. Sorry.'

'Jake.'

Telling me he was sorry, with the sweat running down his face, hardly able to breathe, telling me he was sorry.

'Mrs Brewer, if you can just support the leg here, under the thigh, then I can see what I'm doing.'

I can't remember much more. Jake had his face buried against my shoulder, his teeth clenched in the cloth of my jacket. I saw it later, he'd bitten right through it. Dr Crutchley gave him an injection, and in a little while it was better. By then the men were there with the stretcher, talking about how best to get him onto it, how to do it without hurting him, and in the end they slid to the bottom of the bank with the stretcher. Four of us half lifted and half dragged Jake those last few feet, but he was unconscious again.

Don't wake up. Please, don't wake up yet.

I walked beside him, and Glen and Toby rode on, each leading a horse. I'd told them to go home. Do whatever was necessary at the stables, I'd be back as soon as I could.

'I expect they'll operate tonight,' said Dr Crutchley. 'Try not to worry.'

Worry wasn't what I was feeling. I went to the hospital in the ambulance, and I answered questions and I signed a form, and then I was told I could see Jake for a while. He'd been sedated, and he didn't seem to be in pain. He said he was sorry, and I smiled at him, and I wondered, how do I make amends? What can atone for this?

Back to the stables, and I made Morry ride The Greek, half an hour of work and a few jumps, to make sure he hadn't been hurt in the fall, and that his confidence hadn't been shaken.

'He's all right,' said Morry, and I agreed with him.

We rubbed him down when he was cool. His eyes were calm and intelligent again, and he followed Morry back into his box.

'Lucky,' commented Morry, and I nodded.

We could not look each other in the eye. None of us could do that, not that evening. Some time soon we'd rationalise it, talk about something having spooked The Greek, funny how horses catch that sort of thing. But we wouldn't say any more. Nobody would mention Glen's tears, and Morry would never say what it was he had seen, his white face tense and terrified as he uttered the single word, 'There'.

I telephoned the hospital. Jake was being prepared for the operation. At eight, it was scheduled for eight. Will you be here, Mrs Brewer?

'As soon as I can,' I said. 'Please will you tell him the horse is all right? It's important to him. He'll be worried.'

I sat in a room in the hospital, trying to read the magazines, waiting, watching the clock, wondering. A young nurse brought me cups of tea and kept telling me not to worry, Mr Richards was a marvellous surgeon. Ten o'clock. Eleven. Twelve. Four hours, what were they doing? What damage had they found? What was happening to Jake's knee?

I'm so sorry. I am so very sorry. I wish there was something I could do. And I wish most desperately there was something I could undo.

A riding accident. It was coincidence.

The horses are all right, Jake. And I'll keep them that way, I do promise. I promise. For better for worse, for richer for poorer, in sickness and in health. Those I promised, and those are promises I will keep. Not, keeping only unto you, and probably not as long as we both shall live, but what matters to us, to old friends, I will keep.

For the first time, Jake, I think I could say, I love you, and feel something of truth in the words.

In the early hours of the morning they told me the operation had been a success, as far as they could tell. There'd been extensive damage, but the leg had been saved, and there would be some movement in the knee once it had healed.

Mr Richards was tall and thin, with a circle of almost white hair clipped around a bald crown, and he looked very tired. He kept suppressing yawns as he explained what he had found, and what he had done to repair it.

'Will he be able to ride?' I asked.

'Yes. But don't ask me when.'

'May I see him?'

'Tomorrow. He's in the recovery room now.'

I took a taxi back to the forge, and I had a bath, and then lay on my bed staring up out of the window at the dark sky until the first streaks of light glimmered on the horizon. Then I went downstairs and made coffee, and I wrote a list, things I would do, and how I would do them, and when.

I went outside, and I looked at the two horses grazing in the paddock, and I smiled when Polaris lifted his head and looked towards me, his ears pricked for the first time when he recognised me. Lyric grazed closer and closer to the gate, and when I went back a few minutes later she was standing there, looking over it at me.

My dear old mare, the friend that Jake had sold me.

I drove to the stables, and lights were coming on in the yard. Toby appeared at the tack-room door at the sound of the van pulling in, and came across to meet me.

'They saved his leg,' I said, and he smiled.

I cooked bacon and eggs and Toby made piles of toast. There was a feeling of camaraderie in the big kitchen, and I was pleased, even though I felt it was inappropriate, perhaps even wrong. Soon, I would have to start giving orders, and then we would see whether I could indeed manage these stables.

We would, I said, have to change the routine to allow for Jake's absence.

Morry leaned back in his chair and said we'd have to hire somebody.

'I'm not asking for suggestions, thank you.'

There was silence, and I let it linger.

'I'll pay overtime,' I said at last, 'but the afternoon break is a thing of the past. It's an eleven-hour day from now on. Is there anybody who can't handle that?'

'I'm not working eleven bloody hours,' said Glen belligerently.

'All right. You can work the same hours until the end of the month. Or, if you'd prefer, I'll pay you off now.'

He looked at me as though I'd hit him, and I pushed my chair away from the table. 'Let me know what you decide before the end of the day,' I said to Glen, and then, to everybody, 'Have the first string ready in fifteen minutes.'

In the yard I called to Toby, and he came across, looking worried.

'As long as Jake or I have a stable, Toby, you have a job,' I said, and he nodded at me, relief on his face.

Morry had heard that. He would notice I had no such reassurance for him.

I would ride Barbarian. It would be a statement of my authority, and one I could risk, because I knew I could handle the horse. I saddled him, and noticed my hands shaking as I lifted the bridle onto his head.

So much would depend on how I managed these next few hours. I had said I could run these stables, but I truly hadn't known I would be called upon to prove it.

When I led Barbarian out into the yard Glen and Morry were talking. They stopped when they saw me, and Morry shrugged. He wouldn't look at Glen.

I stayed with Jake's routine for both the strings, and nothing out of the ordinary happened. For the second one I rode the same mare I'd been on when Jake had been injured, and I told Morry I wanted him to concentrate on the two new horses. They were to take priority. He could give Toby one of the hunters. I would also be giving him Polaris to school in a couple of weeks' time, but by then some of the other horses would have gone.

'Gone where?' demanded Glen, and I let my eyes travel

across his face, keeping my expression remote. I didn't answer his question.

'What are you going to do?' asked Toby later that morning when we met in the kitchen. All the horses were back and resting in their boxes, and there was time for a short break.

I gestured at a chair and poured him a coffee.

'I'm selling off about half the horses, Toby.'

His jaw dropped.

'Half?'

'Everything that's been here for more than six months. Except Barbarian.'

That included some of his favourites. Toby was inclined to make pets of horses, when he got to know them. He didn't like it when they were sold.

'And that mare with the splint Jake took when Flycatcher went.'

'You won't get much for her.'

I wouldn't get much for any of them. That wasn't the point.

'I'm off to see Jake,' I said, and Toby nodded, his face worried again as he thought of the horses that were going.

'Auction? There'll be knackers.'

'I know.'

I didn't like it either.

A nurse told me Jake had passed a comfortable night, and we smiled at each other, knowing it was hardly more than a half-truth. He was in a side ward by himself, drowsy with drugs. I sat by his bed for half an hour, as seemed to be expected, and I told him all the horses were doing well. We were managing, although we missed him.

Now and then he nodded as I spoke, but he wasn't listening. He fell asleep before I left.

On the way back I stopped at the auctioneer's office and picked up the forms. I wanted thirty, I said, and the girl looked at me.

'Thirteen?' she asked doubtfully, and I repeated, thirty.

She went into the back office, and Mr Marchant himself came out a moment later.

'Thirty horses, Mrs Brewer?'

I told him about Jake's accident, and he said he was sorry to hear it, very sorry indeed. He hoped there'd be a speedy recovery. But, thirty horses?

I explained that I had my own business to run, and now the stables as well. The only way I could possibly manage was by streamlining, and it would have to be drastic.

This, please, Mr Marchant, is the reason for so many of Jake Brewer's horses coming onto the market all at once.

'I see.'

'I have to keep the stable out of trouble,' I said. 'I can't take on extra staff, not because we can't afford them, but because I can't supervise them. You know what it's like with new people.'

He did indeed. And I was probably right. Yes, this was, he supposed, the best course of action. But what a pity.

Get this rumour off the ground, please, Mr Marchant. This is why all these horses are in the auction: Jake's accident, not because the stable's in trouble.

'We might buy some of them back later,' I said to him, wondering if he could possibly be convinced by such a statement. 'Some of them are quite promising.'

I spent most of the rest of the day on the telephone, trying not to become impatient with the ritual of commiseration and best wishes. Jake would recover, but would be in hospital for a while. In the meantime, I was running the business, and I was having to sell off several good horses. They'd be in next month's auction if I hadn't sold them by then. In some cases it would mean making a loss, but what could I do? I simply didn't have the time, or the staff.

Come on, vultures. Pickings.

I sold ten horses that week, and made a profit on two of them. When Glen told me he thought he might manage an

335

eleven-hour day after all, I said I didn't need him. He could work until the end of the month, and then I'd see about a reference.

Tommy asked if he was being sacked too, and I said no. Why? Why should I want to get rid of you, Tommy?

I showed him how to strip the paint off the loose-box doors, and told him I'd pay him a pound extra for every one he finished. Did he understand? His usual wages, and a pound for every door with no paint left on it. And you do it during working hours. Yes, Tommy, it's a sort of pay rise.

That had been stupid. I should have kept Glen, and sacked Tommy. At least Glen could ride.

'If I say I'm sorry,' said Glen truculently, 'can I stay?'

'No. Somebody was going to have to go anyway, Glen, and you volunteered.'

He went to see Jake in hospital, and told him I was selling all the horses at half their value.

'I've sold ten,' I said when Jake challenged me with Glen's accusations, and then I lied to him about their prices. 'I told all the customers what had happened, and said I'd have to cut down on the horses. They came around sniffing for bargains.'

Jake shifted uncomfortably, and swore under his breath. He was refusing to take the full dosage of painkillers. He had convinced himself they would slow his recovery.

'I am going to have to cut down the numbers,' I said. 'I can't manage them all, Jake.'

'Not the good ones,' he said quickly. 'Not the good ones.'

He listed the horses I was not to sell, not at any price. Barbarian, of course. Weaver's Dream and The Greek. Pennyroyal, Rise and Shine, Nicefella.

Toby and I went through the list of the horses, and I filled in the forms for the auction. Fifteen horses, unless they were sold in the meantime, and Toby almost had tears in his eyes. Who was going to buy old Superman, then? And

336

Milord? It'd be the knackers, wouldn't it? There was still a couple of seasons in them, wasn't there?

I sent Morry over to the forge with the trailer. Bring back Lyric and Polaris, and don't get yourself kicked. Please. Let's see what happens when we put a saddle on Polaris.

He kicked out as Morry tightened the girth, but Morry was quick enough to get out of the way. Toby held the horse's head, and I picked up one of his forefeet. Morry muttered to himself, but Polaris was saddled, bridled, and standing ready, with flattened ears and a swishing tail, for whatever came next.

We took him into the smaller of the two schooling rings, which was deep in loose sand, and Morry mounted, with the fast, smooth movements that left the horse balanced but with no time to back away. Toby let go of the reins, and we both stepped clear.

Polaris was nervous and jumpy, but Morry rode him on a long rein, sitting very still and upright in the saddle, and after a few minutes the horse began to move more easily, in a long, low canter, his hooves scuffing the sand.

Toby went back to the stables, but I stayed for a while to watch.

Round and round they went, Morry almost motionless, just keeping Polly cantering a little faster than he wanted, but letting his head stay loose, leaving his mouth alone, driving him forward with the pressure of his legs. It was slow, quiet work, and there was weeks of this ahead for the little chestnut. Weeks we didn't have. Morry had other horses to school.

I would have to plan this. I would have to find answers to the problems, and I didn't know where, or how.

What have I done?

Tommy finished stripping the paint off the loose-box doors, and I bought primer and undercoat, and showed him what I wanted him to do. Easier than stripping, I said. Once the gloss is on, it's the same deal. A pound a door.

337

I sold Superman to a woman with a bad heart who'd been advised by her doctor to take up some sort of gentle exercise. Superman was quiet and kind, and the woman liked him. She didn't want anything young or active, she said.

Toby was relieved. He'd been fond of Superman.

Only a week to the auction now.

Rainy weather set in, heavy and steady, and the rides on Gorsedown became slippery with mud. We rode carefully, just keeping the horses fit, but not trying to teach them anything new on the treacherous surfaces. The stable yard stood deep in dirty puddles, and wet straw always seemed to be lying soggily on the cobbles, no matter how often Tommy swept it up.

Tommy was irritable, because he couldn't paint the doors in the rain. He liked painting, and he'd been glad of the extra money.

I sold a Welsh cob to a local farmer, Guy Robins, for his two daughters, who'd outgrown their pony. Prince Hal was a handsome horse, too big for them, but he was a safe and easy ride, and the girls liked him. I refused to take the pony. Robins protested Jake had promised they could do a deal, but I said Misty would only be sent to the auction, and would probably be bought by the knackers. The girls rebelled, and Robins made it fairly clear that this piece of information could have been kept private. However, he bought the cob, and when he'd left I made a few telephone calls and found somebody who was looking for a safe pony for her grandchild. I gave her Robins's telephone number.

He rang me a couple of days later to thank me.

It was worth the effort. Sooner or later somebody would mention they were looking for a horse, and Robins would remember a dealer who'd sold him a good one and done a bit extra to help him.

Glen left, asking rather sullenly what sort of a reference

338

I'd be giving him. Quite a good one, I said. He could ride well.

He hadn't found another job. He was going back to his mother, in Birmingham, and would probably end up working in a factory.

Morry told me he couldn't manage all the horses I'd given him. He simply didn't have time. It was quite true.

'Look,' he said, 'how's this for an idea? Tommy doesn't like riding, right? So, you, me and Toby, we do the riding, right? Tommy does the tack, mixes the feeds, and all that. Bit of strapping, mucking out, give us more time.'

'Tommy does all the boring work, you mean,' I said, but it was a good idea. Tommy liked horses, but losing Crown Prince had destroyed his confidence. He didn't want to ride.

I put the idea to him, and he was happy to agree.

'Look, I can't do all this work on Polly,' said Morry. 'Not with the other two to school, and the hunters.'

How was I to manage this?

'Could Toby do it?'

Morry shook his head.

'Not good enough, and neither are you.'

It wasn't rude. It was simply his assessment, and it was a fair and honest one. Polaris was quieter and calmer, but he was still a very difficult horse. He would never be an easy ride.

I should have kept Glen, and sacked Tommy, I thought again. Glen could have worked Polly.

But the stable doors were painted, and they were smooth and shiny, the work very well done. Tommy liked being an odd-job man.

I was visiting Jake every day, and telling him how the horses were coming on, and he listened, interested.

'What do I do about Polaris?' I asked, and he shrugged.

'That's your problem. You bought him.'

His knee was hurting. It was taking longer than he'd

hoped. In one way he wanted to come home, and yet he was glad to leave the problems to me for a while, not to meet the postman every day with his heart in his mouth, not to wonder, when he went into the bank, whether the cashier would say Mr Crichton would be glad of a word, if you could wait a moment please, Mr Brewer.

Everybody needs a holiday sometimes.

Mr Crichton said he would like to see a business plan, if I could draw one up for him. I didn't know what he was talking about, so I telephoned Glory, and asked her, what's a business plan?

'I'll do it,' she said. 'If he asked for it, it probably means he wants to help. He's just covering his back. Are you managing?'

'We're still here,' I said. 'The horses are still eating.'

Twelve went to the auction, and three, including old Milord, were bought by Johnson, the horse slaughterer. Toby and I couldn't think of much to say to each other that evening.

'It's a hard old world,' he said the next morning, and that was as close as we came to talking about it.

I tried to ride Polly. Morry held him while I mounted, and then stood back. I'd watched Morry canter him round and round the schooling ring, on a long rein, and I couldn't see why I shouldn't do that. I knew, even before I put my foot in the stirrup, that Morry could make anything look easy where horses were concerned, and yet surely I could just ride round and round the ring, as he did?

As soon as Morry stepped back, Polaris threw himself into a gallop, charging for the fence, and I hauled on the reins and tried to pull him round. He went back onto his haunches, and I slammed my face into his neck. Pain flooded across my nose and my eyes were streaming as the horse turned, fast. I was unbalanced, not ready for the speed. I felt myself sliding across his shoulder, my knee slipping up the side of the saddle, and then I was off, rolling

on the sand, and the horse was backing away from me, jerking at the reins.

I wasn't badly hurt. I'd thought at first my nose was
broken, and I was slightly winded from the impact of the
fall, but I was all right. I couldn't see through my streaming
eyes. Morry took Polaris from me. He didn't say anything,
he just swung himself up into the saddle and began to ride
as usual, slowly and quietly, until the horse was calm.

I was never going to be able to ride Polaris, and neither
was Toby.

I wiped my eyes, and felt the sides of my nose, trying to
assess the damage, wincing as I did so. Nothing seemed to
move that hadn't moved before, so I assumed nothing was
broken. But my vision was still blurred.

There were two people standing at the gate, watching
Morry and the horse, looking at me, talking quietly to each
other.

'We came to see how you're managing,' said Bess, and
then there was another voice.

'We've missed you, Ann.'

Gwen.

341

23

'Jake's knee was broken,' I said, and my voice was thick, not only because of my bruised nose. 'It was a compound fracture. Do you know what that means?'

'Poor Jake,' said Gwen.

'It'll never be the same again. His knee. It was a horrible injury. He was in *agony*.'

I rubbed at my eyes, furious, wanting to see clearly and unable to do so. What would I see, when I looked into their faces?

Still blurred, still smeared, I could see only that they were looking at me. I brushed at the sand on my jacket. I wanted them to say something. Perhaps I would hear in their voices, perhaps there would be something, and then I could accuse them, and demand an answer.

What was it? What did you summon?

But they were silent. I could not ask the questions.

'Is there anything we can do to help?'

'Not unless you can ride.'

'Well, actually, I can.'

It was Bess who had spoken. That clear, public school voice was unmistakable.

Of course she'd be able to ride. She'd probably never known what it was not to have a pony. Daddy would have bought it for her and stabled it with his hunters and his polo ponies. It would have been traded in for something bigger and better every second birthday, and the young Bess would have taken part in local gymkhanas and Pony Club events.

Morry had dismounted and was loosening Polly's girths. I watched, waiting to see whether the horse would kick, but he stood quietly, sweating slightly from the exercise, his ribs moving. Morry had said he was getting easier.

I'd stayed in the saddle for about seven seconds.

I nodded towards them.

'If you can ride that one, you'd be of some use to me.'

Bess was in jeans and sandals, her feet spattered with mud. She glanced down at them, and grimaced.

'I'll have a go, if you like.'

Jake's leg, bent at that hideous angle, his teeth in the sleeve of my jacket. The cloth bitten through. He'd said he was sorry. He'd screamed with the pain, and then said he was sorry.

So, ride him.

She wasn't as good as Morry, not by a very long way, but Bess could certainly ride. Polaris jumped around uneasily as soon as Morry let him go, but she sat much as he had, upright and relaxed, with her hands low, the reins long, and she was supple and confident. She let Polaris dance around, tossing his head, stepping sideways, swishing his tail, giving him a few moments to accept her, and then she gathered up the reins and her legs moved.

Enough, horse. Now, work.

She took him in a tight figure of eight, a collected canter with his head a little over-bent, and he changed legs at her signal and turned with the rein against his neck. She did it twice, then drew him back into a slow trot, and a walk, and rode him towards us.

'I can ride him,' she said, and if it was an answer to a challenge there was nothing in her voice to indicate it.

She wanted to ride. She could give me a couple of hours every evening, schooling horses, or, if I wanted more, four hours every morning, but for that I'd have to pay, because it would mean losing work. Tam could ride too, she mentioned, although Western style, if it was the same thing.

That was a glint of the old Bess, the ironic sense of humour that could either offend or amuse, depending on whether it was recognised.

I'll have to shoe Polaris, I thought, and then, what do I do now? I procrastinate with my thinking when I'm perplexed, looking down the footpaths beside the main track of the problem. Shoe Polly, because he'll be doing regular work soon. Do I offer Bess a job? Had they done something, something I would never understand and never want to know, something that had nearly maimed Jake?

Morry will have to take time to help with Polaris when I shoe him, or he'll kick. Was it them? Or was it a freak accident? Some sort of infectious hysteria that had caught us, too?

That must have been it.

Zack Paulson. He was a threat to us.

'I'd love a cup of tea,' said Gwen, and I tried to smile at her.

There had been cases of that sort of hysteria. It was how crowds turned into lynch mobs. There were many well-documented occasions of that kind.

And the horses?

'Tea,' I said. 'Yes, of course. Bess, could Tam manage that horse?'

'No.'

No conceit, no 'I'm a better rider than Tam', just an answer to the question. Polaris would only ever be a horse for an expert, a professional.

Bess slipped down from the saddle and stood alongside Polly's shoulder, patting his neck in an almost automatic gesture.

344

'He kicks,' Morry warned. 'I mean, seriously, right?'

I hadn't told her. Her eyes moved from his face to mine, but there was no expression.

'Tea?'

Gwen, playing peacemaker, smiling at me, smiling at Morry, a small shake of her head towards Bess.

Four hours a day, then, we agreed over tea in the kitchen, and she'd ask Tam about some schooling in the evenings. Just keeping a few horses up to the mark, nothing too difficult. Bess herself had trained a couple of jumpers, and thought she could do it again. Not Polaris, not to his real potential. He was too much.

Was there any chance she might ride Barbarian? She'd seen him race, on television. Not ride him in races, of course, but out at exercise? Or was he too much of a handful?

'I can ride him,' I said, and we smiled at each other, the question answered.

'How's Glory?' asked Gwen.

Glory had been down for a weekend, and we'd drawn up a business plan. She'd done most of it, telling me what figures she was entering, and why, and how I was to present it. The prospects for the stables, the plans, how we proposed to win back old customers and find new ones, what we would do if the plans failed. How much money we would need, how much we had, how much we might want to borrow.

'They'll never lend any more,' I'd protested, but she'd shaken her head.

'That's not the point.'

Crichton wanted realism, she'd said. He wanted to know what I was going to do about the financial situation. He didn't want fairy tales, he didn't want dreams, he wanted to be sure I knew what I was doing. He didn't want the business to fail. Apart from anything else, it would reflect badly on his judgement.

When she'd finished she leaned forward and touched me, and I nearly jumped. Glory doesn't do that very often; she's a rather reserved person. It's only when she's in very bad trouble, or thinks I am, that she touches me.

'Ann, please get this partnership broken.'

'I can't.'

'You're not responsible for this. The fact that he's in hospital doesn't change anything. He tricked you.'

But it was my fault. Wasn't it? If you ill-wish a person, and evil comes to that person, are you not guilty?

This is superstitious nonsense. Something frightened the horses and there was an accident. More people are killed riding horses than in any other sporting activity; it is the most dangerous of them all.

'Ann?'

'I can't.'

I have to atone for this. I can only do it by saving the stables for Jake. There was something on Gorsedown that day, and it had been summoned by my will, at my request.

Rubbish.

'Ann, I've done my best with this business plan, but I don't think you'll succeed. I think the cost of the debt is too high. The interest, I mean, it's too much. I think you'll lose the stables, and the forge. What do you hope to gain?'

Crichton asked the same question, when I took the plan to him and sat opposite him while he read it. Mrs Brewer, wouldn't it be better to cut your losses now?

But Glory's business plan was good. He would, in effect, stand back and watch me try to make it work. He wished me luck.

Frederick Hoffmann came to the stables and offered me eight thousand pounds for Weaver's Dream.

I'd taken a lesson from Glory, and kept a record of every horse, what we'd paid for them, the time spent on them,

346

their food: every penny went down in their own books. Frogface, Toby called him affectionately, rubbing the horse's nose. Heading for the top, jump the Berlin Wall and run a mile a minute up a cliff face. Stood me in at five thousand now, did Frogface.

'No,' I said. 'Sorry, Fred. Give me six months, and you can have him for twenty.'

Hoffmann bared his teeth at me in what he imagined was a smile.

'Nine?' he said, and I shook my head.

'Nineteen.'

He shrugged, smiled again, and drove away with the luxurious trailer empty behind the new Bentley.

He hadn't bought Weaver's Dream, but he hadn't laughed at me either.

'He'll be back,' said Jake when I told him that evening, but he was fretful about it. 'Maybe you should have let him have him. He might find another horse. Oh, shit.'

His knee was infected. It wasn't serious, he'd been assured. A few days on a course of antibiotics would soon clear it up.

I thought Frederick Hoffmann wanted that horse, and only that horse, and would try for him again. He was the sort of man who was used to getting what he wanted. He'd leave it for a couple of weeks, hoping I'd worry, just as Jake was doing now, and then he'd telephone to ask if I had anything else that might suit him. There'd be a few questions about the other horses, and then a casual enquiry, had I sold that bay gelding yet?

Not yet, I'd say. I don't want to sell him yet. I want him in the events in Jake's name. Weaver's Dream is down as advertising expenses in the accounts.

Tam could ride well, but in a long-legged, sloppy sort of style that made Toby stare disapprovingly. She didn't like our saddles. Might as well sit on a pancake, getting bunions on my arse.

Toby became even more disapproving. Ladies don't use such words.

Miss Bess was a proper lady, who spoke nicely and always said good morning. Miss Bess might be a credit to the stables in the West of England show if we had a few horses to enter, in the right classes.

'The upper ones, you mean?' I asked, and he chuckled.

Miss Bess was damned if she'd fart about in the bloody West of England show, she'd probably meet a few people better forgotten, like her total arsehole of a father.

But this was in the kitchen, and Toby was out of earshot.

It was Bess who helped me shoe Polaris, and although he flattened his ears he didn't try to kick either of us.

Tommy painted the drainpipes in the stable yard, and cleared the drains and the gutters. Most of the gutters needed renewing, but there wasn't enough money. Tommy patched them from the inside with flattened-out beer cans stuck down with paint and putty, and he used some sort of filler to repair the joins. Then he sanded them, and brought out his paints and brushes.

I filed two of my own bills in the pending tray, and spent money on ladders and weatherproof paint.

'Tommy can't ride,' said Jake. 'He isn't earning his keep.'

The antibiotics were making him sick, he complained. And his knee hurt. Also he had headaches, really bad ones, and a pain under his shoulder. How much longer was he going to be stuck in here?

I should sack Tommy and find somebody who could pull his weight in the stables.

'He's good at cleaning tack,' I said. 'He does all that, and he mixes the feeds. It gives Morry and Toby time to school two more horses each.'

This was not the way it had been in his father's time. And what about these women?

'How did you find out about them?' I was genuinely curious.

Jake said he had his sources, but then he smiled, and told me Clive Laverton had been in for a visit, and had described the blonde as a very tasty piece of pastry.

'Bess *will* be flattered.'

Bess said she had got as far as she could with Polaris, and now it would have to be Morry. Clive Laverton was welcome to impale himself, rear end first, on a splintered broomstick that had been dipped in creosote. Tasty piece of pastry.

She rode Barbarian on Gorsedown the next day, and we took the long track over the hill and past the house into the woods at a gallop. After three miles Barbarian was still ready for more, and Morry said he reckoned she wasn't that bad. At least she could sit still, not bounce around knocking all the breath out of a horse.

'Have you ever ridden in a point-to-point?' I asked, and she threw me a flashing smile.

'Not yet.'

Not Barbarian, not in a ladies' race, but Pennyroyal, and they came third.

'Should have won,' somebody grumbled at me in the unsaddling enclosure, and I snapped at him.

'It's her first race.'

'That's a gelding, not a her.'

'I meant the rider, you cretin.'

Pennyroyal was sweating heavily, and tired, with his head low, but he was sound and he'd done his best. Tommy led him away, patting his neck and murmuring endearments, and I looked round into the red face of a short, fat man with a spoilt-child pout.

'I'm not a cretin, I'm a baronet. A stupid baronet if you like, but not a cretin. Is that horse for sale?'

I sold him Pennyroyal for twelve thousand pounds, and the money paid the last of the bills and most of the overdue mortgage. I telephoned Glory that evening with the news, and she congratulated me.

'Ann, before you lash out on champagne, check the business plan.'

She had calculated we'd sell at least one good horse every two months. It had taken me two and a half.

I would have to do better.

'I told you not to sell Pennyroyal,' said Jake.

'Twelve thousand pounds and a new customer.'

'Oh, all right.'

He was in a wheelchair with his leg strapped to a board out in front of him. He was beginning to look very tired, and puffy around the eyes. He wanted to come home. He wanted the plaster off. Why was it all taking so long? And his headaches were getting worse.

'It was a horrible break,' I said. 'And then there was the infection. Try to be patient.'

Lord Greenford's estate manager telephoned to say His Lordship would like to exchange Pennyroyal for another horse, perhaps something better, a steeplechaser. Pennyroyal's performance in the point-to-point had been a flash in the pan, in His Lordship's opinion.

The tone of the voice was dry, and a little resigned.

'Has His Lordship been riding Pennyroyal himself?'

'Ah. Well, His Lordship does enjoy riding, yes. Perhaps the horse is a little flighty?'

'Racehorses often are. What, in your opinion, would suit him?'

In the estate manager's opinion, His Lordship would be best suited by a stuffed horse on a concrete stand. However, was there any chance of an exchange? He, personally, would see to it that the stable didn't suffer financially from the transaction.

Morry drove the horsebox to the big house. The Greek and Nicefella were in it, both fast, good-looking horses, not difficult to ride. Nicefella was the best I could offer, and I didn't believe he'd buy The Greek. I had to take two horses at least, or he'd refuse to do a deal, feeling he was being put under pressure.

I went myself later in the Volvo, and met the fat little man in the stable yard. Pennyroyal was already back in the horsebox.

'Not blaming you,' said the baronet, 'but the horse isn't as good as he looked. Not got the guts for what I want.'

Nicefella was a strong-looking chestnut with a white blaze, the sort to catch the eye, and quite patient.

'The grey's still a bit green,' I said. 'He's very promising, but he needs a lot of quiet work.'

'No time for that, I want to use him this winter. What's the chestnut done?'

A straight exchange for Pennyroyal, which I calculated had made us a two thousand pound profit. The estate manager telephoned that evening.

'You'll probably have him back early in the New Year,' he said. 'Have something else ready about then.'

Pennyroyal had developed a habit of running out at his fences, the result of not being ridden strongly enough, and he was cautious and shy of them, jumping slowly and not enjoying it. Bess said she thought the fat little bugger had been snatching at the poor boy's mouth. She rode him on Gorsedown with Toby and Morry on slower hunters, the three of them riding abreast, so Pennyroyal began to pick up the taste for a challenge again. It wouldn't take long to put him right, provided nobody else hurt his mouth.

'Pennyroyal's back, but Nicefella's gone,' I told Jake, and he grunted. 'It was Lord Greenford,' I reminded him, and Jake said he knew the fat fool, he rode like a bag of saddles, and what sort of a mess had he made of Pennyroyal?

I would have to sell another good horse that month to pay the mortgage, and soon I would need to buy some, or we wouldn't have a good enough selection to offer potential customers.

I didn't want to do it. I didn't know enough about

horses to spot the ones that could be improved. Not unless it was something like Polaris, where I'd been lucky.

'What should I do?' I asked Jake, but he didn't know. He had the auction catalogues, but he hadn't seen the horses, not recently.

He became fretful and anxious. It was going to be another six weeks, the bloody knee would not heal, it just would not. What the hell were they playing at here? He used to heal up like a cat, nothing had ever taken this long before. They must have done something wrong.

Don't buy in any horses, he said. You don't know enough.

Dominic Mont-Blering came to the house. He was sorry to hear about Jake's accident, he said, but he was still owed money, and would now have to insist.

'I don't believe you. Prove it.'

'Mrs Brewer, gentlemen do not normally find it necessary to exchange documentary proof of their financial transactions.'

'Gentlemen don't race ringers. Crooks do that. I don't know how to deal with crooks, but I suppose I could always ask the police.'

I made my voice as contemptuous as I could, and he looked angry. Calling the police would be most unwise, unless I actually wanted my husband in the dock. He, personally, would not be standing beside him. Think about it, Mrs Brewer.

'Perhaps the Jockey Club could advise me,' I answered. 'The racing world's only a very small part of our business. And I think I can wriggle out of Jake's side of it. I have an excellent lawyer.'

The excellent lawyer was my next unexpected visitor. My Uncle John, Henry Mayall's older brother, a little thinner, the grey hair a little wispier, but still upright, still driving himself in the latest-model Rover, and greeting me on my return from riding out with the second string with a quiet word and a reserved smile.

Tommy took my horse, and Uncle John and I went into the house.

'How's the blacksmith?' he asked.

'Not doing much work in the forge,' I admitted.

Three days a week was all I could manage now. It was enough to pay the mortgage on my home, but there was nothing left over. I tried very hard to keep the accounts separate, and usually I managed, but there were times when it wasn't possible. The horses at the stable had to be shod, and feed bills paid. My own bills lay at the bottom of the pending tray, and I hardly dared look at them.

My customers complained they could never find me. They were having to wait too long between appointments. I'd said Ginger's shoes should be taken off every month and his feet dressed, how could that be done if I was never available? Look at the state of Narnia's feet, Ann. They should have been done weeks ago. Can you fit me in next week? Well, the week after, then? I can't leave it any longer.

I needed to buy in more steel, more fuel, there was a cracked drain at the kitchen corner of the cottage that would have to be repaired soon before the leaking water did structural damage, and I couldn't afford it, I just couldn't afford it.

I gave Uncle John a sherry, and we sat in the old leather chairs in Jake's study. It was cold and dusty, but there was nowhere else that wasn't full of horse papers, riding boots, and general mess. The place was neglected and untidy, even dirty, and I couldn't help it. I couldn't do any more than I was doing. Even I had to sleep sometimes.

'Sorry about the state of the place,' I said, a little curtly, and he smiled.

'It looks rather better than I remember. The paint helps.'

I knew why he'd come. He wanted me to break the

partnership, and save the forge. He could see me heading for disaster, and wanted to stop me before it was too late.

'It's already too late,' I said. 'I can't leave Jake like this.'

Uncle John didn't look at me as he spoke. His eyes were lowered onto the sherry in the lovely old crystal glass, his fingers trailing gently across the cut surface. He likes antiques.

Promises are important, he said, marriage vows perhaps especially so. Without trust, nothing could work. Personal relationships, business, even the law, it was all, to some extent, based on trust.

'Ann, I think you are one of the most trustworthy people I have ever known,' he said, and I was surprised, and almost embarrassed. I glanced away, and when I turned back he was, for the first time, looking straight into my face.

'I believe you would find it easier to break a leg than break a promise,' he said, and I flinched.

My own leg, yes, perhaps. Jake. Sorry, Jake.

'What did Jake promise you?' asked Uncle John.

'He promised to work as hard as he could. To do everything he could to make a success of the stables. He kept that promise.'

'When did he make it? Before or after he made you a partner? Time is of the essence here, and I use that phrase with its legal meaning.'

I looked away again.

He used legal arguments, and he used persuasion, but he did not once say that Uncle Henry had trusted me to look after the forge. We both knew what that good man had meant to me, and why he had left me the place we loved.

It was the weapon that might have worked, and it was the weapon he would not touch.

'Do you know anybody who could help me buy horses?' I asked when he had finished speaking, when there had been silence for some minutes. He looked up, curious.

'I can do everything else. I can even sell. I didn't think I'd

354

be able to, but I can. I don't know enough to buy horses, Uncle John. I know a good horse when I see one, but I don't know a horse that can be improved and sold at a profit. I'm stuck, and I'm going to lose if I can't do this. I don't know who to ask. I can't let people know ... I can't let it be known that I don't know enough.'

'It sounds as if you need an agent. Surely there are such people?'

'For racehorses, yes.' I was doubtful, but he could be right.

'A man who can spot a good racehorse can probably spot a good hack. You could ask. Put the idea to Jake.'

I did put the idea to Jake that evening, and he said it might be worth a shot.

'What else did he say?'

Jake liked John Mayall, but he was a little wary of him. He knew Uncle John was a lawyer, and a shrewd and clever one, and Jake's experiences with lawyers had not always been happy.

Uncle John had said I was too thin, and that I was looking tired. After he'd gone I looked at myself in the big mirror in the dark hall. The evening light gilded the old glass, and the woman who looked back at me was indeed gaunt, with shadows in her face, and her clothes crumpled at the waist where the leather belt held them in.

'When will you feel you've paid your share?' he'd asked when I'd refused, for the last time, to break the partnership, and I hadn't been able to answer. Ten per cent, I'd thought at the beginning, ten per cent was my share of this burden, and if I paid that, wouldn't I have dealt fairly with the man who was now my husband?

What is fair, for a crippled knee?

'When the business is out of danger,' I'd said at last, and Uncle John had raised his eyebrows, and smiled.

The horse world is a small one. Libby Donnington's father was an agent, the third I tried. The others had said they worked only with bloodstock, and didn't want to branch out. Chuck Donnington said sure, he'd give it a go, why not? Wasn't I the one Libby had talked about? Clive Ulverton's friend? What did I think of Libby's riding?

'Good enough to earn what she asks,' I said. 'But I can't afford her.'

'Have you got anything good enough for her to ride?'

'Yes.'

I'd often wondered if I could tempt Libby back with the little liver chestnut. She knew enough to see the promise in the horse, and she might see in him an opportunity to go further in her chosen world.

'I think she's good enough to handle him,' I said, letting a shade of doubt creep into my voice. 'He's a horse for a professional. He's too small for Morry.'

I was running out of time with Polly. He was going well. He'd become supple and obedient under Morry's care and he was beginning to jump without throwing his head around in wild panic. Bess refused to ride him. She couldn't take him any further, she said. She'd do more harm than good, jumping him.

Chuck said Libby would be round in the morning, and she was.

'You keep out of this,' I warned Morry. 'She's just what I need for Polly.'

'Lesbian,' he muttered sullenly, staring at her as she climbed out of her car. 'I hate lesbians.'

I warned her that the horse kicked, and she nodded. It was his ability that interested her, not his temper. She looked him over when I led him out of his box, her eyes travelling up and down his legs, over the short, powerful body, and for the first time since I'd known her I saw the beginnings of a smile.

'Well,' she murmured. 'Yes. Let's see.'

She wasted no time at all. Twice around the schooling ring to warm him up, and then the jumps, small ones at first, slowly, and then faster, and then the bigger jumps, and yet bigger, and she gave him no rest. She shouted at me and Tam: get those poles up, higher! Right. Then again, higher, and another six inches. Right.

Polaris was sweating and his eyes were beginning to roll, his head up high, but she pulled him in and rode him up into his bridle so his steps became short and bouncy, and she turned him towards the big fence, giving him enough time to see it, enough room to judge, and then she drove him forward, and hit him twice, two hard cracks with her whip, and his ears went back but he was in under the jump, his legs gathered under him, and I held my breath as he took off.

It seemed for ever that he was in the air, straining for the extra height, his back rounded, his legs curled up, and Libby sat forward, all her weight over his shoulders, her hands reaching along his neck, everything in her telling him to go on, he could do it, she knew he could do it, and he could trust her.

One hoof clipped the pole and it rattled, but it stayed in place, and he was clear, galloping away from it as she swung her hand against his neck in a grateful salute to the effort he had made.

'Yes,' she said as she rode back towards us. 'Well, yes. Right.'

She and only she would ride Polaris from now on, and she would ride him every day. She wanted complete charge of the little horse. What he needed he was to have. She'd use her own saddle for a start. By summer he'd be clearing at least another eighteen inches, and she'd prove it at Hickstead, no less.

Tam was looking resentful and unhappy. Libby had been very hard on the horse. She'd hit him, and they hadn't been love taps. He'd grunted with the effort of that last jump. He was tired and sweating.

I thought it would work. Polaris was a tough horse, and

Libby was a tough rider. Together, they could do well. She wasn't cruel, but she was demanding, and determined, and strong enough to handle him.

This was why I'd bought him.

'All right,' I said. 'So long as you're good enough to ride him, I'll back you. Don't let me down.'

24

Libby's presence caused an unpleasant atmosphere. Morry referred to her as 'that dyke', in tones of loathing, until I told him to stop.

'Were you planning to seduce her?' I demanded.

'You joking?'

'Then her tastes don't matter, do they?'

Tam's objections were more serious. Tam said she was cruel to Polly. I knew she was hard on the horse, but I doubted cruelty. He was looking well, and cleaning up his feed every day; an ill-treated horse would not do that. He was still bad-tempered, but the fear was dying away.

'Ann, she hits him. God, she really does, Ann.'

There are cruel ways of training jumpers, and they're still used. They're illegal, and certainly banned by the show-jumping authorities, but they work. I didn't know whether Libby would have used them given a chance, but she knew I wouldn't have condoned it, and that I would have spotted them instantly.

'Ann, please, come and see Polly. She's marked him.'

Bess was standing a little behind Tam, not taking her part, but looking noncommittal. When I glanced at her, she shrugged.

There were marks on the horse's coat, three raised weals

on his flank. But he was eating quite contentedly, although he laid his ears back and swung his head as I looked over the door.

'Don't hit him so hard,' I said to Libby the next day.

'He's tough. He can take it.'

'I can't. If a customer sees those marks I could be in trouble. Show me your whip.'

I looked at it, handed it back, and told her not to use it again.

She was annoyed, but she had to do as I said. The whip she brought to replace it wasn't much of an improvement. However, Polaris was growing fitter, and he didn't seem to be frightened of his rider, no matter that she rode him to the limit.

'I'll never understand horses,' I said to Jake one evening when we were talking about Polly, and he smiled at me.

'None of us do, if we're honest.'

He was on crutches, swinging himself up and down the corridor.

'I'll be home soon.'

I hoped he was right. Chuck Donnington was finding me horses, and I was making a profit on them, but it was a very small margin once I'd paid his commission.

Fred Hoffmann came back, and offered me ten thousand for Weaver's Dream. Fifteen, I said, and, Fred, let's not bother haggling. I will not drop his price below that, I mean it. In a year he'll be worth twenty, and I'd have the publicity from him.

Fred gritted his teeth, and his eyes flicked between me and the lovely horse. He knew my assessment of his value was fair.

'It's a lot of money,' he muttered.

'You've got a lot of money, and I need some of it,' I retorted, and Hoffmann laughed.

Toby was rubbing the horse's nose, his face twisted with regret. He knew Hoffmann would buy him now, his pal Frogface, and he'd miss him.

'Fifteen thousand, and he's never been in an event,' complained Hoffmann, and I replied,

'Oh, I'll put him in one if you like, but his price won't stay at fifteen if I do.'

He grinned again. He knew a winner when he saw one, and Weaver's Dream was as good as anything he'd see that year.

Jake agreed that night I'd done well to get fifteen thousand. He wished he could find a few more like old Frogface. How was The Greek?

Second string, the handsome grey. We'd make a profit, but it wouldn't be the sort of quick and big one we'd made with the bay. I, too, wished we could find a few more like old Frogface.

I didn't tell him Polaris was my hope for big money. Jake had bought and sold showjumpers, but had never had an exceptional one, and wasn't particularly interested.

Libby was certainly holding to her part of our bargain. She worked with Polly every day, and she could judge to the finest edge exactly what the horse could do. He was faster, he was confident, and on those rare days when she did turn him to the big obstacles, rather than building him up on the smaller ones, he went at them with his ears pricked, he gathered himself, and he put every ounce of effort she demanded into his jump.

'I sure do hope that horse is good,' Chuck grumbled when I spoke to him on the telephone. 'She's turned down some races.'

It must have been a hard decision for her, but I thought it was probably the right one. It will be years yet before women can ride in steeplechases on equal terms with men, no matter how good they are. In show-jumping, if a woman's good enough, and brave enough, there's no such problem. Libby was being realistic.

As some sort of compensation for the sacrifice, I let her ride in point-to-points, but I warned her, if she brought a horse back marked, that would stop. I would not allow the stable to get a name for being hard on horses. Protesters were causing enough trouble without competitors handing them ammunition.

We did sell horses to two of Jake's old customers, and there were a few new ones, but it was a painfully slow process. When I looked at the account books and the interest on the mortgage I had to admit I wasn't making progress. Another rise in interest rates could be the final straw.

I tried to be optimistic when I saw Jake. Another new customer, and he'd smile, but a horse dealer is not a grocer. One horse a year is quite good; more is unusual, unless the customer is himself a professional. And if we didn't have a horse to suit that customer, there was nothing to keep him. Nobody feels much in the way of loyalty in this business.

Jake could not, or would not, believe his old customers were not coming back. It must be because he wasn't there.

'You're doing well,' he said, but it was with an abstracted air, as though he was trying to be supportive.

Morry drove the horsebox to the events, and I wasn't happy about it. Like many competitive people, he was aggressive on the road as well as in the saddle, and on the one occasion when Libby had gone with them Toby came back and told me he'd never travel with the pair of them again. It was a miracle they hadn't crashed.

'Use your own car in future,' I said to Libby, and to Morry: 'She's not far off as good as you. Don't forget it.'

I didn't go myself. Competition days, for me, had the air of a holiday. I spent them at the forge. I made wrought-iron ornaments or gates, or I mended tools. They were the days when I telephoned old friends whom I'd previously thought of as customers. Got a day to myself on Saturday, Garth. The drop bar for the barn door? Yes, I'll do that for you. Hello, Alan, I'm at the forge on Saturday. Yes, I can do your gate catch. How do you want it?

Perhaps I should have gone. Horses can be sold at the events, but I hated the crowds. Strangers stared at me when they thought I wasn't looking. I told myself, if somebody wanted to buy one of the horses I could be contacted the next day. And Toby was there.

Lord Greenford's estate manager, I never did learn his name, telephoned to say His Lordship had had a bad accident. Nicefella had broken his neck, and His Lordship had broken his hip. He would not be riding again. Sorry to have bad news about the horse.

I allowed myself a brief moment of sheer anger and threw a hammer across the forge. It slammed into the oak door, and clattered onto the flagstones. That good horse, with his brave, kind nature, killed by an incompetent rider.

As Toby had said, it's a tough old world.

I could allow myself anger, but there were times I found I was fighting despair. I will never be free of this, never. Eternity is selling horses, and buying horses, and paying the bills, and trying to keep up with the mortgage, and the wages, and planning without enough knowledge, with all the hope of release pinned on one little horse.

Ridiculous.

Arno, I do so want you. I lie awake and remember the time when there was no empty space beside me in this bed, when I could touch warm skin, and listen to you breathing. When my hands moved slowly over a body at once familiar and exciting, waiting and listening for the change in the breathing that meant you were awake, and would, in just a moment, turn to me.

I haven't sold your car. It doesn't matter, does it? When you told me to sell it, it was only to make sure I understood. It was another way of saying: Ann, don't wait for me.

I love you, Arno. I love you, and I do wish you well, you and your Brita.

But only late at night, when there was nothing else to be done, when the working day was finally finished, did I allow myself to think of Arno. Yes, it would sometimes be as though I was praying to him, and my face would be wet with tears. This I could not allow when there was still work to be done.

How do I make the stables profitable? Where can I cut corners? What can I do?

Oh, dear God, get me out of this.

My friends did try to support me, but they didn't understand. Jane Laverton telephoned me every time she heard that somebody might be in the market for a pony, a cob, something quiet for an old friend, had I got anything suitable?

There was very little time for the ponies and the nice quiet rides for a pensioner who'd never lost her interest in horses. I did buy them if somebody offered me one and I could get it at the right price, but my only hope was good horses, a good profit on them, and then back to Chuck Donnington to bring in replacements. Morry worked as hard as he could: a horse with a mouth like a plank needing it corrected, a failed hunter who panicked at jumps, calm him down and make him sensible and confident and safe. Dear old Toby Joliot stolidly rode horses at exercise and left the skilled work to Morry, never resenting it. Bess listened to Morry and did as she was told, riding for the love of it and a few pounds at the end of the week. Tam in the evenings, again just exercise, but she was reliable and good enough. I couldn't have managed without my friends.

Tommy cleaned tack and mended it, and weeded the overgrown flowerbeds, and told me, if I got in some sand he'd take up some of the sunken cobblestones and level them up. He mucked out the loose boxes while we had the horses out at exercise, so we brought them back to clean wood shavings and filled hay nets. Since he'd stopped riding Tommy had become less anxious, and I wondered if Glen's departure had something to do with his increased self-assurance.

When Jake complained again that Tommy, if he didn't ride, could not be pulling his weight, I retorted that we couldn't possibly manage without Tommy. He worked harder than anybody.

I'd always thought Tommy was slightly simple, but I began to wonder if I'd been wrong. Now his work was within his capabilities, and he knew exactly what he was to do, he became talkative, and he had ideas. When we get the hay delivered, stack it at the other end next time, so it doesn't block off the old lot. Some of those bales at the back don't half smell musty. If we get rid of all that old timber round the back we could put up rails and hang the rugs out there to air. Catches the sun mornings, that bit. Now there's no real flowers in the tubs, can I get some of them plastic ones from down Woolie's?

No, I'd said, and then; oh, hell. Why not? Go on, then, Tommy.

He noticed a big scrape on one of his newly painted doors. He sanded it down, applied primer, undercoat and gloss, then stood back and looked at it, and gave a brief nod. Done it.

It was a mannerism I began to notice. When he'd finished a piece of work he'd stand back and examine it. If it was good enough, there was a little nod, as though he told himself it would do. If he wasn't satisfied he'd suck his teeth in a discontented way, and go back to it and work until it met his standards.

'This place, it's lucky,' Tommy said, and I asked him why.

There'd been no accidents since Mr Jake, nothing bad, just a few grazes, right? Well, that's lucky, isn't it? And there's that cough, half the stables in the county's got that cough, and not us. That's lucky, too. And there's four-leafed clovers in that patch by the paddock gate, that's lucky.

The cough: I thanked Tommy, because I'd taken risks here and I didn't need to. Any new horse, I said, anything that comes in goes out to grass for three weeks, just to make sure. We don't need that bloody cough.

An Anglo-Arab mare I bought from a riding school that was selling her because she was too flighty went out into the big field, and two days later she was coughing. It could have gone through the whole stable and brought us to a complete standstill.

Bless you, Tommy.

It seemed to be a happy place, too. It looked bright, with its new paint and its dreadful plastic flowers which made people smile. We all talked and laughed in the stables, Toby whistled as he worked, and Tam sang folk songs to her horses as she rode them, in a pleasant, contralto voice.

'Do they listen?' I asked.

'You bet.'

Bess and Tam both knew how close we were to disaster, but neither ever spoke of it. There was no money at all to spare. One big, unexpected expense could finish us. Even one month when I didn't sell a good horse.

Jansy Neville started to sleep at the cottage. She said she didn't like her home any more, she couldn't work there, she couldn't bring her friends there, and, Missus, would you believe they turn the telly *on* for game shows?

'I'll keep it nice,' she said. 'I will, Missus. Anyway, you're never here, are you? There could be burglars.'

But I was there, I told myself, I was often there. Three days a week I was Ann Mayall. I could keep my old customers that way, on three days a week. I could just pay the mortgage.

Somehow, I had to get that broken drain fixed, but it was going to be expensive.

'Jansy, can you manage without using the kitchen sink?' I asked. It meant carrying the dirty plates upstairs and washing them in the bathroom.

Five hundred pounds to dig out the drain and replace it, and more if they found any damage once they began.

366

There was still money in the bank left from what I'd raised, but I spent it as slowly as I could, on a horse here, on two new saddles because the old ones were really beyond repair, on the bank loan when I didn't sell a good one that month. It was dwindling away, as Glory and Uncle John had said it would.

But the cottage was my home, and Jansy said carrying crocks up those stairs was stupid.

Those stairs, I noticed, and tried to stop myself smiling. Only a few months ago it would have been them stairs, but only a few months ago Jansy Neville had been a scruffy schoolgirl, and now she was a young woman. The friends she couldn't take home weren't girls.

I telephoned the builder and asked him to start work as soon as he could.

'I was going to ring you,' he said. 'You want to do that before the frost starts. Could be bad, then.'

So I stopped sleeping at the cottage, and left it to Jansy, and because of that our luck did not quite run out.

In the early hours of the morning, on a Monday night when I would have been at the cottage, I woke to the smell of smoke.

It was in the hay loft, and I put it out, sousing the corner with buckets of water until it was a sodden mess. I telephoned the fire brigade, and they dragged out the wet hay and the charred timbers, and they damped it down some more. The man in charge came over to see me and said I should call the police. He thought it was arson.

'By, you were lucky!' he said. 'By! That was luck. If that had got into the new stuff you'd have lost the whole place.'

The horses were still stamping around in their boxes, uneasy, and upset by the smell of the smoke. I hadn't attempted to move them. My only hope had been to douse the fire before it took hold; I could never have done that if I'd taken the time to lead fifteen frightened horses out of the stable.

'Who uses hair spray?' asked one of the policemen who came to investigate. The rafters had been coated with the stuff, he thought, and maybe the hay, too. It was the old hay, which had been damp and, as Tommy said, musty. Could have been written off as spontaneous combustion, couldn't it? How's your insurance, Mrs Brewer?

But it was I who had put the fire out before it had taken hold, and although one of the detectives suggested I'd changed my mind because of the horses it was a half-hearted attempt to pin the blame on me. They didn't believe I'd done it, and they genuinely wanted to know who had.

'Dominic Mont-Blering,' I said.

I kept Jake's part of the story as much in the background as I could. He'd bought some horses from Mont-Blering, but had become suspicious, and had stopped. Mont-Blering claimed a gambling debt.

Was there anybody else who might have done it?

I could think of nobody.

If I was right, said a detective constable, Mont-Blering would have an alibi, but his associates would be investigated.

'You know him, then?' I asked, and he blinked. He hadn't said that, he protested.

Jake was upset about the fire, but when I told him I'd mentioned Mont-Blering he was at first incredulous, and then furious. How could I have been so stupid? Did I really want to see him in jail, or crippled? Had I no idea of what I'd started this time, with this can of worms I'd opened? Could I *never* let sleeping dogs lie? Stupid, interfering, what had I been thinking of, if I'd been thinking at all?

As I listened to him I realised I was no longer angry, or tired, or even despairing. What I felt now was a sort of weariness that had nothing to do with the ache in the evenings from a day's hard physical work, from the strain of laughing and joking in the stable yard when it seemed nothing could ever be funny again, from the worry of trying to stretch two pounds into three, ten thousand into thirty.

What I felt now was self-pity, and if I let it take hold I might as well give up, because I could not win carrying that. I would lose the stables, I would lose the forge, it would be finished.

I could have lost the whole stable, just for a miserable fifteen thousand, said Jake.

'Is that what you owe him?' I asked, but I didn't really care.

Fifteen thousand, and he'd paid . . . how much? Seven or eight that I knew of, and probably more that he'd kept from me. There'd have been interest added to the debt.

Jake flushed, and said it would all have been OK if I hadn't been so stupid about buying Dom's horses. Why did I have to be so pure and high and mighty? Why did I think I was so much better than anybody else? Why couldn't I just keep my big mouth shut and let sleeping dogs lie, and mind my own business?

Because a can of worms is still a can of worms, even if unopened, and a sleeping dog will wake one day. I'd never had to cheat. Would I, if the pressure was hard enough?

I didn't even say goodbye to Jake. I climbed out of my chair, noting with vague surprise that it took an effort to uncross my legs, to push myself off the seat, and to turn to the door, and I walked out of the ward with an idea half formed in my mind of going back to the forge and lying on the blue blanket on my bed and letting it all happen, whatever it was that was going to happen.

But I was looking after five horses at the stable, and if I didn't feed them and rug them up for the night I couldn't be sure anybody else would. They might, but they might assume I'd been delayed, and would do my work when I finally got home. Little white-faced Picket, peering anxiously over the door of his box, always seeming to be worried that he might be forgotten. Big, slow Jack, who felt the cold and liked to have his ears rubbed as a goodnight gesture, my dear old Lyric, Nightfire and Salome, all hungry and unfed.

So I went back to the stable, and I fed my horses, and I laughed at Morry's jokes, and cleaned out Jack's feet because he'd been in the field that day and they were muddy. I checked the tarpaulin Tommy had rigged in the hay loft, tightened one of the corners and wondered what the insurance would pay.

I could tell them it was new hay that had burned, over a ton of it, not just a handful of bales that had anyway gone musty.

But the firemen knew, and the insurance company might check.

I didn't know how to cheat. How could you cover yourself against everything? And what would happen if you were caught?

Naive, and pure and simple-minded, and holier-than-thou. Why couldn't I be like other people, and leave well alone? Would Glory know how to write up the accounts so we'd stretch the money a bit further and not pay tax, or something like that?

There'd been woodworm in that corner, in those burned rafters. No, I would not tell the insurance company that. I'd treated the things anyway, and what would they do? Drill little holes in the new wood to make it just as it had been before?

I should have said, I don't know who started the fire, I can't imagine why anybody would want to do such a thing.

What will Mont-Blering do next?

Jake telephoned late that night, just as I was falling asleep. Dom had been in touch, it was all right, listen. All we had to do was buy a horse. Just, yes, like before. One or two like this, and he'd write off the debt. Ann, are you listening?

Who cares? People bet on horse-races, they're stupid. So,

put money on a good horse, and it isn't the good horse that runs, it might not have won anyway. Who cares?

'All right,' I said, and I put the telephone down without saying goodnight to Jake, and I fell asleep almost immediately.

I woke the next morning instantly alert, and more angry than I had ever been before in my life. I could not remember such a boiling of rage.

It was still dark, quite early, so I went down to the kitchen and made coffee, fresh coffee, the way Arno liked it, and then I went out into the yard and I rubbed little Picket's white face as he craned it over the door towards me. I did not need the picture of him dying in the flames to fuel my anger. It would not leave me.

I will not. I will not buy your horses, you dirty little man. Nobody, nobody who would risk burning horses to death has any place in racing, and I will drive you out. I will fight you, Mont-Blering, and I will win, even if you take Jake down with you, I will win.

'Are you all right?' asked Libby, and I was so startled by the question I could only stare at her. She had never shown the slightest interest in anybody's well-being before.

'You're very pale. There's something funny about your eyes.'

She seemed uneasy. She was almost backing away from me.

She'd always been lean, but now she was even thinner. Chuck had told me she was running eight miles a day and working with weights to make herself stronger, as well as riding his horses and training Polaris. Before, she'd been determined; he hoped she wasn't becoming obsessive.

It was ten o'clock when I telephoned the Jockey Club, and I told the woman on the switchboard about Mont-Blering. I hadn't said much before she stopped me, and said she was connecting me with somebody who could deal with the matter.

All old school tie and no balls, that was how Mont-Blering had described the Jockey Club to Jake, but the man who spoke to me had a North Country accent. He asked his questions quietly, and he wasn't afraid of the silences between them as he considered my answers. His name was Cartwright, David Cartwright.

I told him Jake had bought horses and sold them for Mont-Blering, but once suspicion had hardened into certainty he'd stopped.

'Can you buy the horse and not send him to the next auction?'

A farrier who couldn't build a convincing limp into a horseshoe would hardly be worth her salt, and nobody would send a lame horse to auction.

'Yes,' I said, 'of course I can.'

Over to you, David Cartwright, I thought, and found it strange that the rage had now changed to a sort of impatience. I will deal with you, Mont-Blering, but I hope it won't take up too much of my time, because I've got more important ways of spending it.

'We were lucky,' said Tommy complacently, seeing the luck over the fire as vindication of his opinion.

'Yes,' I agreed, 'we were lucky. Tommy, would you like to try your hand at carpentry? Those rafters. Don't worry if you can't do it, but if you'd like to try, that would be great.'

Jack was sold that afternoon, big, slow Jack of Hearts, to a solicitor who'd put on too much weight to ride the mare who'd carried him the year before. Would I buy the mare?

I'd look at her, I said cautiously.

Somebody had told him this was the stable that had found Weaver's Dream for Fred Hoffmann, was that right? People were saying he'd get into the team with that horse.

'Yes, Weaver's Dream came from here,' I said, and I gave Jack's rump a friendly slap as Tam led him up the ramp into the trailer.

Fred Hoffmann telephoned me that evening to tell me he

was delighted with the horse, and he'd been told he was on the short list for the team. There was nothing the horse wouldn't jump, nothing that scared him, and he was fast as well as brave.

'I owe you one, Ann,' he said, and I replied, tell people where you got him.

I sold The Greek the next day to somebody who told me quite frankly he was looking for something that might beat Fred on his new horse, and where better to come?

'He's not as good as Weaver's Dream,' I said, 'but they're cousins, and if you meet when Fred or the horse are having an off day . . .'

I paid the mortgage out of the earnings, the first time I'd managed to do it. Had I turned the corner?

'No,' said Glory, 'not yet. You're doing better than I'd have thought possible, but you're still just holding your own, aren't you?'

Then Chuck Donnington told me he'd got his eye on two horses that were over my price limit. People were talking about Weaver's Dream and the place that had sold him to Fred, so I'd better have something for the shop window, hadn't I? Since I was trying to get back into the top market?

'No,' I said. 'No, Chuck, I'm sticking to four thousand. I can't risk more.'

But he had two propositions. Four thousand was half the value of these two horses, but if Morry schooled them there should be a big profit at the end. Would I be prepared to take him in on the deal? Half each, and split what we made sixty–forty?

And then: 'Ann, Libby wants to take Polaris to the States. I'll cover the costs. We reckon she can make it there, with that horse.'

373

25

The next few days saw me dealing with one crisis after another, with never, it seemed, a moment to myself.

Mont-Blering telephoned. The horse was to be collected from an address in Kent, had I a pen handy?

'You may have forced us to buy your ringers, but you're not turning me into your courier service. You get the thing over here yourself, and you pay for it.'

And then I hung up.

When I telephoned David Cartwright and told him he said, in very level tones, that perhaps it had been a pity. It was essential to know exactly where the horse had been before it arrived at Brewer's, and if I'd collected it, that would have been easy.

'Your problem,' I retorted, and went back into the kitchen to talk to Chuck, who had come over to discuss Polaris.

Libby knew I had to sell the horse. She wanted to find a sponsor who would buy him and let her continue to ride him. She had dual nationality, and felt she had a better chance in the United States.

I'd asked Tam's advice, and Tam said Libby was probably right.

Then Jake came out of hospital, and began to talk about restocking the stable, because there were hardly any horses.

How much money did we have? Why had I let the number of horses get so low?

'Who's going to look after them?' I asked.

I shouldn't have sacked Glen, he grumbled, but he did have to admit Tommy had done well, and the new system of giving him the work everybody else regarded as boring seemed to be successful.

Tommy, however, was no carpenter. He made a mess of repairing the rafters. I sighed, and told him it didn't matter. I called in the firm that was repairing the drain at the forge. The insurance company had said there would be a delay while the police investigated the arson; no money would be forthcoming until the case was closed.

Jake told Chuck that, if the two horses he had in mind were good enough, we'd buy them outright. He didn't like the idea of sharing profits, not when he'd done all the work on training and schooling.

'Ann, eight thousand isn't a high price for a good horse.'

'Fine. I hope you've got it.'

So the first evening he was home was spent in a quarrel. I did have some money left, didn't I? How was the stable supposed to make money if it didn't have good horses to sell? Why was I being so stupid and so stubborn?

And my replies: we only had Morry who was good enough to train horses at that level. It would be weeks before Jake could ride again. We were looking after five horses each already, it was ridiculous to expect us to do more. And would he please look at the accounts? We had turned the corner, Jake. We were almost on the way up again.

Chuck wanted to know: was he to buy these horses or not?

Yes.

No.

Mont-Blering's horse arrived in the middle of this discussion, and I went out into the yard to see him. He was a nondescript brown colt, and he made his way cautiously down the ramp, slithering a little on the loose straw. There were other horses in the hired horsebox, on their way to Stourbridge and Wolverhampton.

I didn't tell Jake about David Cartwright, and I'd warned David that Jake was not to know; he was frightened of Mont-Blering.

'And you're not?'

I'd never even thought about it. He'd always seemed so insignificant, when I'd seen him, but that could be a dangerous miscalculation.

'No,' I said, and then added, as a sop to fortune, 'Not yet.'

Chuck had left by then, saying he'd wait to hear from us, so I was telephoning from Jake's office, the cold and dusty room in which Uncle John had warned me I stood no chance of saving the stable.

But I almost had. If Jake had been in hospital for just a few more weeks, I might have done it.

I pushed the thought away. I was glad he was out of hospital, I told myself, glad he'd come through those injuries without permanent damage. It was good that he was home again.

He did at least like the horses Chuck had found for us, although he remarked, predictably, that Picket was too small.

'Clever as a cat on his feet,' said Bess, who'd been riding him.

The next day he watched Libby on Polaris, and came away looking thoughtful. Perhaps I'd done well, to buy Polly.

But we need more horses, he insisted. There aren't enough. We should be cashing in on Weaver's Dream, people are coming, aren't they? Looking for another one? So why was I being so stupid?

'All the bills have been paid,' I told him. 'We're catching up on the mortgage.'

'So our credit's good?'

And then, catching sight of my face, he insisted again: we must have more horses. Those two Chuck's found. Come on, Ann. Why throw away a chance like Weaver's Dream? Make the most of it while people remember where Fred found him.

But Weaver's Dream had only cost four thousand. No, Jake, I will not. Four thousand is still my limit. We have turned the corner, but it's taken nearly everything I've raised on the forge. You'll throw it all away if we go into debt. We could still lose everything, the stables, the forge, everything. Jake, please look at the accounts.

Eight thousand is not a lot for a good horse.

They don't come better than Weaver's Dream, not unless you're going seriously into racing. Not just Barbarian and Pennyroyal in point-to-points and a couple of steeplechases a year, but seriously training racehorses. Is that the plan? Should we change direction again and train racehorses?

Why wouldn't I listen to him?

Why wouldn't he listen to me?

David Cartwright came down from London to see the brown colt. He looked at four other horses, and then pretended to notice that one over there, grazing by the hedge: he thought that might suit him.

He'd brought a camera. He was discreet with it, but he was very thorough in his examination, and in the notes he wrote.

He didn't tell me anything about his investigations, but he seemed satisfied when he left. He shook my hand, and smiled at me.

'That should do it,' he said.

The paperwork involved in shipping Polaris to California seemed extraordinary. Chuck handled most of it, but I had to sign documents stating that I owned the horse and believed he was healthy, and agreed to his export, and there were examinations by veterinary surgeons. I wondered if it would ever end.

'He's not a KGB spy,' I said, but the American vet didn't think it was very funny.

Then David Cartwright came back, with a double horse trailer and a friendly young man who said David had told him about a little horse that might be what he wanted for his sister.

Picket.

'We're taking the brown colt, too,' said David, and Jake said he bloody well wasn't, then; the horse wasn't for sale.

'You'll be given a receipt on Jockey Club paper,' replied David, and when Jake stared at him, the colour draining out of his face, he added, 'If you don't co-operate, you'll be very sorry. I guarantee that.'

Why had I imagined he'd continue to be pleasant, once he'd got what he wanted?

When he'd recovered enough to speak at all, Jake told me I'd cost him his licence, his livelihood, his reputation, and Dom would probably cripple him, too. He hoped I was satisfied. And now he still owed Dom fifteen thousand, had I thought of that before I'd mounted my white charger and gone off on my stupid holy crusade?

'I think I thought of everything,' I said, after I'd pretended to mull over his question. 'Nothing unexpected has happened so far.'

Polaris went a week later, with Libby fussing over him as much as she could ever be said to fuss. He wore a smart scarlet and white rug, and his legs were carefully padded and bandaged.

I should have patted him, or rubbed his nose, or made some gesture to the little liver chestnut, but he'd probably have tried to kick me. I was aware of a brief pang of regret.

Barring accidents, he could make us a good name in showjumping, I said to Jake, who wasn't interested. He'd had a letter from the Jockey Club requesting him to attend a hearing.

Mont-Blering telephoned him that afternoon, almost hysterical. For Christ's sake shoot that horse, bury it. Or, better, burn it. Just, for fuck's sake, get rid of the thing, permanently, and do it now, Brewer, or we're all so deep in the shit we'll never get out.

'It's too late,' said Jake. 'They've got him.'

Mont-Blering didn't know how they'd found out, then.

Libby telephoned from California, getting the times wrong so she woke me at four in the morning. Polly had travelled well, except for kicking the pilot, who shouldn't have been anywhere near the horses anyway, stupid man. He'd settled into the new stables and he was eating well. She thought I'd like to know.

'Thank you,' I said sleepily. 'Good luck.'

'Ann?'

'Hmm?'

There was a long hesitation, and I thought, she's steeling herself to give me bad news. What's happened?

'God bless,' said Libby, and hung up before I could reply.

Jake tried to ride Salome, but came back after a quarter of an hour, sweating and grey in the face with pain. There was no strength at all in his knee, he complained. Absolutely bloody nothing there. Help me down, love.

One hand on my shoulder, the other on the pommel of the saddle, and Toby held the mare's head as Jake slowly eased himself down to the ground and smiled his thanks at us both.

Had he thought he could just pick up where he'd left off? I demanded that evening, and he replied, don't get at me, Annie love.

He seemed to be close to tears.

The hearing was only two days away.

Chuck said one of the horses had been sold, so we'd lost him. He might get the other for seven thousand. What should he do?

'No,' I said. 'Sorry, Chuck, but my limit still stands.'

'OK,' he said equably. 'There's a horse in Yorkshire might be that price. Libby sends her best. She's in her first competition next week.'

I already knew that. I'd had to countersign the entry form.

I went to London with Jake, but I wouldn't go to the hearing. I said I doubted if I'd be allowed in anyway. So the taxi dropped me off at a burger bar, and I sat in a corner as far away from the front as I could get, and I tried to read a book while I waited, two and a half hours, for Jake to come back.

Dom had been warned off for life, he said, and the evidence had been passed on to the police.

Jake seemed to be in a state of shock, so I went to the counter and bought three plastic mugs of coffee for him. It should have been brandy.

It wasn't just the brown colt. There'd been four other ringers they'd proved, and all the names he'd used, they knew the lot. How had they found out?

'They're not stupid,' I said. 'There've been cheats in horse-racing for as long as horses have raced. What do you think the Jockey Club wouldn't know about cheating?'

Jake didn't seem to have heard me.

'Dom couldn't believe it. He was just, sort of, amazed. Like, this is me. You can't treat me like this. Don't you know who I am?'

And still, I waited.

'They knew the lot,' he said. 'They knew everything. You know what? They'd just been waiting, just till they could get one of the horses. Just one.'

'What about you?' I asked, when he'd fallen silent again, and he flushed.

'Nothing,' he muttered.

I reached out, and covered his hand with my own.

'Jake.'

Dom would go to prison, he said. The police had been waiting; how the hell had the Jockey Club persuaded the police to let them have him first?

'Why not you?' I asked, and then he almost shouted at me.

'Because of you. All right? Because you told them. What they as near as bloody dammit already knew, but you got the colt for them.'

'Let's go home,' I said. He nodded, and finished the last mug of coffee.

In the taxi on the way to the station he rubbed at his forehead, and his voice was tight and dry.

'They could reel me in at any time, Ann. They've got the lot, all the evidence. All those names he used.'

Glory had spotted those names, I remembered.

'Like a bloody great cat,' he muttered. 'And I'm the mouse it's watching.'

David Cartwright telephoned that afternoon. The brown colt was at Newmarket. Did I want him back? Or should he be sent to auction from there, once the police had finished with him?

'From there,' I said.

There were no thanks, no good wishes, just the hard North Country accent checking off details, impersonal and businesslike. Had he believed I'd been involved in the fraud?

Probably not, but he couldn't be sure.

Jake brooded over the hearing for about two days, hardly speaking to anybody, just drinking coffee and sitting in his study, his stiff leg propped up on a chair. I lit the fire for him, but he hadn't noticed the cold.

'Did you like Dom?' I asked, and he frowned.

'Not much.' And then: 'No. No, I didn't. He was a slimy little shit.'

We were using the past tense, I noticed. Dom was finished, gone. It was as if he was dead.

The horse Chuck went to see in Yorkshire wasn't worth buying, he said. Should he go on looking for horses? Or was Jake back in the saddle now?

'Keep looking, please, Chuck.'

I bought two myself from a breeder in Worcestershire, three-year-olds. The dams were thoroughbreds, the sire a Cleveland Bay with a growing name for getting jumpers. Jake said I should go ahead if I wanted to, but remember he couldn't risk breaking a youngster yet.

Fred Hoffmann was picked for the national team to go to Buenos Aires, and he sent us a case of champagne, with a note to the effect that a child could ride Weaver's Dream, but don't tell the selectors.

Polaris came second in his competition, and Libby telephoned, furious and apologetic. She'd set him at a triple wrong, and he'd cleared it but he'd lost momentum, so they'd been beaten by half a second.

'These things happen,' I said, trying to console her, and failing. Losing was for losers, said Libby. Sorry, Ann.

There was snow, so we spread straw in the yard and led the horses around to exercise them. Gorsedown was clear, at least under the trees, but the road to it was packed with snow, and there was something wrong with the steering on the horsebox. I wouldn't risk using it until it had been repaired.

Jake grumbled at the setback, but he came out of the study and said he might manage a bit of long-reining. What about those three-year-olds? He could make a start on them, and didn't I think Starling was a bit long in the back?

'That's why he was cheaper than Fieldfare,' I answered.

He had to go to the hospital twice a week for physiotherapy, and I was usually the one who drove him.

There seemed to be even more work, since he'd returned. I had less time to spend at the forge, and Jansy told me she thought I was losing customers. People would come, hang around for a while, then drive away again.

There was a patch of raw earth at the corner of the cottage where the builders had dug out the cracked drain. She planted some sort of climber in it, and said it would be nice in summer. A bit of colour.

Chrissie had the baby in February, a little girl. She and Peter called her Rachel. I went to see them in the hospital, and Chrissie looked dazed with happiness with the baby in her arms. She hardly seemed to be aware of anything else, smiling around at her visitors and thanking them for their good wishes, but only briefly, before her eyes returned to the face of the sleeping child.

'She's lovely,' I said dutifully, but I've never known what to say in such circumstances.

'We'll find her a pony,' said Jake, and added: 'when she's a bit older.'

He seemed surprised when I laughed.

Polaris won his next competition, and Libby was ecstatic.

'He *flew* it!' she yelled down the telephone. 'He knew what he was there for. In that last jump-off, he *flew*. He's never gone so fast. He was four seconds ahead of the runner-up, four seconds. Are you still there?'

'Waiting to get a word in edgeways,' I said. 'Well done.'

I asked Jake to come to Wolverhampton with me to deliver two hunters and look at a pair of Welsh cobs, but he said he didn't feel like it.

I'd done it, I said to myself at nights as I lay in bed beside him, staring up at the ceiling and listening to him breathing in a deep sleep. I'd done it. I'd pulled the stable round, it was making a profit. I'd saved it. Nobody believed I could do it, but I had. Hadn't I? Didn't anybody realise what I'd achieved?

'Jake, I have to spend more time at the forge, I'm losing customers. You're going to have to take over here. Jake?'

'All right.'

Toby telephoned me at the forge. If I wasn't there, who was to ride Nightjar in the second string?

Jake said we'd have to hire somebody else. We needed more horses anyway.

'We can't afford it,' I said.

'I thought you said we'd turned the corner?'

'When are you going to try riding again?'

A computer company in Los Angeles made a sponsorship offer on Polaris, but wanted one of their own employees to ride him.

'I can't turn it down,' I said to Libby. 'I'm sorry.'

She rang me back the next night, triumphant.

'Polly dumped him. Stupid bastard can't ride. They've withdrawn the offer.'

He came third in the next competition, dropping a hind leg on a pole in the final jump-off, but he'd been faster than ever before. This time it had been the horse's fault, and Libby didn't apologise.

There was another sponsorship offer, but again the rider couldn't handle the horse. I accused Libby of teaching him rodeo tricks, and she laughed.

'How long did this one stay in the saddle?' I demanded, and she said she thought about five seconds. Polaris was very fit now.

'I once managed seven,' I said proudly, and she laughed again.

I told Jake, but he barely raised a smile.

'What's the matter?'

'Nothing.'

That night I woke to hear him crying.

There was nothing wrong, he insisted. It was a bad dream. Go back to sleep.

Hadn't I saved the stable? Hadn't anybody noticed what I'd done?

'I want to go back to the forge,' I said again a week later. 'I don't want to work here any more. Jake, are you listening to me?'

'In spring?' he asked. 'Will that do?'

Libby sent us a video recording of Polly jumping at Santa Rosa. It had been on television. Jake and I watched it that night, and the commentator spoke of the popularity of both rider and horse, the horse hardly bigger than a pony.

When they came into the ring there was a roar from the crowd. Libby had Polly a little over-bent, so his chin was tucked in, his neck arched, and he pricked his ears at the applause. He trotted in, his knees lifting high, Libby showing him off. She made a graceful acknowledgement of the judges, and then the reins slid through her fingers and the little horse began to canter, turning obediently at the touch of the rein on his neck.

She made it look so easy, those first two rounds.

The other horses were all big, typical American showjumpers, long-striding and powerful, and beside them Polly did indeed look no bigger than a pony. I watched them as they came out of an awkward triple, turned, and then galloped for the water jump, needing speed and momentum to carry them across it, and I didn't think he could do it. They were having to reach so wide for it, those big horses, then regain their balance to circle the wall and come back the other way, meeting a double on a short stride, and then gallop for the line. It was a very difficult combination of jumps.

When Polly came in, with two left to go after him, there were only three horses who had gone clear in the jump-off against the clock, and eight had had one down.

He trotted in, as before, lifting his knees high, his ears flicking as the applause rose, and Libby smiled and raised her hand, waving to the crowd as Polly broke into a canter.

He made two large circles, then lowered his head and went for the first jump.

He put everything into it, throwing himself at the big obstacles and straining to make up the speed between them. He skidded his way around the turns; twice I thought he'd lost his footing and would fall.

Then there was the big triple, and Libby reined him in, losing time but gaining his balance and his concentration. This was where two of the horses had lost, on the third jump.

He bounced his way out of the second, but he was too close to it when he landed, and I heard Jake swear beside me.

But Libby had him balanced, and somehow he managed an extra stride, three where the others had only found room for two. His powerful quarters bunched underneath him as he launched himself over the third, and cleared it.

There were people on their feet in the crowd, cheering him.

That fast turn, again skidding, but finding his feet, and he was flat out on his way to the water jump with Libby over his shoulders, her arms reaching along his neck, Polly's ears right back with the effort. As he reached the take-off bar there was one quick moment as he adjusted his stride, then he was over it, wide and safe, with the commentator yelling with excitement and the crowd behind him shouting at Libby, come on, come on.

But she was a second behind the leader.

He turned inside the wall. Where all the others had circled it, Polly scrambled round the impossibly short turn, his hind legs almost sliding from under him: he only had three strides in which to take the first big jump of the double, three strides where the others had had five, and had only just made it.

He did it.

He was right in under that jump before he took off, with the springy, bouncy action I'd seen Libby perfecting in the paddock here, one long reach for the second, and then he took off again, his head almost down between his knees as he strained for the height, with Libby high and still over his shoulders: he seemed to hang in the air for long, long moments before the neat little hooves thudded down onto the turf, and Polaris was galloping for the line, Libby waving her whip in triumph and the crowd roaring the horse's name.

She telephoned two days later, because the computer company had made another offer. A hundred and fifty thousand dollars, and she would ride Polaris in their name.

26

'I'll give it to you,' I said to Jake. 'Every penny. Every cent, I mean, I'll give it to you, if you'll agree to dissolve the partnership.'

I had resigned myself to years of struggle, but the offer for Polaris, so much higher than I had dreamed possible, seemed to have thrown open the doors. It made me frantic.

Jake was bewildered by my attitude.

'Why? Why do you want to give up the partnership? I told you, it's going to be all right.'

He spread his hands in a gesture close to pleading, his elbows resting on the kitchen table, his face screwed up as he stared at me.

'Listen, you can use some of it to pay off part of the mortgage on the forge. Isn't that what you want? And we can buy some good horses, hire two more lads, we can . . .'

'Polaris is *mine*!' I yelled at him. 'Mine. I bought him. He's mine, he's not yours, not even a share of him. Do you understand?'

He shook his head, staring at me.

'Why are you shouting at me?'

I forced myself to breathe slowly. I leaned my hands on the edge of the table and looked down at the scrubbed wood. Be calm, I said to myself. Be calm.

'Jake.'

What could I say to him? I didn't want to hurt him, but I had to get out. I had to get away. Let me go.

'Jake, listen to me.'

'I'm listening.'

Think. Put this in the right way, and he'll agree. Get it wrong, and he may not.

'Jake, I mortgaged the forge for everything I could raise on it.'

'I know. And it's worked, hasn't it? I told you it would be all right, and it is.'

Don't answer that. Don't turn it into an argument.

'I used . . . We spent the money on horses, and we did quite well, thanks to Frogface, and we paid the bills, and we sorted out the bank loan and got up to date on the mortgage. It wasn't easy, and it could have gone wrong at any moment, but we were lucky. So now, even without the money for Polly, the stable is just making a profit again. You've got Gorsedown, so you're back where you were before you lost Ashlands.'

'Ann, we can be *far* better than that! We've had a big stroke of luck with Polaris, can't you see what we can do?'

It was the first of many arguments. Jake could not understand why I would want to give up the partnership just when it was about to succeed. He said he needed me, he couldn't run the stable on his own any more. He needed my help.

'I'm a blacksmith. I've done my best here, but it's not my life. I don't like running the stable.'

I could be both, Jake insisted. It would be different, now he was back. Of course it had been a strain, with him in hospital, but now it would be different. A chance for a fresh start for the stables, and even for the marriage.

'I'm going for a ride,' I said.

Jake said his knee still hurt quite badly after only a short time in the saddle, so Lyric was my escape. I used her often.

A man came from the London branch of the computer company to talk about the sponsorship. His name was Geof Adams, and he said he was delighted to meet us both. That sure was some little horse. The American public loved Polaris and Libby both, and his company loved the American public, so everybody could be happy, couldn't they?

It was to be an All-American Dream, the pretty little girl and her pretty little horse, beating the best in the world, and the company would just like to be sure we understood that policy.

'Polaris is to be American?' I ventured, and Geof Adams smiled at me, beautiful even teeth gleaming in a carefully tanned face.

The company did not have one thing against British horses, this was just for the publicity. The American public had taken Libby and her little horse to its heart, and there might be just a little of the gloss taken off this story if it came out that the horse was British.

'He's Dutch, as it happens,' I said, but this was not the point. A slight hint of impatience crept into Geof's voice. It would be a better story, from the point of view of the company, which was the party putting up the money, if Polaris was American. Nobody was going to tell lies about it, but nobody was to shout out the truth either. You can't tell a horse's nationality from his accent, and Libby's was pure Oklahoma. It was just a matter of publicity, there was no . . .

'We need publicity, too,' Jake interrupted. 'The horse came from this stable, and he learned to jump here. It wasn't only Libby who trained him, either. Maurice Old did the bulk of the work. Libby Donnington took over because we were short-staffed.'

But Polaris was in the United States now, and, much as he admired the little horse, Geof couldn't see him making the national team. Could we? Realistically? So, who's to benefit from this publicity? Not the stables, surely? Not unless we were planning on opening a branch in California.

He wasn't unreasonable, Geof Adams. The company wanted an all-American success story, but he didn't want us to suffer in any way. Far from it. A hundred and fifty thousand dollars was surely a damn fine price for what his President had called 'half a pint of pony'.

In the end he agreed that there would be nothing in Libby's contract forbidding her from telling anybody, in private, where Polaris had come from. That way, somebody who was truly looking for a horse from our stable could find out, from Libby, where to look. But no press. Not from Libby and not from us either.

It was fair, and I agreed. I knew Libby was grateful to me for the chance with Polaris, and would return the favour if she could.

'We should look into showjumping,' said Jake after Geof had gone, briskly shaking our hands on the way out to his chauffeur-driven German car. 'I mean, seriously.'

'Only if we can find another Libby, I think,' I replied, and he thought about that, and nodded. Without Libby, Polaris would never have become as good as he was. It was Libby who had made him exceptional.

But instead of dropping the idea Jake telephoned Clive Ulverton and asked if he knew of any more girl jump jockeys who might like to train showjumpers instead.

'We can't afford more staff,' I said. 'Jake, please don't get us into debt again.'

'Why did you buy Starling and Fieldfare, then? That's jumping breeding.'

It was true, I had bought the horses with the idea of selling them as showjumpers, and possibly cashing in on Polly's success as we had with Weaver's Dream. But I had planned to sell them as promising young horses, needing work in the hands of their new owners.

'Polly's nine years old,' I said helplessly. 'It takes years.'

Let me out. Please, let me out.

Glory said she found my attitude incomprehensible. Why didn't I break the partnership anyway?

'Ann, you asked my advice before, and you didn't take it then. I didn't think you could drag that business out of trouble, but you did, so I was wrong. Are you still there?'

'Yes,' I said, holding the telephone close against my ear in case Jake should overhear.

'It cost you all your money. And now you want to give him *more*? Money you could use to pay off most of the mortgage? Have you lost your mind?'

I certainly seemed to have lost something, and at times in the confusion of what I saw as planning my escape I wondered if it was indeed my mind. My sense of balance, of proportion, had disappeared. Words kept repeating themselves in my head, a refrain that took on different beats, depending upon what I was doing at the time.

Let me *out*, let me *out*, the thud of hooves, horses cantering on the tracks, let me *out*, let me *out*. My hammer on iron took on the same rhythm; at times even the wind in the bare trees seemed to be echoing the words. *Let* me *out*, *let* me *out*.

'I don't like running the stables,' I said to Jake over and over again. 'I did my best, but I don't like it.'

'I can't manage without you. I can't even ride yet.'

The physiotherapist asked him if he was doing the exercises she'd prescribed, and he said he was.

'When do you do them?' I asked him on the way home, and he didn't answer.

'Don't you think you could drive yourself now? It's not far.'

'Just another week, love. It really does hurt.'

He'd never complained about pain before. Over the years I'd known him I'd seen him with riding injuries, broken bones, and he'd muttered and cursed, but he'd

392

never complained. Just another week. It really does hurt. I'd never heard him speak like that before, that affected whimper.

Sometimes when I heard him crying in the night I'd ask, is it the pain, Jake? Where does it hurt?

It's nothing. A bad dream. Go back to sleep.

Morry started teaching Starling and Fieldfare to jump, trotting them over poles laid on the ground, and then gradually raising the poles. He said Starling might be quite good. Pity Libby wasn't here to take him on.

I stared at him, and he grinned.

'I never said she couldn't ride, did I?'

Jake began to drive himself to the hospital for his appointments. He thought he might try to ride again soon, but not just yet. It hurt too much.

I asked Geof Adams how much longer it would be before the company paid for Polaris, and he replied that the company wanted to get the contract just right, in everybody's interests.

'I hope they won't be too much longer, for their sake,' I said. 'There'll be more than one company wanting to hitch its wagon to that bright, particular star.'

'Hey, that's good!' he exclaimed. 'Can we use that?'

Libby and Polaris had come third in the State of California Jumping Championship, and their photographs were even appearing in Europe.

'Little girl and her pet pony hit the big time.'

Even Morry laughed at that.

I cut out the magazine photograph and its caption and stapled it to the tack-room wall.

'Why don't you ride Barbarian?' I asked Jake. 'He's a darling, he can be a real armchair when he's in the right mood.'

'Yes. Maybe tomorrow. I'll think about it.'

He was crying again that night, and for a while I pretended to be asleep, but then I rolled over and switched on the light.

'Only a bad dream,' he said, but this time I sat up in bed and pulled on my dressing gown.

'Tell me about this bad dream.'

It was the hearing at the Jockey Club. He couldn't believe what had happened, how he'd come so close to losing his licence to train racehorses, even to being warned off, and prosecuted for fraud. It was like those dreams where everything starts with something quite commonplace and it becomes more and more difficult, more and more precarious, until you're falling, or you're trapped, and you don't know how it happened, and when you wake up you can't believe it wasn't true.

'But it was true,' said Jake. 'I hear his voice in the dream, and I can't see his face. Saying they're watching me. They'll always be watching me.'

'It won't matter,' I said, stroking his face where the tears were wet on his cheeks. 'It won't matter. You haven't got to buy ringers any more, have you? So they can watch. There's nothing to see.'

The contempt there'd been in the voice. Not just the dream, but the remembered reality. We won't need a reason, Brewer. Give us a flimsy excuse.

'If you hadn't given them the colt . . .'

He couldn't go on, so we sat in silence, with my hand still resting on his face. I didn't know what to say to him. I'd agreed to buy the ringers again, because I'd been too tired to care, and I'd only gone back on it because I'd been too angry to think.

'I wanted it to be me, who saved the stable,' cried Jake. 'I wanted to do it. I thought I could do it, with Gorsedown, and the money from the forge. A few more of Dom's horses, and just a bit of luck. I wanted it to be me.'

What could I say to him?

'You found Weaver's Dream.'

'You got Fred Hoffmann back to buy him. You did it. You changed things here, and it worked. But I wanted to do

that. I wanted to be able to say to you, look, here it is. I said
I'd do it, and I have.'

He reached up and took my hand, holding it in a grip so
hard it almost hurt.

'Ann, why do you want to leave now? I can't manage
without you. I don't understand why you want to go. I
don't want you to go. Ann?'

His face was almost frantic, and he was kissing my hand,
turning it and stroking it, kissing the fingers.

'Can't you see how much I love you?'

Was this part of his dream? I asked myself. Or was it one
of mine? Jake, telling me he loved me. I hadn't known. I
hadn't seen, I'd never imagined he felt anything more than
liking, and sometimes not even that. Love me? Jake loves
me?

But I don't love him, I thought. I've never loved him.

This isn't fair. This wasn't what we agreed. There was no
talk of love, there'd never been that.

'Ann?'

I can't tell him I love him. I can't lie to him. I don't want
this.

Poor Jake.

'Please don't go.'

'I'm not looking for a divorce,' I said at last. 'That's not
what I want. I don't want the partnership, the business partnership. That's all. I don't want that responsibility any
more.'

There was such desolation and misery in his face I could
hardly bear to look at him.

'But we could do it together. Ann? Now I'm back, we
could do it together. If I start riding again. Darling Ann, I
will, I'll start tomorrow. I can do that. I'll ride Barbarian,
like you said. I can do that. I will, I'll start tomorrow.'

I don't know what to do, I thought. I've never had to face
this before, and I don't know what to do. Arno, I wish you
were here.

He came back the next day.

I heard a car draw up at the gate, a door slam, and then the car drove away again. There were footsteps on the gravel, and I raised my head to listen, lowering the hammer onto the anvil, and feeling my heart beginning to race.

I was still leaning over the glowing horseshoe when he appeared at the door, standing with the light behind him.

We looked at each other, and then I stood up.

'I didn't sell the Riley.'

'I hoped you hadn't.'

He came in, and I walked towards him, and we stood holding each other, close and still, and silent, and I remember thinking: I am still here. I said I would be here when he returned, and I am still here.

Arno.

He was very thin, and there was a drawn and tired look on his face with dark shadows around his eyes. I knew before he told me these were the signs of grief and sadness.

She had died, then, his beloved Brita. So soon?

'Are you hungry?' I asked, and he nodded.

Bacon sandwiches and fresh coffee, and if there was dust on the blue mugs he didn't comment as I rinsed them under the tap, and allowed my fingers to run lovingly over the deep glaze.

'Jansy lives here now.'

'Oh?'

We smiled at each other. I had never interfered with Jansy's life here, and she would have to extend the same forbearance to me.

'I'm married.'

The same steady smile, but there were questions in the blue eyes. Does this matter, this marriage? What has it changed between you and me?

'It was a sort of business arrangement,' I said, and he nodded.

'Why are you so thin?' he asked late that night as we lay

on the blue blankets. I felt his hand on my ribs, the fingers running slowly over the ridges the bones made under the taut skin.

'It's a long story,' I said, and he kissed me, gently and lovingly, and asked me to tell him the long story.

I told him I had married Jake for friendship, because of Gorsedown, and what had happened. The partnership I had thought was a kind present that was a trap, but how I thought I had escaped. Weaver's Dream and Polaris, Pennyroyal and Nicefella, the other horses, and how they and luck had brought me through. Jake's accident. I said: it was an accident, something startled the horse.

'I owe him the stable,' I said, hoping he would understand. 'That was the bargain we made, I think. The promise under the wedding vows. But I think that was all, and now the stable should be safe. If he uses the money for Polaris carefully, he'll be all right. I think I did keep my promise to Jake.'

His hand was on my face, smoothing the lines between my eyebrows. They were new to him. I hadn't had those lines when he'd left.

'And so you are free again?' he asked, and I knew he had understood. I turned my face into his hand and kissed the palm of it, and pressed my cheek against his shoulder.

'Now he says he loves me.'

He had nothing to say to this, because there were no answers, but his lips were moving on my hair and his arms were around me, holding me close against him, and I felt the familiar drowsiness I had thought I might never know again.

'I never promised him love, and I never stopped loving you.'

'My Ann.'

I thought, these are the hands I remembered when I seemed to be praying to you, and these lips, and the eyes smiling down into mine, and the question in them that I

397

answer with my own eyes, and my own lips. I remembered smooth skin and firm muscle, and long bones, and I remembered the way we touched each other, and how the drowsiness became warm and alive, and I didn't want gentleness any more.

I remembered this, I thought: our bodies arching together, arms clasping and holding, and the long moment when the demand was first answered when we seemed to be still. The smiles that held relief, and joy, and the strength that surged through us, wild and fierce, the wanting and the eagerness and the pride, he is mine, this is for me, now, this is for me, the exhilaration of being wanted in return, of giving what is asked, and knowing it is enough.

I remembered all this, my Arno, my love, when I prayed to you.

Later, the warm smiles, sleepy now, and close, holding him close, no need for memories any more. Oh, God, I have missed you so, my love, my Arno, I thought I would die.

My Ann. I missed you too, my magnificent Ann.

Lying close together, my face against his shoulder, arm across his chest, his hands gentle, stroking my back, dreamy and content.

Am I dreaming now?

No. No, my Ann, you're not dreaming now. I'm here.

Quietness, just his hand, the slow movement of his hand, stroking my back. Will he ever say to me, as I say to him, I love you?

Arno, can you tell me what happened?

There was stillness in his face as I looked, and I noted again the drawn thinness, the tired bruises around his blue eyes. Oh, my poor love. My poor, sad love.

She had known what was happening to her. The disease had not even spared her that. She had known, and she had tried to be as she had always been, his bright Brita, smiling, and caring. And capable.

She had tried, but she could not.

398

Sometimes she had become violent. Mostly to him, but also in the end to the children. One day she had hit the boy, and broken his cheekbone. Arno had taken him and the girl to hospital, and a neighbour had come to sit with Brita.

She had said she wanted to go for a walk, so they had walked, she and the neighbour, along the paths to the woods, across the bridge over the motorway.

She had thrown herself from the bridge into the path of a lorry.

I lay in silence and I thought, last night with Jake my hand was on his face, and it was wet with tears, and tonight Arno's tears are touching this same hand. Perhaps there is something I can do to comfort Arno, but I have nothing to offer Jake.

Arno turned towards me, turned his face into the pillow, and as I put my arms around him he cried out, her name, and something in Swedish. I held him, and I thought, please do not let this be a barrier between us. Please, let him know he can grieve for his Brita with me. Please, when this stops, don't let him say he is sorry.

He fell asleep without speaking again, and he slept very deeply. I think it had been a while since he had slept well. I lay awake beside him for most of the night, my hand resting on his head, where the dark blond curls were turning grey now, and I didn't even wonder about the future for us.

Some time early in the morning I slept, and when I woke he had already left the bed, and there was a smell of coffee, and quiet sounds from the kitchen. I lay, listening, and I heard footsteps on the path, the door opening, and Jansy's voice, a startled shout, then Arno, soothing, explaining. Jansy appeared at the bedroom door with a very disapproving expression on her face, and I began to laugh, and couldn't stop. Arno came up the stairs carrying the two mugs of coffee, and he was grinning.

He sat on the edge of the bed and we drank our coffee. I cannot remember a time when I felt more contented, but then Arno smiled down at me, and asked what I would do about Jake.

'I'll tell him. I can't live with him any more. Not now.'

Arno stroked the hair back from my forehead; his face was quite grave even though he was still smiling at me.

'Would you like me to come with you? When you tell him?'

I went back to the stable that morning, and I think Jake knew what I intended to say, even though it had never occurred to him that Arno might play a part in my decision.

I tried to be kind, but that seemed to give him hope. One day we might live together again, he said. Perhaps, after a time, we could try again? He was sorry, whatever it was he'd done wrong.

'You did nothing wrong. Except, perhaps, the partnership. Well, that's all right now, isn't it? You can have the money for Polly, if you'll dissolve the partnership.'

'You should have that. Don't you need it for the mortgage on the forge?'

I shook my head. I could work that off, that was no problem. I wouldn't need much money, I never had. It wouldn't take very long to build up that business again.

'Could you ask Toby to bring Lyric back to the forge when he's next coming past with the trailer?' I asked, and Jake nodded, then turned away.

I knew when I had gone he would cry.

EPILOGUE

It's nearly four years since Arno came back to me. Later that year he took me to Greece for two weeks, because he said I was tired to the point of exhaustion. He cancelled all my appointments, and he asked Jansy to stay at the cottage to look after Lyric.

We spent the time on an island. There were laboratories, where some of the work which was carried out was done for NATO, so there was high security, with fast boats cruising in apparently aimless circles, and very courteous young men in Greek army uniforms, who seemed embarrassed by the guns they carried.

Arno spent most of the time in the laboratories. I lay on the beach and read books, and tried not to be bored while he was away from me. I've never really enjoyed inactivity.

One day we took mules and rode up into the hills, where there were deep caves.

We lay naked on the mossy floor, and Arno said that he loved me very much. He asked me if I would like to be married to him, and he apologised for putting it in such a way, but somehow it seemed appropriate.

'I don't want to leave the forge,' I said, and he smiled, and said he didn't want to leave Sweden, and then the smile became a little mischievous.

'If you would like a wedding, I would be very happy to play the part of the bridegroom.'

'I think,' I said, 'that I would rather you just played the part of my lover.'

I no longer had to remember. It would never be necessary for me to look back, to recall colours, and textures, and words. Everything would happen again, because he loved me and he would return.

I remember everything of that afternoon. I remember the reflected light on the roof of the cave, the way it flickered as the sunlight played on the stream. The sounds of the mules cropping the grass on the little pasture at the mouth of the cave.

I remember Arno's cheek against mine, the soft words whispered into my ear. His hands on my breasts, the still-ness that seemed to question, the sense of timelessness, and then both our heads turning so that we faced each other.

I remember the way he smiled.

His skin was smooth, and clean, and brown. It smelled faintly of sweat, and there was the tang of salt on my tongue. The curve of his spine, and the way his shoulders moved under my hands, I remember.

Do that again, he whispered, and I said, like this?

Yes. Yes.

All our movements were slow, and deliberate, and caring. There were long moments when we lay motionless and my mind traced the sensations of my body, wonder-ingly, almost marvelling.

It has never been like this.

'I love you,' he said.

Remembering, from a lifetime ago.

'Teach me to fly?' I asked, and his blue eyes looking down into mine.

Learning to forget. Learning to believe that Arno finds me beautiful, to believe that he loves me. Listening to his voice as he whispers in my ear. No, Ann, now you do not think of what pleases me, you think only of what pleases you.

Listen to the professor? I ask, and he smiles again.

So laugh, then.

I love you. I love you.

I listen, and I try to believe.

The sounds of water on sunlit stones, the light on the roof of the cave, the mules quietly cropping the grass, and Arno speaking gentle words of love. Wind in the cypress trees. The smell of salt from the sea, the taste of sweat.

Teach me to fly. Please, teach me to fly.

That night, drinking red wine in our room, with the candles on the table, he seemed sad. Women who have been hurt, he said, these scars are so deep. But Ann, I do love you.

I sat on the rug beside his chair, my head resting against his knee, listening to his voice.

I love you, Arno. Nothing else matters.

I'm still married to Jake, although I rarely go to his stables now. He uses Gorsedown to train his young horses, and he has regained the position he once held in his world. Jake Brewer's name is back in the winning lists.

He used the money from Polaris to buy good young horses, and he hired another groom, a French boy, who wants to train showjumpers.

Polaris. He never did make the national team, but he was famous. Television advertisements featured him jumping through a computer screen. The little system with the big heart. You don't have to be a high-flyer to own one.

There was a report of a terrorist scare about him, and security guards. I telephoned Libby, and she laughed. There had to be some reason for the guards keeping Polly's adoring public at a safe distance, she said. One or two had tried to treat him as though he really was the children's pet of the press stories.

'They got kicked?' I asked.

403

'Yes.'

Lyric grazes in the paddock at the forge, and occasionally I take her for a short ride on Gorsedown. She can still run away with me, although it doesn't take me long to bring her back under control now. She's very old, and although the fire is still there, it's beginning to fade. Usually, if I want to go for a long ride, I borrow one of Jake's horses. I kept one at the forge for a few weeks, but I missed him when he was sold, and I worried that he might not have gone to a good home.

Perhaps I'll buy another horse soon, and then I can allow myself to become fond of it.

Most of the women still live at the old railway station in Anford. Tam married a civil engineer, and went back to the USA with him, but six months later she came back to England, and her husband followed her. She said she didn't like the violence in the States.

When Arno isn't here I spend time with my friends, in the building they've turned into a home, or here at the forge. It's difficult for me to imagine life without them now. They've become a part of my existence. Just as the iron snakes in the gate twine their way through the leaves and branches, supporting and enhancing them, so the witches are a part of my life, and I, they tell me, am a part of theirs.

Chrissie and Peter had another child, a little boy they named Mark. I understand now, but Peter remembers my outrage, and although he teases me, I think my words did hurt him. His still hurt me, even though he smiles as he says them.

'I will not pretend spending the occasional night in Chrissie's bed is an unpleasant duty,' he said. 'She wants sex and we both want children, so lump it, big sister.'

He's trying to teach Rachel to play cricket, and my paddock is the preferred ground. Rachel is intrigued by the game. When Peter bowls to her she follows the ball to wherever it comes to rest, and then tries to hammer it into the earth with her bat.

Peter explains this is not a technique likely to stand up to a sustained attack from a fast bowler, but Rachel is not interested.

'Owzat?' she demands imperiously, and he sighs.

Chrissie refuses to take sides, and Glory sits in a deckchair and watches them both, smiling.

Glory and Chrissie are very good friends.

Jansy's doing well at university. She's studying veterinary medicine now, and says she will go on to specialise in large animal treatment, because there's plenty of competition for work in African game reserves. She says, once she's got her doctorate the competition can eat her dust; how many qualified veterinary surgeons have her experience as a poacher?

In the meantime she's discovered she's a highly talented tennis and squash player.

She and Lord Robert enjoy each other's company. He has albums full of photographs taken in Africa many years ago, some of them of elephants. He has stories to tell.

He has a gamekeeper, who is teaching her to shoot.

I am managing the repayments on the mortgage, and the forge is doing quite well again. I know how much money I have, and it's enough. I still shoe Jake's horses and mend gates for him, and I don't often have to remind him to pay his bill.

We're good friends again now, Jake and I. One day he did admit his main motive in marrying me had been Gorsedown, and I replied I'd only married him for his horses, so we grinned at each other. Then his smile faded, and he told me it had all been true, when he'd proposed, what he'd said, that he'd always liked me. It was only later that he'd grown to love me. He hadn't even realised at first.

'If it doesn't work out with Arno and you,' he began, but I leaned across the table and laid my hand on his, and he stopped. He shrugged, and gave me a wry smile.

Arno comes to the forge whenever he can. In the school

holidays he brings his children, and I like them. I've given them the two bedrooms in the front of the house, and they spent their three weeks last summer decorating them, and building their own furniture. Every now and then something collapses, but then it's rebuilt, slightly differently, and mistakes aren't repeated.

Historians still come sometimes, and speculate aloud about the place. I listen, and answer what questions I can.

I sit on the gate to the paddock in the evenings after I've finished my work, and I watch my old horse, and I look at the sunsets and wonder about the person I've become.

At least now I'm at peace with myself. I can accept what has happened, and who I am, and I think I'm happy. I believe I am. And if other people can love me, and I can love them, then sometimes I think perhaps one day I might even be able to love myself.

It's a strange idea, but it might happen. One day.